No Rest for the Wicked
[And I Ain't Slept Lately]

Basil B. Clark

WALDENHOUSE PUBLISHERS, INC.
WALDEN, TENNESSEE

No Rest for the Wicked [And I Ain't Slept Lately]

Published by Waldenhouse Publishers, Inc.
100 Clegg Street, Signal Mountain, Tennessee 37377 USA
423-886-2721 www.waldenhouse.com
Cover art by Alex Young
Type and Design by Karen Paul Stone
Printed in the United States of America
ISBN: 978-1-947589-67-4
Library of Congress Control Number: 2023947548

Suspense, romance, conflict, and a touch of humor, with a surprise ending that combines the misconduct of a drug-dealer with the oft-irrational acts of a run-away wife, the deeds of a crew of State Troopers, and the karma of an aging war veteran -- provided by Publisher

FIC000000   FICTION / General
HUM000000 HUMOR / General
DRA000000 DRAMA / General

THEME:

Even though we
may not understand everything
that is going on right now, it is all
part of a larger story being written,
and, in the long run, it may actually
even favor those who are trying
to do the right thing.

Dedication

To Cora Larson. You, being curious about the picture in the profile on eHarmony, and then deciding to contact this university professor wearing a doo-rag atop Seneca Rocks, WV (at a spot where he was not supposed to climb to), changed my life forever in positive ways. Life truly turns on a dime!

Cora and I connected on eHarmony in November 2008, corresponded for a while and met in person January 3, 2009. Sadly, fourteen years to the day, January 3, 2023, I sat in the Townson-Smith Funeral Home and made arrangements for her Celebration of Life service and then burial at Carver Cemetery in Graham County, NC.

We dated for over two years before our marriage on March 13, 2011. It was a beautiful 60+ degrees day for our outside wedding with grandkids participating, from the girls circling you while scattering petals from Bradford Pear blossoms picked from trees in our front yard, to the boys alternating as ring bearers.

And then the involvement of our three sons; Troy gave you away, Rocky was my best man, and Ralph officiated at his first wedding after being ordained.

Thank you Cora for reading and rereading this manuscript so many times, proofing and making suggestions, and by the way, I made sure to keep in the line you thought would be best for one of the characters (who liked to sleep in provocative, hot pink, form-fitting T-shirts which showed off her long legs to perfection.) You nailed it Babe; I miss you!

Foreword

You're going to love *No Rest for the Wicked*.

Basil Clark and I have been friends for over fifty years, having soldiered together as infantry with the 1st Cavalry Division in Vietnam in 1969. More recently we shared the experience of speaking at the 50th Anniversary Memorial for our good friend Rodney J. Evans, who sacrificed his life in Vietnam to save the lives of some of his comrades, and who was posthumously awarded the Medal of Honor for his incredible selfless courage.

Basil is a war hero in his own right, a recipient of the Silver Star for his own remarkable act of bravery on September 18, 1969, when he single-handedly saved the men from his squad's listening post from almost certain annihilation by the North Vietnamese Army regulars who surrounded us, and were attacking us with mortars, machine guns, and hand grenades. After that amazing act, and seemingly taking it well in stride, Baz stepped in to replace me as platoon sergeant, as I had been wounded during the first few minutes of fighting.

In case you're wondering, we both survived that nearly all-night battle.

After the war, Baz, a spiritual man, became a husband, and father to two wonderful sons, an accomplished university professor, a fine writer and actor, and a man who gave and continues to give enormously of himself, to help others.

Along the way he developed a keen sense of humor, a great sense of drama, and a very strong writing style.

In *No Rest for the Wicked,* Baz formulates a rich cast of characters and brings them together in an intricate but spellbinding plot, all the while mesmerizing the reader with his expert turn of phrase. There is suspense, excitement, romance, conflict, a touch of humor, and a well-crafted surprise ending that will leave you shaking your head. This first novel (by an author who has already published several excellent works of non-fiction) interweaves the shenanigans of a drug-dealer / part time car thief, with the oft-irrational acts of a run-away wife, the deeds and misdeeds of a highly-believable crew of State Troopers, the karma of an aging war veteran, and the unpredictable but very human behaviors of a number of other rich characters, into a story that you'll have a hard time putting down.

But I don't want to give too much away. Turn the page, and get ready for a great ride. I know you'll enjoy *No Rest for the Wicked*!

Gary DeRigne – Former U.S. Army Platoon Sergeant – Vietnam
Author of *One Young Soldier* and *Angie's War*

Endorsements

The decisions you make define the life you lead, whether or not you've been given time to carefully make those decisions in the moment at hand. *No Rest for the Wicked (and I Ain't Slept Lately)* is about the forks in life's road and how some people traveled this one or that one, the life choices they made to do so, and for some, the cost of those choices.

This book is about the forks in life's road and how some people traveled this one or that one and the life choices they made to do so. Now, you the reader, now also have decisions to make. For good or bad, you will judge the merit of the choices the travelers made in this book. So pull up a comfortable chair with good lighting for reading and crack open this book with a gavel handily nearby.

Glen Sparks, Buck SGT Photographer and Philosopher

I work with airplanes, and that gives me an appreciation for having to look at things from a different perspective, and the development of these characters in *No Rest for the Wicked (and I Ain't Slept Lately)* also gives the reader a different perspective on why people sometimes behave the way they do. The characters kept me wondering what was coming next, occasionally laughing, and even though this was a fictional novel, I found many places that had me thinking about real life situations.

Dairton Antonio, Fortaleza, Brazil, Aircraft Technical Maintenance Service

Contents

CHAPTER 1:
Usually No Police

Roscoe Knowles slowed down to 111 miles per hour to reflect a moment. He felt like the sad truth of his life was that after all the parts were added up, the total was something between minus three and minus four. And the real sad part, to him, was that he felt like he was going out with such a whimper. The potential for going out with a bang was there, had always been there, but it seemed that every time, Roscoe somehow managed to wind up 50 calories shy of a milkshake.

There was traffic in the right lane ahead, so Roscoe pulled into the left lane. As he accelerated back toward 133 miles per hour, his peripheral vision caught a glimpse of the Kentucky State Trooper that he was passing. Roscoe realized that things were back to normal; the rubber duck in his tub was leaking again, and if he stopped now, he would have to give some money to the big, bad policeman.

So Smokey gets the tag number, Roscoe thought. *If I can ditch him and then wipe prints off the steering wheel, an abandoned stolen car won't leave any evidence of me.* He pushed the accelerator of the 2022 Infiniti Q50 all the way to the floor. There weren't many places along the Kentucky Bourbon Parkway where one could get a car much over a hundred, but the section from Exit 87 near Microtown to Exit 118 near Frankenberry allowed for more. And the thing that Roscoe liked most about this stretch was that usually, today being an exception, but usually, there were no police around.

Under normal circumstances, Trooper Phillip Cordella would never have let the Infiniti get away, but he had been on his cell to Deanna Fine when the black blur went past. By the time he exchanged three "I love you, I love you more's" and a "Really have to go. Love," turned his siren on and then pulled out; two tractor trailers were side by side. It wasn't much of an incline, but the driver of the 'Papa Bear's Hauler' eighteen wheeler was inspired by the sight of Roscoe flying by, and decided to pass the Food Village tractor trailer. He laughed over the CB, "Catch me if you can!" and all traffic behind slowed as the truckers played out their uphill competition. Both drivers were focused on their mini-NASCAR battle and did not even glance into their rear view mirrors. Any siren noise was superseded by the sound of their diesel engines. Phillip didn't quite think that he could squeeze past on the apron, so he stared at 1-888-SEE-TRUX on the mudflaps as he called the 58th Kentucky State Police Headquarters to inform them that he was attempting to engage in a high-speed chase.

CHAPTER 2:
Enter Heather

The road ahead was clear for Roscoe and his recently acquired Infiniti. After a couple miles, three curves, and still nothing in his rear view mirror, he decided to try an escape off Exit 118. Less than a minute after he pulled under the bridge and parked, he heard the sound of a siren go overhead as Trooper Cordella hotly pursued a car no longer traveling the Bourbon Parkway. Roscoe breathed deeply, and thought that, just maybe, he had adjusted his life up to a minus one.

As he thought about moving to a better location for vehicle abandonment, and perhaps confiscation of another, a Mustang pulled in behind him. Roscoe's eyes widened as he got a fairly good look at the woman stepping out of the vehicle.

Well, she looks mighty fine, Roscoe thought. *What the hell is she doing here?* He decided to check it out, rather than run.

Heather Lamech's curiosity had compelled her to get off the 118 exit ramp, and see if the cop had been given the slip. She wasn't sure why it mattered, but her life had been quite a mess lately, so watching the Infiniti accelerate and eventually disappear triggered a desire to see if she could be a part of the excitement. As she opened the door to get out of her Mustang she thought, *Three shades of purple; if Jackson could see me now, he'd be cussing three shades.*

Heather walked to the Infiniti and leaned toward the window Roscoe had just rolled down. She knew she was being totally irrational, but didn't care. She had vowed yesterday she was through with Jackson, and by the gods who oversaw revenge in the universe, she was determined she would get back at him somehow. Now she was looking at a man about twenty-five years old, with curly blondish-brown hair that covered most of his ears, freckles accented by a boyish grin, and a relatively firm looking body. Heather consciously looked down at the driver's lap, then back into his inquisitive eyes. "Hi," she said, "I'm Heather. And I like your style. Anything I can do to help?"

Roscoe deliberately let his eyes travel slowly from her long, ginger red hair, to her faded denim mini-skirt. Looking back into her deep brown eyes he puckered his lips into a bit of a smile and then answered, "And I'm Roscoe. I guess I could use a lift." He got out of the car and used a handkerchief to wipe off the steering wheel and door handle, and then stuffed it back into his right rear Levis pocket.

As they walked back to the ingot silver Mustang, Heather thought about what to do next. She obviously couldn't go home. And if Jackson ever found out what she had just done, he would hypocritically start on a stupid rampage about marriage licenses, and fidelity. But he thought that a marriage license gave him a license to hit her, and the closest thing he knew to fidelity was their insurance company. Well, Jackson could just kiss what he referred to as her boring little ass.

Roscoe held back a couple steps so that he could further scrutinize Heather. She looked to be around his age with long legs made even more enticing by calf-high, fur-trimmed, brown suede boots. Roscoe noted her buttocks were well formed by his cultural descriptions, and that included no visible signs of body sagging. If questioned, Roscoe would have to admit that his definition of nice woman started with the shape of her body, and typically, never dealt much with personality. But Roscoe never stayed in a relationship long enough to care about that. While looking Heather over, he wondered if perhaps he had wrecked the Infiniti during the chase and somehow arrived at the Pearly Gates. He thought, hardcore terrorist suicide bombers who are expecting seventy young virgins can have them all. I'll settle for this one experienced-looking young woman.

CHAPTER 3:
Randall Knowles

A Cherry Red Grand Cherokee approached and slowed a bit before proceeding up the road.

"Guy seemed a little curious," Roscoe said; "although it's kind of hard to see him through the tinted windows."

"Probably just on his way home and wondering why we were stopped. Seeing us walking toward my car probably let him think you had called me to come get you."

"Like an almost new Infiniti is going to break down?"

"Or," Heather smiled, "maybe he thinks we are meeting for a secret rendezvous."

Roscoe shrugged. "Hope you're right."

As they got into the Mustang, Roscoe flashed back to when he was seven years old and had decided to cut a tree limb with his father's new pruning saw.

He positioned himself precariously on the not-so-large branch and started to rip his incision. Unfortunately for Roscoe, he was cutting on the limb between himself and the trunk. It didn't take long for the branch to snap, and Roscoe landed screaming for help on his buttocks. His mother showed sympathy, concern, and just all round TLC. His father laughed until tears came down his cheeks.

Roscoe glanced over at the sexy woman starting the Mustang and thought, *I wish he could see me now; I'll bet he wouldn't be laughing.*

Roscoe knew, of course, that his father couldn't see him; it had been six years since the funeral. But still, the relationship they never had stayed close at hand like a chigger bite. Of course, Roscoe knew he was wrong in thinking the relationship they had never had; an abusive relationship was still that, a relationship, and even after his father's death, Roscoe resented him. On the other hand, Roscoe's mother, Zelda, had seemed to have an unwavering ability to tolerate everything her husband had thrown her way, and still proclaim her love.

Roscoe had not meant to upset his mother the day of the funeral. The services were over with and they were on their way from the Maplewood Valley Church of Saints Awaiting the Imminent Return of Jesus Christ in These Last Days to the hillside behind Randall Knowles' old home place where he was to be buried. Roscoe was bitterly laughing to himself over the preacher's words about how he had talked on many occasions with Randall Knowles about the afterlife, and how he was confident that Randall was now resting in the arms of God's great forgiveness and peace.

Peace, *Roscoe thought,* I hope not. I think that he ought to at the least endure some form of Purgatory for awhile. *About that time, a car approaching from the other direction blew a tire and sideswiped the hearse carrying Randall Knowles' remains. In the ensuing misadventure, the rear door of the hearse swung open, the casket somehow broke free and popped open, and Randall Knowles wound up face down in the ditch. Roscoe couldn't help but laugh, and for the only time that he could recall, his mother backhanded him across the mouth.*

CHAPTER 4:
First Beat Off

The 58th Headquarters of the Kentucky State Police had been located at Frankenberry because it was a growing community in Eastern Kentucky chosen as one of the 'best seventy-seven small towns in America'. Frankenberry itself had fewer than sixteen thousand people in it, with another thirty plus thousand scattered in smaller towns and communities throughout the county, which, geographically, was smaller in size only to Pike County.

Within the 58th Headquarters, Officer Phillip Cordella had set himself up quite nicely for the handle. He was rather full of himself when he started, fresh out of Academy. He had begun working on the first shift, and frequently made sure everyone was aware of that fact. He called it the first beat and had said that he was "A first beat officer". It was inevitable that Julie Wright, dispatcher for the 58th, had started calling him First Beat-Off, a name she had decided was appropriate when he had a prolonged visit in the restroom one day, and emerged with the latest Sports Illustrated Swimsuit Edition. He had turned beet-red when Julie whistled at him and asked if his wrist was cramped.

By the time Phillip Cordella was able to pass the trucks and had clear, but curvy, road ahead of him, the Infiniti was out of sight. He pushed the pedal of his new Dodge Charger cruiser to the floor, but after some five miles with no car in sight, was wondering if his quarry had bailed at Exit 118. He radioed headquarters to update, and to his dismay, Julie answered.

"Did you catch him, First Beat-Off?" she laughed. Phillip had warned her on several occasions to keep it professional on the radio, but Julie prided herself on being a badass girl who could simultaneously enforce the rules, and give hassle to those whom she felt were deserving of it.

Phillip gripped the radio tightly as he told her that the Infiniti was either way ahead, or had gotten off at 118. Phillip said he thought his best bet was to circle back. Julie said he was probably right, that he had better do the circle thing and see if he got off. Phillip clenched his teeth, gripped the radio tighter, and reddened, even though he was all alone.

CHAPTER 5:
Killing the Skunk

When Jackson Lamech's white RAM 1500 pickup rounded the curve as his wife knew it would, she slowly raised her rifle and followed him through its sights. Months of plotting had finally brought her to this point. Heather knew he always slowed to top the hill and that was where she was going to finally bring this fatal intersection of two lives to a conclusion. His will end, and mine will go on, she thought. If I have calculated correctly, I shouldn't get caught, but even if I am, life can't be more miserable than it is right now. *As her husband's head came more clearly into her sights, she slowly squeezed the trigger to send the tiny, spiral-shaped missile on its way to carry out its lethal mission.*

About that time Heather awoke, and realized that Jackson had again escaped her. She slowly eased out of bed to plod out to kitchen to start the coffee. Later, traveling down the Kentucky Bourbon Parkway toward Parkersville and her hairdresser appointment, Heather wondered about the recurring dream. Then Roscoe flew past in the Infiniti. Now he was in the Mustang with her, and she had just been informed she had a car thief as a passenger.

Yesterday, when Jackson backhanded her across the mouth, Heather swore that it would never happen again. She was tired of him thinking he had a personal, real live punching bag. She stood 5'4" in her stocking feet, and her 34C, 28, 36 body weighed in at 121 pounds. At 6'4", Jackson was not only a foot taller, but about ten pounds more than double her weight. He had played football at Frankenberry High and still maintained his athletic body. He was a handsome man, by any standards, and his thick, golden brown hair combed carelessly back, along with his deep, dark brown eyes, had melted many a woman's heart and sent tingles all the way down her body. But unfortunately, some handsome men who could melt hearts were also capable of packing big punches. Jackson Lamech was in that category.

They lived just outside the city limits, so they were able to keep a chicken coop with a few hens in the backyard because Heather liked cooking with eggs she had just gathered. A skunk had gotten into the coop and somehow Jackson had gotten a hold of it by the tail and lifted it up.

"You see," he told Heather the first time she had told him that a skunk was raiding the coop, "if you can get a skunk by the tail and lift him up quickly, he can't spray you."

"Why not?"

"Because, Dummaz, he can't get enough pressure with his back legs to force the spray out. When they're on the ground, he uses them to prime the pump, so to speak."

"Oh," Heather said.

So there was Jackson, holding up a skunk up by the tail, hollering, "Heather, get your ass out here! Now!"

Heather poked her head out the back door. "What do you wa—Jackson! What in the world are you doing?"

"Hurry, Heather! Get a 2X4!"

Heather dashed to the stack of wood near the chicken coop and grabbed an approximately four foot length of 2X4. "Now what?" she shrieked, wondering what her half-crazed husband was up to.

"We've got to kill him!"

"And just how do you propose to do that?" Heather screamed.

"You!" hollered Jackson. "Hit him in the head! Now!"

Heather thought back some eight years plus to her high school softball days as she swung the 2X4 and connected with the polecat's head. Of course, what neither Jackson nor she had counted on was that the force of the blow, while killing the skunk, also forced spray out, which expelled all over Jackson who howled while half-choking, "What in the hell did you do?"

Heather couldn't help it. Jackson looked so ridiculous, hopping up and down, dead skunk in one hand held out as far as possible, the other arm alternating between a clenched fist elbow-bend to outstretched, with fingers twitching, and bellowing out curses with the most bewildered, shocked look on his face she had ever seen. She burst out laughing, and then, right after Jackson hit her, tasted blood.

Heather glared at him and thought, *This is the last time you'll ever do that to me.* She wasn't sure how to carry through, but she knew she wasn't taking anymore.

CHAPTER 6:
John Deere DUI

Julie Wright took the call from Trooper Todd Truitt and decided she'd better double-check what she thought she had just listened to. "Trooper T, would you repeat. I am not sure I heard you correctly."

"Oh, I'll bet you did," said Todd Truitt. "What I said was, I am downtown, at the Red Bird Street intersection and I have just pulled a man who was weaving all over Main Street on a riding lawn mower."

Julie immediately had visions of a Grand Marshal on his lawn-mower leading a parade of automobiles through town as she replied, "I thought that's what you said." Then she asked, "Just for the record, what kind of mower?"

"John Deere. Green. Not sure what year."

Julie laughed. "Well, good work, Trooper T. Keep us informed." Julie shook her head, smiling. Todd Truitt was an older trooper who looked like he was near, or even past, retirement age for State Troopers, but he always seemed motivated and ready to hit the road at the beginning of every shift. When he had transferred to Frankenberry from another post a couple years earlier, he requested to be back out on the road, patrolling. Beyond that, Julie didn't know that much about him. His medium brown hair had traces of gray peeking through but he looked like he kept in excellent shape. When he smiled, it seemed as though he was holding back from letting it develop into a full-blown one, as it never quite reached his hazel-green eyes that seemed to be hiding some sort of sadness. Julie wondered how the man she was visualizing was handling a lawnmower DUI.

On rare occasions, and this was one of them, the hardest part of his job was not laughing at an inappropriate time. If anyone knew, Todd Truitt did, that drunk driving was a serious offense, not at all a laughing matter. He reminded himself of that fact as he walked toward the John Deere, ticket pad already out, with pen drawn and prepared to fire away about the man's transgressions.

"Runs jusht like a deer, don' it?"

That was all it took. Todd bit his tongue to try and keep the corners of his mouth from curling up, but the gravity of the situation was overridden by the human need to find humor wherever one could in life. He had learned long ago during Desert Storm that life, sometimes, was just downright painful. He was close to an age where he could choose, if he so desired, to take one of the State Trooper retirement plans, but after the loss of his wife and two children in an auto accident several years back, Todd had thrown himself wholeheartedly into his work. A drunk driver had crossed over the line at the crest of a hill and Samantha died instantly. The children never regained consciousness before they passed away.

"Well, maybe not exsactly like a deer, but ith still goeth pretty good, don'cha thinks."

Todd regained his composure as he sternly responded, "Sir, I realize this is a small vehicle, not even intended for road use, but drinking and driving is unacceptable, and against the law, no matter what the circumstances."

"But I only had a coupla beer. Honest, offisher."

Todd let the big guns fly. "That is exactly what the man said who crossed a yellow line and hit my wife and children head-on. Killed them all, so, Buddy, I'm the wrong person to try out your 'couple beers' defense on, okay? Now get off the lawnmower and I'm going to have you walk a straight line for me."

Aaron 'Ox' Patterson began to realize that he might be in trouble. The problem he encountered with many of his escapades was, even though they were often much talked about; the reality was slowly sinking into his 34 year old head that most people were laughing at him, not with him. "I … ah … I'm real shorry about your family, shir. I hope you know I had nuthin' to do with that, an' … an'… I'm ready for you to 'rrest me. I need shome help, shir, I really do." Aaron's voice broke and a tear slowly wound its way over the top of his cheekbone. It came to a halt in his unshaven stubble.

CHAPTER 7
The Partnership

Roscoe was experiencing a first, and he didn't want to blow it. He was a mid-to-lower level drug dealer, and occasionally he would let a female score for half-price when accompanied by a favor. But never in his life had a girl approached him in a manner that even hinted of sexual overtones without drugs being somehow involved. His fantasies wanted to kick into high gear, but his curiosity also compelled him to ask, "So why did you stop?"

Heather thought for a moment as she didn't know the answer to that question herself. She shrugged as she replied, "Not real sure. I know my husband wouldn't be real happy if he knew what I was up to."

"Husband!" Roscoe bellowed. Any fantasies developing were suddenly stifled by images of guns and bullets and local news headlines blaring out "Man Shot in Head While Cavorting with Picked-Up Wife." He asked, "Good Lord, woman, why don't you wear a wedding band? And what are you up to?"

"Answer one," Heather replied, "I took my band off for good yesterday, when I decided that my legal headache had hit me for the last time. And as far as what I'm up to, quite frankly, I don't know."

Roscoe felt like he wanted to, had to, know. "So again," he pushed, "why did you stop?"

Heather repeated herself. "Not real sure." She knew that all she did know was beyond a shadow of a doubt, her life was in transition, she was headed into a new phase, and it could only be more positive than the one she was leaving behind. Anything would be better than the, becoming more regular, beatings from Jackson. She continued, "All I know is when your Infiniti flew past me and then it looked like you might have lost the cop, I just wanted to … curiosity, I guess … wondered if you might have gotten off at Exit 118." Heather grinned at Roscoe. "Guess you'd be screwed right now if that cop had had my instincts."

Oh, yeah, thought Roscoe. *Back to the pressing issue. I have a State Trooper looking for me and I don't want him to win this game of hide-and-seek.* "Speaking of which, I need to lay low for awhile. I don't want that trooper to see me."

Heather remembered the first thing she had been aware of while walking toward the car was she didn't know if she was approaching a man or woman, young or old. "Do you think he saw you? I mean, the Infiniti windows are tinted."

"Good point," Roscoe responded. "But just in case he comes back this way and you get stopped, we might ought to have matching responses to some possible questions." Even though he had just stolen a vehicle, which increased the possibility of contact with the police, Roscoe still did not want to have to answer questions from the law related to his modest tax-free living from pot, cocaine, and his most popular product, Opiods, so any questioning by the police was not good. Also, Roscoe was really annoyed at the law at the moment since two recent busts in Franken County had disrupted cocaine and Meth shipments intended for him. He had moved to Franken County about nine months earlier to fill a void which opened up in the area due to a friend of his being arrested and sentenced to eight years in prison for dealing. Roscoe built his business up to around twenty-five regulars and was on track to make approximately $75,000 a year. Roscoe knew his friend had not been careful enough, so he operated alone; was his own sales manager, bookkeeper, and CEO. He carried two cell phones at all times; one for business, the other personal. So far, he had made it a point to avoid younger buyers, as he had some part in him that didn't want to be labeled as a school grounds pusher. Actually, the majority of his regular customers were considered productive members of society; he even had a couple doctors and a lawyer in the mix. But the law had recently been hurting Roscoe's business, and he was not a happy camper. He had even started thinking if he was going to survive in the industry; he might have to expand to "Moon Rocks" and "Buttons", and maybe even recruiting younger users.

"So, anyway," Roscoe continued to Heather, "we really ought to have stories that are reasonably similar for questions like, 'Where are you going?', 'Why we're together?', 'What are we doing?' you know, that sort of stuff. Unless, of course, you just want to drop me off somewhere."

Heather took in a deep breath. She was having some questions about her cognitive processes and abilities. But, she decided, she stopped of her own volition, so she was now by choice a part of this. She thought of the numerous times Jackson's hand had stuck across her face, and his legion of infidelities. Emotionally she was near the edge and buzzing with thoughts of revenge as she replied, "No, I don't want to just drop you off somewhere. A minute ago I said something about if the cop had had my instincts, you'd be screwed right now. What say we let me have my own instincts, and follow up on that thought? Screwed? Do you want to?"

"I like your way with words," Roscoe said, thinking, *Looks like life might have moved over to the plus side, and I believe this milkshake has just increased by several hundred calories.*

CHAPTER 8
Bradley Miller

Bradley Miller recently turned seventy-four, but still had the energy of a forty-year-old. Brad and his mother Barbara had lived with her father for as far back as Brad could remember because after he was born his father had departed for God only knows where. Brad lived with them until he was sixteen, that is. Then he moved to a remote area of Franken County on property left to him by his grandfather.

Brad's grandfather, Rodney Overstreet, taught him to hunt and fish, and basic survival skills in the woods. By the time he was in the 10th grade, Brad found himself daydreaming of trekking through the woods a lot more than paying attention to the teacher. As soon as he turned sixteen he dropped out of school. His mother wasn't very happy about it, but his grandfather told her to give Brad some time and space. "I just think he needs to spend some time in nature, reflecting. He'll decide his future with a clear head, not jumbled up with facts and figures and dates that just don't mean anything to him right now."

"That's it?"

"Look," Brad's grandfather replied, "I'm going to give him our cabin…"

"The one in that thickly wooded area near the Swisher Glen Forest Preserve?"

"Yeah. That's the better of the two."

"And money?"

"I'm putting a couple thousand dollars into his bank account so he won't have to worry about finances. If he's careful, and lives simply, the money should last … maybe a year. I can add if I need to."

"Hmpf," Barbara said. "I don't recall this kind of set-up when I was having trouble in school."

"For one, I couldn't afford what I can now, and two, the situation was different."

"Well, it sounds to me like you two have already worked this situation out, and I doubt if you all'd listen to me anyway."

"You're right, but don't worry, Brad will be okay."

CHAPTER 9
G Ride Traced

Phillip Cordella radioed headquarters again, cursing himself for not immediately reacting when Roscoe flew past. The two truckers slowing traffic down had certainly become an unintended consequence of Phillip's slowness in responding. He wasn't sure how, or if, to explain the delay in his chasing the Infiniti. Julie answered and Phillip grimaced and told her, "Listen, I was right about him getting off at Exit 118. I'm here with the car at the Parkway underpass. Driver's gone. Will you run this tag for me?"

"Sure thing," Julie responded as she asked, "Did you get a look at the driver? You said he got off at Exit 118?"

Phillip wanted to ask Julie what percentage of people arrested for auto theft were female, but he didn't. Instead he told her the windows were tinted and he assumed the driver was a male.

Julie reminded him of the old saying, "It makes an ASS of U and ME". Then she asked him what the tag number was. Phillip resisted sarcastically answering Julie as he responded "Turnquist County, BSC 591."

Julie typed in the information, and a minute later said, "Hey, First Beat Off, you've got a live one. Black Infiniti reported stolen about two hours ago. Turnquist County, BSC 591."

Phillip cringed at the nickname again, but just radioed back his thanks. He told Julie he would scout around for awhile and see if he could locate the driver. He felt guilty he hadn't just told Deanna, "Gotta go", and started immediate pursuit. Now there was a car thief running loose, and God only knew what else he might be running from. Phillip knew the gamut could run from a teenage prank to something a lot more serious.

He was surprised when Julie only replied "Sounds like a plan", and actually ended the transmission by telling him to be careful.

CHAPTER 10
If Heather Isn't Home

After stripping down to his under shorts on the front porch, Jackson Lamech told Heather to take care of getting the polecat's smell out of his clothes, quickly went into the house, and showered, and then showered again. After finally feeling like he was clean, he got out of the shower and asked her what she had done with them. She told him she'd buried them in a corner of her garden, and, for once, he agreed she had done the right thing.

The next evening, as usual, Jackson stopped on his way home from work at Rourke's Beer Palace and noticed the woman wearing a bright red mini-skirt sitting alone at the bar. A wide strand of light brown hair covered one eye and curled around to end resting about a foot below her shoulders. The top of her black Dingo fashion boots were about six inches below her knees. Jackson had seen her there a few nights earlier, but she was with someone else. He slid on the stool next to her and asked if he could buy her a drink.

"Margarita," she replied, so Jackson ordered one, plus a Bud Lite for himself. She told him her name was Brenda; he introduced himself and asked her if she wanted to sit at a table. When the drinks came, they moved. As they were talking, Jackson noticed that Brenda slightly crinkled her nose. He wondered if she might be detecting *eau de skunk* so he decided he would tell her the previous day's story, which by now, he was even seeing some of the humor laced within. Naturally, he left out the part about hitting Heather.

There was a local band on stage, The Kentucky Regioneers, so Jackson requested them to play 'For the Good Times' and asked Brenda to dance. They immediately pressed tightly against each other, and she rested her head against his chest. Brenda started to feel a slight hardening in the area of his pudendal artery, so at the song's conclusion, she squeezed Jackson around the waist and suggested they have one more drink, and then go by her place for awhile. Naturally Jackson agreed, and soon thereafter they left the bar.

About ten minutes after their arrival, Jackson sat up in bed, reached for his cigarettes on the bed stand, tapped one out of the pack, and lit it as Brenda asked, "Was it good for you?"

Kind of a dumb question, Jackson thought, since, to him, there weren't any bad times in bed. So he grunted and told her, "You were fine," thinking, *for a while, anyway.*

Brenda had had her eyes on Jackson for over eight years, ever since her sophomore high school days, but doubted if he had ever even noticed her. He'd always hung out with other jocks from the football team, and then with Heather. But he was with her now, and had made love to her, albeit rather quickly, and so she asked him, "Do you plan on leaving Heather?"

"Why? What makes you ask that?"

"Just wondering. I mean, you're not exactly committed to her, are you?"

"And just what do you mean by that?" Jackson was starting to get aggravated. The last thing he wanted after a roll in the hay was to talk. He wondered why she couldn't at least let him finish his cigarette.

Brenda decided to see if Jackson was at all the settling type, or just another man on the run, and so she said, "Well, I know I'm not the first woman you've cheated on Heather with. Word gets around, you know."

Go to bed with a girl and she thinks she owns you, Jackson thought. What is it with the female race? "Look, baby," he said, "there's marriage, and there's life, and there's reality. I live with Heather and pay the bills, and occasionally go to bed with her. That's marriage. I just fucked you, that's life. Now, if you don't mind, I'd like to cut out the philosophical discussion and finish my cigarette. That's reality."

Good grief, Brenda thought. *If this is his idea of philosophical talks, I'm glad to see the light before I possibly made the mistake of thinking he might be a prize to pursue. I wonder how Heather lives with him.* Brenda started to get out of bed to go to the bathroom and Jackson reached out his arm and threw it over hers.

"Now don't go too far, baby," he said. "In a half hour or so, I think I'll want a little more. You know, something to hold me over until next time."

Right, Brenda thought. *Next time. In your dreams.*

In less than an hour, Jackson was driving home in a foul mood. Brenda not only didn't want a second time around, she had topped the unpleasant bit of news off by telling him she had made a mistake, and that she didn't want to see him again. When he asked her, "Why not?" she said, "I just don't want to. I made a mistake."

Jackson didn't like it if a woman started getting possessive with him. He surmised Brenda probably figured that after a bounce on the bedsprings he would drop to his knees, propose to her out of sheer gratefulness, and promise to leave his wife. *Well,* he thought, *even on her bad days, at least Heather's still a good cook.* Jackson pulled into his driveway and cursed because her Mustang wasn't there.

He called Heather's cell and got her voice mail. "Heather," he snarled, "I don't know where you are right now, but I know where you should be. Now, unless you're in the hospital, or in jail, you'd best be getting your ass to the house." After he left the message, he dialed Meredith. She might be a little on the ugly side, but Jackson liked her bedside manners. She'd also been good in the backseat of her car, in the shower, and on the kitchen table.

Meredith had not been home when Jackson called, so he decided to go back to the bar to see if he could find someone else. When he walked into Rourke's, he saw her sitting at a table with a man he did not recognize. Jackson went to the bar and ordered a Bud Lite. When Kevin brought it, Jackson asked, "Who's the jerk sitting with Meredith?"

Kevin hesitated a moment, then figured, *what the hell, honesty is always the best policy,* so he answered, "Now, Jackson, you may not be happy over this, but remember you are a married man, and Meredith is single. So when my cousin asked me if I knew someone --"

"Your cousin!" Jackson spoke in near whisper, but fiercely. "Kevin, you know she and I have a thing going!"

Kevin outweighed Jackson by about forty pounds, so he wasn't overly worried as he replied, "Yeah, with her and about fifteen other women. And by the way, I don't appreciate you calling my cousin a jerk, okay?"

Jackson thought he would play an economic card and so he retorted, "You know, Kevin, this doesn't seem the best way to keep customers coming back."

A minute later Jackson left the bar and got into his truck muttering, "If Heather isn't home when I get there, there'll be hell to pay … as soon as she gets there."

CHAPTER 11
Nastywatchers.com

It was nearing the end of Phillip's shift, which he usually looked forward to, but he was still frustrated over the Infiniti driver vanishing. He radioed Julie, and said he might stay out a little longer. "Hey, First Beat," she responded, "you're not the only cop to ever lose one. But look at it this way, you recovered a stolen car, there is one Mr. Richard Dewar who is a happy man right now. So why don't you take Deanna out and celebrate what you did accomplish?"

Phillip knew Deanna was working late shift at the Electric Blue Steakhouse and that he would most likely just make a quick stop at Wendy's for supper to go, but he didn't see any sense mentioning it to Julie, so he just said, "You're right. I did get a stolen car reunited with its owner. Guess that's enough to call it quits on. But I am totally frustrated."

"Then I'll see you in a few minutes. And take it easy coming in First Beat, okay? Save dealing with your frustrations until you get home."

Phillip shook his head. Sometimes Julie could be almost decent, and then there were times she just wouldn't let something go. The thing that bothered him the most was how close to the truth she was. Phillip knew as soon as he got home he would crank up his computer, check his e-mail, and then type in nastywatchers.com/main.html. The main page listed all the porno sites he needed. It was like an escape from life's pressures, but Phillip lived with a nagging fear that someday he would pass out or have a heart attack or something while at some porn site, and be found like that.

CHAPTER 12
Jackpot Motel

Roscoe asked Heather if she wanted to go to the Grand Illusion Hotel, but she replied, "Too close to where I live, maybe instead, we should go to the other end of town to the Jackpot Motel."

"Well, I'd rather hit the Jackpot anyhow. Somehow the Grand Illusion sounds like a set-up for a let-down."

A few minutes later Roscoe checked in to the Jackpot Motel, signing Charles Coleman on the registration card. Heather thought it might be better if Roscoe checked in so that she could stay as low-key as possible. When he came to the blank asking for the vehicle license plate, he said, "I, ah, I can't remember the tag number. I'll have to go check. It's, ah, my wife's car."

The night clerk had recognized Heather when they pulled in, so he smiled, then looked down at the registration form and said, "That's okay Mr. … ah … Coleman, most people don't stay long enough for it to matter anyway, the room is $74.50 total, and you are in Room 123."

"Well that's reasonable. My wife and I were sure relieved when we saw the 'Vacancy' sign."

"Yeah," said the night clerk nonchalantly. "A lot of people who stay here are. Gives them a place to stay for an hour or so to ah, attend to some business matters, if you know what I mean." He added, "Let me know if you need anything."

Roscoe was beginning to get a little riled as he replied, "We are staying the night, and might even stay longer, if we like the area." He let a little hostility ooze into his voice. "Or if we like the people." He turned and walked out the door, and over to where Heather was waiting in the Mustang."

The clerk watched as Roscoe got in the Mustang, and then as Heather pulled it around to the side where they had taken a room. *Must think I'm stupid, or something*, he thought. *Like I didn't go to high school with Heather for four years. I'll bet her husband wouldn't be happy to know about this, but, hey, it's none of my business.*

Roscoe and Heather opened the door to the room and entered. It obviously wasn't a Fairfield Inn, but it would suffice for their purposes. Roscoe closed the door, pulled Heather toward him and told her he was ready for the follow-up on her instincts. Heather smiled nervously and started to undress, feeling surreal. She couldn't believe she was alone in a motel room with a man besides Jackson. Not that she hadn't fantasized occasionally but this was her first in the flesh infidelity. Jackson, on the other hand, was like a dog that wouldn't eat from his own dish because he was always dining at the neighbor's. And for a long time, Heather had tried to make sure that sexually she was putting out more than just store brand generics. She had finally decided it didn't make what she did or offered, Jackson just couldn't keep himself to one woman. She had contemplated leaving, but was afraid to strike out on her own. Now, here she was getting ready to fornicate with a man she hadn't even known an hour. Of course she knew he was an Infiniti robber, which made him pretty close to a pirate, so Heather decided she was just caught up in an adventure, let the consequences fall where they may.

When they finished making love, Roscoe lay back on the pillow, trying to make sense of his day. He didn't understand why he did what he did sometimes, and today was really one for the records. It was like sometimes he just got a real bad case of just don't give a single damn, and when the better part of one's livelihood came from dealing drugs, just don't give a damn days could be dangerous.

But stealing had been a part of his life for as far back as he could remember. He just liked to take stuff. His father used to tell him he would wind up in prison someday, and whenever he heard that, Roscoe would just chuckle in his mind; like he'd never heard his father bragging about cheating on taxes.

Roscoe recalled feeling bad about stealing, once, when he was twelve.

He had been in the hobby shop, and had confiscated two tubes of model glue. A couple days later he was back in the store looking at a model '57 Chevy. It cost $4.95, but the manager, told him he could have it for 4 dollars. Roscoe felt guilty, and confessed that two days earlier he had stolen some glue. The manager said he was just glad that Roscoe *had listened to his conscience and that now he could stay on the good path.*

A couple weeks later, he had been back in the store, and Roscoe just couldn't resist slipping another tube of glue in his pocket.

Not being able to resist a good chance to snatch something was how he had wound up in the Infiniti. Whatever idiot owned it had left the windows down where Roscoe could see the keys dangling from the ignition. It didn't matter his own car was a 2014 Sand-dust colored Toyota Camry he had paid a little over $16,000 for. He just couldn't resist taking off in that Infiniti. Maybe it was because he really wanted one, but was afraid it would stand out too much for his occupation and put him at greater risk for being busted. *Of course,* Roscoe wryly thought, *so does stealing one, but it was like I just couldn't help myself.*

Heather was lying with her head on Roscoe's chest, and after a few minutes realized she felt like she was in the middle of an irrational movie. *I guess I'm a lot angrier at Jackson then I realized,* she thought. *Here I am being a whore to this guy that I picked up about an hour ago, and I can't seem to muster up a single ounce of regret.* She looked into Roscoe's eyes and smiled.

Roscoe smiled back and told her he thought they made a good team; that he owed her big time.

All of a sudden a new passion overwhelmed Heather. *I didn't have to stop for him,* she thought. *If that cop had circled back, Roscoe might be in a jail cell right now, instead of getting a ride to heaven. He is right, he does owe me big time. I'll bet I can get him to help me get back at Jackson. Maybe even get rid of him.* Heather couldn't believe the path that her mind was going down. *What am I thinking? I'm no murderer!* Yet …

CHAPTER 13
Wanna Grab a Bite to Eat?

Todd was through taking care of all the paperwork concerning Aaron Patterson's DUI. He knew local reporters would probably have a field day with the arrest, but that was the way it worked sometimes in the life of a law enforcement officer. As he went past the dispatcher's desk, Julie Wright asked, "So, Trooper T, did you bag any other deer today besides the big green one?"

Todd grinned, looked down at his shoes, and then back at Julie as he replied, "We are in John Deere season and the limit is one."

Julie liked to verbally spar, and frequently imagined herself in fencing mode in her conversations. She let Todd Truitt know he had just scored one. "Touché."

Todd grinned again. "You don't know how hard it was approaching that lawn mower. And then when he said to me 'Runs jusht like a deer, don' it?' It was one of those sad, but funny situations."

"Aaron seemed pretty contrite when you brought him in. Just what did you say to him?"

Todd hesitated. He had transferred to the Frankenberry Post from the western part of the state a little over two years ago. He hadn't talked to anyone about his wife, and had no intentions of doing so. He knew some at the Post were aware, but they seemed to follow his cue on not discussing the situation. He answered, "I just let him know that even though he was on a small vehicle, not even intended for road use, that drinking and driving was unacceptable, and against the law, no matter what the circumstances."

Julie knew the sight of a State Trooper made a lot of people become more sobered, but there was something unusual about the look on Aaron Patterson's face that she didn't have a handle on, and so she pushed again. "And that straightened him up? You must have had a very persuasive manner."

She flashed back to when she was about six years old and had asked her mother about her Aunt Dottie, whom Julie had never met.

All Julie knew was that her Uncle David used to have a wife and she had been killed in a car accident. Julie remembered her mother saying, "people have died from drunk drivers", and "there was no excuse for what he was doing". And there was something else, but Julie couldn't think of what it was, for the life of her.

Julie realized there was something bigger going on than what Todd was telling, and she decided that she was going to find out what it was. "Say, Todd, I'm done for the day too. Wanna grab a bite to eat?"

Again Todd slightly delayed his answer and then decided he really didn't have any good reasons not to. "Sure, why not? Do you have anyplace particular in mind?"

"How about the Electric Blue Steakhouse? I live near there, so if you want to follow me home, I can drop off my car and ride with you."

"Sounds good to me; lead on."

Julie parked her car in her drive, and then walked to Todd's 1967 Oldsmobile. It had been restored to mint condition, a four-speed, hardtop, eggshell colored leather interior, Safron yellow exterior, 442, that he had paid a little over $62,000 for a year ago. He got out and opened the passenger door for her. "Nice car," she said. "I've thought that before, but don't guess I've ever told you. So, anyway, Trooper T, take me away to the Electric Blue Steakhouse, and watch out for deer, John, that is." Todd grinned as he walked back around to the driver's side door, put the car into first gear and pulled out.

CHAPTER 14
God's Impending Judgment

Tira Furcologna had swirling images in her mind of a lost locket, a destroyed music box, a missing ruby ring, a slashed evening gown passed down from her mother along with several other dresses, the missing Revolutionary War era silver tea set, and always, the image of her mother's picture with eyes that had been poked out with a pen, and then a large mustache scribbled on it. In the course of her prayer ritual before leaving the house, she had had to adjust, due to the missing tea set. She faced the crucifixes as usual, and she still held the porcelain dove with both hands, but much more carefully so she wouldn't cut herself on the jagged edges from when it had been broken. At the conclusion of her prayer for guided concentration during the task she needed to accomplish, Tira carefully transferred the broken dove as usual to her left hand, and then made the sign of the cross. More than ever now she had to let God know she loved him with all her heart, soul, mind and strength. Then she left the house and walked several blocks east. She wandered into Wendy's and approached the counter. Kari Turner was at the register, and asked, "May I help you?"

Tira was on a mission. She now knew more than ever how evil the world was, and that God had commissioned her to seek out any salvageable human beings, and so she asked the girl taking orders if she was ready to meet the Lord.

The question caught Kari off-guard as she was expecting something more along the lines of Number Three with a Coke, so she responded, "Pardon me?"

"Honey," Tira took the response as an indication of a hungry soul opening her heart to receive a message direct from God. "You need to make sure you are ready to meet Jesus. His day of judgment is almost here. God has been revealing things to me in dreams and visions. Terrible things are about to happen to this town if we don't repent."

"That's nice," said Kari, "but this is Wendy's, and I'm here to take orders for food. Would you like something to eat?"

Phillip Cordella came out of the restroom and got behind Tira. After completing the paperwork portion of his day, he concurred with his earlier thoughts about what to do for supper, so on the way home he stopped at Wendy's to get a small Fries and a Jr. Bacon Cheese-burger off the Value Menu. He would soon wash them down with a cold beer at the house.

Tira just stared at Kari Turner. She couldn't believe anyone could be complacent with God's impending judgment hanging over the town, so she adamantly told the cashier that it was not a time to be eating, that she, herself, had been fasting for three days, ever since God had started showing her his plans for Frankenberry.

Good Lord, thought Kari. *I gave up watching Looney Tunes in the sixth grade and now I'm caught in one.* She told Tira, "I'm real sorry but I don't have time to talk about judgment at the moment; my job is to take orders for food and I don't want to get into trouble with the manager." Tira couldn't believe how badly people ignored prophets of God. She felt camaraderie with Jeremiah, Hosea, and other Old Testament figures as she tried to convince Kari that trouble with the manager would be nothing compared to being in trouble with God.

Phillip listened for a moment, thinking, *What is it with my Karma today?* He shook his head, and then spoke. "Is there a problem, Ma'am?"

"Big problems," said Tira, turning to face Phillip. "Oh good, you're a policeman." She was relieved she had finally received a positive sign from God; he was sending her someone in a position of authority to help her rescue the few who would listen to her.

Phillip appreciated the local police, but he wanted people to know there was a hierarchy of law enforcement officers within any given State. He was at the higher level and he wanted to clarify the fact to Tira, so he replied, "Yes, Ma'am, I'm a State Trooper."

Tira didn't care what level of law enforcement Phillip was at. She just knew that God had sent her one of his messengers in uniform to help bring higher plans to fruition, and so she told Phillip, "Either way, you can help me spread the word. People will listen to you."

Don't I wish, thought Phillip. He eventually had found out there was only a small jump on the authority scale when he donned his

State Trooper uniform. It seemed as many people were as interested in running from him as listening to him. "Just what word is it you want me to spread?"

"Officer," Tira began. "You won't believe the judgment God is about to bring on this town for all it's wickedness. I have been receiving the messages through dreams and visions. There is going to be an earthquake of Biblical proportions just south of here on the Little Sourdough River which will cause it to overflow its banks. Frankenberry is going to be totally under water, along with other towns as far north as Grayson."

"Well, you're right," said Phillip. He decided that he might as well be blunt. "You said I won't believe it, and I don't."

Tira was shocked that someone in authority, someone indicated in the scriptures as ordained by God to be a part of the Almighty Chain of Command was ignoring her, and so she frantically told Phillip that it was imperative for him to help her spread the word so that maybe together they could see the town spared. She begged him to think of his duty.

Phillip's tired frustration came through as he said rather shortly, "Ma'am, I just got off duty. It has not been a good day, so actually, what I am really thinking of, is how I am going to get some food to go, take it home, and wash it down with a nice, cold beer. Now, I am sure you mean well, but --"

"Tira?" About that time Albert Furcologna came up behind them. "Tira," he repeated. "I've been looking for you. Are you okay?"

Tira glanced downward, and then answered, "I'm all right, Albert. I'm just trying to warn people of the coming disaster."

Albert was quite disturbed. At some level on their marital scale of devolution, he really did love Tira and was concerned over the direction her emotional state had been heading ever since her mother's illness and then death. "Tira," he said, "let's go home." He looked rather sheepishly at Phillip as he said, "I hope she wasn't bothering you, Officer. She's been having a little trouble lately. We're the folks over on Sumbat Avenue who had our house vandalized a few days ago. A lot of irreplaceable mementos of her mother were destroyed."

Phillip had heard and read about the break-in. He knew the local police were handling the situation, but he was suddenly overwhelmed with a feeling of sadness for Tira as it appeared that the unpleasant incident had probably pushed her over some kind of edge. He told the Furcolgnas he was truly sorry for their losses.

Albert thanked Phillip. "The whole break-in had no rhyme or reason to it and has been extremely difficult on my wife."

Tira became immediately defensive. "You don't need to explain me away; I'm fine."

Phillip saw a man walking a tightrope as Albert Furcologna told Tira he knew she was okay, and then told Phillip again, he hoped she hadn't been bothering him. Phillip looked to the register at Kari and asked her if she was okay.

"I'm fine," Kari responded. "I just didn't know what to do."

Tira threw up her hands. "I tried to tell you what you need to do. You wouldn't listen."

"Come on, let's go home," Albert said, as he took Tira's hand and led her toward the door.

Trooper Phillip Cordella shook his head at Kari, and then watched as Albert and Tira Furcologna went out to their car, got into it, and drove off. Then he placed his order.

CHAPTER 15
Medical Career?

As he whittled a face into the block of wood sitting on the hand-made table in front of him, Brad was tortured by images of people dying. Even though he had helped many, errors of judgment, or in some cases, reactions to given circumstances, just would not let him go. He thought of when he first became interested in the field of medicine.

He was sitting in the camp chair when he saw a rabbit limping slowly toward him. It seemed he instinctively knew Brad could help. "What's the matter, little guy? Did something hurt you?" He saw it was favoring its right paw and remembered his grandfather saying that a fairly common problem for rabbits was a sore hock. The wounded critter let him pick it up and Brad saw there was some loss of hair on the paw. He set the rabbit into an empty box next to the shelter. "Not real original, but do you care if I call you Peter? Of course, on a closer examination I may have to change it to Flopsie. Now you stay here Peter while I go get a brush and my first aid kit." Peter was still in the box when he came back, so Brad brushed a small amount of hair off, got out an adhesive bandage and made a small fur patch. Then he placed it over the spot where the hair was worn thin, and used more bandage to secure it to the paw. Brad placed Peter back into the box, but the rabbit lifted his paws up, almost like a cat or small dog wanting to be petted.

"Okay, little man, you can come up." Brad sat back down in the chair and then lifted Peter onto his lap and began to stroke his neck and back. Peter hunkered down in obvious enjoyment. Two days later Peter was still asking to be held and stroked.

Brad started thinking about becoming a veterinarian. The only problem he saw with the idea is it would involve going back to high school, and that didn't particularly appeal to him. On his occasional trips to Frankenberry for supplies he picked up a newspaper to stay somewhat updated on news, and was aware that the war in Vietnam was still ongoing, and in mid 1967 he felt he should fulfill his duty and enlist. A stint as an Airborne Ranger sounded exciting.

Brad sighed deeply and chipped away at his current project. *Exciting doesn't always turn out as advertised*, he thought.

A while later he looked his finished carving over and then sighed again. He shrugged and then carried it over to the small shed he had eventually had to build in order to house his creations. *Don't even know why I save all these damn things; don't mean nuthin'.*

Brad faced a problem with Peter. The rabbit seemed to enjoy life as a domestic pet rather that running wild in the woods so Brad's grandfather agreed to keep Peter for as long as he was in the military, which was a huge relief. He had grown quite fond of the little guy.

After Basic Training the next destination for Brad was supposed to be Advanced Infantry Training, and then off to Airborne and Ranger School. However, he was told that his scores indicated he might do well as a Combat Medic. Brad saw this as a signal that maybe he was on the right track. In order to continue training in this area though, he first waived Jump School and Ranger Training, and passed his GED.

After Training he received his first assignment, lining up with what he thought it would be, Vietnam.

CHAPTER 16
Aaron "Ox" Patterson

Aaron Patterson was unable to stop the tears as he sat alone in his jail cell. The look on the trooper's face as he had told him about a drunk driver killing his family was etched in Aaron's mind and the tape was playing repeatedly. He flashed back to college days, years earlier, Fall Semester.

He really hadn't been college material to start with, but his grandparents, whom he had been raised by, wanted him to attend their alma mater, so he found himself enrolled at Rolling River College by the Woods. When someone in the dorm had asked him his name, Aaron replied, "Ox, just call me Ox." The name, actually, quite appropriate, stuck. Ox Patterson soon become the butt of many jokes, but he hadn't enough sense to figure out he was being laughed at, not with.

One Friday October evening, several of the Rolling River students had gone to a hillside overlooking the lower end of town, got a good bonfire going, and partied. For the fun of it, they invited Ox along. Ox bragged he would put away at least a case of beer before the night was out. He opened a can, drank a little, and then, discreetly, in his mind, poured the rest out. This continued. "Eight," he hollered. "Eight, and counting!" Later, "Seventeen, twenty, twenty-two, and counting!"

Although they didn't intervene, some of the guys were pissed that he was letting the better part of a case of Coors mingle with the dirt. "It just ain't right," one of the students grumbled the next day. "We have got to teach this sucker a lesson he won't forget."

The next weekend, basically the same group invited Ox to another bonfire party. "Want to see you put away another case of Coors," the upset student from the other night said. "I'm telling you, Ox, I don't think I've ever seen anyone else put it down like you do."

Ox grinned as he said, "Now, I can hold my liquor."

"You sure can," the student nodded. "And I think everyone is looking forward to seeing just how you do it."

Soon a crowd had gathered around Ox cheering him on. Ox felt good knowing he was popular with so many of his fellow students. He'd have to let his grandparents know he was a BMOC. After his second beer, he started getting concerned. With everyone right around him, goading him on, he had no way of pouring anything out.

And so he drank. The students made sure that they kept attention on him, and chanted as he drank. "Nine! Nine! Nine!" Later, "Thirteen! Fifteen!" Then Ox vomited and passed out. The ring-leading student, with the assistance of others, loaded OX into the bed of his pick-up truck, drove him back to campus, and left him lying in the parking lot. Later a security guard found him and called an ambulance. At the hospital, the doctor said the alcohol poisoning was severe enough, that had it been another couple hours before he was discovered, he would not have lived. A scared student told campus police about the events on the hill. Upon his release from the hospital, Aaron Ox Patterson returned home, in shame, to his grandparents.

He sat at the kitchen table as he said, "I'm sorry, Nana, Pop. I didn't mean to get kicked out of Rolling River."

"I guess you should have thought of that before you got drunk, Aaron." His grandfather was upset, and Aaron knew it. "From what the Dean of Students told us, you thought you were being the life of the party, and were too damned stupid to know everyone was making you the ass of the party."

Aaron's Nana told his Pop that Aaron had made a mistake as everyone did at one point or another. Aaron appreciated his Nana coming to his defense, the one thing he could always count on.

But his Pop wasn't ready to let it go. "Actually I phrased that wrong. Those students weren't making you the ass; you did that all by yourself! You're lucky you didn't kill your damn self!"

"Monroe, now that's enough. Can't you see that he is sorry?"

"Yeah, I can see that he's sorry," Aaron's grandfather hollered. "Sorry is a good word to describe him right now. And add in embarrassment. You ought to be embarrassed, Aaron. I sure am. For God's sake, this is my alma mater we're talking about! I wanted to see you graduate and be someone we could be proud of, not the college laughingstock!"

Evelyn let fly. Aaron had never heard her talk back to Pop, never use a swear word; nor had he ever heard this story. "Monroe, you just stop right now with being such a damn, self-righteous hypocrite! If I remember right from your Army days, someone, I won't mention any names, wrote me telling me about almost getting into a little trouble with the Company Commander, but fortunately the First Sergeant got to work that morning before the Captain!"

Monroe didn't think pointing out his own earlier drinking escapades would help Aaron get a handle on the current problem and so he retorted, "Can it, Evelyn!"

That put Evelyn over the edge. "You can it! Wrote and told me about coming in drunk and parking your car part way up the front steps to the Company Headquarters; First Sergeant waking you, telling you to get your ass up and move the car before the CO arrived and busted you! Monroe, I never told you this, but I almost broke up with you right then and there. Scared to death I might have a drunk on my hands. But you straightened up – as far as drinking goes. But I've had to listen to your self-righteous drivel since then, and I'm tired of it! Lord knows we've had trouble with Janice over the years, and we've had to raise Aaron, but I'm telling you this, and I want you to remember it, you short-memoried bastard, Aaron's the best thing that's ever happened in my life! So just shut up, you hear me?"

Aaron sat in a mixture of embarrassment and pride as his grandfather slammed out the door. He loved his Nana more than ever, and wondered what his next conversation with his Pop would be like.

What he did not realize as he sat on the bed in the cell was that as much as she loved and accepted him, his Nana also unwittingly enabled him. But he did know he was letting her down, and he determined he was going to show her that all her faith in him had not been in vain. He was not going to embarrass her any more.

CHAPTER 17
Man of Sorrows

The Electric Blue Steakhouse was about half full, and soon after Todd Truitt and Julie Wright sat down in the booth, Deanna Fine came over to take their order. Julie had met her once, months before at a Post picnic. "May I get you something to drink while you look these over?" she asked as she set the menus on the table in front of them. Todd and Julie both ordered Root Beer.

"Aren't you Deanna Fine, Phillip Cordella's fiancée?" Julie asked.

Deanna smiled as she replied, "Julie, right?"

"With a 'W', right."

"I thought you looked familiar," Deanna said. "We met at the annual picnic, I believe."

Julie figured that Phillip had surely talked about her harassment of him to his fiancée, so she thought she would face the issue head on. "Right," she said, "I remember you from the picnic, too. Plus I imagine Phillip's mentioned me, oh, at least a time or two. Giving him a hard time, and all that."

Deanna half smiled, half pursed her lips. "Well, I wasn't going to mention it …"

Julie grinned as she said, "Don't take it wrong. I only irritate people I like." Todd broke in and said he was thinking that perhaps he should make a request to be put on Julie's "hate list". Julie told him to give her a break and said, "Did I forget to mention I'm buying?"

"I'll be right back with your drinks," Deanna said.

"Okay," Julie said, as she told Deanna they hadn't known she was working the Electric Blue that evening. Julie said she had told Phillip earlier to take Deanna out and celebrate his recovery of a stolen vehicle. Deanna said she hadn't talked to Phillip for awhile, and didn't know anything about a stolen vehicle, so Julie briefly filled her in on the details.

After Deanna left, Julie asked Todd if he thought she had managed to squirm out of the hot seat with Deanna or not. She said, "I'll bet Phillip's got her thinking I'm some kind of fire-breathing Dragon lady."

Todd had actually felt sorry for Phillip a couple of times when Julie had been particularly rough on him and he broke into a broad smile, saying, "I don't know why Phillip would ever consider sharing with Deanna that impression of you."

"Me neither," Julie laughed, "But enough of my charms. Truth is, I'm curious about your incident with Aaron Patterson. He's been booked before for public drunkenness, and usually gives the arresting officer a hard time. I hardly recognized him today, due to his remorseful behavior."

Todd deliberated a moment before answering. He had pretty much decided after Samantha died that he was not going to get involved with anyone again. He'd been somewhat of a loner as a young person and had quite easily reverted back to that status after losing his family. It had been working for him the past eight years, so, he wondered, *Why now should I open the door a crack? And especially with Julie who is not particularly known for her sensitivity?* He decided to choose his answers carefully. "Maybe he's just ready to face up to the seriousness of some of his behaviors."

"Now, Todd," Julie replied, "I'm not making light of the situation, but DUI on a John Deere riding lawn mower? This becomes the moment he chooses to get serious?"

Todd hesitated as he thought, *Damn it, she's got me cornered, stuck her foot in the door. Now what?* "Well," he started, "Like I said earlier, it was hard approaching him, because it struck me as wildly inappropriate, but still funny. And I had to bite my lip to keep from laughing when he said, 'Runs jusht like a deer, don' it?' But when he pulled his 'I only had a couple of beers' crap on me, I let him have it. I told him …" Todd hesitated slightly and felt a choking sensation that he hadn't counted on. "I told him … that … sometimes … sometimes people die after someone's 'only had a couple beers', and he had picked the wrong person to pull that defense on." Todd blinked back a tear.

Suddenly the something else that Julie had been trying to remember earlier clicked. "Wait a minute," she said. "Pardon my ignorance, but was it your family … drunk driver … about eight years ago?"

Todd swallowed and couldn't believe that he had lost control of a tear that started down his cheek. "That's me," he said.

"I'm so sorry for not putting that together earlier." Julie was embarrassed, a position she wasn't used to being in as she continued, "Actually, I was on a month-long vacation when it occurred, and only heard something about it when I got back. And, of course, back then, a twenty-seven year old, recently divorced, full-of-her-own-problems woman, I never really … Todd, I'm awfully embarrassed to say this, but I never really gave it much thought."

Todd realized he was seeing a side to Julie he had never seen before. And, to this point, he had only communicated with her at work, where naturally everyone worked on impression management with his or her colleagues, and it seemed the impression Julie wanted to convey was she was capable of holding her own with men, or, as was the case with Phillip Cordella, hold the advantage. And although he was committed to loner and self-sufficiency, Todd did not suffer from blindness. From day one he had been quite aware of Julie's striking features, over the shoulder length, dirty blonde hair usually held back in a pony tail, and a pretty oval-shaped face with dark eyes that flashed a combination of fun-loving and challenge. She also had dimples which added a certain innocence to her innate sensuality. Todd answered, "You have no reason to apologize, Julie. Number one, Murray is over four hundred miles away, and, number two, it sounds like your own plate was rather full at the time."

Deanna returned with their drinks. "Are you ready to order yet? Here is your Root Beer. Made it myself," she said as she set them down.

"I'm supposing," laughed Julie, "the reason was so you could slip in the arsenic to get revenge for Phillip."

"Of course, and I'll serve the strychnine with the entrée. But first you'll have to tell me what the entrée will be, so I'll be sure to add it to the right one, pun intended."

"Actually," Julie replied, "we've been talking the whole time you were gone and haven't even looked over the menu yet. Could you check back with us in a couple minutes?"

As they opened their menus Julie said she had eaten there awhile back, and the Kentucky Hot Brown was delicious.

"Picture of it looks good," Todd replied, "and the truth is, I had some about a month ago, and you're right."

When Deanna returned Todd and Julie ordered and then continued with their conversation. Todd was sharing about the accident that destroyed his family and Julie was listening to Todd with more seriousness than she had ever listened to anyone before. She realized she was in the presence of a man who had tasted deeply of sorrow, and she sensed he was someone who could teach her a thing or two about how to deal with life. And that was something that Julie needed to do better. Her badass girl attitude worked for the veneer, but deep inside she knew there were issues she still had to resolve. It struck her that Todd reminded her of her Uncle David. Not physically, but personality-wise. And she was aware that her unresolved issues were the ones that she had debated sharing with her Uncle David, but had never had the chance to.

"So, how did you ever deal with getting rid of toys and books and things like that?" she asked Todd.

"I'll not pretend it was easy. I know I often felt like no one knew what I was thinking as I gave some of the things to Goodwill, a church yard sale, or the Murray Helping Hands Foundation. The fact is most people aren't at all aware of when and how someone is going through a particular rite of passage in the healing process, even if they've been through a similar experience. I believe each one has to walk the valley alone, so to speak."

Julie thoughtfully spoke. "That is so true, and I guess I would have to admit I'm probably more careless than some in being aware of what others are feeling. Kind of a wall I put up years ago." As she said that, Julie seriously wondered, for the first time in years, about how someone else might be feeling. "Todd?" she asked, "does it bother you to talk about this?"

He smiled sadly and said, "Actually, I really haven't much at all. Just stayed busy and tried to deal with it that way. I realized earlier today with Aaron Patterson there are still some pains real close to the surface. Maybe it's time to share a little."

"Promise you'll tell me if I'm being too intrusive."

"That's okay." Tears welled up in Todd's eyes, and one started down his cheek. He wiped it away and smiled. "I'm glad you asked me out to dinner. The timing's good. Like I said, earlier today I realized I still need to let some things go. When Aaron pulled that couple of beers line on me, I wanted to slap the shit out of him."

"And quite understandably so."

"But," Todd shook his head, "sometimes, I can't seem to incorporate into this situation some of the things I learned when I was in Desert Storm. I guess it's because the memories are more personal."

"Losing family is hard," Julie said, "but I agree with you, each experience, and relationship, is different."

"Something I believe we can glean from all of them though is learning the value of hope and perseverance."

"Hope and perseverance?" Julie looked down and shook her head a little, then looked back at Todd. "Perseverance I understand. Hope; I don't know so much about that one."

"I'm not saying it's easy. I was divorced when Samantha and I met. She was fifteen years younger than me. I loved her, but we were still a very typical husband and wife with all the very typical problems. But it was different with JR and Mindy. They were children, only seven and ten years old. From the time they were born, I did my best to be a good father to them, and quite frankly, I think I did a good job. We laughed, we played, and there have been times when I have been thrown violently back into one of those memories by just the slightest of triggers. I've been attacked by commercials, by people talking, by the sight of other children, and always by those memories; memories that were being built into a solid relationship; memories suddenly twisted and turned into damned knives stabbing my emotions and cutting out my heart." Todd choked up. "I'm sorry, Julie. You asked me to dinner, and I'm turning it into the song, 'Crying Time Again'."

Julie decided to be honest, something she sometimes held in reserve. "Todd, the reason I asked you to dinner was I sensed that with Aaron Patterson there was something more going on than what you were telling. I decided to find out what it was, although, to be honest, I'm really not even sure why. I hope you won't hold that against me, because I am glad we're talking. I don't want to bring up painful memories, but if my listening can help you in the healing process you mentioned earlier then I'd like to be your listener." As she spoke Julie wondered if it was her talking, or did she have a nice-person clone somewhere that had slipped into the conversation.

Todd smiled and told her he wasn't complaining; that truthfully he was seeing quite a different side of her than what she usually made available for them at work. "In fact," he grinned as he said, "I really think I might somehow be helping you through the fire-breathing Dragon lady process."

At that, Julie laughed, and lightly kicked him.

Deanna returned with their meals, and Todd and Julie continued to converse as they ate. They shifted the discussion to Phillip recovering the stolen Infiniti, and other events of the day.

Later, when Todd dropped Julie off, she asked if he wanted to come in for awhile. Although he didn't want to offend her, he didn't feel real comfortable with the idea, so he politely declined, "If you don't mind, I am really getting tired, and since I have to get up early, I should probably just take a rain check."

"I understand the whole early morning thing, but I will remember, and hold you to, the rain check."

"Aha," Todd laughed. "Sounds to me like you're maybe learning hope to add to your perseverance."

CHAPTER 18
Uncle David

Julie squeezed Todd's hand, thanked him for going to dinner with her, and started to get out of the car. Todd said he would walk her to the door, but Julie said it was okay, that he didn't need to, said goodnight, closed the car door, and walked up the sidewalk. Then she turned and waved as Todd drove off. After his car was out of sight, Julie checked her mailbox, and then went inside. *Thank goodness computer spam hasn't totally done away with junk mail*, she thought, *otherwise I'd have nothing to throw away.*

She decided to draw a tub of hot water and enjoy a nice bubble bath. As she unbuttoned her pants, and then unzipped and stepped out of them, Julie wondered if Todd had declined her invitation to come in for awhile because maybe he had thought she was trying to put some moves on him. She realized it might have looked like that, but decided that if that was the case, then the pieces would have to lie where they fell. A few minutes later she added Champagne Caress bubble bath to the water, slipped into the tub, leaned back, and sighed contentedly.

Her mind went serenely neutral for a few moments, and then slowly started to wander. Again she thought of how, personality-wise, Todd reminded her of her Uncle David. Julie reflected back to her mother's oldest brother. She recalled when asking her mother about how Aunt Dottie had died, the answer was that Aunt Dottie had been in a car accident; hit by someone who had been drinking a lot of beer. When Julie had asked, "So drinking a lot of beer before driving is bad?" that was when her mother said those words, "people have died from drunk drivers", and "no excuse for what he was doing."

Julie had never known her Aunt Dottie, but she knew she loved her Uncle David. She was seven, and they were riding home from Vacation Bible School. He was her favorite uncle, and she liked to go places with him. He always stopped for ice cream, and he was fun to talk to. Tonight she had an important question for him. "Uncle David?"

"Yes, Pumpkin, what is it?"

"Well," she continued, dragging out the word. "There's a song we sing in church sometimes, when it's church for everybody, and there's something in it that I don't understand."

"Well, your old Uncle David will see if he can help you out, okay?"

"Okay. It's the one where we sing, 'My spear it was made strong. For Jesus took my burden, and left me with a song'."

"Okay," Uncle David said. "I remember that one. What's your question?"

"Well," she dragged out the word again, "I don't see anybody in church with spears, so how can they be made strong? And what's a burden? Why does Jesus take it? Where does he keep them all? And does he have a music store? I mean, otherwise, it must cost him a lot to get all those songs for everybody."

"Phew," Uncle David replied, "Those are a lot of questions. I'll see what I can do. First, the word is spirit, like the feelings you have inside. So what it means is he can help you feel better when you feel sad. And a burden is also when you feel bad inside, so not only can he help you feel better, but maybe even feel good enough that you feel like singing. And, no, Jesus doesn't have a music store, though I guess he could if he wanted to. Does that help any?"

"I think so," she replied although she was still a bit confused. "Thanks, Uncle David."

"Are you ready for some ice cream?"

"That might make me feel like singing. Are you Jesus?"

"No, Pumpkin," Uncle David laughed, "but I try to act the way I think he might."

Julie wondered if she should share her "burden" with Uncle David. Her fifteen year old brother Adam had come into her room the other night, and had rubbed her inside her panties. He had told her not to tell anyone, because, he said, they wouldn't believe her because she was so little. But what Adam was doing to her didn't seem right, she felt bad inside about it, and she didn't know what to do.

"Is everything all right, Pumpkin?" Uncle David asked.

Julie thought maybe she should just wait to talk to Uncle David about it until some other time. Adam was right, she was little. Maybe Uncle David wouldn't believe her, or, even, worse, maybe he wouldn't like her anymore. So she just answered, "Yeah, I'm okay. And I'm ready for some ice cream."

The next morning Julie came downstairs to her mother's crying. "What's the matter, Mommy?" she asked.

"It's your Uncle David, Honey."

Julie felt a frigid current run through her as she asked, "What about Uncle David?"

Her mother held her close and wept. "He had something called an aneurysm, Honey. No one knew. After he went home last night it burst and killed him." She clutched Julie as they both broke down sobbing.

Tears running down her cheeks stirred Julie from her reflections, and then her thoughts went back to Todd. Their personalities had really seemed to click. She didn't feel like she was engaged in conversation with a man old enough to be her father, but rather, just sharing with a friend, a handsome male friend, who just happened to have a little salt invading the pepper portion of his hair.

CHAPTER 19
Afraid of Gettin' Some

While he was showering, after he had gotten home from dropping Julie off, Todd's thoughts tumbled around like colored shapes in a kaleidoscope. He had wanted to take up Julie on her offer to go in with her for awhile, but he had not been sure what all that might lead to. He wasn't sure exactly why he was afraid it might have ended up in the bedroom, but he was. Then he told himself he was engaging in completely irrational thinking, that Julie had no interest in him for sexual reasons, and she was just being a friend. Todd contemplated on the fact he had allowed some bricks to break away from the wall he had been building from eight years ago, he did have an interest in Julie beyond conversation, and he was afraid. Afraid of another close relationship. And in his adult life, close relationships had started with laughter and ended with pain. Then he grinned as he thought, for some reason, probably linked to the kaleidoscope side of his brain, about a scene from Desert Storm.

Desert Storm 1991. Sergeant Todd Truitt greeted a newly assigned man, Paul Warmble. "Glad to have you out here, Paul. We're a tight team, and we take care of each other. Main thing you've got to remember for awhile is you are the new guy, so act, and learn, accordingly. Now, that's not meant as an insult, it's just a reality. Until you get some experience under your belt, you need to learn from us, work with us, and let us work with you. And remember, time spent on anything, and experience, are not necessarily the same thing. And something else, all the experience in the world still doesn't outweigh plain old common sense."

"Yes, Sir," said Paul.

"Don't remember a damn thing from training, do you? Don't Sir me, I work for a living."

"Sorry, Sarge."

"'S all right. Just don't let it happen again. Now, first question, a ritual out here when a new guy arrives, got any pictures in your wallet?"

"Yes."

Todd turned to the rest of the squad. "Hey, guys, come on over here for a couple minutes. We've got some pictures."

Paul took out his wallet and started telling who was in each photo. At one, a squad leader nicknamed Slim Jim whistled, and asked admiringly, "Wow! Who's that?"

"My sister," Paul replied.

Slim Jim grinned. "Does she fuck?"

Paul was taken back by the bluntness of the question and just stammered, "Well, I... I don't know. I ... don't think so."

Enjoying the moment, Slim Jim asked, "How come it is, nobody's sister fucks, but everybody's gettin' some?"

Todd laughed and spoke out loud as he continued to rinse off. "That's what my problem is, I'm just afraid of gettin' some."

CHAPTER 20
Hello Vietnam

Brad stared at the two tombstones standing at attention near the holly bush he had planted over the grave of his pet rabbit Peter. For three decades he had been keeping the small cemetery neatly groomed, in contrast to the natural growth surrounding it. He shook his head sadly. Thirty years ago today a couple State Troopers came by to inform him that his mother and grandfather had been killed in a car wreck, and he determined they should be laid to rest next to his abode. Today he was thinking of almost fifty years ago when he left for Southeast Asia.

Emotions were mixed as he peered through the glass; an edgy sense of excitement over leaving for Vietnam as a Combat Medic, but also seeing his mother peering through the airport terminal window at the plane. He was suddenly overwhelmed by the fact that this was most difficult for her, seeing her only child off to war. Brad swallowed a choking sensation and waved, aware that because of the distance involved, his mother probably wouldn't know who it was. She waved back.

One could only wonder if there had ever been a time where anything in the military happened without long lines, and waiting in them. The day at Ft. Dix, NJ was spent processing final paperwork for departure to Southeast Asia. It was not real exciting stuff, but there was a lot of speculative talk taking place.

Early the next morning the men were awakened and told to grab their belongings and fall out for the chow hall. A few minutes later all were lined up in formation.

"Hey, Sarge," one of the guys asked. "Is it true our orders have been changed and we're going to Hawaii?"

"Actually," the Sargent replied. "You all are going to Hawaii, but don't get excited. It's just a refueling stop on your way to sunny Vietnam."

A collective groan went up from the ranks, as they were called to attention and then marched over for a breakfast of sausage, toast and eggs. Brad managed to sit next to Steve, a guy he had earlier struck up conversation with. Someone next to them joked about enjoying his last meal.

"I prefer to think of it as my last meal for a while on American soil," Steve said. Brad agreed.

After they ate everyone grabbed their duffel bags and loaded buses waiting to take them to the airfield to catch a westbound flight. Steve and Brad managed to get seats next to each other, and as the plane took off Steve mentioned his mother's words to him as she said goodbye, "Well, you're in God's hands now."

"Okay," Brad said. "But what does it mean to be in God's hands?"

Steve shrugged. "Believe that he'll take care of us, I guess."

"So, does he play favorites? I'll bet that most, if not all, mothers seeing their kids leave off to war put them in God's hands, so to speak, but the nightly news just keeps reporting rising death tolls. So what's happened to God?"

"I don't know, man," Steve said. "I don't think about that stuff. I just want to get my ass back home alive."

The stop in Hawaii was only for a couple hours, and they all had to wait in the airport lobby, but Brad figured he could at least say that he had been to Hawaii.

The plane circled at a higher altitude and then dropped rather quickly to what the men on board were told was Tan Son Nhut Airbase. There was a SGT sitting in the row ahead who was returning to Vietnam for his second Infantry tour, and he announced rather loudly, "The descent into hell begins, my friends. Give your souls to God, because the Devil has just claimed the rest of your life!" Brad wondered if they would be facing gunfire upon leaving the plane.

When the plane doors were opened the change in temperature was immediate, and the heat just sucked breath away. "I told you!" the SGT spoke again, "but you didn't want to believe me. Maybe you will now."

Brad wistfully smiled at the marble stones and turned to go back to his cabin.

CHAPTER 21
Little Boy Lets God Down

Phillip took his food and beer to the computer table and sat down. Most of the e-mail was spam. He thought, *thank goodness most of it is labeled as such because it sure saves a lot of time.* Every now and then he liked to look and laugh at some of the on-line degree information. There was a particularly good one today. "Earn yore degree with no classes on campus. Masters, doctors, whatever you need. Degrees taylored to fit yore needs. This cuold be the opportunities you has been wating for. Click to recieve more informashun".

Yup, thought Phillip, *this sounds like my chance of a lifetime, but I think I'll let it go fester in the delete file with the others.* He wondered how some people could be so stupid to think anyone would actually reply. *But then again,* he thought, *some must take the bait; otherwise, the spammers wouldn't keep sending the garbage out. But why do some people do what they do; what is it with certain members of the human race?* Phillip thought if there was a God, and if said God was watching over humanity then he or she must have a strange sense of humor because, frequently, it was a really weird show going on.

Phillip took a bite of his Jr. Bacon Cheeseburger, a swig of beer, and just sat there thinking. *And why didn't this God give more attention to the children and what often went on with them?* One of his earliest religious recollections was when he was five years old and there had been an Evangelist at the little church his folks attended, Rev. Scareski, pronounced Scare - ski, emphasis Phillip decided in later years on the SCARE. He preached something, Phillip couldn't recall exactly what, but it had gotten the attention of a five-year-old. Phillip did remember it was something about heaven and hell, and he hadn't wanted to go to the hell the preacher was talking about, and so he had gone down front to the altar to be saved AND sanctified. Big Night! Within the doctrinal beliefs of that particular group, sanctification was having the sin nature removed, so one didn't sin anymore. *Real important stuff,* Phillip thought. *They must not have wanted another five-year-old running the streets, spewing out his sins everywhere.*

Well, not only did Phillip get saved that night, but the preacher asked for volunteers who were dedicated enough to fast and pray all the next day for a real outpouring of God's blessings on the next evening's services. Well, after making such a big decision, Phillip knew God wanted him to volunteer.

Of course the next day, naturally, he got quite hungry around noon, and finally gave in and ate something around two p.m. He quit praying for awhile, too. His mother told him not to worry, that God understood, but Phillip only understood one thing. He had made a commitment to God the night before, and on his first day, had failed him. He had let God down. God was counting on him in order to be able to bless the services that evening, and he couldn't go all day without food, and he couldn't concentrate enough to stay in prayer all day.

No one except Phillip went down to the altar that evening, and he knew it was a sign from God. He knew there was trouble in the heavens, because so early in life, he had been an unreliable five-year-old boy. It didn't matter what his mother said. He had failed God.

And that wasn't the last time. According to the messages he kept hearing in church, try though he did, Phillip just couldn't measure up. And he did try. Phillip was willing to bet he walked the aisle to that altar at least three hundred times between the ages of five and sixteen. It became a real problem from the ages of thirteen to sixteen, because somehow, Phillip had discovered thoughts about girls, especially ones with some of their clothes missing.

Sears catalogue provided a pretty good array of women, but then one of Phillip's friends showed him a Playboy, and told him they might be able to find some magazines showing men with the women, kissing, touching, and even more. Phillip was hooked, and after awhile, the trips down the aisle decreased, because they didn't feel as good as Phillip's trips to his bedroom closet. The guilt always tried to creep in, but Phillip knew it was just God messing with the little boy that had let him down.

As he grew older, and took some psychology courses in college, Phillip began to have a better understanding of himself, and how he pretty much was a visualizer, and, again, he found himself typing in nastywatchers.com/main.html.

Deanna was tired when she got off work, but she went ahead and dialed Phillip's number. It would be rare for him to be sleeping this early. The phone startled Phillip. He looked at the caller ID, and then turned the volume off on the computer before he picked up the receiver.

"Hi, Hon," Deanna said as he picked up. "I just got home, and I'm worn out, but I want to let you know that I love you before I drift into dreamland. You doing okay?"

Phillip wanted to have an open, honest relationship with Deanna, but he didn't think it was the appropriate time to start talking about the particular aspect of his life that her phone call had just interrupted. And she might not appreciate the sounds of lovemaking from the PornoLuv video.

Phillip told Deanna he was just taking it easy after kind of a rough day, and Deanna told him Julie told her about him recovering a stolen vehicle.

"Julie?" Phillip asked, "Where did you talk to her?" As he said that, he thought, *Thank goodness that Julie can't see me now.* Deanna told him about Julie and Todd Truitt eating dinner at the Electric Blue. She told him she had talked with them a little, and Julie had actually seemed pretty nice.

"More than likely she was trying to impress Todd," Phillip replied. "Setting him up for the kill."

After a little more conversation Deanna said that she was going to get ready for bed and told Phillip "Goodnight".

After she hung up, Phillip just sat a couple moments. He felt a bit guilty about not being open in this area with Deanna, but he wasn't quite sure how to start the conversation. Besides, in some respects, he saw his "porn time" on the computer as a form of staying faithful to Deanna in a "safe sex" alternative kind of way.

For the moment though, had his thoughts a visual form, one would have seen the good angel - bad angel debate in progress. Phillip had problems distinguishing one from the other at times.

"Phillip, show a little more maturity."

"Maturity? This is adult material, why don't you leave him alone?"

"Face it, Phillip; you're hooked like a crack head scrambling for his next fix."

"Bad comparison. This is harmless."

"Not quite. Do you really think this will help with your relationship with Deanna?"

"Hey, what guy doesn't think of watching a little erotica with a chick that enjoys it?"

"You think she wants Phillip thinking of Brianna Banks instead of her?"

"Harmless fantasies. Everyone does it."

"More than just fantasies."

"How so? For God's sake, so what? At least he's keeping it in his pants. Not running around like a lot of guys."

"So instead, he looks at pictures of others running around. What's the difference? Morally, I mean."

"Keep you damn moral arguments out. Not applicable to this conversation. And there is a huge difference in consequences."

"Hey, Phillip, want anyone at Headquarters to see how you spend an evening?"

"He's unwinding, for God's sake. Stop being so damn critical!"

"Just pushing for him to be a better person."

"Trying to turn him into a guilt-ridden neurotic. And trust me; they can't be all they can be."

"This isn't an Army of one. How's this for a headline? State Trooper accesses porn sites? Hey, on the other hand, a headline like that would make your whole life worth living for, wouldn't it?"

"Oh, give it a break, will you?

Phillip shook his head and brushed his angels aside. The link to 'Mature redhead fucks neighbor' looked inviting, and so he clicked on it.

CHAPTER 22
You Could Stay With Me

Heather snuggled in Roscoe's arms. She was basking in the afterglow of one of the strongest orgasms she had had in a long time. "Mmm, thanks, Roscoe," she contentedly breathed. "That was great." Roscoe mumbled something Heather that couldn't understand to the effect of "nnh huh, mmm", and burrowed deeper into the pillow. Heather knew that eventually Jackson would get to the house, find out she was gone, and start to realize something wasn't right. "Roscoe," she asked, "So what are we going to do?"

"Hunh?"

"What are we going to do?" Heather repeated.

"Mm. About what?"

When Heather sharply repeated his name, she surprised herself at her authoritarian sound as Roscoe bolted upright and asked "What?"

"Sorry, didn't mean to sound so harsh, but we've got to do some planning about what comes next. For one, we can't stay here too long. If my husband gets to prowling around and finds the car, there's going to be a scene." Heather made sure her voice was smothered in concern. "And that won't be good for you, Baby. I think for your safety, we're going to have to get a little further away from the area, and then plan what to do longer range." The webs were clearing from Roscoe's mind; he was again surprised Heather wanted to stay with him, and so he asked if she was planning on sticking around.

Heather reminded him she had said earlier it had been her choice to stop for him at the Infiniti, so she was there for him.

"If I can get back home, no one's going to know anything. I don't see paying money to get away from the area."

"Good point," Heather said, "but what about me?"

Roscoe thought a moment. This milkshake was gaining more and more calories by the minute. Lately, his life seemed to have been going down fast, losing motivation, losing direction, near misses by an ever-active local drug enforcement agency. He had foolishly stolen a car and it was a given the police were most certainly looking for him, and now, here's this hot damn broad wanting to be with him. *Kill me right now,* he thought, *and I'll tell you "Life has been good."*

"You could stay with me," he said.

That might work for a while, Heather thought, so she asked Roscoe what they could do about her car.

Roscoe thought a moment. "My mother lives on the far end of Armstrong County. We could leave it there; she has a barn we could pull it into. And, she has a car we can borrow to get back home in."

Heather realized that what she could offer Roscoe, he wanted more of, and she could use it to her advantage. She was thoroughly convinced she was now at a point of no return with Jackson, and also, that she couldn't do what she had to do alone, so she responded in the most innocent-sounding voice she could find, "Baby, you'd really do that for me?"

Roscoe thought, *what part of heaven have I relocated to?* as he replied, "Sure, Baby Doll; that and more."

"When are we going to leave?" Heather asked. "I'm thinking the sooner the better."

"I agree," Roscoe said, "but let me get a little catnap first."

***

About forty-five minutes later, Heather decided they had better get going, so she gently ran her fingers through Roscoe's hair and lifted it off his ears. Roscoe moaned softly, wiggled his nose, and then suddenly his eyes shot open. When he saw Heather, he remembered where he was and grinned. "Didn't mean for you to see my ears," he said.

He was in the sixth grade and the teacher had given the class scripts the day before to read over and decide what parts that they wanted to try out for in the Christmas play. "Roscoe," she asked, "Do you know what part you want to play?"

Roscoe laughed and said, "The only part I can play, an elf. Look at these ears!"

He told Heather, "My mother always said I had my father's ears, and that when I was a baby she prayed my hair would grow long enough to cover them."

Heather laughed and replied she didn't care; if she was remembering correctly, Roscoe hadn't made love with his ears.

***

It was closing in on 4 a.m. and Jackson was not happy. He'd dozed off in the recliner, and when he awakened, Heather still hadn't returned.

It wouldn't have mattered as much, of course, if he could have awakened at 4 a.m. in Meredith's bed with her legs entangled in his, but that piss-ass Kevin had ruined that possibility.

But he wasn't with Meredith, and Heather wasn't home. *If she's out screwing around with someone else, I'll kill her,* Jackson thought. He was wide awake now, so he decided to go looking for her. He'd drive looking through the parking lots in Frankenberry first, and then expand his search. "Damn bitch better hope I don't find her Mustang parked outside of the Grand Illusion Hotel," he muttered. "Or worse, yet, some other sleazy motel room."

***

About 5:15 a.m., Roscoe and Heather pulled the door to Room 123 shut and walked to the Mustang. "You probably ought to drive," Heather said. "Be easier than giving me directions. Just don't get us a ticket."

Roscoe slid behind the wheel and pulled the door shut. As he started the engine, he felt connected to the power coming to life under the hood. He felt like he was invincible. And it had all started with a stolen Infiniti. *Life is funny,* he thought, *the way things pull together.* The night clerk heard the Mustang come to life, looked out the window, and watched as Roscoe and Heather pulled out. Heather laid a hand on Roscoe's thigh as he looked both ways, and turned left onto Copperhead Avenue where he would go two blocks south and turn right to pick up 473 W.

Less than fifteen seconds after Roscoe turned on Route 473 toward Armstrong County, Jackson turned left off Zoology Drive onto Copperhead. He saw the flashing kettle on the Jackpot Motel sign. *I'm tired*, he thought. *If her car's not there, I'm going back home. I'll call in sick for work. I've got to sleep.*

The clerk saw the familiar RAM pickup pull in and drive slowly around the motel. *The gods must be smiling on Heather*, he thought. *Damned if I'm going to interfere.*

Jackson stopped at the lobby and got out. "Looking for … a friend," he said. "Drives a silver Mustang. Haven't seen it, have you?"

The motel clerk had been three years behind Jackson in school, had lost sixty-five pounds and grown a beard since his graduation ten years ago, so he felt certain that Jackson wouldn't recognize him from those days. Of course, he knew Jackson's habits as he had checked him in for short stays on more than one occasion with another woman, but the clerk had always thought it prudent not to mention to Jackson that he knew him. *So Heather is screwing around on her old man*, he thought. *Think I'll just keep this info to myself. Who knows, maybe someday I can get lucky with her.* He looked at Jackson, pursed his lips, furrowed his brows slightly as if thinking, and then lied, "No." He furrowed his brows even deeper. "Of course," he said, "I don't always see every car people get out of. They come and go here a lot. You know how that is. Who is it you're looking for?"

"A … ah," Jackson was caught a little off guard. He really hadn't intended on giving out his wife's name." He went on. "Heather Lamech is my friend's name."

The clerk said, "The name doesn't ring a bell, but I'll check the resister." He looked and then said that no one named Lamech had checked in, and asked Jackson what his friend looked like.

"Well," Jackson started, "she's a real pretty woman, 'bout five foot- four, with ginger red shoulder-length hair."

A pretty women I wouldn't cheat on, thought the motel clerk. Then he said, "Sorry, I haven't seen any one with red hair tonight."

"Thanks anyway," Jackson told the clerk, as he turned toward the door.

"If I see any woman fits the description and name, I'll tell her you're looking for her," the clerk said. Then he watched Jackson get back in his pick-up and turn back right on Copperhead.

When he got to the house, Jackson decided to stay up until after seven a.m. when he knew there would be someone at the shop to take his call about not being able to come to work. Along with being majorly pissed, he was actually a little worried about Heather. This was not like her. *Maybe I shouldn't have hit her the other day,* he thought, *but she was wrong to laugh at me. Stupid ass skunk. It wouldn't have even been there if it hadn't been for her fucking chickens to begin with. Chickens,* his thoughts continued, *she'd best get home soon, because I'm not taking care of them … and I didn't hit her that hard. God knows the time she cussed me out running her damn mouth about missing dinner was worse than this time. Hell, then, and the time I knocked her out, she had a black eye. This was just a little backhand; she's had plenty of them, ought to be used to it by now.* Jackson fixed himself a sandwich to eat while he waited for the time to pass. As soon as he was able to make his call, he went straight to bed, and immediately fell into a deep sleep.

CHAPTER 23
Bad Medic

As he worked on chipping wood away to form the nose on his latest carving, Brad smiled pensively at a memory that flashed through his mind.

Upon deplaning the men started processing, and soon Brad found out he and Steve were assigned to the 1st Air Cavalry Division, and headed to An Khe for several days to go through what was called FNG Training, aka Fucking New Guy Training, aka Cherry School, aka Charm School. Along with about fifty other men they boarded a C-130 and settled in for a noisy trip north. The first thing noticed when Camp Radcliff came into sight was a humongous 1st Cav Patch painted on the side of Hon Cong Mountain. After disembarking the airplane they could see they were in a fairly large camp in a mountainous area. A lot of the training seemed redundant, but he did enjoy repelling from the tower.

The FNG's were about halfway through training at Charm School and one night he was assigned to pull guard on the perimeter. He was leaving out the Supply Room door when the Supply Sargent hollered at him, "Hey, Miller. Get your ass back here!"

"Yes, Sir!"

"And I ain't no Sir; I work for a goddamn living!"

"Yes, Sargent!"

"That's better. Now on your way out of here en route to the perimeter, don't you think it would be a good idea to take along the ammunition I just gave you? Or do you plan on leaving it here on the counter and just throwing your rifle at any NVA that might try to sneak in tonight?"

Brad's face turned red as he took his ammo. "Sorry Sargent," he mumbled. "Thank you."

"And I guess I'd best leave you with another warning. Just a couple months ago a couple guys fell asleep on guard duty and we found them the next morning with their throats slashed and their balls cut off. Don't let that happen to you. It's a really difficult letter the Commander has to write to the family, explaining all that."

Although Brad questioned the veracity of the story, he still felt a tingling sensation below the belt line, and accepted the motivation to stay awake and alert.

Nicknames; for whatever reasons it seemed like everyone in the Nam was given a nickname. Some matched from the get-go; some never did; some were grown into.

The day before Christmas, 1968, Brad, Steve, and several other FNGs were flown by helicopter to LZ Ellen where their new unit, D 1/12th, was on perimeter duty for a week. Upon landing, they were told report to the Headquarters tent where one by one they were assigned to a platoon by CPT Kiser, the Commanding Officer, and the First Sargent, SFC Monroe. When it was Brad's turn the First Sargent said, "Okay, welcome to Delta; name?"

"Bradley Miller, Brad."

"Ah, the new medic. Good. Did you say Badly?"

"No, Bradley, Brad."

CPT Kiser jumped in. "And a medic, Top. Bad Medic."

"I plan on being a good medic," Brad replied.

"Well then," the First Sargent came back, "that would make you a ba...aa...ad medic; that's good."

"Whatever."

"Hey, Bad M," CPT Kiser said, "take it easy; don't mean nuthin'."

"By the way," SFC Monroe said, "You did remember to bring your ammunition with you, right?"

Brad reddened as CPT Kiser added, "Yes, Bad M, Now I see you're a medic who carries a weapon, so keep in mind that here in Delta Company we believe in carrying our ammo with us at all times. Otherwise, it could be bad, Medic."

CHAPTER 24
The Porcelain Dove

Karen Esterbean, Tira's mother carefully got the porcelain dove down from the mantle. "Tira," she said. "I know I have told you many times not to touch this because it's special. Well, Sweetheart, you are four years old now, getting to be a big girl who can understand things better, and it's time I told you why. This is so important because my mother, your Granny Lisa, gave it to me, her mother, Granny Thelma, who's in heaven now, gave it to her, and her mother, Granny Marta, who's also in heaven, gave it to her. When you get bigger, I'm going to give it to you. And when you get bigger and have a little girl, someday you can give it to her. That's why this is special. Do you understand?"

"I think so," Tira said, "No one really wants it, so they keep giving it away."

***

Tira Furcologna was ten. Her mother was a very spiritual Catholic who did not happen to believe her attendance at Mass, or, more to the point, lack of attendance, had any real impact on her being accepted by any Divine Power who monitored the universe. However, she had started Tira in catechism classes, and regularly spent some time in meditation every day, sitting in her lounge chair, facing her large wooden crucifix on the wall. Tira had observed this, and at the age of nine decided she, too, would spend time staring at the figure on the wall. Tira asked her mother if it would be all right for her to hold the porcelain dove so she could make the crucifixion meditation event more special by clasping it with both hands while praying. Her mother had responded that she could, as long as she was always very careful with it. Now, a year into her habit, Tira decided when she was done she would transfer the dove to her left hand and then make the sign of the cross again. In catechism the priest had said they should cross themselves before praying, but Tira figured that she would be even better off by doing it before and after.

***

Frankenberry Middle School housed the 6th, 7th, and 8th grades. Tira was eleven when she made the transition into that academic realm and Karen Esterbean decided the time was appropriate to transfer dove ownership. She told Tira, "Honey, whenever you have a child of your own, you too will know when the time is right to pass this along."

Tira's tears flowed as she clutched the porcelain bird and faced the crucifix. She promised the figure, "I will always guard and protect this dove with all my heart."

When Tira was fifteen, a friend invited her to Frankenberry Community Church It had a large, active youth group and Tira liked it, so she asked her mother if she could start attending there. Karen Esterbean shrugged. "I have no problem with that."

The Preacher's name was Ulysses Brock, and Tira liked listening to him when he talked to them after their social activity times. Tira did not remember her father, but she thought that if she'd had one, he would probably have been someone like Pastor Brock. The service formats were quite different between the community church and the Catholic Church. Tira enjoyed the community church more, but she still kept her daily ritual of praying to the crucifix while holding the dove. She was not only comfortable with, and comforted by, the routine; she figured it wouldn't hurt her to have the extra safety net.

When Tira turned sixteen and passed her driver's license test she spent an extra ten minutes in front of the crucifix, since Pastor Brock had said at one of their youth meetings they could pray for protection, and God would give it to them. As she held the dove and meditated on the wooden figure, she wondered if she should ever say anything to Pastor Brock about her daily ceremony. Not too long ago, during a Sunday morning service he had said when they prayed they didn't need crucifixes like the Catholics, or any other human devised rites. Tira really liked Pastor Brock, but she felt a calming hope in what she did, so she decided she would just keep information about her prayer routine to herself. She felt a slight twinge of guilt whenever she thought about what she considered deceiving Pastor Brock, but when she clutched the dove tightly and looked square into the wooden eyes of the man on the cross, she always felt the guilt subside.

CHAPTER 25
Enter Albert

Sometimes Albert Furcologna was surprised at the fact that he and Tira Esterbean were married. In the early years it was surprised pleasantly, and in later years the element of surprise came from the fact that they were still married.

A few years back, when he was twenty-two, and finishing up his undergraduate degree in Business at Periwinkle College, a friend, George Rostenburg, asked him to a church picnic at the Frankenberry Community Church. Albert wasn't a regular church attendee anywhere else and he didn't have anything planned for that day, so he agreed.

Tira Esterbean was wearing rather tight jeans, a top that showed occasional glimpses of her navel, and Albert's thoughts were of heaven, though not necessarily church-oriented.

Albert and Tira wound up on the same volleyball team, and he took a moderate approach; polite, showing interest, but not behaving like a dog looking for a bitch in heat. At the conclusion of the day's activities, the pastor conducted closing prayer, and reminded his congregation about the next evening's special music, Bill and Gloria Gaither. Tira was next to Albert, and asked, "You going?"

"I might," Albert shrugged, "but I have to admit, I don't know anything about them."

"I've got a couple of their tapes," Tira said. "I was really happy when Pastor Brock said he was bringing them in. They've been around a while, and usually they do larger Christian concerts, but Pastor Brock and his wife know Bill Gaither from school years, and anyway, Bill said he and Gloria would love to come here. I think it is so cool." Albert reiterated he wasn't familiar with them, but it sounded good to him.

"I have their 'Because He Lives' CD in my car," Tira said. "I could lend it to you, or, if you want to, we could go listen to a couple of the songs right now."

Albert couldn't believe this good looking, apparently single, young woman was asking him to her car to listen to some music, but he vaguely remembered a prayer, he thought it was by Peter found somewhere in the Gospels. He wasn't even sure why it had been prayed, or what it meant, but from what he could remember how it went, it seemed appropriate for the occasion; "Lord, I believe; help my unbelief."

**

Albert had a disability most people didn't know about. According to the doctor, probably due to not wearing earplugs while hunting, it appeared he had nerve damage which contributed to a condition called tinnitus, a loud, continual ringing in his ears. Sometimes it bothered him more than others; most of the time, it only drove him crazy.

Albert had already discovered that in life most things were a mixed blessing. He had enjoyed tromping through the woods with his father as a young boy. And it was not just the fact he had learned to really enjoy nature, it was also about the only conditions under which his father spent time with him. But when it came to hunting, Albert's father had taken a hard-core approach with things like protecting yourself - from yourself. "Earplugs are for sissies," he used to say. After a particularly successful day in the hunting department, when Albert was thirteen, he started to become aware of the loud, ringing sensation.

After a few days of the noise not calming down, Albert's mother took him to the doctor, who referred him to a specialist. After a battery of hearing tests, he was informed it appeared to be nerve damage. The specialist tried to insert some jocularity, saying, "Actually you don't hear too badly, for a hunter." By then, the noise was so distracting to Albert that he didn't find humor in the statement.

He found it difficult to speak about, because he was the only one aware of it. When he had tried to talk about it to his father one time, the response was, "Guess you'll just have to learn to live with it. Probably need to cut back on the hunting trips." One day, when he was seventeen, he was so aggravated and depressed he thought aspirin might be the cure, lots of aspirin. Albert took about twenty, thinking that would probably be enough to kill himself, and lay down. It wasn't.

For some reason, he felt very calm and peaceful. So this is what it feels like to die, *he thought. He drifted off to sleep, and later awakened to the loudest ringing to date. Albert was scared, and told his mother what he had done.*

Her response was, "What is the matter with you? Don't you think of anyone else's feelings except your own? That was a really stupid thing to do!"

She took him to the emergency room, but by then most of the aspirin were in his system. Although, by this time, it was obvious he hadn't taken a lethal dose, they pumped his stomach, and the doctor told his mother to make an appointment for Albert with a psychiatrist. Then he passed on to Albert what he jokingly referred to as the really good news.

"I hate to tell you this, Wild Man, but too many aspirin can cause a temporary ringing in the ears."

On the way home, Albert asked, "Do we have to tell Dad about this?"

"A little late. I called him from the emergency room."

"Oh," said Albert, "so why didn't he come?"

"He was getting ready to go to Floyd County to close a land deal that was the end result of several weeks' work. He said he really had to go, but told me to call him if it looked like it was going to be an emergency."

"Well," thought Albert, "I guess I'll just have to learn to live with it."

Now, five years later, as he sat in the car with Tira listening to 'Because He Lives' and 'It Is Finished' by the Gaithers, he was glad he hadn't taken a fatal dose of aspirin. Dealing with the ringing was easier when he stayed occupied and concentrated on something. And he thought Tira seemed like someone he might want to concentrate on. He was in his own place as he had moved away from his parents as soon as possible, and after two years of living alone, he was feeling like he wanted someone to share his life with. Albert had several female friends, but he had not gotten romantically involved with any of them, probably for a variety of reasons which included working a full-time job, being enrolled in college, and generally being a loner, whether linked to the ringing or not, he didn't know.

Albert agreed to come to the church concert the next evening, and then he and Tira sat and talked. He told her about his desire to become a Business Professor at Periwinkle College and that he had at least his Masters to complete before that became a reality, and he hoped to do that at Marshall University in Huntington, West Virginia.

"I work for my mother at the Petal Pushing Floral Shop in Frankenberry," Tira said. "I really enjoy it. I'm extremely busy this week as my mother is out of town at the Kentucky Florists Annual Convention."

"I didn't even know florists had conventions," Albert said.

"Well, my mother hasn't been a member of the Association, but recently heard about, applied for, and received a Rodger Vannatter Grant."

"What's a Rodger Vannatter Grant?"

"It was established apparently in honor of some guy named Rodger Vannatter to help encourage people who had chosen the floral industry as a profession to gain more knowledge within their field. The conference includes sessions in everything from customer relations to advertising and several classes on working with established and new floral designs. Mother said if the conference is beneficial she'll likely send me next year."

After another couple hours of sitting in the car and talking, Albert and Tira parted ways to their separate homes. Albert had gleaned from the conversation that Tira and her mother were close and thought it was kind of nice for someone to be close to a parent. A little different than his situation, but that was life. Tira had said her father walked out when she was two, and they had never heard from him again. Albert told her his father was still around, but they hadn't really communicated in years.

"Although, I could be wrong. I guess one could say that his hollering at me occasionally is a form of communication."

The next evening Albert went to the concert and sat with Tira. He had already figured he would enjoy her company, but, a little to his surprise, he also found himself enjoying the concert. Afterward, Pastor Ulysses Brock and his wife Eloise had coordinated a pizza party where people could visit with Bill and Gloria Gaither, and just enjoy time with each other. Albert was having a good time with Tira, and he realized it stemmed from more than just the glimpse of navel he had caught the night before.

When the pizza party was over, Albert asked Tira if she wanted to go to the movies with him the next evening. She agreed, and by the end of the week they had seen four movies together at the Cinemawatchee II. Friday evening, Tira asked Albert if he wanted to go to church with her Sunday and Albert agreed. Tira said her mother would be back from the conference Sunday evening and had said she wanted to meet Albert.

Sunday found Albert sitting next to Tira and listening to the preacher. During announcements, Pastor Ulysses Brock said, "And after the meeting tonight, Eloise and I will coordinate a time of fun and games in the rec room, with more pizza. Of course, we can vote on the pizza, if anyone objects. And it's only for those young people who are under the age of ninety-six."

Tira leaned into Albert and said, "The reason Pastor Brock said ninety-six, is because Mr. Hobbin just turned ninety-five and he still comes to most of the evening services."

Pastor Brock continued, "Now Mr. Hobbin, naturally we will up the age limit if you start going out with an older woman."

Everyone laughed as Mr. Hobbin said, "I just might surprise you one day."

Pastor Brock countered, "Naturally Mr. Hobbin, you will have to bring said hypothetical older woman to church."

Everyone laughed again as Mr. Hobbin replied, "I wouldn't go out with any other kind; she'd have to come to church with me, and if she didn't like pizza, she would have to allow me to still keep eating it."

Albert liked the relaxed atmosphere, and felt like he was really lucky to have met Tira. He still couldn't believe, foremost, that she wasn't going with any else, and next, that she was interested in him.

Later, after the evening service, while sitting at a table eating pizza, Albert and Tira talked some with Mr. Hobbin.

"I look like I'm a young man, only seventy or so, instead of ninety-five, don't I?" he said to Albert.

"You look like you've learned the secret to enjoying life."

"Treat others the way you want to be treated, and ride horses," Mr. Hobbin came back.

"Ride horses?" Albert queried, thinking maybe it had something to do with what his father used to say about really feeling alive when out hunting.

"Son," Mr. Hobbin continued, "my father bought me my first horse when I was five years old. Been riding most of my life since then. Actually, I had to quit about ten years back, but I still like to go to my son's stable and be around them."

"Five years old?" Albert was trying to remember if he had even seen a real horse by the time he was five.

"Yes sir," said Mr. Hobbin with a smile in his eyes as he mind-traveled back some ninety years. "Everyone laughed because of the name I gave him. My last name was Hobbin, so I named him Mr. Dobbin. I'd tell my mother it was time for Hobbin and Dobbin to go out riding. I used to race him against some of the other horses in our section of the county. We beat everyone, except that little upstart Lucinda riding her bay called Sugarbush. Hobbin and Dobbin never could beat her. But I fixed her one day." He broke into a big smile.

"What did you do?" Albert took the bait.

"Why son, I married her."

"How old was Mr. Dobbin?" Albert asked.

"About sixteen."

"Is that old for a horse?"

"Not at all; he lived for another twelve years."

"So," Tira asked. "How long were you and your wife married?"

"Lived with her for sixty-five wonderful years. Fixed her real good."

Albert and Tira laughed. "Sixty-five years," said Tira dreamily, "that's neat."

"And what was your secret for that long a marriage?" Albert asked.

"Kept on letting her and Sugarbush beat old Hobbin and Dobbin. Well," he laughed, "until they got too old to race – the horses, that is."

"Let?" Tira smiled as she said it, and then laughed as Mr. Hobbin asked her not to kick the props out from under an old man's fantasies at this stage of his life.

Albert asked Mr. Hobbin how long he had known Lucinda before he married her, and Mr. Hobbin hesitated a moment, then replied, "A while. Remember, things was different back when I was younger, and besides I knew from the moment I first saw that sweet little girl I wanted to marry her." Tira asked how old Lucinda was when they got married and Mr. Hobbin replied, "Sixteen, but like I just said, things was different."

"Sixteen? How old were you?"

"A little older," said Mr. Hobbin. "I was nineteen."

Albert suddenly felt bold. "Tira, when I first laid eyes on you ... well, we're both older than they were ... Will you marry me?"

"Now like I said," Mr. Hobbin interjected, "times was different then."

"If you get down on one knee and ask proper-like," Tira answered.

Albert grinned as he slid out of his chair and on to his right knee. He stretched his hands upward to Tira. "Tira, Honey, will you marry me."

"Sure, why not," said Tira.

Mr. Hobbin shook his head as he said, "Maybe things haven't changed as much as I thought they had. Albert, you need to buy horses for yourself and Tira, and, by the way, make sure you get her the faster one."

Later around ten p.m. when Tira and Albert entered Tira's house, Karen Esterbean was sitting in her Navy blue velvet wingback chair reading. "Was church good, Sweetheart?" she asked, setting her book down. "And is this your friend, Albert?"

"Church was nice, and so was the rec time afterwards. And, yes, this is Albert Furcologna."

"Well hello Albert. Tira mentioned you are working on a college degree; sounds like you have good goals for yourself."

"I'm trying," Albert smiled.

"If you don't mind my asking, are you any kin to Brent Furcologna, Franken County Sheriff a few years back?"

"He's my uncle."

"Well," Karen started, "I've always thought Brent Furcologna was a good man; voted for him all three times he ran for sheriff."

"I'll pass that bit of information on to him," Albert said.

"Albert, did you enjoy church and the pizza party?"

"I did, Thanks for asking. We sat with Mr. Hobbin and really enjoyed ourselves."

Karen laughed. "Then I'm sure you heard about Hobbin and Dobbin."

"We did," Albert said. "Mr. Hobbin seems like a real nice man and it sounds like he had a good marriage with Lucinda."

"From what I could tell when I was younger, he did. Even though they had very different religious directions, my family has known Mr. Hobbin for as far back as I can remember," Karen responded.

Tira shifted somewhat uncomfortably. "Mother, did he ever ... did he ever tell you how old he was when he and his wife got married."

"Uh huh," said Karen, looking closely at Tira. "Why, are you thinking of getting married?"

"Ma'am," Albert nervously started, his speech rate increasing with each word, "Mr. Hobbin was telling us he knew from the minute he met his wife he wanted to marry her, and they got married right away, and they were happily married for sixty-five years, and I was wondering, would you please let me marry your daughter?"

Karen Louise Esterbean stared at Albert for a moment then broke into smile and started laughing. "Albert," she said, "Tira's father and I dated for four and a half years before we got married, and three years later, when Tira was two, he walked out on us, left us high and dry and I never heard from him again after the divorce was final. And old Mr. Hobbin and his wife stayed married for sixty-five years. What the heck, you two, try it his way; my way sure didn't work. Welcome to the family, Albert Furcologna."

They visited for quite awhile and discussed all the changes that would be coming about. After they were married, of course, Tira would be moving into Albert's apartment. She said she was making enough at her work to be able to allow him to continue on with his schooling.

Albert said, "As soon as I receive my BBA I plan on pursuing my MBA at Marshall University. I planned on moving there, but since we're getting married, I'll just commute."

"Won't that be too far?" Tira asked.

"Not at all. About forty-three miles one way, so round trip daily approximately eighty-five, eighty-six miles. I can still work about thirty hours a week at my current job, and even though things might get tight at times, I think we'll be all right financially."

"Well," said Karen, "I experienced rough times when my husband walked out years ago, but with hard work and hope I came out on top. If you two tackle your problems head-on as one, I'm sure you will successfully weather your own storms. I don't mean to surprise you, but there will be storms, you know."

As he drove home later, Albert's mind was whirling with the sudden change in direction his life was taking, and, the dichotomies; feeling he was truly being welcomed into a new family, and, of course, distraction by his constant companion, the infernal tinnitus.

After Albert left, and her mother retired for the night, Tira went to the mantle and carefully got down the porcelain dove. After she made the sign of the cross, she held the dove with both hands, like she had done so many times before, and started meditating on the man looking back at her with his arms outstretched. She decided she would look for a crucifix as close as possible to the one she was gazing at to take with her when she set up house with Albert.

CHAPTER 26
Loco 6, Permission Denied

Brad looked his cabin over and decided he should make a list of repair work to do. Money was no object as after the accident he had sold his grandfather's other property and hired a CPA to provide guidance in establishing a balance between everyday living needs and long term investments. As he got out a pen and yellow legal pad he thought about the many paradoxes of life. Over time he had grown to love the rides in the Bell UH-1 helicopters, otherwise known as Hueys, with their specific thumping blade noise, an almost soothing sound to him. But he knew he would not have had those rides were it not for combat assaults. The Birds were also a welcome sight and sound when delivering food or mail, or coming to take someone to the field hospital, but the paradox was that, although still a welcome sound, they sometimes had to be called because someone needed to go to the hospital, or worse, the morgue. He loved and had many pictures of beautiful sights in the jungle, but he was aware he never would have seen them without including the images of the aftermath of artillery and air strikes, firefights, napalm drops, and the defoliation caused by Agent Orange.

Brad sighed, and started on his list of needed repairs. As he worked he recalled a time when his platoon leader made a serious request from the Company Commander, but all that happened was the CO made light of it.

On December 29th, 1968, Delta Company made a combat assault into the outskirts of a small village. Brad followed suit of his 3rd platoon leader whom he was sitting next to on the floor of the chopper, and let his legs hang out. At around 7-10 feet the Huey hovered and the door gunners were hollering, "Jump! Jump!" Brad was thankful for all his prior physical training up to this time, also aware of the impact on legs and back on landing with around 85 pounds in the ruck on his back. There was some firing generally westward into the jungle edging the village; one of the platoons had made contact with some enemy. There were no casualties, and soon the entire company moved out Northwest into an extremely thick jungle where after some four hours of humping they dug in for the night.

The next day of reconnaissance proved uneventful, but tiring. December 31st was different, and foreshadowing. Shortly before dusk on New Year's Eve, the resupply chopper was landing when a couple of NVA fired at it from the 3rd platoon side of the perimeter. The supplies were kicked out and the pilots managed to lift off and escape with no hits.

The LT called the Company Commander on the radio.

"Crackerjack 6, this is Tonto Loco 6; Over."

"Go ahead, Loco 6."

"Crackerjack 6, request permission for a mad minute in the direction enemy fire received from earlier."

"Loco 6, this is Crackerjack 6, permission denied."

LT handed the handset back to his RTO and cursed. "Damn CO seems to not understand yet how to handle these situations, but I know better than to argue with him. Just hope we don't have any New Year's Eve fireworks!"

After dark LT got on the radio again, whispering, "Crackerjack 6, this is Tonto Loco 6. My Listening Post is hearing what sounds like people climbing trees, also hearing verbal communication."

In response the entire company could hear, "Tonto Loco 6, tuck your men in and tell them 'Goodnight'. This is Crackerjack 6; out!"

"Fucking idiot," LT whispered to Brad as he put down the handset.

More than we thought, *Brad reflected;* way more than we thought.

CHAPTER 27
Enough is Enough

A jailer brought some breakfast by, and Aaron couldn't believe how good the Cheerios and milk tasted. There was also a piece of toast with a rectangular-shaped grape jelly container accompanying it, and as he spread the jelly on his toast, Aaron thought about the many times he had done that as he was eating a breakfast fixed for him by his Nana before he left for work. But work was another area where Aaron had not done real well, and had created difficulties for himself over the years.

Aaron lifted one of the boxes of books up and headed for the car. "What are you going to do with these, Nana?"

"We're going to stop by the Franken County Library and leave them there. They've been around this house collecting dust on the shelves for too long. They all look as good as the day I bought them. Might as well see them used by someone."

Aaron had to admit, none of them looked even vaguely familiar. "I don't ever remember reading any of these."

"You didn't, Aaron," his Nana said, "that's exactly why we're getting rid of them. You never were much for reading. You liked to play outside with your bicycle, and later, tinker with a vehicle all the time. I've always said, people are just smart in different ways. Book learning just didn't happen to be yours."

"But I'm doing okay now, Nana, I've got another job." Aaron knew that at age twenty-eight most guys didn't still live with their grandparents, and he wondered if she was disappointed in him. "I'm hired on as a mechanic down at Tadpole's Service Station."

"I know Aaron, and I'm glad you enjoy your work."

"Pop doesn't seem too happy."

"You can't worry about that. Your Pop just had something different in mind for you, that's all. But we can't live someone else's life for them. We each gotta do what we gotta do."

Aaron thought that maybe he could find his way back into his Pop's good graces, so he told his Nana, "If Pop has car trouble, I could probably get him a good deal on it."

"That won't happen. Pop always takes his car to the dealership."

"Doesn't make sense, not if I can get him a discount at Tadpole's."

"Aaron, you get what you pay for in life; when you pay for Tadpole, you get Tadpole. I have to agree with your Pop on that one. Now help me get the rest of these books into the trunk."

Aaron thought his Nana sounded a bit impatient, but he shrugged it off. She was probably just tired or something, nothing to worry about.

As Aaron ate his toast he thought of a situation from about three years earlier. He had finally moved into his own apartment, and waking up for work had become his own responsibility.

He awoke, wrinkled his forehead, and then rubbed it. He glanced over at the clock and groaned. Aaron had decided a few months earlier that Ox was back in style and the night before had been down at O'Rourke's and had run into Jackson Lamech, a friend he occasionally had a few drinks with. Jackson often had a good looking woman with him, usually not the same one, and a couple times had fixed Aaron up with one of his female companion's friends for some horizontal comforts. Jackson was alone last night, and even though they had stayed until closing time, Aaron wasn't worried about getting up for work because he was thinking, No problem. Hell, I'm the Ox. Now he was thinking, How did I not hear the alarm again? I know I didn't have that much to drink last night.

Aaron knew he was screwed. Toolbox, owner of the Brakes and Buggies Service Center was a good boss, but the day before he had told Aaron "Enough is enough." Same thing Aaron had heard a couple years earlier from the owner of Tadpole's Service Station.

"Aaron," Toolbox said, "You can't just show up late for work two, three days a week."

Aaron looked down at the floor as he responded, "It won't happen again."

Toolbox told Aaron, "I wish that were true, but I know better. Damn it, you were supposed to be here two and a half hours ago!"

"Sorry, Boss," Aaron replied.

Toolbox continued, "Mrs. Justice wanted her car first thing this morning, and I had to pull Pliers off a gasket job to finish it."

Aaron again said "Sorry, Boss," for about the 97th time in his life. But Toolboxes' chastening didn't stop there.

"Furthermore, Fiona Washington called me last night and said you were making her feel uncomfortable."

"I didn't do nuthin'," Aaron said defensively.

Toolboxes' voice rose as he said, "Oh yeah, you only stared at her breasts and smacked your lips. Most women would find another garage to go to, but Fiona and I went to school together, and she's been bringing her car here for years."

"Sorry, Boss," Aaron said. Number 98.

"And stop saying, 'Sorry, Boss'."

"Okay, Boss. Sorry." Almost 99.

Toolbox shook his head and told Aaron, "Tell you what. You just said it won't happen again? This is your last chance. You show up late one more time and you're fired, got it?"

"Got it." Aaron breathed a sigh of relief. "Thanks, Boss."

So Aaron just rubbed his forehead again. He knew there was no sense showing up at the garage for work anymore.

Aaron stared at the jail bars as he finished his toast and sat there wondering if there was any way he could get his life into some kind of order. He knew he'd been given all the chances one could ever hope for.

Aaron sat at his grandmother's kitchen table. "Nana, I messed up again." His grandmother brought him a bologna and cheese sandwich and a Dr. Pepper and asked if he'd been fired again. Aaron miserably nodded in the affirmative.

"Drinking again?"

Again Aaron nodded "yes".

"Now Aaron, I don't want to make a comparison because the good Lord knows you are a lot more pleasant to be around than your mother, but you have to accept the fact that your mother had a drinking problem, too."

"I know, and I don't want to be like her because if I ever have kids, I want them to be proud of me."

"I know, Aaron," his grandmother replied, "And I'm proud of you for thinking like that." Aaron smiled at Nana and took a huge bite of bologna and cheese. He already felt better. "Now, Aaron," said Nana, "things will work out for you. And chew, don't just swallow your sandwich."

Aaron knew the sad truth of his life was that after he added up all the parts, the total was right there in front of him, bars on a jail cell door. And the real sad part, to him, was he felt like he really didn't know if there was any potential for his life to be on the plus side. He really didn't know if his Nana even felt that anymore.

CHAPTER 28
Angel Windows

Todd wondered how Aaron Patterson was doing the day after. It looked like he had been seriously jarred by Todd's words the day before, and Todd hoped it would be a turning point for Aaron, or at least another factor pushing him toward one.

Todd had felt totally helpless after his family had been killed. For a long while after the accident, if he was thrown into any incident that involved drinking and driving, Todd felt near uncontrollable hostility, and frequently wished he could take the offenders out somewhere and kill them. In time, it was reduced to just wanting to kick the shit out of them.

Now, for the most part, Todd realized that by arresting and helping prosecute drunk drivers, he was doing something. With every arrest, he was potentially sparing some family the anguish he had suffered.

After Todd came on duty, he got ready to go by Mrs. Walker's house in Frankenberry. It seemed there was some property damage connected to an arrest he had made. A report had already been taken by the local police, and they thought Trooper Truitt should take one also. He had talked with Mrs. Walker on the phone and told her he would be by this morning.

Todd saw Julie wasn't in yet, and asked the man who was covering dispatch for her if he knew where she was. The Dispatcher said she had called in sick. Todd hoped it didn't have anything to do with their conversation of the prior evening, or the fact he had turned down her invitation to visit for awhile. He decided he would try and call her later and see if she was all right.

Todd headed to 1657 Acorn Street. As he parked in front of the house, got out of the cruiser and headed up the sidewalk, he observed obvious damage to the white picket fence. Not only was it completely knocked over in one place, some of the green paint from the John Deere lawnmower had scraped off. It was obvious Aaron Patterson had made a stop here first on his way downtown yesterday.

Later in the day, Aaron was escorted from his cell. The guard told him he had a visitor, and Aaron fully expected it to be his Nana. He was a bit taken back when he saw Todd and realized he was facing the trooper who had arrested him the day before. Todd thanked the guard and told him he would call him when he was done talking with Aaron. As the guard left, Todd asked, "So, Aaron, how are you feeling today?"

"Not so good, sir," said Aaron. "I didn't sleep too good last night. I've been doing a lot of thinking about what I done yesterday, and a lot of other stuff I've done in my life, and I don't feel so good at all. And I want you to know, I'm real sorry about what happened to your family."

Todd replied he accepted that, and he was glad Aaron had been doing some thinking. He asked if Aaron had been serious the day before when he said he knew he needed help.

Aaron said he had been, and was, serious, and that it had really hit him hard that he had a drinking problem and trouble keeping a job. Aaron said he felt certain if he stopped his drinking, his job problem would take care of itself.

"I'm thinking you're probably right," said Todd. "Now let me tell you what else I've been thinking. I talked with Judge Glen Leahy a few minutes ago. I told him something about your demeanor when you were being arrested yesterday got my attention, and I can't help but feel that maybe the timing is right for you to go through a long-term treatment program. In his position, he can court order you into the Angel Windows facility. It is a minimum six month program. Are you willing to commit to it?" Aaron nodded his head somberly as he said he really did need help because he couldn't seem to do it on his own.

Todd added, "And there is another matter that will also need to be taken care of, after you are released from Angel Windows. You will need to get a job and pay restitution to Mrs. Walker on Acorn Street since you paid her lawn a visit, but forgot to stop the lawnmower before climbing her white picket fence. Do you recall that?"

"I kind of remember something about a fence, and … and … I'm real sorry about that too, Sir."

Todd somberly looked at Aaron and replied, "This may be your only opportunity to make a fresh start. It won't be easy; but most things in life worth having come with hard work and sweat attached. Are you prepared to make this kind of commitment?"

Aaron said "Yes, sir," and then asked Todd if he could ask him something.

"You may."

"Don't take me wrong, Sir, but why are you doing this instead of trying to get the book thrown at me?"

"Number one, like I told Judge Leahy earlier today, you seemed like you might be ready for this, and, number two, Aaron, to be honest, if this works, someone in the future may be spared the hell I've had to go through." Todd continued, "And trust me, if you were to hurt or kill someone while under the influence, it would destroy your life, too." Tears flowed down Aaron Patterson's face as he shook hands with Todd Truitt.

In contrast to normal procedures, a few minutes later Aaron humbly stood in front of Judge Leahy. The Judge decided to administer his own testing format on Aaron and asked, "So, are you the guy who had decided to see if Main Street needed mowing yesterday?"

Aaron looked up and quietly answered, "What I did was wrong, Your Honor, and I'm really sorry I caused those problems."

"So, be honest with me, and remember I've had you in this courtroom before, are you really sorry, or just sorry you got caught?"

Despite his best efforts, tears came to Aaron's eyes, and one trickled down his cheek.

"No, Your Honor," he replied, "Why I'm sorry is I got to thinking about what happened to the Trooper's family, and I know there have been times when I was in a car that I ... that ... that I could have been guilty of doing that."

Aaron told the judge he had a Nana who had raised him and he knew she loved him a lot and he had also been doing some thinking about the pain he had caused her.

"And I know," he continued, "if I ever hurt someone, or worse, it would also be hurting my Nana real bad. I've been lucky, Your Honor, and I really am sorry for all the times I have taken chances with other people's lives."

"Well, Mr. Patterson," Judge Leahy sternly said, "You can consider yourself very fortunate for at least three things. First, I believe you are thinking clearly about not wanting to cause your Nana any more pain and grief; second, like you just said, you never hurt or killed anyone while drinking and driving; and third, you are most fortunate Trooper Truitt is the arresting officer and that he thinks you are sincere about wanting to change. Because of what had happened to Trooper Truitt's family, as a judge, I take his recommendations about drunk driving cases very seriously."

Judge Leahy continued, "Mr. Patterson, you are to be taken from here to be admitted to the six month program at the Angel Windows Rehabilitation Facility. Should you fail to complete the program, for any reason, you will be immediately locked up and finish your six month sentence in jail. Furthermore, upon release from Angel Windows, you are to make arrangements through the court to pay complete restitution to Mrs. Walker, whose fence you damaged. Do you understand this sentence?"

"Yes, Your Honor," Aaron said, "and thank you for giving me this chance."

"You need to thank Trooper Truitt, and by the way, he will be the one checking on your progress."

Aaron acknowledged those conditions, and thanked them both again.

CHAPTER 29
New Year's Day 1969

Brad thought about when he learned that wartime truces were sometimes one-way. Tensions were high around 8 a.m. on New Year's Day 1969. Three men from 3rd Squad were heading out for Observation Post to replace the nighttime LP when all hell broke loose. The OP's ran back to the perimeter, saw Chuck, and immediately called out, "Medic!"

"Coming!" Brad hollered as he low crawled to where they were and was faced with his first war casualty, a man he only knew as Chuck leaning back against a tree with two bullet holes in his forehead, still holding a C-Ration can he had been opening. Although he had a shocked look on his face, he probably never knew what hit him. Brad checked his pulse hoping that somehow the obvious was wrong. It wasn't.

About that time he heard another man screaming, "Jesus, I'm hit! Medic! Someone help me! Oh, Sweet Jesus, I'm hit!" A man from Chuck's squad said it was Ray Dickenson who was calling for help.

"There's nothing I can do for Chuck; I'm going to some others who are wounded!"

Brad crouched low and ran to Ray. When he saw blood flowing only from Ray's upper arm he said, "You're going to be okay, man, you got it?" He then cut away the fatigue shirt sleeve around the top part so he could slide it off. It looked like shrapnel had ripped into the muscle, but the injury did not appear to be life-threatening. As Brad worked on Ray he heard other cries for help as the firefight continued to rage. He could hear the crack of gunfire all around, bullets whistling past, and explosions from mortars and hand grenades. As soon as he stopped the blood flow he applied a gauze patch to the wound and tightly wrapped it with a bandage roll. "Get back into your foxhole and try to keep the bandage higher than your heart; I'll be back to check on you soon."

"Medic! Doc Larry's hit! We need a medic over in 2nd Platoon!"

Brad could hear bullets flying by as he again crouched and ran to where the cry came from. Doc Larry was lying on his side clutching his right hand over his heart, his face contorted in agony. "I ain't gonna make it, Brad; ain't gonna make it!"

"You'll be fine, Larry. Hold on." Brad cut cloth away from the wounded area and saw that the bullet was a bit to the left of the heart, more in the shoulder. He got the bleeding stopped and was applying bandages when another volley of enemy gunfire opened up, and Brad instinctively hunkered his head down. He heard a gasp from Larry, and saw he had taken a bullet in the neck. Like Chuck just a few moments earlier, the look of death covered his face. Oh, God, Brad thought. Could I have shielded him? Why did I duck? He furiously tried to stop the bleeding from the neck, but realized there was nothing he could do. Another man just a few feet away screamed out as he took a chunk of shrapnel in his back. It came all the way out the front carrying intestines with it. Brad's mind was in a dazed state as he crawled to Don and started to readjust guts so he could wrap him. According to what he had studied, it actually looked like Don could survive.

In a pain filled voice, Don asked, "How's Doc Larry?"

Brad knew Don was in very fragile condition, and his knowing Doc Larry was dead might trigger shock, so Brad replied, "I just left him; he's fine. You'll get to see him at the hospital. You're both lucky bastards getting to go see all them pretty nurses while we stay out here with this shit." Don smiled weakly and nodded his head.

Artillery barrages had been called in and apparently were the key in quelling the enemy forces, so the company started dealing with the aftermath of the firefight, patching up those with minor wounds and calling in a Medevac to transport the dead and seriously wounded.

The Company Commander came to Brad. "You were working on Doc Larry, Bad M. Goddammit. How the hell did he die?"

"He seemed okay just before the last heavy round of gunfire, Sir. Then he took a bullet in the neck."

"Didn't you have him protected?"

Brad let his own prior questions stay silent as he answered, "I did what I could, Sir."

One of Medic Larry's friends, Rollo, was there and angrily said, "I saw you duck down, Bad M. Larry took the bullet because you left him open."

"I don't like it when one of my good medics dies, Bad M," the CO said. "Next time let your best be just a little fucking better, got it?"

As the CO walked away, the 3rd platoon LT came to Brad and said, "Don't take him personally. He's almost as new as you; he just doesn't learn as quickly. You did all you could. As a matter of fact, I'm putting you in for a Bronze Star for your actions under fire. Chuck and Doc Larry had mortal wounds, there was nothing you could do, and you did save Don's life, and damn sure helped a lot of other people. You did well."

Why didn't that make me feel any better? *Brad thought.*

CHAPTER 30
Keep Our Stories Straight

As he stayed fairly close to the speed limit to try and avoid any encounters with the law, Roscoe talked to Heather a few minutes about what they should say to keep their stories straight with his mother. Heather was feeling empowered as she realized the hold she had over Roscoe. "Can you believe," she started, "that I have never done anything like this before?"

"Well, I'm glad you started now because I am thoroughly enjoying your entrance to the wild side."

After a few more minutes of conversation, Heather asked Roscoe how much further to his mother's place, and he told her it would still be close to another hour and a half or so.

"Armstrong County has got to be one of the weirdest shaped counties in Kentucky," Roscoe said. "It's almost like the town of Huntington, West Virginia, long and narrow; except in this case, long means approximately 65 miles, and narrow is 20 to 25 miles wide, at its widest spots, and mostly curvy roads."

"Do you care if I rest for a few minutes?"

Roscoe told her "No, catch some Zs' and I'll wake you up when we get there."

"Thanks", Heather said as she reclined the passenger's seat back, shifted to get comfortable, and then soon was breathing deeply.

Roscoe grinned as he listened to her and thought of how things were looking up in his life. Then he started working out schedules in his head. He had a long time associate in the drug business coming through Franken County sometime in the next couple days. About a week ago Charlie Cameron had told Roscoe he and his wife Rita were going to head north through Kentucky on the Bourbon Parkway as they combined a visit to her mother with some deliveries of Crack. Roscoe decided to try and get a hold of Charlie and find out two things; "Did he know yet when he would be hitting Franken County?" and "How much can I buy?"

Many curves later, around 7 a.m., Roscoe turned left onto a gravel road and told Heather that it was about a mile up to his mother's place. He added he would go slowly so that no stones would get kicked up onto the paint of her car, but overall, it was actually pretty smooth.

Heather opened her eyes and asked, "Are you talking to me?" Roscoe repeated what he had just said.

A moment later he swung a right turn up a drive that led to a modest wood-frame house halfway up a small hill. His mother came out onto the porch as he and Heather got out of the car. She was 5'4" tall and weighed about 175 pounds. She stood there with curlers in her hair, a cup of coffee in her right hand, and a cigarette dangling from her mouth. She inhaled deeply, blew out the smoke, and then asked Roscoe, "Who you got with you, Son, and what do you want?"

"Thanks, Momma," Roscoe answered. "Good to see you, too. This is my friend … ah … Sarah … and we need to park her car in the barn for awhile. Ah … Sarah, this is my Momma, Zelda. Momma, I need to use the Escort to get back to Frankenberry."

"So what kind of difficulty have you gotten yourself into? You wouldn't be hiding no cars if you wasn't in trouble with the law."

Roscoe ignored his mother's remark and instead responded with what he and Heather had rehearsed on the way there. "Now, Momma, my friend, Sarah, is trying to get away from a real bad boyfriend who's trying to hurt her. She's going to stay with me, but we need to keep her car out of sight for awhile."

Zelda Knowles snorted. "Yeah, and bears don't shit in the woods. I don't believe a word of it, Roscoe, but I don't care, either. Damn it, I always used to tell you there was no rest for the wicked, but it seems like I'm the only one that loses sleep over you."

"Yeah, yeah," Roscoe said. "But don't worry Momma, I ain't slept lately either, so you can just go ahead and start catching up on your beauty sleep."

"Well, if you ain't slept lately," Zelda said, looking Heather up and down, "let me just give you my three guesses as to the reason why, and the first two don't count. But back to your question about the car.

Now that Escort ain't been started for a few months but if you can get it going, you can take it. The tag is expired though."

"Momma, let me take the tag off your car. I'll mail it back as soon as I get home."

"Roscoe, do you take me for a damn fool? Hell no, you ain't taking the tags from my car!"

Roscoe was becoming exasperated and just a little bit embarrassed as he said, "Then, Momma, do you think I could borrow your car, and me and Heath ... I mean ... ah ... Sarah ... can bring it right back. I'll drive your car, and she can drive mine."

Zelda shook her head, and then said, "I guess so, though I don't know why I'm being so damn stupid as to help you again." She looked at Heather and shook her head. "I know your name ain't Sarah, and I don't know why you want to hide your car. I figure you must be the same kind of character as Roscoe. But you're pretty, and you dress clean and kinda nice, though I will say your dress almost shows your moneymaker and makes you look a little slutty. Roscoe's kind of girl I guess. But maybe you're okay, I don't know. I actually don't see you hanging around with someone like Roscoe here."

Heather decided nothing would be gained by giving some smart-ass answer, so she just said, "Ma'am, what Roscoe told you is the truth. And I appreciate you letting me keep my car here. You don't know how bad my boyfriend has been to me."

Zelda said she understood, then told Roscoe he'd best be getting on the road soon because his Uncle Tommy was coming over after awhile. Roscoe wanted to know how soon and hoped that his mother would let the matter die as he wasn't real anxious for Heather to know why there were problems between him and his mother's brother. Zelda told Roscoe his uncle would be there in a couple of hours and reiterated he couldn't stay long. Roscoe agreed he and Heather had better just use the bathroom and get going.

Zelda said to Roscoe, "You might be getting a little smarter, who knows. Just remember, your Uncle Tommy didn't call the law when you stole his collection of over six hundred commemorative quarters, because you was family, not because he forgave you."

Please shut your mouth, Momma, Roscoe thought.

Damn, Heather thought. *One hundred and fifty dollars in quarters to a 2022 Infiniti. At least his activities are increasing in value.* She inwardly smiled. *And if he steals from his own uncle, I believe I can talk him into helping me take care of Jackson.* Heather trailed Roscoe who was following his mother into the house. They used the bathroom, fixed sandwiches quickly, and then got into Zelda's 2010 Volkswagen Rabbit. Heather laughed.

"What?" Roscoe asked.

"From a Mustang to a Rabbit; but hey, if it keeps us from being spotted by Jackson, who cares?"

CHAPTER 31
Not Much of a Lucky Dog Lately

The phone awakened Jackson and he furrowed his eyebrows, scrunched his nose, and then remembered his wife was gone. He looked over to her side of the bed which was still empty, rolled over, picked the phone up and asked, "That you, Heather?"

"No," said a female voice, "this is Marquita. I was just calling to see if Heather wanted to go shopping with me this afternoon."

Jackson was still somewhat groggy, but awake enough to think, *If Marquita's calling for Heather, then she doesn't know that Heather's not here. No sense letting others know Heather has spent the night away.* So he replied, "I was thinking the phone call might be from Heather, because last night she said she was going shopping today. I guess she's already at the Sheltowee Shopping Plaza. Marquita thanked him and said that she would go over there and see if she could find her.

After he hung up, Jackson just lay in the bed for a moment trying to figure out what might be going on. Then he thought, *Now Heather and Marquita were really tight in high school. I'll bet Marquita knows exactly where Heather is, and the phone call was just to try and throw me off track.* He figured he might as well get up, so he headed to the kitchen for coffee. After a couple cups, Jackson decided to drive around some more and see if he could spot Heather or her car. As he zipped up his jeans, he read the tag on the inside of the fly. *That's a lie,* he thought. *Heather's gone; Brenda doesn't want to see me again, and Meredith's busy with another man. It sure hasn't been much of a Lucky Dog lately.*

CHAPTER 32
Confronting Abuse

Julie awoke at 5:45 a.m. to the sound of her drum alarm clock across the room. She moaned, rolled out of bed, and padded to the dresser to stop the beating. As she pushed the button, she received back the daily recording, "Good morning."

"Yeah, yeah," she answered back, "Good morning, my ass." Then she went to the kitchen and started the coffee pot. She went back into her bedroom and reset the clock for 6:15. As she drifted back into the fog zone, Julie thought, *it really is a good morning*. That thought gave a boost of energy which drove the mist away. She lay there awaiting the next round of drumbeats, and reflected on the prior evening.

Julie had enjoyed dinner with Todd immensely, even though a lot of the conversation had been quite serious. It was the longest time period in awhile, according to her memory, she had been out with someone and not held him at emotional bay. She had also kept her smart-ass comments in check. That in and of itself forced reflection. When the alarm went off for the second time, Julie was wide awake, but she reset it again for 6:35, and lay back down. She figured she could hurry and still get out the door in time for work.

She was thinking of the prior evening with Todd when, for reasons known only to her subconscious mind, her thoughts shifted to her last conversation with her brother, Adam. She was twenty-two. During a psychology course she had taken while working on her Bachelors, she decided she needed to confront her brother about his sexual abuse of her when she was younger so she could move on with her life. Julie had pulled into the drive, and was approaching his house when Adam came out onto his porch.

"Hey, Julie, long time, no see. What brings you out to my humble abode?"

"Well, Adam," Julie began as she moved to the bottom of the steps, *"like you said, it's been awhile, and actually, there is something I'd like to talk to you about. Is Sharon working?"*

Adam shifted uncomfortably as he replied, "Yes, why?"

"Because I don't want to talk to you with her around. This is just between the two of us."

Adam drew in his lower lip and bit it. He inhaled deeply through his nostrils, blew it out through pursed lips, and then said, "Look, Julie, I don't want you coming out here and starting trouble, understand?"

Julie realized that with his wife at work, Adam was going to take a more belligerent stance. Well, she thought, ironically, thanks to him, I can dish back anything he throws my way. "Adam," she began, "I'm not here to start trouble. I just think we need to talk about what happened when I was a little girl."

Adam stiffened as he replied there was nothing to talk about; whatever problems she thought she had from her early years, it was time to let them go and to move on.

Julie tried to remain calm at his near admission coupled with the "her problems" outlook. She was not doing so well as she continued, "Adam, I am trying to move on, that's why I am here. I was seven years old, for God's sake, when you started touching, and then screwing me. You kept me afraid with your 'I'll fix you' and 'no one will listen to you' bullshit until I was ten. It probably would have gone on longer, but then you joined the Army, thank God."

Adam stood squarely at the top of the porch steps with his feet planted shoulder-width apart, elbows bent with his index fingers in his pockets, and his chin tucked into his chest. He glared down at Julie and almost spit out the words, "Julie, I told you I don't want no trouble."

Julie looked up at him and for a moment was almost overwhelmed with emotion as she realized this was her brother with whom she was trying to establish a normal relationship with. My brother, she reminded herself, I want to have a brother. "Adam, please," she said, "I don't plan on doing anything, legally. I just want you to acknowledge there was a problem, and that you were wrong, what you did to me."

Adam smirked down at her. "Wrong? I don't know what you're talking about. Besides, you know what; I think you liked it too."

Julie lost it as she screamed, "You son of a bitch! A child isn't old enough to deal with that area. You were abusing me, and that's that!"

"Julie," Adam was moving his head barely up and down in a 'bobble-head' fashion. "It's your word against mine, so don't even think of going back there. I said I didn't want no trouble, and I mean it!"

Julie laughed back at Adam as she retorted, "Boy, this sure sounds familiar! I thought maybe you had matured, and changed, but it looks like that's a laugh. I don't think you'll ever change, you bastard!"

"Julie," her brother said as he slightly turned his left side forward and shifted so most of his weight was on his left leg. "Just take your lunatic ravings and get the hell out of here, okay." He thrust his right hand out and pointed at her. "Just stay the hell away from me - and Sharon."

"You don't have to worry about that," Julie countered. ""I can see there's no hope for any kind of normal sibling relationship between us. The only way I'll ever bother you again is if there is ever any kind of indication you are doing your shit to another minor. Then I'll be all over your ass so bad you'll wish you'd never been born!"

CHAPTER 33
Discovering Hope and Perseverance

Julie's alarm went off again. As she shut it off, she decided she was going to do something she considered almost unprofessional, call in sick. She stared at the clock a moment, and then headed out to the kitchen. As she sat at the table, sipping her coffee, she decided she would go to the Zachary David Nature Preserve and go hiking. There was a trail up to a large rock overlooking a beautiful valley. Julie figured if she couldn't get her thoughts in order out there, then it would never happen; they would just have to tumble around in disarray.

Julie called in sick, got her hiking gear out of a closet, loaded it into her car, and headed south on the Kentucky Bourbon Parkway. She got off where it intersected the Bert T. Combs Mountain Parkway, headed east on it for about thirteen miles to the Blister Pad exit, and then went south on the winding Route 17 toward the preserve. After about five miles, she pulled into the main Zachary David parking area, got out of her car, shouldered her daypack and headed toward Valley View Rock. En route, she went down a side trail for a couple hundred yards to take a short break near the Carved Rock waterfall at a spot where she could watch the ten foot wide stream fall sixty feet to a basin below.

After several minutes of drinking in nature, she again saddled up and retraced her way back to the Valley View Rock Trail. She soon crossed over a small wooden bridge that overlooked an open area to the left filled with some kind of red, star-shaped wildflowers. Julie stopped a few more minutes to get another revitalization vitamin from nature before heading out on the final leg toward her destination. She was about a quarter mile from Valley View Rock when she was startled as a wild hen hurled out of the undergrowth and then, cackling loudly at the top of her fowl lungs, flapped her way up the trail.

I'll bet, Julie thought, *she has young ones nearby, and she is acting as a decoy to lead me away from them.*

A few minutes later she was at the Valley View Rock Overlook, and as she dropped her daypack she thought, *It has been way too long since I've last been here.*

It had, in fact, been the day of her brother's funeral, in June of 2012. Adam had been driving home in heavy rain, hydroplaned, and hit a tree. Julie had reluctantly gone to the emergency room where he was lying unconscious. She realized as she looked at him she was devoid of feeling. Her eyes told her it was her brother Adam lying there, but her heart told her she did not know the man, and didn't want to know him. He died soon after without regaining consciousness. The next day, Julie's mother had been furious when Julie had told her she would not be going to visitations, or attending the funeral.

"For God's sake, Julie, he's your brother! What is the matter with you?"

Julie had never felt like she could share with her mother what Adam had done to her. She wished she had been able to, but she also knew if her mother had known what had happened it would have torn her heart out. Julie also knew even if she could ever share, now was not the time, and so she just said, "I don't have to explain anything; I just can't go."

"I know you and Adam didn't get along well, but you could at least come to his funeral. What do you think the rest of the family is going to say?"

Julie set her jaws. "Quite frankly, Mother, I don't give a damn what anyone says, or thinks. I know what I can and can't do, and I can't go."

"Julie, if you don't go, you will be making a decision you will deeply regret. That's all I have to say to you."

During the funeral, Julie had come up to Valley View Rock. Growing up, she and Adam had done some hiking with their parents, but this had been one place, for whatever reasons, they had never visited as a family. She felt like it was clean here, unblemished by his presence.

And now she returned to again order some thoughts. She knew one of the primary reasons her first marriage had failed, besides Rusty being at a most exceptional level of immaturity, was her failure to relate normally to men. She had been able to camouflage her feelings when she and Rusty were dating because she thought it would be different after marriage. But after the wedding, she just froze up whenever they engaged in sexual relations. She didn't even want Rusty touching her for fear it would culminate in the bedroom. She knew what her brother had done to her when she was between the ages of seven to ten was the primary factor.

After the divorce, Julie just added a few more bricks to her wall, and kept her innermost being well out of sight, letting it only occasionally pop back up to throw out a sarcastic barb, usually at some man's head, or heart. But last night's conversation with Todd was causing a crack to appear in the brick wall, and along with thinking about that, Julie needed to cleanse her soul. As she looked down at the valley below, she was lost in its beauty. Then her thoughts again went to Adam, and the day she had spent here as he was being buried, and the questions that had no answers still bounced off her mind like a barrage of ping pong balls thrown off a twelve-story roof by someone on an old David Letterman show.

Do we really just live in a world of estrangement and chaos? Julie wondered. She felt more optimism than she could ever remember having with reference to being hopeful about life, and she wasn't sure why. *And what is it about Todd?* she asked herself. There just seemed to be an inner peace he had, which, realistically, shouldn't be there after all he had been through. Her thoughts continued. *Does a person need to experience adversity to believe in a message of hope and perseverance? And if that is the case, why have I become so cynical?* A strange thought struck Julie. *I do believe in hope and perseverance and have never realized it until now. Every night I prepare the coffee pot before going to bed, so when I wake up, all I have to do is push the On button. My evening coffee-making ritual ... I am telling myself that morning will come. Hope and perseverance, I've had it all along; now all I have to do is figure out what I am hoping and persevering for.*

Todd was about twenty years older than her, but Julie had felt a kind of spiritual connection when listening to him. Maybe she was just looking for a father, or Uncle David, figure but she didn't think so. *Older brother?* she thought. *Not hardly.*

She had truly enjoyed herself with Todd, and had to admit that she found herself attracted to him. As a fresh breeze picked up, Julie felt like nature was washing over her and scrubbing out some inner dirt. She wished Todd were there with her, wished he was holding her. And then doubts came. Todd probably had no romantic interest in her. On the other hand, he had said Samantha had been fifteen years younger than him. Julie thought, *We have got to go out again, that's all there is to it*. She lay back on the rock, and felt at peace with the world, a totally new concept for her.

CHAPTER 34
Whip-poor-will

Evening in Kentucky woods brought out a variety of singers; one of tonight's was an Eastern whip-poor-will.

Delta Company moved out around 11 a.m. after it got reorganized from the firefight. Third platoon was point; Brad was following the line moving out. He was coming to where Rollo was waiting until his squad moved out, and Brad averted his eyes away.

"Yeah, look away, Motherfucker. That's what you do when you know you've done wrong." Brad just clenched his teeth and kept on moving. Rollo continued, "I hope Medic Larry is your last thought when you die. May you never rest in peace!"

My plan, *Brad thought,* was to become a medic and save lives. Already it looks like things are spinning out of control in that area. From just 3rd platoon, out of twenty-five, there were two killed and thirteen wounded. *Brad began to think his chances for survival over the next year weren't looking so good. Later that evening, he fixed a C-Ration meal and sat by himself trying to piece the day together. Several guys, including some from 3rd platoon were already picking up on the moniker* Bad Medic. After today, I guess it's appropriate, *he thought.*

For whatever reasons he had never been homesick as a child, but reliving Chuck and Medic Larry, he felt like he had just been sucker-punched in the stomach, and he wanted to be able to just sit and talk with his mother and grandfather. Welcome to 1969, *he thought. Following up on the idea that his chances for survival weren't looking so good over the next year, Brad pretty much adopted a new motto, "Hell, I ain't gonna live to be 21 anyway."*

"Whip-poor-will, whip-poor-will, whip-poor-will," the song continued.

Or Brad, he thought. Whip Brad.

The next day the company was working in the area of a rubber plantation where they dug in for the evening. Brad fixed a cup of coffee.

"You look like you've got something on your mind," Steve said as he sat down next to him.

"January 2nd. Just remembered. My mother's birthday."

"Bummer."

"Not really, I guess. I mean I didn't even think of it until I was thinking about our New Year's Day Truce yesterday and then remembered, oh, the 2nd, Mom's birthday."

"How old is she?"

"1969 – she was born in 1930. So 69-30 equals, what, 39?"

"Math skills like that," Steve laughed." You should be working in finances."

"And miss out on this shit? You crazy?"

"Yeah, call me crazy. For sure, a year ago I never dreamed I'd be here in a rubber plantation helping you celebrate your mother's birthday."

Brad looked around the area. "I wonder if anything from this place ever made it to tires on her car."

Brad placed his elbows on the outside work table and rested his chin over his hands as he slipped again back to 1969. He felt that too many times people made erroneous judgments based on quick glances like his CO had with the nickname Bad Medic. The moniker he had assigned Brad remained, although the CO's days with the company were numbered.

The four platoon leaders from Delta Company decided to send a letter to the Battalion Commander about the unprofessional attitude and reckless behavior of the CO. One of the LTs slipped the envelope through the window to the pilot during the next re-supply. As the Huey lifted off, the pilot gave thumbs up.

"What the hell was that about?" The CO asked.

"Friend of mine," the LT curtly replied.

Two days later the Battalion Commander, accompanied by a Captain, came out with the log bird. As soon as the Huey lifted off, he called the four platoon leaders and the Delta Company CO together.

"We'll make this quick," he said. "Dangerous for all of us to be together out here, and, the Huey's coming back in five minutes. CPT Kiser, you're coming back in with me as I called you about earlier; we'll discuss your reassignment there, and effective immediately, CPT Nelson is Delta CO. Kiser, let's go. Nelson, these are your platoon leaders; let them get you up to speed on what needs to be done."

Well at least, Brad thought, *Karma caught up with Kiser, although I don't know what the hell it was caught up with me.* The bird called out once more, "Whip-poor-will, whip-poor-will, whip-poor-will."

CHAPTER 35
A Really Hot Ass Mini Skirt

Phillip headed down the Kentucky Bourbon Parkway toward Exit 118. He was going to check around the bridge again to see if there was anything he might have missed the day before, and then check out a few businesses in the area. He figured whoever had abandoned the Infiniti couldn't have just vanished, so he thought maybe he could find someone who noticed something unusual.

He stopped under the bridge where he had found the Infiniti the day before and carefully looked around. Two boys who looked to be about nine or ten years old were riding bicycles down the road toward him. When they got next to him, he said, "Nice bikes. You boys live around here?"

Phillip liked the comedian Carrot Top; one of the boys reminded Phillip of him, and he replied, "Yes sir, right up the road."

"I'm just wondering," Phillip asked, "if you might have seen anything here yesterday, like someone getting out of a black car?"

"No, sir," miniature Carrot Top said.

The second boy who sported a short buzz hair cut replied, "I think maybe my dad did."

"Why's that?"

The boy puckered his lips to the left side of his face as if he was wondering about whether he should be saying something or not. "I don't know if he knows I was around, but I heard him tell my mother that he saw some guy leaving a black Infiniti under the bridge to get in a Mustang with a girl he thought he went to school with. Said she was wearing a … a … mini-skirt. When my mother asked him who it was, he said Heather something. My mother got mad at him then, I'm not sure why. I … was in my room and didn't hear all of it."

Phillip thanked the detective gods for what might be a break in his search, and asked the boy if his father was at home.

"No. He's at work but my mother is there."

"By the way, what's your name?" Phillip asked.

"William Resnick."

"Where do you live?"

"Just up there," William said, pointing. "Usually our Red Grand Cherokee is in the yard, but it's not right now. Like I said, my dad is at work. But I can ride real fast on my bike and you can follow."

Phillip smiled as he said, "Sounds good to me, William."

"Hey," miniature Carrot Top said, "Don't you want to know my name, and where I live?"

"Sure," Phillip replied.

"I'm Donnie. Donnie Anionic, and I live next door to William."

Phillip told the boys that he was glad that they had come by, that they were being really helpful to him in solving a crime, and asked if they were ready to go.

"Do you want to talk to my mother, too?" Donnie asked Phillip.

"Does she know anything about the driver of the Mustang?"

"I don't know if she knows this Heather lady in the mini-skirt, or not, but my mom's not married and I think you'd like her."

"Well, thanks," said Phillip, "but first, I'm about to get married, and second, I'm really here to find out about the drivers of the Infiniti and Mustang."

Phillip laughed to himself as he followed the boys to William's house. He would have to tell Deanna tonight about Donnie trying to fix him up with his mother, sight unseen, at that.

William's mother was sitting out on the front patio when Phillip pulled up to the house and got out. Her face immediately showed concern as she realized Phillip had been following William and Donnie, and she worriedly asked if there was any problem. Phillip told her that the boys were fine, introduced himself, and then said he thought she might have some information that could be helpful to him.

"I don't know what it could be, but I'll help you if I can. By the way, I'm Francesca Resnick, William's mother."

"Nice to meet you," Phillip replied to her. "I was back there at the underpass when the boys came riding by. I asked if they had seen a black car there yesterday, and William said he thinks his father may have seen the driver of a black Infiniti getting into a car with some girl. Did your husband mention anything to you about that?"

"William?" Francesca asked her son, a rather sheepish look on her face, "I'm assuming you heard your father and me talking last night?"

"Yes, ma'am," William replied, looking down at his feet.

"William, it's okay you told the police officer what you overheard, but tell you what, why don't you and Donnie ride your bikes some more, if that's all right with Trooper Cordella, so we can talk."

Phillip said that was fine with him, but then William asked if he and Donnie could stay, in a begging sort of voice. His mother rather sharply replied that they couldn't, and told the boys to "get along".

Phillip and Francesca watched the boys pedal down the street, and then she spoke. "I didn't realize William was listening to my husband and me talking last night. I … I got angry at him, kind of foolishly I guess, but William shouldn't have to hear that."

Phillip told Mrs. Resnick what William had said, that he heard her get mad at his father, but that he couldn't hear everything, and so he wasn't real sure why.

Francesca said William had probably heard more than what he had told Phillip, and he just didn't want to admit it. Phillip asked Francesca what she could tell him.

"Well," she started, "when my husband, his name's Ted, came in from work, he said he saw some guy leaving a black Infiniti at the underpass to get in a Mustang with a girl he thought he went to school with. Said she was wearing a really hot-ass mini-skirt. Those were his words. Well, when I asked him who it was, he said Heather Lamech, used to be Heather Dupre. I told him I knew who she used to be, and he didn't have to characterize her as wearing a hot-ass mini-skirt, because now I knew full well what he was thinking."

Phillip realized he was in the middle of a touchy conversation, but replied to Francesca he took it she knew this Heather from school too. Francesca replied somewhat testily her husband had dated Heather for awhile before he had started dating her, and he had had the audacity to talk about Heather on their first date. "I almost didn't go out with him again because of that." She went on to say that the prior evening she wouldn't have cared at all about her husband telling her he had seen someone getting into a car with Heather; he just didn't have to describe her in a manner that let Francesca know that he was still thinking of her in a physical way. Then she apologized to Phillip and said she was sorry he had had to hear about the spat between her and her husband.

Phillip told her, "Not a problem, everyone has them." Then he asked, "But about this Heather, you said, Lamech? Was your husband pretty sure it was her? And do you have any idea where she lives?"

Francesca seemed to relax a little once it appeared that Phillip wasn't judging her at all and said, "My husband said he thought it was Heather. I have no idea where she lives," she added, "but you can probably find her address in the phone book; she married a man named Jackson Lamech, one of the football players during our high school days. Of course," she continued, "from what my husband said he thought he had seen, I don't know if Heather is still married to Jackson or not."

Phillip had been taking notes. He put his book away and then said, "Well, either way, you have been a real big help to me, Francesca. Thanks a lot. And by the way, last night's argument is confidential, okay. It's certainly not pertinent information for my report."

"Thanks," said Francesca, a relieved look coming across her face. "I appreciate it."

CHAPTER 36
The Wedding, and Bear Scat Lane

George Rostenburg said he would be Albert's best man, and Mr. Hobbin agreed to give Tira away.

When Albert and Tira had asked Pastor Brock to marry them, he expressed some reservations, primarily concerning the short length of time they had known each other. But after talking with Mr. Hobbin, and Karen Esterbean, he said he would perform the ceremony, if Tira and Albert would agree to wait a couple of weeks and would meet with him for six, one hour, pre-marriage counseling sessions.

They set the date and planned a small ceremony inviting just a few family and friends. Albert's father said he couldn't make it, but Albert's mother came.

At a small reception in the rec room, decorated by Tira in cream and light purple, Albert and Tira opened wedding gifts. Then Tira's mother stood up to address the group. "Tira, my little girl, not so little any more, and Albert, my new son, I wish you the best in your marriage. You have two role models to choose from. First is Mr. Hobbin, who married his wife after a very short courtship and the marriage lasted for sixty-five years. On the other hand, Tira, I dated your father for four and a half years before we got married, and three years later, when you were two years old, he left, and to this day, I have never heard from him again. So, please, Tira and Albert, model your marriage after Mr. Hobbin's. It looks like you have already started that direction."

Then she raised her punch glass and said, "A toast … that you may continue on the path blazed by Mr. Hobbin and Lucinda. And a toast … to sixty-five years of wedded bliss, or more, if you can still drag yourselves into the bedroom by then." As laughter died down, Karen Esterbean continued. "Tira, my gift to you is a precious one, Sweetheart, one that has been in the family for years. George, would you help me now?"

George carefully unveiled one of the tables which displayed a beautiful silver tea set. Tira gasped as she said, "Mother, that's the pre-Revolutionary War set!"

"And now yours. I hope you and Albert will have someone in your future to pass this down to. Until that day, cherish, and enjoy."

A tear rolled down Tira's cheek as she started to become keenly aware of traditions, family histories, and responsibilities. She determined she would place the heirloom on a small table in the living room right below her crucifix so it could be a part of her meditation ritual.

***

Two weeks after they were married, Albert asked Tira if she liked to hike.

"I've never done a lot of hiking," Tira replied, "but my mother used to be an avid bird-watcher, and on a few occasions I went with her. I guess you could call that mini-hiking."

"I never did a lot of hiking either, but I enjoyed it when my dad and I walked in the woods when we went hunting. I'm thinking maybe we could enjoy hiking together, without the sound of gunfire."

"That sounds like fun."

"If I remember right," Albert said, "there is a trail in the Swisher Glen Forest Preserve, the Coyote Trail I think, that my dad and I hiked one time, no hunting involved. I think we could complete the Coyote lower loop in two to three hours." After Albert and Tira got into their car and cleared the Frankenberry limits, he said it was about a half hour drive to the Preserve.

"In time," Albert said, "we might want to take out a membership at the Healthwatch Street YMCA in town, but I'd rather spend the money on gas to get to some areas where we can hike outdoors instead."

"Sounds good to me, at least during warm weather."

A little bit later Albert laughed when they went past the sign for Bear Scat Lane.

"I'd forgotten all about that."

"Forgotten about what?" Tira asked.

"Bear Scat Lane. I think it's hilarious."

Tira asked what was so funny about Bear Scat Lane, and Albert asked her if she knew what bear scat was.

"I don't know, maybe something to do with telling a bear to scat, get away."

"I think bears scat when they want to scat," Albert said laughing. "Usually when they've had their fill of berries." Tira said that she still couldn't see what Albert was laughing about.

"Shit," Albert said.

Tira was surprised, and, also, offended that Albert had said shit to her for no reason, and told him he didn't have to talk to her that way. Albert started laughing again and explained to her about bear excrement. Tira smiled weakly, but was still a little bit upset that Albert hadn't explained the term right away.

"I'm sorry. I assumed you knew what it meant. I didn't mean to sound like I was making fun of you. I'm sorry." Tira smiled, and reached over and took his hand, and said she was sorry for being too sensitive.

There was a sign for the Coyote Trail, so Albert pulled into a small parking area at the trailhead. Markers indicated a lower loop trail 3.8 miles long, and an upper loop trail measuring 8.3 miles. Albert suggested the lower loop for their first time out and Tira agreed.

"I can't believe," Albert said, "how long it has been since I've been over this way."

"Seeing as this is such a pretty area and only a half hour from town," Tira said, "I can't believe I've never seen this area."

Due to the moderate changes in elevation in the terrain, and not being regular hikers, coupled with several stops to just enjoy the scenery, it took Albert and Tira almost three hours to complete the loop. Their stops to look at scenery were not only for the wide views, but also places where they were taken by the minutia along the trail. "I think nature teaches that beauty comes in all shapes and sizes," Albert said.

"I agree. I feel so peaceful, and," Tira paused just a moment as she squeezed Albert's hand, "so full of love for you."

CHAPTER 37
This Jangling Companion

One Sunday a couple of months later Albert and Tira were coming home from church and, for, whatever reasons, the tinnitus was particularly loud. Albert was tense and irritable, so when Tira asked him if he had liked church that morning, Albert shrugged.

"It was okay I guess, but the ringing in my ears is bothering me like crazy and I can hardly stand it."

"Oh, that," said Tira nonchalantly.

"Yeah, that."

"Well it didn't look like you were paying attention in church."

Albert stiffened a little inside as he replied, "I'm okay."

"I noticed you were doodling. I don't think it is respectful to do that during church."

"It gave me something to concentrate on."

"Well, Pastor Brock was talking and it isn't polite to draw while someone else is talking."

Albert was starting to get aggravated, and he knew from experience, that when the ringing was bad, and someone was trying to intrude into that grating, circle of noise, he withdrew. It was his defense mechanism or something. Again he replied. "It gave me something to concentrate on."

"Perhaps you need to pray about it," Tira responded lightly.

"I don't want to talk about it."

"I would think you'd be better off after church, not worse."

"Look," said Albert sharply, "I don't feel better when I am in a situation where I just primarily sit and listen to it for an hour."

"Sounds like someone needs to think a little more about what Pastor Brock said this morning," Tira replied. "Or did you hear what he was saying while you were composing your little cartoon characters?"

"About spending more quiet time with God? Tell you what," Albert answered disdainfully, "I would gladly be rid of this damn ringing in the ears, and spend more quiet time with anyone. I don't think you understand how depressing it is to wake up, and the first thing you are aware of is this noise that you realize, once again, will be with you all day. You can't leave it there in the bed. It's like this jangling companion that you can't get rid of."

Tira asked if he was dropping any hints, and Albert asked, "Hints about what?" He was angry, and just wanted to walk, or sleep, or do anything that would somehow try to offer a little relief.

"Well, I'm your companion, too," Tira said, "at least I thought I was. You're not thinking about me when you say jangling companion you can't get rid of, are you?"

"No, I am not, I am referring to the noise, have been all along. Don't add meanings to things not there."

"Okay, but I swear I don't see how you can have this noise going on in your head, and no one else hears it. How can that be?"

"I guess," Albert retorted, "that was how someone invented the word subjective."

They rode in silence for a few minutes and then Albert asked what she wanted to do for dinner. Tira said she didn't care. Albert decided to try and compensate for his mood and asked if she wanted to go to the house, change into hiking clothes, grab something at a drive through, and go out to the Coyote Trail.

Tira smiled. "That would be nice. Albert," she paused, "And, I'm sorry; I really don't understand what you're talking about, or going through with the ringing."

"It's all right, doesn't really matter. Like a doctor told me a few years ago, I just have to learn to live with it."

After arriving at the trail, they decided to tackle the upper loop. As they were nearing completion of their hike, Tira again commented on how peaceful she felt when out walking, and, again, how much she could feel her love for Albert. Albert told her he loved her, too, and when the ringing was real bad, hiking, or any physical activity

offered more peace than church, or any other situation which primarily just involved sitting, listening to someone else. Tira said she still
didn't understand, but she would try to.

As they drove away from the Coyote Trail area, they passed a
large field sloping up to a tree line. "Sometime," Albert said, "we need
to do some hiking in areas like those woods where we won't have a
trail, but instead will have to rely on a compass."

"Sure, if you think we can do it without getting lost."

CHAPTER 38
Are Some People Just Evil?

Albert graduated from Periwinkle College with his BBA in Accounting, and then went on to acquire his MBA, also in Accounting, from Marshall University. During his last semester at Marshall, he had applied for an Instructor position at his alma mater, Periwinkle College, and was hired with a standard one year contract.

***

About two years later, on their way home from church, Tira asked, "Do you think there are people that are just evil?"

Albert thought a moment. "You mean that there is no hope for them, never will be?"

Tira nodded and said, "Yes."

"I guess you're thinking of what Pastor Brock said about Judas Iscariot during his sermon."

"Yes. I think Judas was born evil and his purpose in life was to betray Jesus."

"I disagree with you," Albert said, "and I think there are a lot of Biblical scholars who do also. I believe Judas had the potential to make choices in either direction, and he made some poor ones that led eventually to the real big, bad one."

"No, you are wrong, Albert." Tira tensed up and became adamant as she said, "Judas was destined to be evil."

"I choose to differ with you, I happen to think there is something in the world called free will which means people are capable of choosing what they do, or don't do."

Tira seemed a little agitated over Albert disagreeing with her as she told him she knew what free will meant, but he only needed to look at the news to see there were people out there who were just plain evil, who would never change because they just weren't capable of it.

"Now we're talking about a new topic," Albert replied. "Enter in, the mass media, and the perception it gives us about what all is going on in the world."

"So they just make up the stories?"

"I didn't say that. But they pick and choose, and of course they are going to pick the sensational over the ordinary. Sensational sells." Albert laughed. "Well, that and sex. So that is why we see so much of both of them in the news and in other forms of mass media. This stuff has always gone on. We just hear about it more now."

"You haven't disproved my point. Now I agree wickedness has always been around, but a lot of it is done by evil people who have no hope, that can't change, and don't want to change."

"By don't want to change, do you mean like you're being about your opinion?" The split-second he asked, Albert had serious, too-late, reservations about his choice of words.

"It is not like that at all," Tira sharply responded. "My opinion isn't evil and isn't hurting anyone."

Albert decided to crawl out on the dangerous limb one more time and said, "Right, you aren't hurting anyone except the people you're condemning as hopeless and incapable of changing."

"You really should have become a lawyer instead of a professor. You could have made a career out of defending evil people. And then I could say, 'My husband, Albert Furcologna, protector of psychopaths and other evil people'."

"But you would be helping me spend their money," said Albert, smiling and shaking his head. "Wouldn't that make you evil, too?"

Tira grew very tight-lipped as she replied, "I ask you a serious question, and you make light of it. That is bordering on evil, Albert. Think about it." When they arrived home, while Albert was changing, and before she started fixing dinner, Tira clasped her dove tightly as she pursed her lips and prayed for strength to deal with Albert.

CHAPTER 39
Some Dreams Re-occur

A log bird was shot at with 51 Calibers; fortunately no one was hit, and the pilot managed to get the crippled Huey safely back to base. Then a trip flare went off and an observation post saw and killed an NVA soldier. 2nd platoon pulled security while 3rd platoon conducted a reconnaissance of the area where they found several bunkers containing caches of B-40 rockets.

Later that night movement around the perimeter was heard which was reminiscent of New Year's Eve. Brad and Steve quietly talked about it, hoping it would not be a repeat. In contrast to New Year's Eve though, this time the CO called the Nighttime LPs in just as dawn was breaking and ordered a Mad Minute with machine gun and small arms fire, hand grenades, and blowing of claymore mines. The rest of the day was uneventful.

When dawn shared its light through the window of Brad's cabin, he awakened, stretched, and swung his feet over the edge of the bed. Some dreams were recurring, and others just worked their way through the subconscious on rare occasions.

CHAPTER 40
We May Have Screwed the Pooch

Jackson had been driving around for awhile and decided that he needed to grab a bite to eat. He had passed the Electric Blue earlier, but Shoney's was just up the road. *I'll just go in grab a quick bite there,* he thought. *Try to wrap my head around whatever's going on.* He continued to himself, *but I haven't been to the Blue for a good while. Maybe I can do it later tonight, see if there are any waitresses looking for a good time.*

***

Soon after they left his mother's house, Heather asked Roscoe if he was still awake enough to drive. "I am," he replied, and Heather said that was good because she was still sleepy, and asked if he cared if she took another nap. Roscoe told her no problem, he was still plenty alert. Again she got comfortable, and soon her breathing became heavier, and then developed into a light snore. Roscoe grinned and concentrated on the road ahead. He wondered when, or if, he should mention to Heather his line of work. So far he hadn't gotten the impression she would dump him over it, but he knew one could never predict those sorts of things. His mind went to his next drug shipment from Charlie Cameron. He had touched base with him earlier on the cell and Charlie said he'd call Roscoe whenever he got into Frankenberry, he still wasn't exactly sure when, but probably sometime in the next twenty-four hours. Charlie told Roscoe he and Rita would most likely eat at the KFC, and Roscoe could meet them afterwards for the transaction, unless, of course, he was craving some Kentucky hot wings.

A couple hours later Roscoe turned off Route 173 and picked up Biscayne Avenue toward Frankenberry.

At the outskirts of town, Heather awakened and asked, "Where are we?"

"Almost home," said Roscoe.

Heather was still a bit sleepy and also trying to shake off a weird dream that she had been having about Roscoe's mother hollering to

Jackson through a cheer-leading megaphone that she thought he should cover his wife's moneymaker before he tried to sell her on eBay.

"I'm hungry," Heather said. "Do you have anything in your refrigerator?"

"Not much at the moment."

"Then," Heather said, "We ought to get something to eat before we go to the house. There's a Shoney's coming up soon."

Roscoe was anxious to get home and rest and responded, "There's also a McDonald's drive-thru, which I believe might be a little quicker, and cheaper."

"Oh, for crying out loud," Heather snapped back, "I'll buy. It's not that much more expensive."

Her response caught Roscoe off guard and he thought, *Well, for whatever reasons, it looks like the honeymoon is over.* They pulled into Shoney's, went in, and were seated.

A waitress came over and asked if she could get them something to drink while they were looking over the menu. Heather noticed Roscoe took a good look at a little cleavage showing as the waitress bent over to lay the menus on the table, so she coldly said, "We'll take the breakfast bar." The waitress said it was being changed over to the lunch bar right then, but she thought they could still get most of what was on it, or they could just order the salad bar, and take from both.

"That sounds good," Heather said, "and we'll have coffee and water." Even though it was most likely what Roscoe would have said, he was somewhat irritated Heather had ordered for him without consulting him first.

The waitress went for the drinks and Heather and Roscoe started toward the food bar when suddenly Heather grabbed Roscoe's arm quietly saying, "Oh damn, Roscoe, damn, damn, damn!" Roscoe felt like his arm was in a vise grip, and he felt dread rising as he asked her what was wrong. Heather stood frozen; staring out the window at her husband's white, RAM pickup entering Jerry's parking lot. "That's Jackson's truck!" she said in a low, but panic-stricken, voice. "We've got to get out of here!"

"I think we may have screwed the pooch on this one," said Roscoe. "What are we going to do? Meet him coming through the door?"

"Oh, think quickly," Heather said half to herself. She knew if Jackson saw her it wouldn't bother him to make a scene in public as he would think he was the one in the right; that the observing crowd was obviously on his side. "Tell you what," she said to Roscoe. "I'm going to the restroom. You wait near the door, and, then, while Jackson is heading toward a seat, knock and let me know. Then I'll slip out the front door and go around to the left. You can get the car and come around for me."

"Hell, girl, have you forgotten I don't even know what Jackson looks like?" Roscoe exclaimed as he watched the white pickup with tinted windows come closer.

Heather threw up her hands in exasperation as she snapped, "Well, watch and see who gets out of that truck, dumbass. Now, I'll be waiting inside the Ladies Room."

Heather went quickly between the rows of booths and then went left into the restroom area. As soon as the man that he assumed was Jackson climbed out of the pickup, Roscoe went to the front entryway area. The waitress who had waited on them came out with a tray with drinks on it, saw Roscoe, and asked if he was leaving. Roscoe said he was sorry but that all of a sudden he had started feeling real sick to his stomach. The waitress turned to return the drinks to the kitchen as she said she hoped he got to feeling better and told him to come back soon. *Not in this life,* thought Roscoe.

Somehow, all this reminds me of yesterday under the bridge, he thought, trying to appear casual as Jackson came in and was approached by a hostess who asked if he was alone.

"Yeah," replied Jackson, looking her over. "Unless you want me to buy you lunch." The hostess smiled and said she was on the job. ""I'll be right back," Jackson said. "I have to use the restroom before eating."

Great, thought Roscoe. *This is just great. We're not only screwing the pooch, it's while everyone is watching. Hope he doesn't take too long to come out. I can just see Heather coming out to see if I'm still here. If they come out together, damned if I'm going to stick around.* He gave quick and serious deliberation to just leaving right then, but another thought struck, *Hell, if I leave, Heather'll turn me in for stealing the Infiniti.*

As soon as the men's restroom door closed on Jackson, Roscoe went to the women's door and tapped on it lightly. As Heather opened it, another lady coming out looked at Roscoe with a questioning look on her face. "Shh," whispered Roscoe to Heather as he pointed to the other door.

The lady leaving smiled knowingly at Heather, and said, "Ah, ha. I understand now. Good luck, honey."

Heather turned left at the front door as Roscoe went out, got into his mother's car which had Jackson's RAM truck parked alongside of it. He was nervous and forgot it was a stick shift, and when he turned the ignition the car jumped forward, and he almost hit a man on the sidewalk.

"Why the hell don't you watch what you're doing?" the man hollered. "Where'd you get your license? Wal-mart?" Roscoe threw up his arms in a gesture meant to indicate he was sorry. The man came over to the window. "Have something to say to me?"

Roscoe cracked the window. "I'm sorry. I just borrowed the car from my mother and forgot it's a stick shift. Again, I'm sorry."

The man looked at him for a few seconds and then broke into a smile. "Tell you what, Buddy. Did something like that myself not to long ago with my girlfriend's car. Except I forgot hers was an automatic. Brakes don't work real well as clutches. Have a good day, okay?"

Roscoe said "Thanks," and then started the car, correctly.

When Jackson came back out, the hostess asked if he was ready to be seated, and Jackson said he was now, that he felt much better, and asked her if she had seen any lady and guy come there in a silver Mustang. As the hostess walked him to a seat she replied that she hadn't, but she usually didn't pay much attention to what people were driving.

Roscoe backed out of the parking space and pulled around to the other side of Shoney's. As Heather got into the Volkswagen Rabbit, she exclaimed, "Oh my God, Roscoe!" and slid down below window level. "That was close."

"Yeah, right," Roscoe said sarcastically, "Oh, but Shoney's isn't that much more expensive. Almost cost us our friggin' lives."

"Just shut up!" Heather fiercely told Roscoe, "You know there was been no way of us knowing Jackson would be going there."

"No, I don't know that; however, have you and Jackson had ever gone to Shoney's before?"

Heather's jaws drew tight as she replied, "As a matter of fact, yes; we've been to Shoney's before, along with Wendy's, Electric Blue, and most of the other eating establishments in town."

"Okay, okay," said Roscoe. "Let's just go through a drive-thru and then get on to my place."

"Fine," said Heather through tight lips, her voice edged with anger. "How 'bout McDonald's?"

CHAPTER 41
Chips and Pop

After going through the drive-thru at McDonald's, Roscoe pulled into a Food 'N' Fuel and Heather asked what he was doing. Roscoe told her he was picking up some chips and pop and asked if she needed anything.

"Not right now," Heather replied. "We can make up a grocery list later." She added, somewhat derisively, "Maybe even something healthy."

Roscoe went into the store and picked up a carton of Ale 8 and a large bag of Ruffles. *Healthy, damn!* he said to himself. As he waited in line, he remembered his mother and father arguing, about a year before his father had a heart attack. *His father had just come in from the grocery store. As Roscoe's father came through the door, Roscoe's mother said, "Thanks for going shopping for me, Randy."*

"No problem, Zelda." Then, "I'm going outside on the deck." He pulled a bag of chips out of one of the grocery bags, and headed for the door.

"Randy," Zelda asked. "You didn't buy regular chips again, did you?"

Randall Knowles laughed. "Only kind that taste good."

"But you know the doctor told you only to eat baked ones, and not too many of them."

"Well, you ain't the doctor, and he ain't here right now."

"Well, then I guess that makes me your conscience," Zelda responded, "and I believe your high cholesterol is still here."

"I don't need a conscience." Randall snapped. "Now just let me eat my chips in peace."

"Okay, okay," Zelda sighed, "but just don't eat the whole bag like you did yesterday, all right?"

"I bought the whole bag because I want the whole bag, okay?"

In exasperation, Zelda retorted, "There's over fifty grams of fat in that bag of chips, do you even care?"

"Of course, I care. That's why I take Tums, so I won't burn so bad after eating them."

Roscoe realized he was hypothetically answering Heather out loud as he said, "I bought the whole bag because I want the whole bag, Okay?"

"Sir?" the Food 'N' Fuel clerk looked questioningly at him. "Did you have any gas?"

"No, just the chips and pop." He paid for them, and on the way out the door thought, *I don't want to be taken out early like my father, with a heart attack, but I don't want to give up my Ruffles, either.*

When Roscoe and Heather arrived at his house, they quickly went inside. He called his mother to tell her they had arrived okay, and they would bring her car back as soon as they had a chance to rest up, and that he would call again before they left to make sure his Uncle Tommy wasn't going to be there. Zelda complimented him on his good sense, and told him to behave himself. She suspected her son dealt drugs, but she didn't want to confront him over it. She had decided that, especially concerning one's children, there were just some areas where it was better to not stay abreast of the situation. At a deeper level, she knew society, right or wrong, tended to judge parents by what their children went on to become, and she wasn't ready to deal with that. Zelda wondered what was going on with the girl Roscoe was hiding out, but decided she probably didn't want to know too much there either.

Roscoe opened the bag of Ruffles and asked Heather, "You want any?"

Heather frowned. "The only thing I want at the moment is to rest some more." She flopped down on the couch and added, "If you don't care, this is where I'm going to sleep."

"Fine with me," Roscoe said as he went into the kitchen where he ate about half the bag of chips and drank an Ale-8. Then he took a leak and went into his room where he stretched out on the bed and fell asleep immediately.

CHAPTER 42
Some Days You're the Statue

Deanna Fine awoke, fixed a cup of coffee, and went out to her porch to enjoy the start of the day. She loved where her house was located in a rural section of the county. Several years earlier, her parents had moved from Franken County back to their long-time home in Arkansas to be closer to both sets of her grandparents. Her father, especially, had relished the idea of moving back to the home of his youth. They sold Deanna her childhood home for a dollar.

As she sipped her coffee and watched a robin feed her young in a nearby nest, Deanna felt completely peaceful. Garbage pick up had been the day before, and the cover was still off the fifty-five gallon barrel she used as a trash can. She set her coffee cup on the arm of the glider and went to place the cover on the barrel. A bird flying overhead shit on her arm. Deanna laughed and said out loud, "Some days you're the pigeon; some days you're the statue; most days you don't know which." She looked up and smiled, and then added, "Thank you, God, for clarifying the issue so early today."

Deanna had been waitressing for almost five years now at the Electric Blue Steakhouse, and knew a little about the difference between being the pigeon or the statue. She often wondered what happened to some folks between church and the Sunday buffet. *Obviously,* she thought *sometimes, there are those who do not interpret God's love the way that I was taught.* Deanna thought any relationship with a Universal Higher Power should somehow permeate into one's attitudes and actions toward others, including the waitresses who served them at the local restaurants after church. She had realized some time back what the cold reality was. Overall, she worked harder, got less tips, and took more verbal abuse when she worked Sundays than on any other day – the statue.

She went back into the house to get ready for work. She didn't mind waitressing, but she also didn't want to make a career out of it. She had two years of college, and she and Phillip were in agreement she should finish school after they got married. All her core requirement classes were out of the way, and she had already declared a major in Communication. When she had taken the introductory course, it was like things had clicked in her head, and she knew she wanted to pursue a career in the field.

"Exactly, what," she had told Phillip, "I am still not sure of yet. I might even want to teach. The only problem I have already come to realize is, with communication, the more I knows about it, the worser I gets at it." Phillip had laughed and told Deanna she communicated quite well that she loved him, and that was all he cared about.

I am concerned about Phillip being a State Trooper, she thought. *And I know I will worry about his safety, a lot.* When Deanna entered the Electric Blue Steakhouse, she sighed. The place was packed, and it looked like another tiring day was ahead.

CHAPTER 43
Call from Valley View Rock

From the time he had left Acorn Street and the damaged picket fence through the end of the court session with Aaron and Judge Leahy, Todd had kept his mind quite occupied. As he pulled out of the court house parking lot and headed east he took a few moments to reflect on the night before.

Damn, he thought, *I hope I didn't lay stuff on too heavy. Julie probably thinks I'm hung up on Samantha.* About then, his cell vibrated and he answered it. It was Julie asking him if it was a good time to talk. Todd said it was, and that when he had found out earlier she'd called in sick, he'd been worried and was wondering if she was okay.

"I'm fine," Julie said. "To be honest, I'm not sick; I just need a day to get some thoughts in order. I'm calling from Valley View Rock in the Zachary David Nature Preserve."

"Well I'm envious and feeling a bit sick myself, because I know you are looking at some of the best scenery in our part of the State."

"No," Julie laughed. "It is probably the best scenery in the whole State, and I assume from your comment you are familiar with where I am."

"I think it's tied with Sky Bridge in the Red River Gorge as one of my favorite thinking spots. I wish was there with you," he said, but then quickly added, "Although I realize you might wish otherwise."

"I wish you were here too, although earlier I really did need to have some alone time."

"I understand," Todd replied. "I've been in those situations before, and the fact is, I really needed to get done what I just did." He told Julie about coordinating with Judge Leahy and that he had been able to get Aaron Patterson into the six month program at Angel Windows.

Julie said, "Sounds good. From what you said last night it could well be a turning point for Aaron. Todd, you have done a good thing with Aaron; I'm proud to be your colleague."

Todd chuckled. "I'm just doing my best to keep downtown Frankenberry safe from stray lawnmowers."

Julie laughed. "Also, Trooper T, although we both probably need to avoid using sick days, perhaps we could plan a hike up here soon … together."

"Sounds good to me, matter of fact, I'm off this weekend; you?"

Julie breathed in deeply of the fresh air as she said, "Me too."

"Funny that last night we missed that Valley View was a favorite spot for both of us."

"Hey," Julie responded, "give us a break. We can't discover everything all at once."

"True," Todd answered back. He wanted to keep talking, but he knew that he couldn't, and so he told Julie, "Listen, I've got to get on to some other duties, you know all about that. But I'm glad you called. Made my day."

"Yeah, I know all about duty calling," Julie responded. "And, Todd, your last statement … that makes my day. Thanks, and talk to you later."

Okay," said Todd, "and by the way, if you want, call me again later this afternoon."

"Sure will. Maybe we could even coordinate dinner again?"

"Sounds good," said Todd, and then closed his cell.

Real good, thought Julie as she lay back on Valley View Rock and closed her eyes.

CHAPTER 44
Rita Never Should Have Done That

Phillip's cell vibrated and he saw it was Deanna. He rather instinctively looked around to make sure there was not a black Infiniti in sight, and then took the call.

"Hi," Deanna said. "I'm on a break and just calling to tell you that I love you."

"Love you too; glad you called. Have you had a busy day so far?"

"I have, but I'm hoping we can spend some time together this evening."

"Sure," Phillip replied, and then told her, "Sorry, I've got to go, someone just turned against a red arrow; love you." He closed the cell, turned on his flashing lights, and a few seconds later pulled in behind the Cayenne Red Nissan Altima. He radioed in his stop, then got out and walked to the driver's window. Phillip smelled what he was quite sure was the sweet odor of marijuana coming from the car. He looked down at a woman who was about thirty years old with disheveled, shoulder length, ash-blonde hair. When she scowled at Phillip, it magnified the wrinkles under her eyes that looked like they belonged to a forty year old who had put at least fifty years on them. "Excuse me, Ma'am," Phillip asked. "Do you know you just turned left against a red arrow?"

"I'm sorry, Officer." The woman behind the wheel looked visibly upset, and spoke with a slight slur. "I asked my husband if there were any cops around." She glared over at the man beside her. He looked to be in his early to mid thirties, sported a dark brown goatee and a clean-shaven head. There was a scar trace which ran for about three inches at about a ninety degree angle from his left temple toward the top of his head.

Charles Cameron spoke. "Didn't realize you were there, Sir. Rita never should have done that, I agree."

Rita turned at Charles and screamed, "I never should have done that?" She turned back to Phillip. "Why weren't you out on the Kentucky Bourbon Parkway about twenty minutes ago when Mr. Lead-foot here wanted to see how fast our new car would go?"

"Shut up, will you?" Charles tersely spoke.

"You wanna to know how fast it goes Officer? We don't know! At one hundred and twenty-five miles an hour he had to slow down for the curve coming up."

A hundred twenty-five, Phillip thought. *Must have been on the Black Infiniti stretch.*

"One hundred and twenty-five miles an hour, Officer; is that fast enough for you?" Rita continued ranting. "He could have killed me, so I took over, kept the speed limit, and get pulled for going through a red arrow, but only after he failed to warn me that, in fact, there was a doughnut lover in the area!"

"I told you to shut up, damn it!" Charles hollered.

I hate the arguing spouse stops, Phillip thought. *I'd trade this to Todd for a John Deere any day.*

Rita told Phillip if he was going to give her a ticket he'd better arrest her husband also, for speeding.

"Sorry, Ma'am, I didn't catch you, or your husband, speeding, but I did observe you turning left on a red arrow."

"Where were you, on a doughnut break, when my husband was speeding?"

"Excuse me, but I need to see your driver's license, and registration."

"You're not getting my license unless my husband is written up too!"

"Sorry, Ma'am, but the system doesn't work that way. Again, I need to see your driver's license and registration."

Rita challenged, "So what if I just put our nice new car in gear and take off? What are you going to do? Shoot out my tires?"

Charles couldn't believe Rita was acting so stupid. He knew she had gotten a little crazy on pot before, but never like this. *Then again,* he thought, *this is the first time that she's been pulled by a cop while smoking.*

"That is an option, Ma'am," Phillip replied. "However; I'd recommend you just keep it right here, parked, while I call for back-up."

"But," Rita threw down the gloves again, "the nice policeman wouldn't want to shoot out my tires, would he? No, because they remind him of doughnuts."

"Rita!" Charles spoke even more sharply, "Shut-up!"

Rita looked at her husband. "You and your lousy damn eyesight! They're probably going to search the car now. Do you realize how much money we're going to lose because of you?"

"Me?" Charles rolled his eyes and shook his head. Every thought bearing any semblance to common sense had just flown out the window, but he continued talking anyway. "We're going to be late for our drop to Roscoe. All you had to do was quietly hand the doughnut lover your license. But no, make a scene, you did good this time. Lose money, hell; you probably just put our asses in jail."

Rita snapped back, "Like you weren't taking a chance when you went a hundred twenty-five!"

Phillip spoke again, with his hand on his revolver. "Both of you, be quiet, get out of the car, put your hands on top of it, and keep them there until another trooper arrives." Following directions, Charles and Rita Cameron glared at each other across the Altima roof. After his back-up arrived, Phillip said he was going to search the car.

"Do you have a search warrant?" Charles asked.

"Due to comments you made about a drop to Roscoe, I have probable cause."

"Officer," Rita said, "You won't find anything except some boxes of toys we're taking to Roscoe. He, ah, manages the Safe Shelter for Women in Portsmouth, Ohio."

When Phillip opened the trunk, the cargo area's standard cover was in place. He lifted the rigid cover and where there was usually a spare tire he saw eight medium size teddy bears lying on top of a quilt. Phillip lifted the quilt and whistled as he said "I'll bet these aren't just bags of pretty rocks back here. Rough guess, I'll estimate close to three-quarter million street value."

Rita still glared at her husband as she said, "What, Officer? Are you telling me we don't have boxes of toys back there? Charlie, what are you trying to pull off here?"

CHAPTER 45
No Party, No Boom Boom, Nothing

For a while before entering the service, Brad went out on a couple dates with a girl named Christy that he knew from before he quit school. When he got ready to head out for Vietnam they promised to write each other. He sent a letter to her in early January and was glad when she wrote back.

During early morning hours February 14th, the men in Delta were hearing noise in the jungle all around the company perimeter, so at the crack of daylight the CO ordered a mad minute.

"It's one hell of a way to start off Valentine's Day," Steve remarked afterward.

"Huh. Forgot about it until you said that."

"Heard from Christy lately?"

Brad shrugged. "Not in a couple weeks."

"She still thinking of joining the Navy?"

"Like I said, last letter was a couple weeks ago; first time she's mentioned it. Talking about God and country and all that shit."

"Hey guys," SGT Young said as he approached the men. "3rd is going to set up an ambush with 2nd. Leaving in half hour."

"Damn, Sarge," Steve joked. "We were planning on a Valentine's Day Party with some Boom Boom Girls."

"Tell you what," SGT Young replied. "You get some fucking NVA walk into your ambush; have a Boom Boom party with them."

Brad smiled in recollection. Turned out to be no party, no boom boom, nothing.

CHAPTER 46
Coffee, Tea, or You?

Deanna was glad it was nearing the end of her shift. It had been busy almost all day, and tips were good, but she was tired. She approached the table where a customer had just sat down, and handed him a menu. "May I bring you something to drink while you look this over?"

Jackson looked her over. "Coffee, tea, or you?"

"No, sir," Deanna said, "that line is only good with my fiancé. But the coffee or tea is available."

"Make it coffee." Jackson said as he thought, *My lucky dog curse continues.* He was caught somewhere in the middle of anger and worry. He had been hunting for Heather most of the day with a few stops back by the house to see if she had returned, to no avail.

He was pent-up over his fruitless searching and doubly frustrated over his recent attempts to get laid, so after a good meal, he intended to cruise down to Hedgehog Brook Street area. It had been a while since he'd paid for sex, but he decided, *By God I am going to get something tonight, one way or another. Hell,* he thought, *I might even get one that will spend the night with me, and if Heather comes back home during it, too bad.*

He had already determined that if Heather was going to act the fool, and take off on him, then she would pay, and pay dearly whenever he got up with her. Jackson decided if Heather wasn't home by the next evening, he would give Marquita Snyder a call and see if she would meet with him. He still wasn't convinced Marquita wasn't involved somehow, or at least aware of, Heather's disappearance. Deanna returned with Jackson's coffee and asked if he was ready to order.

"Actually, I placed it earlier, Darling, but you turned me down. Care to reconsider?"

Deanna smiled because she knew that was what waitresses were supposed to do, even when serving assholes, and asked if he was ready to order from the menu. When Jackson asked if the food was any warmer than she was, Deanna smiled, and said, "Oh, much more," thinking, *Lord, help me make it through the next half hour.* Jackson ordered sirloin tips smothered in onions and peppers, rolls, and a baked potato with extra sour cream and butter. He said he would pass on dessert since he had already been served ice-cold shoulder.

About forty-five minutes later Phillip opened the door for Deanna and asked if she was all right. Deanna sighed and said she was beat, particularly since one of her last customers had been an ass.

"What kind of an ass?"

"A trying to make a move, didn't understand 'No', that kind of ass," Deanna replied.

"Do you think he'll be back?"

"Unfortunately, it seems like those kind always came back."

"If he does come back, and continues to bother, maybe you could point him out to me sometime." Phillip grinned. "Of course, I would never harass him, but I could make sure he followed the traffic rules to the letter of the law."

"That might be stretching it," Deanna said, "but tell you what, not to change subjects, but about eating, let's do something different. How about we go to that all-night diner in Goodman Village, The Roasted Bread and Gravy?"

CHAPTER 47
Subs, and Life Lessons

Todd pulled his car into Julie's drive, and she came down from her deck to greet him. She was wearing a light coffee colored pants set that was highlighted with scalloped embroidery and wooden beads. Todd realized that, except for the Headquarters picnic, where he really hadn't paid a lot of attention to her, he had never seen her dressed in anything other than her uniform before, and he liked what he was seeing. He grinned as he handed her a Get-Well card. Julie thanked him and said she appreciated it, although it might be coming a little late as she believed the long overdue dose of Nature she had taken earlier in the day had pretty much made her better.

"That is good news." Todd responded. "So I'm guessing you have an appetite, and are ready to go, the question being, where to?"

"Do you like subs?" Julie asked,

"I've been known to put them away."

"Cold-cut combos from Subway?"

"That's fine," Todd said. "Sounds like you already have them."

Julie laughed. "Actually I don't, but since you've admitted you like them I'm thinking maybe we could go to Food Village, get a cart, and stroll the aisles together."

"Sounds like good exercise to me."

"Then," Julie went on, "after we get all the fixings, we can come back and make our own."

"Sounds like a plan, and a good enough one at that," Todd replied. "One I wish I'd thought of."

"Pretend you did," Julie told him as she walked to the passenger side of the Delta 88. "By the way, I want another ride in your car."

"Want to drive it?"

"I can't," Julie jokingly replied. "Because of a recurring nightmare I have."

"Which is?"

"Where I'm on a first date and wreck the guy's car."

Todd handed her the keys as he said, "Well then, here; I'm figuring last night was a first date, so this is the second."

"All right, if you insist," Julie laughed.

On their way to the grocery, they passed the new Frankenberry Convention Center which was in its final stages of construction and Julie said that she hoped that once it was completed that it would give a boost to the local economy. Todd chuckled as he said, "It should, but it seems to me they might have to get a director with a more progressive outlook. Did you read in the *Franken Daily Times* the center has already booked its first convention?"

"Really?"

"Going to be a good one from all I can tell," Todd said, "although we might have to assist the local police in crowd control."

"Well, don't keep me in suspense. Who have they got coming?"

"Don't you dare laugh so hard that you lose control and wreck my car, but make your reservations now to attend the August 2023 Annual Convention of Former Redneck Rooster Owners."

"You serious?"

"Sure am," Todd replied. "Not quite as good a catch as Pikeville got once landing a Harley convention, but I suppose Frankenberry has to start somewhere." Julie was still smiling when she pulled into the Food Village parking lot and they got out.

After they got a cart, they proceeded through Food Village, picking out wheat hoagie rolls, bologna, thinly sliced honey ham and honey turkey, a head of lettuce, a large tomato, one red onion, a green bell pepper, provolone cheese, mild cheddar cheese, and low-fat mayonnaise. "Chips?" Julie asked.

Todd puckered his lips a bit to the left, looked upward and then at Julie. "Why not? And since we're using low-fat mayo, maybe we could get some of those high fat Kettle chips."

"I'll see your Kettles and raise you a half gallon of Breyers ice cream; what's the call for liquid refreshments?"

"You like Root Beer?"

Back at Julie's, they worked together on the subs at her kitchen table. Todd told Julie he'd been worried when he found out she had called in sick, and quite frankly, afraid he might have been too dark and heavy in their conversation the night before and possibly scared her off.

"Oh, no. First, I asked questions; and, second, I was … am … intrigued by what as I see as an inner peace despite everything that's happened to you."

"I was afraid you would think I was hung up on Samantha. Truth is, I do think of the accident at times, but after it happened, I really just threw myself into my work and enclosed myself inside a little barrier. But I think I have fully dealt with losing her. But, honestly, I can't say that I'm still not bothered … often times … by the children."

Julie asked if JR was short for Junior and Todd nodded "yes" and added that Mindy was short for Miranda.

"Miranda, that's a pretty name. And in reference to what you just said about still dealing with the past at times, everyone has a past that they will never be totally freed from. That's life."

Todd smiled and asked lightly what deep and dark secrets she had lurking in the shadows.

Julie answered that they actually entered into part of what she had been thinking about at the Rock, and that if Todd really wanted to listen, she could give him an earful.

"Well, I'm not meaning to pry, but I am available for listening, if you want to talk."

"Tell you what; it looks like we've done all the damage we can to these subs. Glasses are on the shelf over the toaster. Pour us some Root Beer, and I'll spill my guts out while we eat. Sound appetizing?"

"Good enough for me." Todd said as he pulled down a couple glasses, put ice in them, and slowly poured the drinks. Then they sat opposite each other at the small table.

"My earful won't be long, just blunt," she started. "If you want, you may label me juliewrightdirect.com. I'm just going to get to the heart of my dark side. When I was seven, my fifteen-year-old brother, Adam, started sexually abusing me, and it continued for three years until he joined the Army. When I was twenty-two, I tried confronting him about it, but he went back into his threatening mode. Anyway, almost three years ago, he was killed in a car accident, and I just could not bring myself to go to the visitations, or the funeral. As a matter of fact, the day of his funeral was the last time I had been to the Valley View Rock before today. Of course, my refusal to attend his services has set me in good shape with my family, and sometimes I use that term loosely. So, Mr. Truitt, have I scared you off?"

"Not at all," Todd said as he shook his head. "Like you said, we all have a past. I'm sorry about everything that has happened to you, and I'd like to give you something to think on. You may have already thought of this, and I'm just a day and a half late, and three dollars short. We both have had some rough spots in our roads, maybe even more than most folks, but the consequences of all that good, bad, and ugly stuff, all those consequences have somehow come together so that you and I are now sitting at this table, enjoying our subs, and, damn it, Julie, I like that."

Julie replied she had never quite looked at it that way and said, "Damn it, I like it, too. Part of why I want to know you better is there is a part of you that I think needs to rub off on me."

Todd took a drink of pop and looked at Julie, grinning, as he said, "So that's it, rub a little of me off, make me a lesser man, and then throw me away?"

Julie dished right back. "When the time comes, we should both be involved in the rubbing, and I have no plans to put you in the garbage can, okay?"

"I'm hitting my 'save' button as fast as I can."

"But, seriously, Todd, I have let what I just told you control parts of my life for a long time. Is there a way to break free?"

"In Chekhov's play, *The Cherry Orchard*, Trofimov talks about the importance of work, and I have come to believe that honest, hard work is truly part of the solution to moving on in life. It keeps you constructively occupied, and frequently puts you in situations where you are other-centered, and not so focused on yourself, and your problems."

"So," Julie interjected, "like I said earlier, there are just parts that will always be there. Everyone has a past that we will never totally be freed from, and that's life."

"That's so true," Todd replied. "Forgive my military analogies, but they have helped me through the years. I recall traveling from Piers County to Daniel Boone State University to some summer classes I was enrolled in, Directed Studies, so it had been a week since my last time over the road. One trip, there was a dead dog on the side of the road, apparently killed several days earlier, and the bloating was at its peak. It didn't do any good to close the windows as the putrid odor was already inside and taking my mind back to another hot day, but this time the decayed flesh belong to an Iraqi soldier, not a canine. Smells were the same, though separated by years, and the odor of those days was back again. It filled my senses like ads take over TV during an election."

Julie was thinking back to an eerily similar experience and thought pattern that she had gone through just a few months earlier, and she wondered what part of the cosmos was trying to exert its influence on her now.

Todd continued, "I wondered if life's journey would ever take me far enough to get beyond the smell, or if part of it had already permeated into my soul to always linger. I have learned that osmosis doesn't undo itself, at least not easily. And the adage time heals is good, if you keep that time positively occupied, like your hike to the Rock today, good stuff, about as positive as it gets."

"I hear you," Julie said, "and I guess what you just said aligns with some of my thoughts earlier today. Actually, I had my own epiphany of sorts over my nightly coffee-making routine. A new thought struck me while up at Valley View today. I do believe in hope and persever-ance, and had never realized it until this morning. Each night I pre-pare the coffee pot before going to bed, so when I wake up, all I have to do is push the 'On' button. My evening coffee-making ritual … I am telling myself morning will come … the coffee filters of our lives, hope and perseverance. I've had them all along; now all I have to do is figure out what I am hoping and persevering for. Do you suppose you can help me figure it out?"

"Sure," Todd replied, "back to my earlier statement about consequences. We've been both hoping and persevering for this time together over a sub sandwich."

"You know, Todd, I am starting to believe what you just said is a lot deeper, and more philosophic, than it seems on the surface."

"That's what hiking is for, brushing up on what we didn't learn in our philosophy courses."

"Oh, yeah, good old philosophy class. I remember Dr. Hansel talking about reality, and if someone came into the class, half high, and they perceived the piano in the corner as a pink elephant, was it, in fact, a piano, or a pink elephant? Several students engaged him in a lively discussion, and after a few moments of what I perceived as a circular argumentative pattern settling in, with no solid answers looming on the horizon, I raised my hand and, while adding a slight slur to my voice, asked why everyone was calling the pink elephant in the corner, a piano. I recall one girl getting quite upset with me. Said I was making light of a serious discussion. Really surprised me. I mean, I would never even consider doing anything like that."

Todd chuckled as he said, "I agree, you would never do anything along those lines; just ask Phillip Cordella." As she had the night before, Julie lightly kicked him.

When Todd and Julie finished eating the subs and chips, Julie asked if he wanted coffee with his ice cream. Todd answered that if she didn't mind, he thought he'd wait a few minutes before engaging in her coffee-perseverance ritual. Julie said she would perseverance him, but that, seriously, she was wondering how many of life's lessons were missed because people were walking along, looking down at their feet, so to speak.

"Julie," Todd asked, "have you ever done any major backpack hikes?"

"Mostly day hikes, although I did complete a couple short sections of the Appalachian Trail, about seventy miles one time, and twenty-five another."

"Do you use trekking poles?"

"Not usually," Julie replied. "Does it count that for one of the steeper climbs in a Smoky Mountain section of the AT, I used a stick I found alongside the trail?"

Todd smiled. "We'll count it. Why did you do that?"

"Well, it did make it easier."

"There you go. Life lessons. Think about this. I read an article in an older *Backpacker* magazine about how much weight is displaced by use of trekking poles. I tested it with my pack and poles on my scales at home. Results vary, of course, by the weight of your pack, how you position your poles, and how much pressure you apply to them. But if you are carrying a fifty-pound pack and put approximately thirty pounds of pressure per second on the poles, you are looking at about 1800 pounds per minute, and 90,000 pounds in a fifty-minute hour. As you can see, Darling, I'm going to allow you a ten minute break every hour. Now, if you hike a six hour day, that is 540,000 pounds in a day, or over two hundred and fifty tons. That is weight that has been kept from bearing on your lower skeletal structure."

"Wow," Julie exclaimed, "that's a lot."

"Now, anyone who hikes knows there are times when you wax philosophical. So far, my longest single pack was the southern hundred-forty miles of the Vermont Long Trail. Out of one of my periods of jumbled thoughts came the names for my trekking poles, Faith in my right hand; Perseverance in my left. I have discovered, both in hiking and in life, you can have one of these without the other, but it really works best when you have both."

"Again, I understand. But faith? Faith in what?" Julie asked. "Yourself?"

"More than that. I think it's threefold; faith in yourself, in others, and in a Higher Power."

Julie shook her head. "I have trouble sometimes with the others part, and with a God. I mean, when my brother started abusing me … where were the others, and where the hell was God, and what was he thinking of the day that he allowed all of that to start? Like maybe he was out having an oxygen-deprived moment that led to short-term memory loss, and he forgot that little seven-year-old girls aren't supposed to have those kinds of experiences."

Todd nodded. "Trust me, Julie; I have been through what you are expressing. I came upon a fatal accident a couple years after my family was killed where a drunk driver ran a stop sign and killed a teenage girl. And I specifically remember thinking to myself, *A few years ago, if this driver had been in another country, born to a mother of a different culture, in an army of a different name, I could shoot him, and my bullet would be blessed by my country, my superiors, the God of their construction. But he's here, and killing is not justified for his offense,* and so I slowly awakened from my fantasy to the reality that I had to help him into the ambulance. I had some serious questions that day about any so-called God, and whatever attributes this being might have."

"So what conclusions did you arrive at?"

"Back to hiking, and life in general," Todd said. "I'm still working on it. I do know that as humans we have the ability to make choices, and we can't blame them on some higher being."

"So what choice did a seven-year-old girl have when her fifteen year old brother started fucking her? That was his choice, wasn't it? By the way, pardon my English, because, contrary to what some folks say, that wasn't French."

"All I know," Todd replied, "is the more that I know, the more questions I find need answering. I once wrote a short story called 'To Choose, or Not to Choose, That is the Consequence'. Now what the hell that means, I have no idea. What do you think?"

"What do I think?" Julie asked. "Is it too soon to say I think I might be falling for you?"

Todd smiled as he said, "Only as long as you don't insist it's a one-way street."

"Trust me," Julie laughed, "I'd have you arrested for not driving the right way."

Todd sat back in his chair and replied that he didn't mean to be bringing up old subjects, but all the talk about hiking, perseverance, and consequences had made him ready for dessert and he wondered if the offer was still on for coffee with Breyers.

"There is only one condition," Julie said. "You have to promise not to stop seeing me just because I'm twenty years younger than you."

"What? And lose the chance to have people comment on my trophy-girl?"

After they finished the dessert, Todd and Julie stayed at the kitchen table and continued their conversation for some time until Todd glanced at the clock on Julie's stove. "Good Lord," he commented, "I sure lost track of time, and I have got to be in early tomorrow." Julie asked if he really had to go and Todd responded, "Unfortunately, what we have to do, and what we want to do, don't always line up with each other at the right time, but, yes, knowing what time my alarm clock is going to go off, I really have to go. But, what are your plans for tomorrow night?"

"If you had asked me that a week ago," Julie laughed, "I'd have told you, 'Hell, I have no idea. I just take each lousy day as it comes.' But that was a week ago. Fix something here? Go out to eat? Pick your poison. I don't even want to suggest a movie, or anything, because all I feel like doing is talking with you, getting to know you better."

Todd liked what he was hearing and how he felt as he replied, "Tell you what. I'll be filling out my usual crapola at the end of the shift, so let's decide then."

"Sounds good to me. And, at the same time, maybe we could plan a day hike to Valley View or something."

"How about the or something first? Have you ever been to Carter Caves State Resort Park?"

Julie nodded. "Years back, with my parents."

"So you've been in some of the caves?"

Julie shook her head. "No. Only the hikes. I've had this thing about caves ever since I was a little girl."

"Want to try?"

Julie flashed back to her mother almost hysterically telling her to stop screaming because she was using up air as she replied a bit tentatively, "Just the thought of it kind of scares me, Todd, but I'm willing to try."

"Then," said Todd, missing her hesitance, "let's try Saturday. We'll plan the specifics of it tomorrow night."

As Julie and Todd embraced, she leaned back to look him in the eyes. "Todd, when I was five, a friend and I were playing in an old fashion luggage trunk, just taking turns climbing in and out, and letting the other one put the lid down. You know how kids can play. Well, somehow it locked on one of my turns, and for several searing moments I screamed as my friend cried for my mother who then frantically searched for the key. Of course, the fact I'm in your arms now confirms she found it, but that's why I've never wanted to go in caves, before now. But with you … I … want to try. Of course, the irony of it all is, from that experience I went on to learn and grow in a world which hid a myriad of old trunks."

Having just heard what had happened to Julie in her early years with the trunk, Todd wondered if maybe he had made a mistake by asking her to go caving, and so he said, "We can skip the caves and just go hiking if you'd rather."

Julie had felt a near panic-attack when Todd mentioned caves, but she also simultaneously had an inner sense that everything happening was good for her. "No," she said. "Maybe cave exploration will do me good. Whether you realize it, or not, I feel like our conversations are helping me find a key that unlocks the lid to a particular trunk that has held me captive for years. I can't even begin to describe what I am feeling right now."

"I'm think I'm feeling the same thing," said Todd as he brushed her lips, "and I love it."

CHAPTER 48
Nothing More Than the Usual

Albert was singing along with the Gatlin Brothers on his way home from work. The tinnitus was near driving him to distraction, and he was doing anything to try and refocus. Classes were underway in a new semester and he felt pretty good about that. At home, Tira had been rather moody lately, and Albert wasn't quite sure how to deal with it. When he got down, it seemed the ringing was louder, and then he just wanted to withdraw. Tira thought he was withdrawing from her, and he couldn't seem to explain what he was feeling, and, actually, when depressed, didn't feel like explaining, and then he got down even more. And he was even more frustrated because Tira kept trying to make his physical tormentor into a spiritual issue.

As he walked through the door, the smell of bacon wafted through the air and Albert said, "Smells good, Hon. And," he added, "I'm hungry."

"Well", Tira replied, "wash up, because BLTs are ready."

As they were eating, Tira said there were going to be special services at the church, and Pastor Brock had mentioned to her she should encourage Albert to attend so he could receive healing from the ringing in his ears.

"It might be a little more complicated than that," Albert replied.

"It's only as complicated as you want it to be; you're just letting unbelief stand in the way of a better life. Furthermore," Tira added, "you resist any solutions I come up with."

"Just forget it, okay!" Albert angrily reached for his BLT.

His voice tone triggered Tira's response as she snapped, "That's it Albert, the whole problem is you don't want to listen to me when the fact is I know what you need to do! Pastor Brock and I are concerned about you, but it seems to be wasted effort because you don't even care about yourself!"

Between the damnable ringing in his ears and the direction the conversation had somehow gone Albert felt like he was going to explode. He was a sole jogger on the streets of Pamplona during the feast of San Fermin, and the bulls were fast closing in. He went into the bedroom and closed the door, hoping Tira would stay in the living room for a while, thinking *How can I rationally deal with an irrational woman?* Meanwhile, out in the living room, Tira went to the mantle and carefully got down her dove, gazed at her tea set, and then asked the figure on the wall to help her deal with her irrational, unspiritual husband.

The next morning Albert sat at the kitchen table, tiredly staring at his cup of coffee, and thinking, *Why does it have to be the first damn thing I hear every morning as I awaken?* He knew the tinnitus was connected to the physical body, so whenever he was freed from clay, it would be gone. The thought was a sort of comfort, but also served as a tormenting tempter. *Of course*, his thoughts continued, *if after I die, I still hear the noise, then I know where I've gone.* He thought back to the argument the night before which had eventually included Tira calling him sacrilegious because he wouldn't let her lay hands on him and pray he would change his mind about attending special services at church.

Tira came out of the bedroom into the kitchen. "Albert?" she asked. "What's wrong? You look like something's bothering you."

Albert sighed and said, "Nothing more than the usual."

Tira said she wished she knew what to say, but she didn't even know how to identify with something like the ringing. She told Albert, like she had many times before, "It just doesn't make sense to me. You say you hear it all the time, but I sleep right next to you and never hear anything. Again, Albert, it just doesn't make sense."

"Forget it," said Albert acrimoniously, "we've been through this before. Subjective things are that way. If you had a pain in your ass, would I feel it?"

"Now, Albert, you don't have to be sarcastic, and you don't have to talk that way to me. I'm just trying to be nice, saying that I wish I could help."

"All right," Albert said. "You just said you wished there was some way you could identify. I told you once that the ringing I hear is like sitting next to our teapot when it's whistling, loud. If I get within a foot of it when it's going full blast, then I might not hear mine. Try that and, say, reading for an hour and see how well you can concentrate."

Tira went to the refrigerator and got out a can of Dr. Pepper. She felt quite smug as she popped the lid because she knew Albert was not expecting what she was about to say. She felt like he felt she didn't care about his noises he heard, and she was about to open his eyes to the fact she really had made an attempt to relate to him and his stupid ringing.

"I tried it." Tira said. "I never told you, because I didn't want to discuss the ringing, and possibly make you think of it … if you weren't."

"Don't worry about that because it's always there."

"Well," Tira continued, "Like I said, I tried, but the sound of the constant tea kettle about made me sick to my stomach, so it seemed rather dumb for me to continue listening to it for an hour."

Albert pulled in his lips over his teeth and then puckered them out a little as he leaned his cheek into his fist. He sighed again, deeply. "And I suppose the sound that makes you sick just bounces off of me?" he asked.

Tira said it was different, even according to him, because he had said his noise came from inside his head, and that was different than noise coming from the tea kettle. She smiled and took a large swallow of Dr. Pepper.

"Whatever," Albert said. "At least it's connected to the physical, so that its days are numbered … I hope. After I'm dead, if there's silence, I'm in a good place; if not, mercy on us all."

Tira took another swig of her drink and replied he knew that was not the way it was, and she thought perhaps he needed to go to church with her more, and pay more attention to Pastor Brock.

"I am getting tired of everything somehow being connected to church and Pastor Brock. I have a mind of my own you know, and I'm capable of thinking too."

Tira belched. "Excuse me," she said, "but, Albert, you know better than to think where you are in an afterlife is connected to the ringing in your ears." Visibly upset she reiterated, "You do know better, Albert!"

"As a matter of fact," Albert sharply replied, "Maybe I don't. And also, as a matter of fact, I think a person ought to be allowed to speak facetiously now and again. It's good for the soul. All I have ever said is the ringing is linked to the physical, so I know after I'm dead it will be gone. Now, if I am wrong, and I were to wake up in some sort of an afterlife hearing it, then, baby, it'll be a continuation of what I'm going through now, and it is hell! Now if I'm dead and gone, and I awaken in the middle of a desert, looking for water, feeling like I'm parched with flames, and it's quiet, then praise the Lord, and pass a teaspoon of sand please, because, baby, without the noise, I will at least think I am in heaven."

Tira boiled over. "Albert I swear you can be so blasphemous sometimes! If I had known this was how you were going to turn out, believe me I never would have married you!"

"Really? Well, my response. Tira, you still look good, you've taken good care of yourself, and I would still classify you as hot, if you were wearing the right stuff, and had the right attitude. You know, that was also part of what attracted me when I first saw you. But you know what, it's sure been awhile since we've gotten it on, hasn't it?"

"Well, maybe that's part of the problem, Albert! Think about what you just said. 'Gotten it on'. Real turn-on, you know. And speaking of attitude changes, you've sure gone through quite a few since our first date. Or do you even remember the Bill and Gloria Gaither concert?" Tira took another big swallow of Dr. Pepper. "Sometimes, Albert, the way you talk, I wonder if you haven't just given yourself over to the evil one."

"Damn it, Tira, let's not get started on this again, and I know, 'but Albert, that's not what Pastor Brock would say'." Albert knew he was treading in dangerous territory, but he was reaching a point where he didn't much care anymore. "Well, I think Mr. Brock has collected himself some spiritual groupies, and we husbands stop in occasionally to see what he's telling his harem this week. Actually, I wonder sometimes what his wife Eloise thinks about the Pastor Brock Fan Club."

Tira squeezed her half-empty can of pop hard enough to crush it and force some Dr. Pepper out the top. Because she had jerked her hand upward in the process, a little of the drink went up her nose and the rest just dribbled off her chin and over her clenched fist. She threw the can at Albert who saw it coming and ducked. It bounced off the refrigerator as she screamed, "Albert Furcologna, you are crossing the line! Now, Pastor Brock says, if possible, we are to stay with our unbelieving husbands, because there is a chance they might be saved through our belief. But, trust me, you are making it difficult!"

"Tell you what," Albert said, "Why don't you go back to bed and dream of your special services, and don't forget to include Pastor Brock in them."

Albert went into the bathroom to get ready to go into his office at Periwinkle College. After she spent a few minutes in meditation while holding her dove, Tira went to the phone to call her mother.

CHAPTER 49
Enter Delayah

After teaching his 10 o'clock MWF class in Intermediate Accounting, Albert went to his office to finish up grading a quiz that he had given in Principles of Accounting I. A short time later there was a knock on his office door and Albert called, "Come on in."

Delayah, one of his sophomore advisees and also a student in his Introduction to Business class entered. She was wearing a pink cotton jacket with bell sleeves over a pencil skirt with a feminine below-the-knee length hemline. There was a large, tasteful, rhinestone brooch pinned to her left lapel. Her outfit flattered her well-kept body, and Albert noted her brunette hair, shoulder length, straight, and combed back off her face and forehead.

"I was wondering if you could help me out?" she said.

"I could tell you it's the opposite of the way you came in, but I won't. What do you need help with?"

Delayah looked puzzled, and then smiled at Albert's weak joke. "I have an appointment next week on Tuesday morning in Ashland and I'll have to miss class. I was wondering if I could come in Monday to take the chapter quiz early."

Albert asked her if she would be back on campus Tuesday afternoon after the appointment and Delayah said she expected to be, by two. She asked Albert if he wanted her to take the quiz then, and Albert told her that that would be fine, just come by his office.

"I really apologize about missing," Delayah said, "but it is hard to get appointments with this doctor, and I really have to have one."

"I know that's how it is sometimes, particularly with specialists," Albert responded.

"I wish I didn't have to see him," said Delayah, feeling like she owed some kind of explanation to her instructor. "I know this is going to sound crazy to you, but I have this loud buzzing noise in my ears, my family doctor calls it *tintus, tinitus,* something like that."

Albert couldn't quite believe what he was hearing. "Why don't you have a seat," he said, indicating the chair next to his desk. "And it's called tinnitus. Having a ringing in your ears is not at all crazy, though it may drive you there some day."

Delayah looked surprised as she said, "You know what I'm talking about?" but there was also a tone to her voice that indicated she was ready to talk to someone who understood. She sat, crossed her legs, and smoothed her skirt down.

"Oh, yeah," said Albert. "Actually, and this may sound funny coming from a Business Professor, but I am working on a book of poetry about it. Going to call it, Strings May Be Broken, But the Music Goes On."

"Holy Shit," said Delayah. "Pardon my French, but I can't believe this. My younger brother has been asking me, 'If it's really there, why can't I hear it?'"

"I know how frustrating it is to try and explain about the tinnitus to some people." Albert smiled to himself as he thought, *Tira would have my scalp if she could hear what I'm about to say, but I guess it doesn't matter anymore.* He continued, "You see, I've heard that same question before … many times … from my wife."

"You're kidding me," Delayah looked truly shocked but then caught herself. "I … I didn't mean anything bad by that, Mr. Furcologna."

Albert chuckled. "I know you didn't," he said, "and, please, call me Albert." He continued, "It doesn't feel too good, does it, when people think you're crazy, and you know what's bothering you really does exist?"

Delayah had an expression on her face that seemed a mixture of disbelief and relief over finding someone to talk to as she said, "Not real good, no. You said you were writing a book of poems about it. Funny you should mention that because I wrote a couple short poems the other night. Didn't make the noise go away, but I felt like I was doing something besides just sitting there going nuts." Albert asked her if she could remember what she had written and Delayah replied she had written them in her notebook. She uncrossed her legs and set her books on the edge of Albert's desk as she asked him if he was sure he wanted to hear them; she didn't think they were any good as writing went, but she had been trying to express what she was feeling at that given moment.

Albert nodded his head in understanding. "That's what the writing has to be about," he said. "Expressing what you are feeling."

Delayah drew in a deep breath and started. "Here's the first one. I called it 'Circle of Noise', goes like this.

Circle of noise, closed in sphere.
Settling down with depression, fear.
Tension, paralysis, all give shove.
Seeming like I can't give out
Or take in love."

Delayah smiled sheepishly as she asked. "Pretty bad, huh?"

Albert stared at her for a moment. "No ... it's not bad. I think anyone wrestling with tinnitus would identify with what you wrote. And, what also makes it good is, although you and I know it's about the noise, there are a hundred other things, physical, emotional, psychological, you name it, where people could say, 'Hey. She's talking about what's bothering me'."

Delayah had been greatly agitated by the ringing when her brother had last given her grief over it, and she had gotten extremely pissed off at him, so she was relieved upon finding someone who identified with her and related to what she had written. She straightened. "You really think so?"

"I know so," said Albert. "You said you wrote a couple ...?"

"Well, there's just one more, for right now. Pardon my French again, I ... I'm ... a little angry in this one. I ... kinda ... cuss."

"Yeah," Albert chuckled as he said, "the noise will help you there sometimes. Go for it."

Delayah hesitated a little and Albert could tell that she was somewhat uncomfortable with what she was about to say. "I wrote this one right after my brother was harassing me about the noise the other night," she said. "It's in acrostic format, so I guess the title is ... uhm ... 'Fuck You'."

Albert leaned back in his chair and laughed. "I love it," he said. "I can't wait to hear it."

Delayah said, "Well, here goes, my first public reading of 'Fuck You'.

"For a while I thought you were a good friend
Until you made fun of me and said, 'I
Can't hear the noise. How do I
Know you're not making it up?'

"You sniveling bastard, you don't even care,
Or else you're stupid, ignorant.
Until I decide which, kiss my ass."

Albert shook his head. "Oh my God," he said, "Beautiful. If that doesn't capture the way we with this unpleasant symphony feel sometimes, then nothing does."

Delayah put one elbow on the desk, raised her hand and rested her chin against it, and half-cocked her head as she asked, "You're not just saying that?"

"No, Ma'am." Albert was feeling a jolt to his spirit like he had not experienced in a long time. "I told you I've written some myself, and I think you have a good grasp on capturing some of the feelings one has with tinnitus at times. But I should warn you, writing temporarily helps, but the noise will still drive you to the brink of desperation at times. Longevity with this affliction doesn't mean a damn thing. No special privileges."

"I didn't mean to come in here and take you away from your work," Delayah said, "but I can hardly believe I've run into someone who knows what I'm going through."

"Sounds like you're thinking like I've been thinking," Albert said. "And trust me; if this is an interruption, it's a welcome one." Delayah smiled at Albert and asked if he would read something he had written. "Sure, I'd love to," Albert said, thinking, *Tira can have her special services with Pastor Brock; I'll have my own version, without the good pastor.* "Tell you what," he continued, "I'll read you a little something that I wrote when the muse last struck me. It's my latest attempt to unseat Robert Frost. Sure you want to hear it?"

"You know I do."

Albert got up from his desk saying he had to get it out of his writing files. Delayah noted his file cabinet looked like so many others in the faculty offices at the small college; older, dented from years of use, and papers piled on top that should have been sorted through and, most of them file-thirteened months, or even, years ago. Albert opened the second drawer down and shifted a manila folder up. He pulled out the first sheet in the file and sat back down, leaving the drawer open and the folder standing watch over the others below it.

"Well, here goes nothing. It's called 'Subjective Things'." He paused. Delayah smiled and told him that she was ready. Albert cleared his throat and said again, "'Subjective Things'.

If I were set in a wheelchair, and hit a big old bump,
And slipped a little on my side and fell out on my rump,
Some assistance would soon be with me, for evident problems would show,
And seeing me lying flat on my ass, others would quickly know I needed help.
But my handicap is subjective, so even if it lays me low,
And batters and beats me all about, no one will ever know…unless I tell them.
But who wants to share in a defect? And who really cares how it beats?
For subjective things are the hardest to share, and the easiest to cause defeats."

Delayah shifted once during the reading like she was trying to concentrate even more on Albert's words, giving him a sense of excitement he hadn't felt for some time.

"So," he asked, "what do you think, is Robert Frost worried about being replaced?"

"Fortunately for him, Robert Frost will never have to worry about being replaced, but I think he would recognize the poem for what it is, good, and right on target. I tried to explain to my brother about subjective things, and it was like he couldn't comprehend. I got so mad because I just feel like he doesn't want to comprehend it."

Albert agreed, thinking about his many disconcerting discussions with Tira about the ringing. "I believe I know exactly what you are talking about, and, I concur, it is frustrating."

"Yes, it is. But you want to know what I'm really thinking right now? You've inspired me. After my latest incident with my brother, I felt an almost abject hopelessness and a feeling of, I don't know, I guess you would say, powerlessness. But I am seeing now that instead of lapsing into those feelings, we can look the universe straight in the eyes with all the dignity we can muster, and turn our pain into a work of art. I didn't realize that's what I was doing until now. Thanks, Mr. Furco … I mean, Albert."

"You're welcome." Albert glanced at his wall. He was enjoying himself and had lost track of time. There was a department meeting in just a few minutes, and since his Chair had been on his case lately in a couple areas, Albert felt it would behoove him not to be late. He said somewhat apologetically, "I'm really sorry, Delayah, but there's a meeting coming up I have to get to."

"No need to be sorry. I'm the one who should be sorry. Like I said earlier, I only planned on stopping in quick-like and checking on the quiz."

Albert told her never to apologize for brightening up someone's day, and added, "And like I said earlier, a welcome interruption. Manna from the gods, and all that good stuff." Then he smiled. "A question. When you come by to take the quiz, do you have a class, or anything else, right afterwards?"

"I have a class at three. I'll be free until then."

"Then maybe we could visit a few minutes. And who knows, before then, you may get motivated and turn some more pain into poetry. You really need to keep doing that, especially if you're angry."

"I will," Delayah laughed. "And I'll see if I can get a 'fuck this' motif going."

As Albert and Delayah were laughing, Tira came through the door. "Sorry, Albert," she said coldly. "I was in the area, and thought I'd stop by and see how you were doing." Tira stared callously at Delayah as she said, "Hope I didn't interrupt anything."

Albert reddened a little as he told Tira she hadn't and then added that Delayah was a student in his Introduction to Business class. He said to Delayah, "My wife, Tira."

Delayah looked Tira up and down, as she thought, *Look up subjective, woman, you might learn something. But most likely, something you wouldn't want to know.* Then she reached out her hand, "Nice to meet you, Mrs. Furcologna. I just stopped by to coordinate a make-up quiz I have to take. Doctor's appointments and all, you know how it is. Well, I really should be going." She turned back to Albert. "See you next week, ah, Mr. Furcologna. And I'll see if I can get any more writing done on my … ah … project."

Tira waited until Delayah was gone and then asked, "Albert, I'm curious about something I heard as I was coming in. Just what does that, uhm … motif … she was talking about have to do with a make-up quiz?"

Albert was glad he had a valid excuse for leaving as he said, "Tira, I'll talk with you about it later, but if I don't leave right now, I'm going to be late for a meeting."

CHAPTER 50
I Accept Your Invitation

At precisely two p.m. on Tuesday afternoon, Delayah poked her head into Albert's doorway as she gave a little knock and asked, "Safe to come in?"

Albert emotionally jumped at the sight of her as he said "Yes." The other day her clothing was very feminine, but professional, looking. She still looked very feminine, but in a much more sensual way, wearing an olive colored jersey dress with a mid-thigh hemline with small side slits, long sleeves, and a deep v-neck with a mixed stone necklace. Albert couldn't help noticing Delayah was journeying through this particular day sans bra. He couldn't help but wonder if she had selected the dress specifically with the make-up quiz in mind. He hoped so, and also hoped that his voice didn't give away his nervousness as he said, "Hi Delayah, nice to see you. I have your quiz ready."

Delayah flashed a warm smile and said, "Mr. Furcologna, I hope my talking to you didn't cause any problems the other day", although inwardly she smiled and thought, *Hope he knows I'm lying, and I also hope if his wife walks in on us today she notices how carefully I have planned my apparel.*

Albert broke into a half smile and shook his head a little as he replied, "First, like I said the other day, call me Albert. Second, like I also said the other day, a welcome interruption, manna from the gods, and all the good stuff." He continued as he concentrated on trying to look at her eyes, "And, third, it is nice to see you again. Let me get you your quiz."

Delayah took the paper and sat at a small desk in the office and started writing. A few minutes later, she handed the completed sheet to Albert and said "Finished." As he took the quiz from her, Albert indicated for her to sit in the chair next to his desk. She did, and as she crossed her legs her skirt rode up revealing a little more thigh. Albert asked how her appointment had gone, and had the medical field come up with any magic cures for tinnitus in the past few months.

Delayah sighed as she re-crossed her legs. "No, it doesn't look like there are any magician's tricks on the immediate horizon, although the doctor did say there's some medicine, Ativan, I believe, that offers some relief to about twenty-five percent of the people who have taken it. I'm not sure; some relief to about twenty-five percent? Those odds are kind of low for a medicine I don't want to use while driving. With my schedule I just don't want to take anything that might make me sleepy or impaired in any way."

"I understand what you mean there," Albert replied. "Sounds like a couple conversations I've had with my doctor. However, jumping to another point, have you done any writing? And more specifically, did the muse of your chosen motif inspire you?"

"I was hoping you'd ask; that I could talk to you again. I went home after our last conversation inspired, and started writing immediately. So now I have three more acrostic poems with a 'fuck this' title."

Albert felt like a teenage boy getting ready for his first date as he said, "Good. I want to hear them." He got up from his desk and closed the door to where it was barely cracked. He explained, "This will allow for some privacy. I hope you don't mind. I don't want anyone overhearing and misunderstanding."

"No problem." Delayah was secretly glad that he had closed the door and wished that it had been pulled all the way shut. She pulled some pages out of her notebook. "So here we go, 'Fuck This', number one.

> *Functioning with it is so hard some days*
> *Until I tell myself that it*
> *Can't go on forever. Lord*
> *Knows I need a break. Then,*
>
> *The noise comes back.*
> *Has to always come back*
> *Into its usual*
> *Superior place."*

Albert smiled and nodded knowingly as Delayah continued. "'Fuck This' two; 'tee, double-u, oh', or 'tee, oh, oh', your choice.

> *Finding myself exhausted again.*
> *Under, over, all around me.*
> *Continually, incessantly,*
> *Knocking at my ears.*
>
> *This relationship with the noise*
> *Has to stop. But how?*
> *Is there any assistance?*
> *Somewhere, someone has to know."*

"And now," Delayah uncrossed her legs and shifted to get more comfortable, then crossed them again. Albert noticed as her dress edged a little higher on her thigh, and he liked what he saw. "'Fuck This' number three.

> *For a while I listened to this*
> *Unwelcome sound, then thought,*
> *Can I find relief? Does anyone*
> *Know what I'm feeling?*
>
> *Then I found someone who identified.*
> *He understood exactly what I was feeling.*
> *I couldn't believe it was true, But then the*
> *Sound jarred me back to reality."*

Albert leaned toward the desk, one elbow on it, resting his head against the outer flat portion of his closed fist. When he was dating and first married to Tira he never dreamed he would be thinking what he was currently thinking, and that was, he wanted desperately to make love to this woman he was not married to. He said, "You really strike a chord, Delayah, pun intended."

Delayah shifted her legs again before she spoke. "Thanks for listening to my writing. After high school, I worked five years before starting college. I started dating this guy at work, and we went steady for almost four years. I wrote occasionally, but I learned not to share it with him as he always picked it apart, and was always reading things into it that he shouldn't have. We broke up a few weeks ago and now I feel freer to write."

Albert looked at his blank computer screen, then back at Delayah as he said, "Even though business is my chosen field, I feel as if writing's my mental health counselor. I guess we all need some way to cope. And like you implied in your last poem, it's nice if you feel there is someone else who really understands." He paused a moment, and then continued, "I don't know if I should mention this or not, but Tira overheard you mention the 'Fuck This' motif, and after you left, she was asking what that had to do with a business quiz. I didn't even try to explain the tinnitus connection because I knew she wouldn't understand. I really did have to get to the department meeting, but later that evening I told her, as an advisee, you were just talking about a writing project you had for an English class."

Delayah felt like she and Albert had similar agendas winding subtexts through their words as she replied, "Well, like I said earlier, I didn't mean to cause problems with your wife, but, I wonder, what is going on when you're going through difficult times, and then all of a sudden, through no choice of your own, you cross paths with someone who understands? Seriously, all I did was come in here to set up a quiz time, and all you did was act like a decent, human being, but then, boom, we found a common link, and, I don't know about you, but I felt, I feel, a pretty strong bonding."

Albert let even more of the weight of his head rest against his fist and grew very thoughtful. It seemed everyone was vulnerable in times of loneliness, and fancies ran free, and common sense, well, common sense just wasn't so common after all. But, who was responsible for Delayah and him clicking? Neither of them had been out rooting around in the mud looking for someone. They had both been minding their own business, just going through a day.

"Delayah," he started, "I also felt, and feel, the same, and I don't know the answer to your question about what's going on. Are we talking chance, identification through common needs, maybe even love? What part do circumstances play when there is that bonding? Who makes the rules? I do know I've thought of you a lot since our conversation last week."

Delayah glanced at the door and then spoke non-stop, softly and somewhat nervously, "I've really been thinking a lot about you too, Albert, and I know you're an instructor and I'm a student. You're probably about five years older than me, and you're married. I may be totally out of line, but I'd like to spend more time with you at my place where I could explore more aggressively a Fuck This motif, if you catch my drift." She paused and looked straight into Albert's eyes and then continued, "And if I'm being too forward, I promise, I'll leave right now, and we'll never mention it again."

Albert also glanced at the door knowing this would not be a good moment for Tira to accidentally overhear anything. "One more time," he spoke softly, "welcome interruption, manna from the gods, all the good stuff. And, yes, I definitely accept your invitation to, ah, visit with you, and, ah, help your motif exploration."

CHAPTER 51
Look Out! He's Moving!

Dreams and memories of that day always left Brad restless, un-settled. He sometimes wished there was someone he could talk to about it, but these things had been bottled up for years. He had tried to just forget Vietnam when he returned back home and never even talked with his grandfather about it. And the ringing in the ears, he knew it was called tinnitus; it just never let up, and it made some things hard to forget.

3rd Platoon was going out on an ambush, and due to a shortage of men, Brad was also in the role of Rifleman. He was assigned a position with Alijandro, nicknamed Andro, a Puerto Rican man who was kidded about looking like a Vietnamese. "Make sure you let everyone know when you're out digging a cathole," the squad leader had told Andro when he was first assigned, "We don't want to accidently shoot you."

About fifteen minutes after setting up they saw several NVA soldiers coming down the trail and waited until they were all in the kill zone. One of the NVA stopped and squatted down and looked in the direction of Brad and Alijandro, saw them, and a real quizzical look crossed his face. "He must think I'm one of them," Alijandro whispered. Then the NVA start-ed raising his AK-47 and said something in Vietnamese. Brad squeezed the clicker for the M18A1. The mine was camouflaged about three feet from the NVA and when it blasted, he gave a little cry and fell to the trail. The other positions blew their mines and several NVA were down.

After a strip search was conducted, the squad leader, Mark Sanders, said, "Bad Medic, you and Fat Billy follow this trail south and see if we got anyone else. Alijandro, you and Kevin follow it north."

Brad led the way as he and Fat Billy cautiously moved out. The trail widened a little as it curved around a large ant hill to the right which they could not see over, and Fat Billy moved alongside Brad. As they edged past the hill they could see where the trail straightened out again, and lying a few feet in front of them was another NVA. "We've got another one!" Fat Billy yelled back.

"Look out! He's moving!" called out Brad, as he and Fat Billy reacted simultaneously and fired 20 rounds on automatic into the body. There was a loud explosion and Brad thought he was dead; sure another NVA was behind the ant hill and had thrown a grenade at them. Then he was immediately aware of three things; the NVA had been ripped apart when the bullets hit explosives he was carrying, he felt a sharp pain in his shoulder from a piece of shrapnel, and Fat Billy had fallen backward with a gurgling cry. Brad saw blood flowing from a gash that looked like it had cut Bill's carotid arteries and jugular veins.

"No! Fat Billy! Damn it, Sanders, we need help down here!" Ignoring his own wound, Brad furiously started to try to stop the blood flow from Fat Billy's neck, but sensed he was engaged in a futile effort. Tears flowed down his cheeks and mingled with blood as he realized yet another soldier had died right out from under him. God, maybe I am a Bad Medic, he thought. What the hell is going on?

SGT Sanders arrived with a couple other men and immediately asked, "What the fuck happened, Bad M?"

"He started moving and we shot him. Apparently he had grenades that blew up."

"Couldn't you have just taken him? For Christ's sake, you had him covered!"

"We both reacted at the same time!" Brad was feeling a mixture of anger over the interrogation, and sorrow over the loss of Fat Billy. He continued to hold a bandage tight to the neck but could tell from his training it was too severe a wound; eyes were already rolled back in death.

"RTO, give me the horn," SGT Sanders hollered. He took the receiver and called, "Loco 6; this is Hellman 3-3. We have a casualty at ambush site; Bad Medic lost another one, Fat Billy. We need another squad out here to pull security for us. Is it possible for a Jungle Penetrator?"

"3-3, I'll tell 6. 2nd squad will be to your location in less than fifteen."

SGT Sanders swung around to Brad. "Now explain to me again just why you had to shoot that little bastard instead of taking him alive?"

Fifty plus years later, Brad still lived with that question. Furthermore, after the chaos and noise of that morning settled down, Brad became aware of a loud ringing in each ear, similar to the shrill whistle of a tea kettle. He knew then that it could be a temporary thing, or more. Now, over fifty years later, Brad knew it was permanent.

Brad examined his own shoulder and asked SGT Sanders if he would help put gauze and a large bandage over the wound.

"And I suppose you're going to want to be medevaced?"

"Hell fucking No!" Brad retorted.

"Well, good!" SGT Sanders said. "Let's just hope that a hovering chopper waiting while we load a body doesn't draw any more attention to our presence in the area than we already have!"

That statement still kept Brad awake at night at times; had off and on for the past fifty years. Later that afternoon the company was hit again and four more people were killed. Had his choice to shoot the wounded NVA contributed to four additional deaths that day? Medics were supposed to save lives, not add to the death toll.

CHAPTER 52
A Man of My Choice

When Heather Dupre was seventeen, she and her best friend, Marquita Rivera, were talking at a sleepover. They were both honor students, and feeling quite undecided about their futures.

"Do you really think it's over between you and Ted?" Marquita asked.

"Oh, yeah. He's interested in Francesca."

"So, did he break up with you, then? I thought you said last week that you might break things off."

"Well," answered Heather, "I knew it was going to be kind of hard, 'cause like you know, we broke our cherries on each other. But when I started to talk to him about breaking up, he seemed kind of relieved. He said he'd also been wondering lately if maybe we should just be friends, and be seeing others. Then I saw him the next day with Francesca, so I guess it worked out okay for both of us."

"What do you mean, okay? Is there something you've not told me, Heather?"

"About what?"

"Duh. How about 'guess it worked out okay for both of us'? Are you already hooked up with someone else?"

"Nothing definite," Heather giggled, "but Jackson Lamech did ask me if I was going to come watch him at the football game Friday night."

"Jackson Lamech! Quarterback? What'd you say?"

"What do you mean, what did I say? Of course I told him I'd be there ... watching him. He asked if I wanted to go out for something to eat after the game. Now what would you tell him, Quita?"

"That I had to study for my ACT exam?" Both girls broke out with laughter.

"Yeah" said Heather, "that's what my parents would want me to say, too, but I'm tired of always being the good girl, always doing what they think I ought to do. I think it's time I discover what I want to do. That could include the college of their choice, but more likely, a man of my choice."

CHAPTER 53
Dear Christy, Wish You Were Here

Brad sometimes wondered whatever happened to Christy.

After a couple months their letters had taken on a more serious tone and Christy even scribbled the marriage word. Then a couple weeks after Valentine's Day Brad got a letter saying she had decided to join the Navy. Several more weeks went by without hearing from her; he figured she was probably busy with training. Then a couple days after he was wounded and Fat Billy was killed, Brad got a brief letter from her.

"Dear Brad, I love you and hope you are doing okay. We just had a big parade yesterday, and I was one of the ones chosen to be part of the Admiral's Honor Guard. I was so nervous; I spent over two hours shining my shoes the night before. Everything went well though. I'm just so proud to be in uniform serving my God and my country. How are things with you? Love, Christy."

In light of the past few days, the letter just struck a bad place in Brad and he sent off the following reply. "Dear Christy. So glad you're proud to be in uniform serving your God and country. I'm over here up to my ass in mud. Wish you were here. Brad."

He smiled wryly. For some reason he didn't hear back from her and found out later she married some guy she met in the Navy. Then she got out of the Navy in less than a year and moved to California; he didn't know why. He figured maybe God and country let her down.

CHAPTER 54
Hedgehog Brook Street

After Jackson left the Electric Blue Steakhouse, he decided to make a quick run down to Parkersville again. It wasn't but thirty-five minutes away via the Kentucky Bourbon Parkway and there were only two motels there, but if Heather was screwing around on him, she might have decided to go a little south. He hadn't seen the Mustang anywhere in the Parkersville area earlier in the day, but that had been mid-afternoon.

A couple hours later after another fruitless look around, he was back in Frankenberry, and decided, even though it was late, before going home he would follow through on his earlier thoughts, and at least cruise on over to Hedgehog Brook Street and see if any ladies of the night were hanging out on a street corner. The street name came from Hedgehog Brook that ran along the southwestern corner of Frankenberry, and the legend was there was a time when porcupines were in abundance there. Some dissenting locals said Eastern Kentucky was out of the range of porcupines, and even if there were any, they were listed by the Kentucky Department for Fish and Wildlife as threatened. These same animal experts would also make the point that hedgehogs and porcupines were not the same; furthermore, hedgehogs weren't even native to the United States. Nevertheless, someone in power along the way had dubbed the brook hedgehog, and from thus came the street name. As a community area, it had degenerated into a closely spaced row of houses taking comfort from each other in their common need for paint and repair. In Frankenberry, and, by extension, Franken County, Hedgehog Street was known as the place to go for anyone seeking drugs or a relatively cheap sexual encounter.

And Jackson was upset his charm hadn't worked with Deanna. *Damned if there aren't some women*, he thought, *who just don't know what it is to have a real man make love to them. But if they're not willing to find out, I guess that is just their loss.* He didn't feel like going to O'Rourke's and taking another chance on coming up short, and a few weeks back, he had gotten a good quickie on Hedgehog from some chick who said her name was Chantillee. Jackson thought maybe he could spot her again and see if for a little extra cash, she might even go back to the house with him.

As he turned left off Second Street onto Hedgehog Brook Street, Jackson spotted a couple of women halfway down the block. He pulled alongside them and stopped. "Chantillee?" Jackson called.

"You want me, Baby?" she answered back.

"Yeah," said Jackson. "I do. I've been thinking about you, and how good you made me feel last month."

"I thought I'd seen this RAM 1500 before. You're sure running awful late tonight, but you're in luck because I like to say that in my business operation I'm available 24/7."

"That's why I thought of you," said Jackson. "That and the fact, like I said, you made me feel awfully good."

"But it's been awhile since you've been here," Chantillee said in a pouty voice, knowing whatever she heard back would be pure cow chip.

"Well," Jackson responded, "it's this way. I've got a wife, and a couple girlfriends. A man just has to make sure he takes care of them all, you know. He just can't go leaving someone out."

Chantillee knew that in her occupation she was usually paid to do other things with her mouth than just talk so she tried to move things along. "Right, right. So what do you want? Same as last time?"

"Actually, I was wondering if I paid a little extra, if I could get you to come to my place and spend the night."

"Thought you said you was married."

"She's out of town. Gone to her mother's for a week. No problem."

"It's a problem for me," said Chantillee. "I'm not working in another woman's bed. Now I'll give you the same as last time and have you on your way in no time, okay?"

Jackson was a little bit frustrated and a little bit relieved. At least he wouldn't have to worry about getting out of bed to return Chantillee back to her street-based office. But he laid no claim to understanding her sense of economics. He was willing to pay, and in his mind, *why wouldn't a woman want to make a little extra money when it involves what she already does? And I'm offering her a chance to sleep in a nice bed. What difference should it make it's also been occupied by my wife?*

But, Jackson figured, on the other hand, *now my little puppy can make it to the feeding bowl just that much sooner,* so he said, "Okay, climb in. Let's get this show underway."

Chantillee unzipped his trousers, and after about a minute of working him over, Jackson was startled by flashing blue lights appearing behind him. *Son of a bitch,* he thought, *Lucky dog, my ass.*

Two city policeman, Josh Arlington, and his partner, Frank Reaume, walked to the pickup and shone their lights on Jackson and Chantillee.

"Damn it," said Josh. "Frank, take care of Mr. Horny here, I need to talk to the lady a minute." He looked at Chantillee, shook his head, and said, "Get out of the truck, Ma'am." Josh walked a little away from the RAM with Chantillee and then spoke somewhat harshly to her. "Cheryl, when did you start back on the streets, and what the hell are you thinking?"

"Screw you!" Chantillee retorted. "I don't have to answer to you, or anyone else."

"Maybe not," Josh replied. "But I guess you will have to answer to the law."

"So, are you going to arrest me? Or will you put it off on your partner?"

Josh sighed deeply. "Believe it or not, Cheryl, I really love you. I just can't believe this. I really can't. And just what do you suppose Mom is going to say?"

"Spare the lectures, big brother," Cheryl said. "If you're going to read me my rights, just do it, okay?"

Josh shook his head sadly and turned away to walk back to the RAM.

***

Down at the station, Jackson tried to make a phone call. There was still no answer at his house, so he asked if the police would look up the number for Marquita Rivera.

"Don't see a Marquita," said the night desk officer. "Only got about two Riveras in here and Marquita isn't one of them. Is she married?"

Jackson answered "Yes," and then spoke to himself "Who the hell did she wind up with? I think it was Vic. Officer, is Victor Snyder listed?"

"There is. I'll write the number down for you."

"I don't know," said Jackson, "I can't call her in the middle of the night. The only reason I even thought of her is because I think that she knows where my wife is."

"So," the officer smiled as he asked the next question, "is that what you were doing down Hedgehog, looking for your wife?"

Jackson momentarily forgot where he was and who he was talking to, and why. "You son of a bitch!" he exploded. "No, I wasn't down Hedgehog looking for my wife!"

Officer Frank Reaume rushed back over to where Jackson was, told him to settle down before they brought more charges against him, and asked him what the problem was.

"This weasel was asking if my wife's a whore!" Jackson said.

"Wes?" Frank looked inquiringly at his co-worker as they got ready to play off each other.

"I don't think so," said Wesley, "He was arrested with a prostitute, and he said he thought that the woman he was going to make his one call to might know where his wife was. All I asked was if that was why he was down Hedgehog, looking for his wife."

Frank turned to Jackson. "Seems like a reasonable question to me. Was that, in fact, why you were down there?"

"You wait," Jackson angrily replied. "When I get a lawyer the both of you are going to be looking at harassment charges."

Wesley grinned then asked, "Well, listen, have you decided yet who you're going to call?"

Jackson thought of the bar. He had an occasional drinking friend, Aaron Patterson who might come get him out, if Jackson could just find out his phone number. He knew Aaron sometimes lived with his grandparents on his mother's side, but he didn't know their last name. He wondered if the bartender, Kevin, was still up, and figured maybe he could tell him what Aaron's number was. "Could you look up Kevin O'Connor for me? He bartends down Rourke's Beer Palace. He's probably still up."

"Yeah," said Frank, winking at Wesley, "and, who knows, maybe he knows where your wife is."

Jackson bit his tongue to keep from saying anything else as he wanted to get out of the mess he was in as soon as possible, not deeper into it. *Damned Heather,* he thought, *whenever I find that bitch I'm going to slap her silly.*

***

Jackson was pissed as he sat on the edge of the hard bed in the narrow cell. Kevin O'Connor had said he couldn't come down, and when Jackson asked if he knew Aaron Patterson's number, Kevin had said that he wasn't a damned telephone directory, so Jackson waited until morning, and called Marquita.

"What's this again, Jackson?" she asked. "You want me to bail you out of jail? What were you arrested for … my God, you didn't beat Heather up, did you?" Jackson irritably said he hadn't, but then added if he knew where Heather was he might consider it. Marquita's voice raised in anger as she told Jackson, "You must be a total idiot if you think that after the comment you just made I would even consider coming down and bailing your ass out of jail. By the way you didn't tell me what you're in for."

"Oh, hell, never mind," Jackson said as he hung up. He asked the guard if he could get him a phone book so he could look up a lawyer.

CHAPTER 55
Back to the Future

Brad hoisted himself into his '56 Chevy pick-up and headed down the grassy trail that connected near the parking lot for the Coyote Loop Trailhead to the road that led into town. He always had mixed feelings about the occasional trips, as he sometimes found himself caught in the middle of loner and lonely. He was on his way to get a few non-perishable items from the grocery, a couple items from the hardware store and then stop by the Roasted Bread and Gravy Diner in Goodman Village, a quaint little all-nighter. The owner had acquired two, Steam Train carriage, 1920's Pullman cars from the Essex Clipper Dinner Train line located in Essex, Connecticut. He had remodeled with one side taken out of each, and then they were joined. After they were assembled, then he made roof modifications and painted the exterior to resemble a large loaf of bread. The food was home-cooked and the diner seemed to always have customers, no matter the hour.

Brad hoped it wouldn't be real busy when he got to the diner so he could enjoy his meal in relative solitude. He picked up a few staples from the grocery and then a new short bent and straight skew for wood carving from the hardware store. He wasn't really hungry yet so he made the rare decision to take in a movie since the classic "Back to the Future" was in re-run. He purchased his ticket and went in to enjoy the show.

When he finally got to the diner he was glad to see, that unlike some other times when he had been there, it was almost empty. He went in and sat at a booth at the end just in case some others came in. He usually wasn't in a talkative mood; less so tonight. "Back to the Future" had stirred up some things.

He realized after he got back from Vietnam and out of the service that he was subject to mood swings like he had never had before. He did date and eventually marry another girl he had known from before he quit high school, Linda Crowe. Shortly after they married she said she didn't like living in the cabin and wanted to move to town. They were in an argument over it one night, and Linda asked him if he realized that sometimes he could be the biggest goddamn jerk ever. Brad didn't answer and said nothing else the rest of the evening. The next morning she told him she was moving back to her parents and filing for divorce.

Brad realized that for practical purposes he was living the life of a retiree, as he was on his own schedule and didn't have to really keep track of the days, or really even, the time. But he usually did. This day was a reflective one for him as it was his grandfather's birthday. He recalled when it rolled around while he was in Vietnam. *They were conducting reconnaissance missions and found a bunker complex and destroyed hundreds of pounds of rice. As he was digging his foxhole that evening Brad thought about rice being one of his grandfather's favorite meals, and wondered, what would he think if he could see so much of it being wasted.*

CHAPTER 56
Designing a Strategy

After sleeping for about six hours, Roscoe got up, opened a 12 oz. bottle of Ale 8, and guzzled it down. He awakened Heather and remembered they had gone to sleep upset with each other over the Shoney's incident, so he just told her they needed to get ready soon to return his mother's car back to Armstrong County. She lay in the bed for a few moments as if she was trying to recall where she was, and how she had gotten there, and then replied quietly, "Oh, yeah." Roscoe told her he was going to clean up.

Once he had showered, he called his mother again to make sure his Uncle Tommy wasn't at the house, and then told her they would be there with her car in a couple hours. Roscoe gave Heather a red bandanna to tie around her head, and along with one of his Army surplus shirts, it changed her appearance enough that glancing quickly, very few people, if any, would recognize her.

She was very tranquil as they got ready to leave. Roscoe said it would be best if he drove his mother's car and Heather the Camry. She agreed, thinking, *I never saw it any other way.* It was an uneventful trip to Armstrong County where they dropped the car off, fixed a sandwich and used the bathroom, and then headed back toward Franken County. They had ridden in silence most of the way back when Heather spoke. "Roscoe, we need to talk about something."

Damn, Roscoe thought. *Here it goes.*

But Heather was not thinking confrontation. The further into this misadventure she got, the more she was thinking she really wanted to hurt Jackson, bad. But she knew she couldn't do it alone, that her best bet would be to have Roscoe helping her. And she had pretty much figured out what motivated Roscoe. "Roscoe, we were both on edge earlier today, and I got kind of bitchy with you. Forgive me?"

Her words caught Roscoe off-guard as they weren't what he had been expecting, but he wasn't complaining. "That's okay. You're right, I guess we were just feeling a lot of pressure, trying to get here without being seen, and all."

Good, Heather thought. *I think I can get him.* "Roscoe," she said, "tonight, a little before midnight, we need to go by an ATM and I can get a few hundred dollars. That will help. Then we've got to design a strategy. I really need to fix Jackson so he'll leave me alone for good. Then you and I can plan our future."

"Right, Baby. You and me. I can handle it. Let's make up in the bedroom when we get home, okay."

Heather replied "Okay", as she thought, *Home? You and me long-term? I'm not so sure about another long-term man in my life. The last one almost killed me.* But she also realized she had been correct in a motivation for Roscoe. As long as she supplied what he wanted, Roscoe was hers.

They decided that later in the evening they would use the ATM at the Castle Street Branch of Trustworthy Community Bank located in Goodman Village. Heather told Roscoe. "About a year ago, Jackson upped the withdrawal limit to five hundred dollars a day, so I'll withdraw four hundred eighty, leaving a window to cover possible fees. Of course, I'll check our balance first, to see if he's withdrawn anything, and, if so; lower my withdrawal accordingly. Then we can ride around for an hour or so, and after midnight, then I can get another four hundred eighty. Those will be the only withdrawals I can make until after we have done what we need to do to Jackson."

Heather was not aware of it yet, but she had gone over the edge. She still wasn't sure on her revenge, but her thoughts had been ranging from tattooing bastard on his testicles, to even, somehow, killing him. The more she thought about killing Jackson, the more the idea appealed to her. When she mentioned that to Roscoe, he suggested smothering him by wrapping a large roll of duct tape around his head, and dumping his body into a Porta-Potty. Heather thought that was sick but didn't express her opinion, instead saying, "I want to kill Jackson, but nothing spectacular. Plus, a body in a Porta-Potty would probably start to stink rather quickly, and be found. I want any deeds committed against Jackson to be untraceable, in a 'Goodbye Earl' sort of way."

After arriving back at Roscoe's place and going inside, Heather slipped out of her miniskirt and blouse and asked Roscoe, "Would you like to help me finish undressing … and then … ?"

CHAPTER 57
Close Encounters

About 10:30 p.m., Heather again donned Roscoe's bandanna and shirt. He went out and started his Camry and then Heather slipped out to join him, adjusting the seat so she was laying back and barely visible. At the bank, balance information showed Jackson had not used the card during the day, and so Heather withdrew four hundred eighty dollars. Then Roscoe drove around awhile as she again slumped down. They decided to go to the all-night diner in Goodman Village, The Roasted Bread and Gravy. Roscoe would park off to the side, and go order take out meals while Heather lay down in the car.

Roscoe went in and noticed a couple sitting near a window and a couple booths down a man by himself. *I've seen that guy in town before*, Roscoe thought as he glanced at Brad, *but where?* He sat at the counter with his back to the couple.

"May I help you?" asked the woman behind the counter. Roscoe had never watched any episodes of the Alice series on television or he might have wondered if Polly Holliday, aka Flo, had a twin sister. Roscoe ordered two take-out meals of fried chicken, mashed potatoes and gravy, peas, and rolls, and two medium Pepsis. The Flo look-a-like told Roscoe it would be a few minutes on the chicken, and asked him if he wanted something to drink while he waited. Roscoe answered he'd take coffee, black. He shifted to get a little more comfortable on the stool and then stiffened a little as he overheard conversation at a window booth behind him.

"So how is it your fault the Infiniti got away from you?" asked Deanna.

"Because," Phillip answered, "I should have just told you immediately I had to go. By the time I pulled out after it, there were two tractor trailers side by side on a hill, and by the time I got around them, the car was out of sight."

Roscoe listened closely while doing his best to look like he was bored and waiting on his meal.

"Well, I guess I should share the responsibility," said Deanna. "I was the one who called you."

"Not your fault, Honey," Phillip said. "You had no idea what was going on. Besides, we can't change anything now. At least I got the car back for the owner, and it didn't appear to have any damage done to it."

The waitress brought his coffee and Roscoe thanked her while fighting the urge to look at the couple talking. He hadn't paid them much attention when he came in.

Deanna spoke again. "And no clues as to who did it?"

"Actually, there is a lead," Phillip said.

Roscoe froze with fear as Phillip said, "I talked with a woman who lives down the road from where I found the car, and she said her husband saw some guy leaving a black Infiniti under the bridge to get into a Mustang with a girl that he thought he went to school with. His wife said she had gotten mad at her husband because he had told her the girl was wearing a really hot-ass mini-skirt."

Roscoe was now thoroughly convinced it was his episode being talked about, and he was relieved Heather had stayed out in the car. He knew from his experience as a drug dealer there were times you had to maintain absolute cool, and this was one of them. If Heather were in there they not only would have attracted more attention as a couple, but the temptation would be strong to whisper or react in some way. Roscoe knew that what he had to do was wait for the dinners and hope Heather didn't decide she needed bladder relief.

Deanna laughed as she said, "He should have left the hot-ass mini-skirt part out, I take it."

Phillip continued, "Definitely, but think on this. She got upset with her husband and their voices got a bit loud, and their young son overheard them. So when I'm at the underpass, a couple boys come by and I ask them if they know anything about a black car parked there the day before, and because of the argument, this boy says, 'Yes'. I almost certainly wouldn't even have this lead if she hadn't gotten mad at him for saying, what is without a doubt, an unquestionably stupid thing to say to your wife."

Deanna grinned. "Make sure you remember the lessons learned; use discretion in comments about other women, although, I do have to admit, I admire his total honesty."

Phillip reddened slightly, inwardly cringing over nastywatchers.com, and then continued. "So anyway, back to this guy seeing this girl. His wife told me when she asked him who he thought it was, he said Heather Lamech, used to be Heather Dupre. She said that was when she got mad at him as she proceeded to tell him she knew who Heather Lamech used to be, and that he didn't have to characterize her as wearing a hot-ass mini-skirt because she knew damn well what he was thinking."

"So I take it she knew her?" Deanna asked.

"Well, the woman said if it was the girl her husband thought it was, that he had dated this Heather for awhile before he had started dating her. She told me the reason Heather was still such a sore spot with her was because her husband had had the audacity to talk to her about Heather on their first date; that she almost didn't go out with him again because of it. Then she told me she wouldn't have cared at all about him telling her he had seen someone getting into a car with this girl, but he just didn't need to describe Heather the way that he did."

"So," asked Deanna, "Have you located this Heather to see if it was her?"

"Not yet," said Phillip. "I was going to work on it today, and I got caught up in a routine traffic stop. You know when I told you I had to go because someone had just crossed on a red arrow. Bad mistake on their part. It turned into a major break in an on-going drug dealing investigation. I wouldn't have even searched the car except the couple got to arguing and the man said his wife should shut up or they were going to be late for their drop to Roscoe. I've heard that name before, but haven't been able to find out who it is yet. But I do plan on trying to locate Ms. Heather Lamech, trust me."

Roscoe felt like he had been kicked hard somewhere between his testicles and his belly button and that he needed to go to the restroom to feel relief from the ocean that was pounding waves against his stomach from the inside out. He put all his efforts into maintaining his cool and praying Heather stayed in the car.

"Here are your dinners. Do you want me to put that coffee in a cup to go?"

Roscoe was startled by the sound of the waitresses' voice. "Ah … no, that's okay," he said, shooting up a prayer of thanks for the quick service. He paid for the dinners, took a deep breath and then left the diner on what he trusted were not too noticeably wobbly legs, stealing a quick look at Phillip and Deanna on his way out.

"Mmm, smells good," said Heather when he got into the car. Roscoe told her that he didn't know if their restaurant Karma was good or bad and Heather asked what he meant by that.

"Two chance encounters in the past few hours," Roscoe said. "Both involving food. One could have gotten us killed, and the one I just had, Ms. Heather Dupre, might well save our asses from getting caught, in more ways than one."

Heather looked a bit startled as she asked Roscoe "How do you know my maiden name? What had happened in the diner?" Roscoe said what had happened at Shoney's had been bad, but he thought that what he had just found out was good. He started the Camry and carefully turned left onto the highway.

As he put distance between them and the Roasted Bread and Gravy Roscoe told Heather that the cop he passed when he had stolen the Infiniti had been in the diner with his wife or girlfriend or something. Heather asked if he was sure and Roscoe said he knew it was the same cop because he had mentioned the Infiniti getting away from him. Heather asked Roscoe if he was sure he hadn't been recognized, and Roscoe answered, "No, but get this, he was saying he had talked with some woman whose husband saw me getting into a Mustang, and he thought that the woman I was with was you."

Heather was near panic as she asked Roscoe, "Who the hell was the guy that said he thought it was me he had seen, and why do you think what you just heard is good?"

"The cop said the guy's wife told him that her husband used to date this Heather, in other words you, before he dated her."

"Ted Resnick?"

"Cop didn't say any names, but he did say to trust him that he planned on locating Ms. Heather Lamech."

"So how is this good?"

Roscoe decided it was time to reveal his occupation to Heather, and so he told her, "I, ah, I need to let you know I make my living off selling drugs, and my name was also mentioned. Also, while you were sleeping I made a call to a supplier, Charlie Cameron, and I also heard the cop say that Charlie's drop had been intercepted. They know it's for a Roscoe, but don't know who I am yet. So I say this is good because we have a warning." He glanced over at Heather for any reaction, but she was quiet. What he could not tell was she was quickly piecing everything together and thinking that the revenge gods had smiled again and had given her even more ammunition in her arsenal to keep Roscoe in her corner.

"So," Heather asked after a moment, "I just have two questions. First, Frankenberry is not the world's largest town. How have you managed to keep evading the law?"

"I learned a whole lot from the guy who worked the area before I moved in, mainly things not to do. He's in prison."

"Better make that three questions," said Heather. "Because I'm wondering why stealing Infinities doesn't fall under the category of things not to do?"

"I know," Roscoe answered. "Bad on my part. But I have always liked to take things, and whoever owned it just left it sitting there with the windows down and the keys in the ignition. Couldn't help myself; next thing I knew, I was out on the Kentucky Bourbon Parkway questioning what the hell I was doing. World's almost dumbest criminal; something like that?"

"Good enough," Heather responded. "I'll buy that. Third question. Do you have any suggestions about what we should do now?"

Roscoe processed thoughts rapidly. "I think," he started, "we should go to the bank in a few minutes as planned, and then go back to my place. Then, you don't leave the house. I sat next to the cop who even said my name and he didn't know who I was, so there is no way they're going to immediately be at the house looking for you. The pressure is on over the drugs now, but I think we still have a little time to come up with a workable plan to save our asses. Of course," he added, "you could always just go back to your place tonight, and deny it was you."

Heather shook her head. "Maybe you don't listen so good, Roscoe. I told you earlier Jackson has hit me for the last time. Now since I am an accessory to the facts of your stolen car, and now that I know what you do for a living, I think that we are in this together." Roscoe grinned as Heather continued. "Your idea's a good one. After we go to the bank, we lie low at your house. I had been thinking about maybe calling my friend Marquita tomorrow, but I don't think I even dare do that." Thanking his lucky stars Heather wasn't raking him over coals for his livelihood; Roscoe agreed she probably shouldn't contact her friend, at least not for the time being.

"Roscoe?" Heather decided it was time to get some commitment. "You needed me and I helped. Now we need each other. And I really need, well I mean I really want, to plan something bad, really bad, to do to Jackson, and then clear out of Frankenberry. Does that appeal to you?" Roscoe wasn't sure which she was asking him about, doing something to Jackson, or clearing out of Frankenberry, and so he asked her if she was talking about moving.

"Well," Heather said, "the police are looking for you for drugs and now for me as an accomplice in your get away after stealing the Infiniti. And I do want to get out of the area."

Heather realized that in actuality, except for Marquita, there was no one anymore in her life she could really call a close friend, and she figured, in time, she would be able to contact Marquita and swear her to silence, so she said, "Another state, fresh start, no one trying to find out who we are. Interested?" Heather laid her hand over on Roscoe's lap. She knew the male organ had little, if any, conscience and she was counting on that bit of information to keep Roscoe following her like a puppy dog.

Roscoe's voice quavered as he said, "Yes, I'm interested. I think it's a real good idea."

Heather smiled as she said, "We're going to have to be careful, real careful."

"I agree," said Roscoe, "and by the way, do you want to know how I knew for sure the cop was talking about you?"

"How?"

"Because the guy's wife the cop had been talking about," he paused, "what was Ted's last name again?"

Heather replied, "Resnick," as she thought back to the night that she had lost her virginity.

"Yeah, that's the name," said Roscoe. "Well, apparently this guy's wife said her husband told her the girl he saw me getting into the Mustang with was wearing a really hot-ass mini-skirt. And I thought to myself, Bingo."

"Well," Heather responded. "Tell you what, as soon as we get back to the house, as a form of celebration, our version of Bingo, I guess you could say, how about this girl that wears the hot-ass mini-skirt makes love to you again; sound good?"

"Better than good," Roscoe replied as he said with an emotion he was unfamiliar with, "Heather, my life is getting better and better. How could stealing a car wind up being such a turning point for me? I honestly think I love you, Baby."

"And I love you, too," Heather said, thinking, *It really is true that blood can't flow simultaneously to the brain and the penis. I'll be able to get Roscoe to do anything for me.*

***

Deanna watched as Roscoe walked out the door. Then she looked back at Phillip and said, "That guy probably heard us talking about the stolen Infiniti and made a vow to himself to make sure he always locked his car doors from here on out."

"Well if you're right, then I guess overhearing our conversation would be a good thing for him." After Phillip and Deanna finished eating, they paid, and also left.

CHAPTER 58
The Pink Mini Skirt

Jackson sat at the table staring at his cup of coffee. While talking with him about the solicitation charges, his lawyer, Bruce Terry, had also told him he needed to file a missing person report on Heather, and, in addition, to not be talking about wanting to kick her ass. He cautioned that if any foul play had befallen Heather, Jackson would be the one the police looked to first, and violent talk could be entered as circumstantial evidence.

"Okay," Jackson had told his lawyer. "I won't talk about it. But if I find that bitch, I'll damn sure do it."

He decided to drive around looking for her again. He looked up Victor Snyder's address in the phone book and figured he ought to swing that way to see if he just might see Marquita, or possibly, even Heather or her Mustang. If Marquita's old man wasn't home, maybe he could coerce her into telling him what was going on and where Heather was.

Jackson started down Main Street, and stopped at a crosswalk to let a woman in a pink mini-skirt go. She had long, shapely legs, and Jackson felt his, recently unlucky dog, stirring. She waved thank you and Jackson waved back. He rolled down his window and asked if she needed a ride. The woman smiled, but just kept on walking, so Jackson slowly drove alongside trying to coax her into the truck. He didn't notice that the driver ahead of him obeyed a stop sign, and Jackson was thrown forward against the steering wheel as his pick-up, his beautiful RAM, rammed into the back of the brand new, silver Lexus.

"I'll be a horse's ass, I can't believe this!" Jackson put his arms arch-like over the steering wheel of the RAM and put his head down on them. He felt like a quarterback being sacked, his mind slammed. He thought, *Looks like today is another third and twenty-two. It doesn't matter that the coach is protesting, the play is dead, the game continues.*

Within a minute, there was the sound of a siren, and the local police were on the scene. He shook his head as Officers Frank Reaume and Josh Arlington walked toward him. Jackson tried to joke and asked them if they ever got any sleep. Frank Reaume answered. "Sure, then we come right back to work. Or at least that's the way this week's schedule is. So what's the problem?" An irate middle-aged woman got out of the Lexus and came back to where the police were talking to Jackson and told them she had stopped for a stop sign like she was supposed to, and the next thing she knew the truck had rammed into the back of her.

Officer Arlington looked at the chrome plated curved horns on the truck emblem and couldn't keep from smiling as he said, "That he did. Yes, Ma'am."

"I don't see anything funny about this, Officer, do you?"

Josh cleared the smile from his face. "Oh, no, Ma'am. I was just looking at the truck's emblem, and … never mind. No, Ma'am, I apologize. There's nothing funny. He definitely rammed you."

The woman continued. "I think I may have hurt my back. I most certainly will be calling my lawyer. So you had better keep this professional if you don't want to be part of a lawsuit."

Josh bit his tongue to keep the smile from resurfacing and said, "Yes, Ma'am. You are right; he definitely rammed you."

"So, what happened?" Officer Reaume asked Jackson. "Still looking for your wife?"

Jackson rolled his eyes. "No. I guess my foot slipped off the brake, or something. I'm really not sure."

The woman in the pink mini came out from the doorway of the Hot Fox Dress Shop she had stepped into after the accident. "I saw what happened, Officer," she volunteered. "This man was nice and let me cross the street, but then he kept asking me to get into the truck with him. He was looking right at me when he ran into the back of the lady's car."

"Not sure what happened?" Frank Reaume said to Jackson. "Sounds to me like you were looking for everything but your wife … again. I will be issuing you a ticket, but you won't have to come down to the station on this one, unless…" he looked at the woman in the mini-skirt, "unless this lady wants to file harassment charges."

The woman in the pink mini-skirt replied, "No. Now I only want to do my civic duty and make sure the accident is reported correctly so that you know the lady in the silver car is the one in the right."

The driver of the Lexus thanked her for getting involved. "There aren't too many people like you around anymore; the world needs more like you, the good Lord knows that."

Josh Arlington said, "Well, I need to get going on the paperwork for the accident report. And, Ma'am," he added, addressing the woman wearing the pink miniskirt, and looking at Jackson, "If you change your mind about filing harassment charges, feel free to come by the station."

Both vehicles had some very minor exterior damage but were drivable, so after insurance information was exchanged, all went their separate ways.

***

Even though he was pissed at Kevin O'Connor, Jackson decided to go to Rourke's again. As he walked into the bar, he saw Meredith sitting on a bar stool, alone. He talked her into going back to his place, and was feeling pretty good when they pulled into the driveway as he knew from the conversation that his, recently unlucky, dog was about to spring back into action and bury the bone. Jackson assured Meredith that Heather was out of town with her friend Marquita. Meredith's first time with Jackson had been with a similar story, so she had no qualms about going to his place.

As they entered the house, Jackson said, "Been missing you, Baby," and Meredith replied she had missed him, too. Jackson decided to wait until they were in the house before he mentioned the last time he had wanted her. "Wasn't real happy when I saw you with Kevin's cousin last time I was in," he said.

"Oh, him?" Meredith lightly responded. "Kevin asked me to do him a favor. That guy don't mean nothing to me, Jackson."

They went straight to the bedroom, undressed, and got into bed. After about ten minutes, Meredith asked, "What's the matter,

Jackson. You never had trouble before. Something on your mind?"

"Just help me out some more," Jackson said. He couldn't believe his sex life was heading south so quickly. After a half hour with no success, Jackson cussed Meredith out, told her to call a taxi, get the hell out, and that she'd best not ever talk to anyone about what had happened, or more to the point, about what hadn't happened. After she left he watched Paramount Network for an hour or so before drifting off to sleep in the recliner.

Jackson couldn't awaken from his nightmare and he couldn't get away from the woman.

He was in his RAM chasing her in her Lexus convertible down Hedge-hog Brook Street, when the emblem on the grill of his truck started to grow. The woman pulled the Lexus off the side of the road and jumped out of the car. She was wearing a pink-mini skirt, and wielding a large, orange banana in her hand.

"You son-of a-bitch!" she hollered at Jackson.

He stopped his truck to see what was going on, and the emblem grew into a full size ram and leapt from the grill. The woman in the mini-skirt ran toward it, and Jackson saw she held the orange banana in one hand, and a small saddle in the other. She turned and ran toward a police officer just coming out of a shoe store and started screaming. "This man owes me money!"

Jackson ran from his truck as fast as he could down the sidewalk. Randall Knowles, his father, peered through a cloud and dropped something. It was a skunk. Jackson caught it and realized there was no one down-field open; he was going to have to try and make it to the line of scrimmage himself.

He noticed that Heather had driven up in a gold Mustang adorned with purple flames and got out to watch him. The woman in the pink mini-skirt saddled the ram and threw the banana to the cop. "Hold this while I collect my money!" She spurred the ram forward toward Jackson.

"You owe me," she cried. "Don't think you can get my services, and then leave me on the side of the road!"

The line of scrimmage started to slide forward, and as he neared it,

Heather stuck out her foot and tripped him. He fell forward, and as he hit the ground, the skunk slipped out of his hands, and floated back up into the air where his father peeked through the clouds again, and then re- trieved it. The mini-skirted woman caught up to Jackson and got off the ram. Jackson rolled onto his back and then she stood over him, glaring down.

"Take a good look, will you?" she said to him. "Remember me? I'm Chantillee."

Heather called out, "Come on Jackson, you can do it. She's not me or Meredith; look at that hot thing!"

Then the woman saying that she was Chantillee hollered to the police officer, "Arrest this man! He slept with me last night, and now he doesn't want to pay. He says his wife kept the checkbook and wouldn't give him any snack money for recess. Arrest him!"

As the cop put handcuffs on Jackson, Heather waved and called out, "See you later, Jackson. I've got to take my car to the shop to get a new emblem put on it."

Jackson sat upright in bed, and tried to orient himself. He wanted to find the woman in wearing the pink mini-skirt and driving the the Lexus.

CHAPTER 59
If You Change Your Mind

The next day, Jackson decided to try calling Marquita again. She picked up the phone on the third ring.

"Heather?"

"No, this is Jackson," he started, "and, first off, Marquita, I really want to apologize for the last conversation that we had. Having just been arrested, I was under a lot of pressure. Plus," he continued, "That's not mentioning my embarrassment over why I was arrested."

Marquita furrowed her brow. The voice on the phone sounded like Jackson, but the words didn't. She considered hanging up, but she was getting concerned over Heather's absence, and Jackson had to have some reason for calling, so she just answered, "That's putting it mildly." She went on, "When the caller ID showed your number, I thought it was Heather. Has she returned yet?"

Either she really doesn't know, or she and Heather are working really well together, Jackson thought. *I think I'll go along with the assumption for awhile that she really doesn't know,* so he told Marquita, "No, Heather's still missing. I'm just checking to see if you've heard anything. I've told the police she's missing, and I'm worried because it's not like her to just take off."

Marquita decided not to mention that in some of their conversations Heather had indicated she was tired of being Jackson's punching bag. Instead she just said, "Well, I'm worried. Please, if you find out anything let me know."

"I will," Jackson said, "and listen, not too long ago Heather said something about you and Victor having a big argument."

I'll kill her, Marquita thought as she replied, "Oh, I just mentioned a spat we'd had. It was no big deal. We got things smoothed out, no problem."

"Well the only reason I mention it is because if you want to go grab a beer with me somewhere and talk about it, I'm free right now."

"No thanks," Marquita said. "Victor and I are going out to a movie and dinner, and I need to finish getting ready."

"Well," Jackson replied. "Good talking to you, and make sure you let me know if you hear anything from Heather. And listen, if you change your mind about having a beer and talking, you know how to get in touch."

"I will," Marquita answered, hanging up the phone and thinking, *God, Heather was right, that guy would try to fuck a wart hog if you put a skirt on it.*

CHAPTER 60
I'm Done for the Day, Sir

Brad wondered sometimes about whatever happened to Carl Briley. He had tried to help him, but that hadn't gone over so well with the CO – another Bad Medic day.

Carl enlisted when he turned seventeen and wound up in Vietnam one half year later, Infantry, and assigned to Delta Company, 3rd platoon. He was a fairly small kid and he occasionally took some ribbing; his pack probably weighed more than he did, that sort of thing. But there were some days when it was obvious he tired more quickly than most. Brad did his best to encourage him, and on more than one occasion had carried a couple items from his gear if it was scheduled to be a particularly long hump.

One afternoon Carl just sat down on the side of the trail.

"What are you doing?" the squad leader asked.

"I'm done for the day."

"Well, you're not, because we're not to where we're setting up yet."

"Then you just keep on going," Carl said, "but I'm done."

"Let me get the LT on the horn, see if we can take a break."

"Break all you want to. I'm done for the day. I ain't taking another step today."

Brad tried to raise Carl's spirit by telling him that they didn't have much further to go.

In a minute the LT came back to where Carl was sitting. "What the hell is the problem here?" Carl just stared at the LT and rolled his lower lip into his mouth while biting on it. "Are you sick? What's the matter?"

Carl looked at the ground and mumbled something.

"What'd you say? Speak up!" LT said.

"I said I'm done for the day! I ain't going any further!"

The LT spoke quietly but firmly. "You are not done for the day, soldier, and I am giving you a direct order to get back on your feet so we can continue!"

By that time the CO was on the horn. "LT," his RTO said, "The Old Man wants to talk to you."

"What the hell's going on back there?"

"Sir, I have a man who just sat down and refuses to go any further."

"Goddamnit, Lieutenant, don't you know the whole company is being held up? Now get him on his feet so we can move out!"

"He's just sitting here saying he's done for the day, Sir."

"Tell him I'm coming back there, and he'd best be on his feet and moving or he'll be court-martialed!"

By this time several of the guys joined Brad in taking items off Carl's pack to make it lighter and trying to talk him into standing up. By this time his jaws were set, tears were trickling down his cheeks, and he just continued saying, "I'm done. I ain't going nowhere."

Soon the CO arrived on the scene. "Soldier, what's your problem?"

"I'm done for the day, Sir."

"How about we take your weapon and gear and just leave you here where some fucking Charlie can come along and slit your goddamn throat."

"I'm done for the day, Sir."

"Sir," Brad spoke up. "I really do think he is suffering from exhaustion and needs medical attention."

"Look, Bad Medic," Brad cringed at hearing this CO for the first time use that term to his face. "I know you might be trying to make friends and overcome your reputation. But I'm not calling a medevac out here for this pussy. We're already attracting enough attention as it is." He turned back to Carl. "Now let me tell you what's going to happen, son. Your gear is being redistributed, and when we're logged tonight you are getting on that bird and going back to the rear to face court-martial. Now get on your goddamned feet and follow me!"

Carl stood up and quietly said, "I'm gonna shoot you, Sir."

The CO glared at him and then said, "Fine. Now move out, Soldier … and walk in front of me where I can keep an eye on you."

The company started to slowly move out again, Carl left on the log bird that evening, and the guys never saw him again.

Brad stared into the tree line. *We did hear Carl wound up in Long Binh Jail,* he thought. And again Bad Medic let someone down. He needed to be medevaced, allowed to recuperate, and assigned a job that didn't require humping with a fucking pack that weighed damn near what he did. Hell, he never should have been allowed out as a Grunt in the first place.

CHAPTER 61
Angel Windows: I Have Some Connections

Aaron's Nana came to the jail and brought a duffel bag with some clothes and toiletry items and was able to visit with him a few minutes. She told Aaron she was proud of what he was doing, made him promise to drop a note to her in the mail every week, and that she would visit whenever she could.

Then she had to leave, and soon a car and driver from the Angel Windows treatment facility came for him. Aaron exchanged greetings with the driver, and then climbed into the back seat as directed. As they started out, there was some small talk, but Aaron soon lapsed into his own thoughts and rode in silence. He felt hopeful, but also wondered what all lay ahead for him. After about a twenty-five minute ride, the driver pulled into a circular drive lined with bushes and trees and drove up it toward an older-looking stucco configuration which appeared to have once been a series of separate houses later joined together to make the current structure. "We're here," the driver said. "Home, sweet home, for awhile, at least."

Aaron looked at the facility that was probably once white, but now looked almost a light tan-cream, with brick chimneys sticking out of the roof at either end of the main building. It was two stories high with a large wooden double window on a dormer protruding out a few feet. There was a small embossed metal sign by the sidewalk which read "Angel Windows." A young man dressed as an orderly came out to the car, opened the door, and greeted Aaron. As Aaron got out and followed the man toward the entryway, he felt like his mind was breaking with the feelings washing over it. He really did want to change his ways and make his Nana proud of him.

And he still couldn't get the image of Trooper Truitt's eyes out of his head. There was a certain sorrow in them that had gripped a hold of Aaron as he realized that under different circumstances that sorrow could have been caused by him. And then there was also the fact it had been over twenty-four hours since he'd had a drink, and his body wanted a return to the norm.

Aaron knew he was going to have to fight hard if he was going to succeed and make his Nana proud. Again, he wondered what this was going to mean for his life.

Inside, he was taken to a room where he completed in-processing, then followed the same orderly down a hallway and up a staircase with large mahogany banisters that looked like something a young, adventurous child would have the time of his life on. At the top of the stairs, they turned left down the hall, and the orderly stopped at a room three doors down. He knocked, opened the door slightly and said, "Got your new roomie, Quinton. Take care of him."

Aaron followed him into the room and a man who appeared to be about twenty-five to thirty years old got off a bed on the left side of the room and told the orderly he had been expecting him. The orderly introduced the man as Quinton Comfort and told him he would leave it up to him to help get Aaron settled in and then turned and left.

His new roommate flashed a grin. "Like the man said, I'm Quinton Comfort, but you can just call me Quint. I've been here for a couple months already. What are you in here for?"

Aaron hung his head a little and then answered, "To take care of a drinking problem."

"Ah, you don't have to feel bad about that," Quint said, "something like that is why we're all here."

Aaron wanted to affirm aloud what he'd been telling himself, so he took a deep breath and said, "I want to get my life straightened out."

"That's, cool," said Quint. "That's why we're all here. But that doesn't mean you have to totally quit. If you need to get a little something to help you, let me know." Aaron looked puzzled and Quint laughed and continued, "What I mean is, don't worry if you get a hankering for a drink. I've got some connections. Just let me know what your fave drink is, and we will deliver."

Aaron's mind immediately jumped at the thought of a Miller Lite. He shook his head as he said, "That sounds tempting, but I really wanted to work on my problem."

"Did a judge order you into the program?"

"Yes. The State Trooper who arrested me arranged it."

"Really. What were you arrested for?"

After a slight hesitation Aaron answered, "DUI."

Quint asked what he had been driving, and Aaron decided to be honest. "I was on a John Deere lawnmower," he said. "I damaged a woman's fence and then went to downtown Frankenberry."

Quinton burst out laughing. "And they put you in here for that? You don't have a problem, except that you're being cheated. You need to collect back pay, man … for providing entertainment for the five o'clock news."

Aaron felt anger rising. He couldn't shake the image of Todd Truitt's eyes, and was upset his new roommate was making light of something as serious as a DUI. He sharply said to Quint, "Hey, Smar-tass. Have you ever looked into the eyes of a man who has had a wife and two children killed by a drunk driver?"

The smile disappeared from Quinton's face. "No. Guess I can't say that I have. You?"

"Yeah," said Aaron. "The State Trooper that arrested me. And you know what? Ever since that moment I have thanked God it wasn't me. And I intend to make sure it never is. So if you don't like that, go ask for a new roommate."

Quinton looked at Aaron and sneered, "Well, fine, and you got it right, I believe I was the one in the room first. And, by the way, re-member, you just arrived, so your word might not be as established as mine as far as the reasons for you needing a new roommate. So, yeah, you just might be the one who checks out and leaves the room." Quinton turned sharply and walked out, slamming the door.

Aaron sat on the edge of the bed and put his head in his hands. It looked like trying to straighten his life out was going to be a lot harder than he had thought. Although he didn't really know him, he wished Trooper Truitt was there for him to talk to. A few minutes later there was a knock on the door, and then the orderly who had brought him there earlier entered and told him the Program Director wanted him to report to his office. Not knowing what was next, Aaron numbly followed the orderly down the hall to the stairs he had just come up a few minutes ago. As he descended the steps, Aaron wondered if his life was sinking back down to zero again. On first floor he followed the orderly to an office door with a plaque on it that read "Angel Windows Residence Director, Anderson B. Darmenella."

"Go on in, he's expecting you," said the orderly. Aaron's heart was pounding hard as he opened the door, and then he grew even tenser. There was a large desk with a nameplate of Anderson B. Darmenella on it, and two black Captain's chairs about ten feet apart in front of the desk facing it at roughly forty-five degree angles. The director was seated behind his desk, and in the Captain's chair to the left of the desk as Aaron faced it sat Quinton Comfort who just stared at Aaron.

"Please," Director Darmenella said to Aaron, "have a seat." He motioned to the empty chair, and Aaron nervously sat down. He was tempted to say that he didn't mean to start any trouble, but he didn't, because he was afraid it might start trouble.

"The reason I've called you here," the director said, "is I understand there was a difference of opinion between you and Mr. Comfort here, and even though you just arrived less than an hour ago, already you apparently think it might be better if you had another roommate. Would you care to tell me why?"

Aaron felt boxed in. If he said Quinton had offered to get him beer, he probably wouldn't be believed and would be labeled as a troublemaker, even if he got moved to another room. But if he said there really wasn't a problem, just a little misunderstanding that really wasn't important, and he went back to the room with Quinton, that looked like a rough road ahead, too. Aaron started to speak, slowly, carefully. "I didn't mean to cause any problems, Sir. I just said I wanted to get some things in my life straightened out, and I felt like Quinton was joking about it, and I got mad. I'm sorry, Sir. Like I said, I didn't mean to cause any problems."

"Well," said Director Darmenella, "misunderstandings can happen, especially when you are new to a situation. So, tell me, Aaron, just exactly how were you in disagreement with Mr. Comfort?"

Aaron felt the trap increasing its pressure. "Uhm, he ... ah ..., well, I told him how I was arrested for DUI on a lawnmower, and he said it was good entertainment for the five o'clock news."

"So," continued the director, "why were you talking about your arrest, or even alcohol, to begin with?"

Damn, Aaron thought, *there's no way out of this mess except the way I got into it, through what happened.* "Because," he said, "when Quinton asked me what I was in for, I told him I had a drinking problem, and I wanted to get my life straightened up. Then he told me if I needed help, he had connections, and could deliver my favorite drink to me. I'll be honest, Sir, I immediately thought of Miller Lite, but I really do want to straighten up more than anything else. Now, that's the truth."

Director Darmenella looked at Quinton. "Mr. Comfort," he asked, "Did you offer to get Mr. Patterson anything alcoholic to drink if he wanted it?"

Aaron waited for Quinton's reply. Quinton had actually only said his "fave drink," so he honestly could say that he hadn't said he had offered anything alcoholic, so Aaron couldn't believe his ears as Quinton answered, "Yes, Sir, as a matter of fact I did, and just like he said, he told me he was tempted but that he really wanted to work on his problem."

"So, Mr. Comfort," Director Darmenella asked, "Why did you offer to get alcohol for Mr. Patterson?"

"Because you told me to," said Quinton.

Aaron's mind was spinning circles as he felt like he was in a tornado being tossed about. "That's correct," said Director Darmenella. "You see, Mr. Patterson, Mr. Comfort is not a resident of Angel Windows. He's one of our staff psychologists. Judge Leahy, who ordered you here, in consultation with Trooper Truitt, wanted to see if you might be an appropriate candidate for shock probation. Mr. Comfort is recommending you receive it. We told Judge Leahy that if we felt that you should be given the probation, we wanted you to stay with us for a couple days of counseling and instructions, and then you would be released to the custody of a parole officer who will work closely with Trooper Todd Truitt. Conditions of your release will include reporting here one day a week for sessions and spending four hours a week with Trooper Truitt, your arresting officer. This is a very unusual procedure, I'll be the first to admit, but apparently Judge Leahy has full confidence in Trooper Truitt's intuition, and the State Trooper believed that if you passed the test, which we feel that you just did, this would all be in your best interests. So," Director Darmenella looked hard at Aaron, "do you have anything to say?"

"I don't know what to say," said Aaron, fighting back a lump in his throat. "All I know is I can't shake the image from my mind of Trooper Truitt's eyes as he was telling me his wife and two children were killed by a drunk driver. I just can't get that out of my head. Under different circumstances, that could have been me driving the car that hit them."

"Well apparently," said Director Darmenella, "There was something in your eyes that stuck with Trooper Truitt, and he feels compelled to help you straighten your life out. And we want you to know our staff stands ready to assist him and you in any way we can."

Aaron remembered something the Judge had said. "Director Darmenella?"

"Yes?"

"What about Judge Leahy telling me if I failed to complete the Angel Windows program for any reason then I would be immediately be locked up and would have to finish my six month sentence in jail?"

"Right, he did say that," Director Darmenella answered. "However, he said he would rescind the order and replace it with the shock probation order and conditions if you qualified. So you don't have to worry about that. If, however, you violate the probation conditions, then all of the previous order will come back into play. But again, we are here to assist you in preventing that scenario from happening."

A few minutes later, as he sat on the edge of the bed in his room, Aaron again felt like things were moving along almost faster than he could keep up with, but in the midst of it all, he was also starting to feel a sense of peacefulness settle deep inside him. He couldn't wait to talk to his Nana about everything that had happened.

CHAPTER 62
The Old Man in the Burl

Brad looked over the almost basketball size burl in the yard-length section of tree trunk. In it he could see the face of an old man waiting for someone to chip away the wood shielding him from others not so observant. He could almost hear the old man calling, "Medic!" He picked up his straight gouge chisel and carefully started. Working on the protruding bulge called out other things as well.

Delta Company had been humping hard for a couple days without contact. They'd crossed over a large trail with elephant tracks and dung, some which was basketball size. Soon after they found an area where the CO said to dig in for the night. They were about an hour in the area when shots rang out from several areas around the perimeter. SGT Lonnie Quarles, a 2nd platoon squad leader gave a sharp cry as he fell to the ground. Brad saw this and immediately grabbed his First Aid pack.

"Medic!" the assistant squad leader called out. "Bad M! Need you!"

"Coming!" Brad called as he started to run through the gunfire, toward SGT Quarles. When he got closer he could see the blood flowing freely from the squad leader's head where a bullet had cleanly gone through the left temple where the trajectory had been deflected before leaving through the right side of the cheekbone.

"Son of a bitch!" Brad said to the assistant. "Never had a chance!"

"Well, shit, Bad M, isn't there something you can do?"

"Bandage, but he has no pulse. Doubt if he knew what hit him. Same as Chuck."

The company medic came over in a few minutes and confirmed Brad's observation. The firefight continued to rage for almost another hour, and Brad and the Company DOC stayed busy moving amongst the wounded. Fortunately there were no more KIAs. After airstrikes were called in then Medevac Hueys were able to land. There were three in a row to get out SGT Quarles' body and all of the seriously wounded.

A Reconnaissance patrol discovered several bunkers in the area. Delta continued to set up for the night knowing they would be conduct-

ing a thorough search of the complex the next day. Recon the next morning discovered supply hooches that contained several hundred pounds of rice and a lot of cloth most likely used for making uniforms.

Second platoon had a patrol out and the rest of the company heard gunfire their direction. The platoon leader reported back that an NVA had been killed. When they got back in one of the guys said the machine gunner, out of anger over SGT Quarles death, had just kept pumping bullets into the neck area until the NVA's head separated from his body.

When Brad heard that he thought, I wonder if all his anger was directed at the NVA, or was he also releasing some of his anger toward me?

Brad took no comfort from the old man in the burl whispering, "It's okay, Bad Medic; it's okay."

CHAPTER 63
Looking Up Nasturtiums

It had been a rough day at the restaurant and Deanna said she was really tired as she kicked off her shoes.

"Well," Phillip said, "if you are ready for dinner I've been thinking about eating out again."

"Anything sounds good as long as I don't have to put on my apron and serve it," Deanna replied. "But," she added, "If you don't mind, I'd like to use your computer a minute. You know how I love flower gardens. Well, Patty was telling me on break today about some specials on nasturtium.com."

Phillip's mind went numb as he realized he hadn't cleaned his history after he had been surfing earlier, but he knew he couldn't tell Deanna "No".

"Earth calling Phillip," Deanna called in a sing-song voice. "Mind if I use your computer?"

Phillip felt an immediate tenseness in his throat that seemed to jump his pitch up about half an octave as he said, "Not at all," while thinking, *Well, yeah, I do; I just can't say so. I mean, what are my prerogatives here?*

As Deanna went to the computer desk, Phillip tried to look interested in a magazine despite feeling symptoms of hyperventilation. She clicked on the mouse to bring up the screen, and started to type in the address bar. When she got as far as 'nas', the address bar expanded and dropped down, and at the top of the visited sites was nastywatchers.com/main.html. Deanna raised an eyebrow in curiosity. Part of her thought maybe she should just ignore the address and not click on it, but –

I shouldn't, she thought, *but what is this? I had no idea I would find something called nastywatchers on his computer … is he into computer porn? Good Lord, he's a State Trooper.*

Phillip cleared his throat and called from the living room, "Have you found your nasturtiums?"

"I found something," she answered.

I hope her name doesn't start with Monique, Phillip thought.

Deanna looked at the home page for nastywatchers. "Phillip?" she called.

Phillip felt like he was just a heartbeat away from a heart attack as he answered, "Ah, yeah?"

"Could I talk to you for a minute?"

As Phillip walked toward Deanna he was flooded with a combination of dread, defensiveness, and relief. *I remember*, he thought, *one time when I was a kid playing with some ants, messing with them really, always changing their direction with a stick to thwart them from whatever they were trying to do. My quickly evolving theology now includes the possibility that God is a large ant – seeking revenge.*

Deanna looked at Phillip. "Phillip, I love you –"

"Honey," Phillip cut her off, "I've … I've wanted to have a discussion with you about this, really, for some time, but I've never quite known how to start the conversation. I guess I was afraid if I tried to talk to you about, ah, what is, um, I guess you might say is, a, ah, a problem for me sometimes, that I might lose you."

"Why's that?" Deanna asked.

Phillip tried to formulate an answer he thought might make sense to Deanna. "How my life, and desires, developed to where I am right now, is a lot more complicated than it may look. A lot of things happened which slowly led to a fascination with visual stuff." Phillip felt his ears burning as he added, "And believe me; I'm not sure if I could be put in a more embarrassing position than I am in right now."

Again Deanna's asked, rather coldly, "Why's that?"

Phillip wasn't sure why, but he started to get defensive. "You don't think this doesn't bother me? That sometimes when I get up from the computer, I'm worried because what if I became real ill, or even died while surfing these sites? And the State Trooper hierarchy can say what it wants to about seeking counseling if you have a personal problem, I'll guarantee you if you do, it will get used against you and come back to haunt you in some way."

"Phillip," Deanna started, "What I …"

Phillip interrupted her again. "Some might say, 'Why didn't he seek counseling?' but trust me; they'll crucify you if you admit you have a problem." He took a quick breath and continued. "I know there are a lot of people out there who only know my name, they really don't know me, but still, I wouldn't want them finding out that Trooper Phillip Cordella got caught surfing nastywatchers.com."

"Phillip," Deanna tried again to get a sentence out. "So anyway, what I'm curious about is, when did you start watching porn?"

"Does it matter?'

"Actually, yes. To me at least. I've been looking forward to a relationship based on honesty and trust, and here I find out you've been, shall we say, a little less than that? I mean, how long have we been together now; a year and a half if I remember correctly?"

"You see," Phillip said, "this is exactly why I didn't want to say anything, because of your response."

"So just hide it and hope you never get exposed? I would hope for a physical relationship based on your desire for me, not imagining me as some woman on your screen."

"Can we talk about this?"

"Phillip, I'm really tired right now, and I just don't know what to think, or how I feel. Can we save it for later?"

"Sure. Whatever."

"And until we get some things sorted out, let me just leave this ring with you."

"What?"

"Phillip, I need to go home and try and get some sleep. I'm drained."

Phillip sank down on the couch as he watched Deanna walk through the door. *Damn*, he thought. *This looks like it could be what former Vice President Biden said one time, a big fucking deal.*

CHAPTER 64
The Whys and Wherefores...and Ironies

Another work shift was over and Todd and Julie decided to do homemade subs again, once more at Julie's. As they worked on making the sandwiches, they picked up the conversation where they had left off the night before. "Todd," Julie asked, "do you suppose if a person could live his life free of trouble that he would accomplish anything?"

Todd thought for a moment about the very question he had asked himself many times, then asked, "Interesting question, where did that come from?"

"Well," said Julie, "you are a State Trooper, and a damn good one from all that I have seen and heard."

"Okay," Todd replied, "if you insist. So what does that have to do with trouble-free lives?"

"I'm being serious, Todd," Julie responded. "Now, between Infantry in Desert Storm, and the accident eight years ago, you've seen close-up death. And I know it hasn't been easy on you. But it does seem that what has happened, and what you have learned from it, has combined to make you a better person."

"I think that is one of those areas where we'll never know the answer, but I do believe the saying that one either learns and grows better, or dwells on things negatively, and grows bitter."

Julie pursed her lips. "So, how does one keep a positive attitude while in combat?"

"Sick humor usually worked."

Julie wryly smiled and asked, "Kind of like my sarcasm?"

Todd laughed as he pulled American cheese slices apart to put on the subs. "I think it's the same basic idea. It's a survival technique. Rodney Short was a good friend in Kuwait. We joked with each other all the time about our watches. Stuff like, 'Hey, Rodney, if you get killed, can I have your watch?' Of course, it wasn't a joke when I was hit, but not before I saw his lifeless body on a stretcher. I was so numb inside that I couldn't cry over him at the time. But it had made for lighter moments in a scramble for survival in a race that Rodney didn't win."

Julie had a very reflective look as she said, "I envy you, Todd. I really do. You seem to have come so much further down the road of life than I have. You take difficult experiences and use them positively. And it's more than just identifying with others experiencing similar difficulties. What you did for Aaron, for example. A lot of people couldn't do that."

"I don't know about that," Todd said as he laid the top halves of rolls over the bottom piles of bread, meat, cheese, tomato, lettuce, and onions.

"I do." Julie spoke adamantly. "What you did would be like me volunteering to help someone who was a child abuser. Lord knows he would need help, but I couldn't be the one to give it to him." As Todd cut the subs in half, she said, "Looks like these puppies are ready to eat. Shall we?"

"It's what I had in mind while working on them."

"Good. I'll pour the Root Beer," Julie said. She was quiet as she poured the drinks, waited for the fizz to settle back down to the ice, then poured some more. Then she screwed the cap back on the two liter bottle, put it back on the counter, and took the glasses to the table where Todd had already set the subs and chips on Styrofoam plates and had gotten out napkins. She spoke again. "Todd, concerning you helping the same kind of person as the one who hurt you, I more than envy you; I greatly admire you."

Todd took a bite of sub, and started chewing. Before taking another bite, he spoke. "What I get from what you just said, is that you might even wish that you were capable of doing the same, helping someone similar to the one who has hurt you. What may be more likely is relating to and helping someone who has suffered the same experiences as you."

Julie had an elbow on the table and raised her arm and pressed her closed fist against her mouth and chin as she reflectively said, "I think you're right. That seems much more likely ... and practical."

"My guess, Julie, is that your day will come. You just aren't ready for it yet."

Julie was still chewing, so she finished, and then took a swig of pop. She couldn't believe Todd was diagnosing her so accurately. She stared thoughtfully at him as she said, "You know what? I hope you're right." Julie quickly lightened and laughed. "God, I can't believe I just said that. Hey, don't ever breathe a word to Phillip First Beat that I might be softening." Todd smiled and told Julie when she was ready Phillip would be the first to know. Julie half seriously asked Todd if he thought that she had been too hard on Phillip.

Todd broke into a laugh. "Are you kidding? Would a rattlesnake bite you in the ass if you stuck it in front of him?"

"Ouch." Julie grimaced. "Speak bluntly, don't you?"

Todd laughed again. "Only to people who can handle it."

Julie said she would take his statement as a compliment and Todd said he meant it as one, that her hike to Valley View Rock the day before was a giveaway she was trying to learn and grow better. Julie smacked her lips and said that once again they had out done themselves with their sub making. She added that the subs could become habit-forming and Todd replied, "Like you."

"Todd," Julie began, "I'm getting the idea your military experience in some ways parallels your trooper experience. Tough at times, probably lighter moments, too, like we have sometimes. Just another reflection of the paradoxes of life."

"Oh, I agree. Although it has been labeled the 100 Hour War, my exposure to combat was full of images, mostly negative, which I'll never forget. We were in an Iraqi Scud missile attack on barracks in Dhahran and two close friends were killed immediately, Jake, from shrapnel to the head, and Wilson, to the heart. I noticed one of my other friends, Tanner, lying out in the open so I crawled out to bring him back in. He was scared shitless to move. When we got back to cover, he said a Scud landed close behind him shortly before I came out to him. When the attack was all over, and all the dead and wounded were medevaced, Tanner and I realized that an irony was that out of our squad, Tanner and I were the only two not wounded, and we were the only two of the squad in the open area."

Julie shook her head as she asked, "Are you saying that was one of your lighter moments?"

"Sometimes you took them where you could find them, but actually, since you mentioned paradoxes, I thought the incident fit."

Julie had stopped eating while Todd was talking and sat with her elbows on the table, chin resting on her hands. She smiled. "I think that I'm falling in love with you. Is that why you weren't wounded? For me?"

Todd got real thoughtful. "I do wonder sometimes about the whys and wherefores … and ironies." He took another bite of sub.

Julie shivered slightly and shook her head as she said, "Me too."

Todd took another drink of pop before he continued. "And the question is, why? So far all I can come up with is, that after Desert Storm, I met Samantha, had two wonderful children with her, and we had some good times, make that great times together. Then I went through terrible pain because of the accident, worse than anything I ever encountered in war, and after eight years of building a wall then this beautiful woman I work with asked me to the Electric Blue Steakhouse, and I felt some of the bricks crumbling." He smiled. "Maybe you're right, for you."

Julie felt her eyes mist over as she looked at Todd, and then a tear started to trickle down her cheek. "I believe you are already helping me to heal."

Todd smiled again. "And you are helping me with another part of my healing process. Plus, in all honesty, ever since my incident with Aaron there has been a crazy little idea tumbling around in my head."

Julie brushed the tear from her cheek and laughed as she asked, "And what might that be? You want to open a John Deere lawnmower store?"

Todd chuckled. "No, not today at least. But, seriously, I've been thinking about Aaron, and the many others like him." He told Julie about what had been worked out for Aaron concerning shock probation, and said he was reaching a point where he realized that just about anyone who really wanted to could do what he did as a Trooper, including arresting people for DUI, but it seemed like there weren't near enough citizens concerned about helping these same people at a later time when they really needed extra support. He continued, "In our area, many others too probably, there ought to be a well-run, half-way house type of facility, specifically geared for recovering alcoholics just released from prison. It seems like that may well be the most critical time for them in choosing which road to take."

Julie picked up a kettle chip and looked at it, and then at Todd. "You'd give up your position as a trooper to do that?"

"Well, if I did embark into something like I'm thinking about, it would come as a result of early retirement, but don't read me wrong, I have no plans to rush out tomorrow or the next day, plus I'm sure there are a lot of things to consider that I'm not even close to discovering yet."

"I suppose funding was one of those things?"

"True, but also, I would have to give thought to my personal situation at that time."

Julie felt an unusual sensation in the pit of her stomach somewhere between excitement and nausea. "And, by that you mean …?"

"There is always the possibility I could find the right woman, and consider settling down again."

"Well," laughed Julie as she felt the sensation spill more toward the excitement side, "as irresponsible as you seem to be, you'd better let me help you. I don't want you making any mistakes in that department."

CHAPTER 65
It was a Normal Dose, to Ease the Pain

Brad smiled at one of the few light memories he had from Vietnam.

He and Steve had to go from an LZ near Bien Hoa to Tan Son Nhut Air Base to catch a Caribou to Phouc Vinh. They had recently come from the field and were still looking rather grungy. As they walked down a sidewalk they were approached by an MP.

"Excuse me, fellows. Are those rifles loaded?"

"Of course."

"Well you need to remove the clips and expel any rounds from the chamber."

"Well damn, we must be in the rear," Brad said as they followed orders. Their clips came out and when the chambers were cleared, two bullets hit the street.

A PFC in starched fatigues was observing and asked, "Are you guys Grunts?"

"You've got it," Steve replied. "Well," he said pointing at Brad, "he's a medic, but he's with us in the field, yeah."

"Do you care if I keep those bullets as souvenirs?"

"Not at all."

He quickly picked up the two rounds and put them in his pocket. Brad and Steve continued their walk to where they would catch the Caribou.

"Damn," Steve laughed. "That guy saving our bullets as souvenirs is enough to put us into the almost feeling important category."

Brad could hear a helicopter in the distance. *Probably a Robinson R-44*, he thought, *searching for pot.*

Delta Company was busting through the dense undergrowth when they heard a Low Observation Helicopter flying in the area. "Probably trying to see if there is a reasonable area where we can park our asses for the night," SGT Sanders said. "Makes the Loach a rather easy target though."

"Plus," said Steve, "it lets the NVA know someone is probably in the area." As Steve finished his statement, they heard the crack of an AK-47, and the unmistakable sound of the Loach falling and crashing.

The CO grabbed the handset from his RTO and called Headquarters. "Loach down! Need assistance! I'm sending a platoon that way immediately!"

All the platoon leaders had headed to the CO's location. 3rd platoon leader arrived first. "LT, get your men headed to the crash site, now! The rest of the company will follow."

"Yes, Sir!"

When 3rd platoon was about a half click away, they started to see the smoke from the burning Loach and could hear someone calling out in agony. "Binder 6, this is Pivotman 6, about 500 meters out; will need Medevac, location XN285176."

The men pushed forward and soon could see the twisted metal still burning. One of the pilots had fallen or crawled out and was now weakly calling, "Help me! Oh dear God, send someone to help me!"

Brad rushed to the pilot beside the Loach as others tried to douse the remaining fire and get the other pilot out. The remainder of the men quickly set up a perimeter to secure the area. Brad could see his crash victim was severely burned, but couldn't tell if there were internal injuries or spinal cord damage. Due to the obvious pain, Brad pulled morphine from his medic bag and gave him an injection. The pilot apparently hallucinated and started screaming again, "Oh, God! Please help me! Oh, Guaa … Gla … Fu … Gluaa … Glmm." He jerked and then suddenly went limp.

"Mother of God! What's going on?" Brad yelled.

"What the hell did you give him?"

"Morphine, to ease the pain."

"Well it looks like he went into respiratory arrest."

"It was a normal dose, to ease the pain."

Brad worked to resuscitate the pilot to no avail as the squad leader popped a smoke grenade to give specific ground position to the Medevac nearing their location.

The sound of the R-44 was fading as the pilot left the area. "it was a normal dose, to ease the pain," Brad said aloud. "All I wanted to do was ease his pain."

CHAPTER 66
Quickies are Okay at My Place

The door to Albert's office was open, but Delayah still knocked. Three times quickly, then once, followed by two more quick knocks, as she walked in. She was wearing the same short olive-colored jersey she'd been wearing the day she had asked Albert if he wanted to spend time with her at her place. "Just me," she said, as she came in and closed the door.

"Just you is enough. How are you doing?"

"Well," Delayah started. "The ringing is just as loud as ever, but my attitude is different." She tossed her head a little. "Thinking it might have something to do with my sex life."

It had been over a month since Albert and Delayah had first entwined, and they had figured out ways to meet about every other day. They also were working on the book of poetry together now that Albert had started, *Strings May Be Broken, But the Music Goes On.* Albert laughed. "It would be nice if great sex was a cure-all for tinnitus because we would be well on our way to complete recovery."

Delayah laughed. "It has to be helping a little bit, because like I just said, my attitude's changed."

"Sex is an interesting phenomenon," Albert said. "It's like a gift … from the Creator … probably an apology, for the dodo bird, and some of the other things that look like they went wrong."

Delayah laughed and responded, "Along those lines, while we are engaged in a good healthy round of pleasure, there is some relief being offered for the ringing. And I know sex isn't the sum total of our relationship, but it's a nice part of it." She continued, "We could have that pleasure with someone else and probably get the same results, but I'm glad that I'm having it with you."

"I miss having you in class," Albert said. After they had started their romantic rendezvous, Delayah had decided, since she didn't need the course for her major, she would drop it because she felt it would be hard not to have others in the class noticing that something was going on between her and Albert.

"Given the choice, I like it the way it is now; you having me out of class."

Albert smiled, then grew serious as he asked, "Does it bother you at all that I'm cheating on my wife?"

Delayah deliberately crossed her legs so her jersey dress rode even higher on her thigh as she asked, "Does it bother you at all that I'm holding on to the idea I may be able to change her status to ex-wife?"

Albert looked pensive. "Not at all. I just don't want to act too quickly. This is major."

Delayah smiled. "Agreed. But if we leave now, quickies are okay at my place."

CHAPTER 67
Sorry I Disturbed You

Phillip knew Deanna would probably be leaving for the diner soon, so he called her and asked, "Hi, I was wondering if you might want to go out for dinner after you got off work tonight?"

"Thanks for asking, but I don't think so."

"Another time?"

"Phillip, I don't think anytime soon. I'm just not at any kind of a good place with us right now."

"How long will it take before you can find it in yourself to forgive me?"

"Forgive; I can probably do that soon. Forget, or get over the lack of trust, not so much."

"I'm sorry, Deanna. I really am."

"And I'm sure you are; at least sorry that you got caught. Now I admit that maybe I'm the one looking at it the wrong way, but if so, that's my problem, and I can't deal with it right now."

"We could talk about it. That might help."

"Look Phillip, I need to leave for work soon, and as I just said I just don't want to talk about it now. I don't know if I ever will."

"Well," Phillip said. "Have a good day at work. Sorry I disturbed you."

CHAPTER 68
I Said, Damn You!

Usually Brad was content with the pieces he carved, but he decided to destroy this particular one; it looked too much like a skull.

Delta was on a sweep of a bunker complex, and the CO was angry over the loss of a fellow West Point Academy classmate killed a couple days before by an NVA sniper. His classmate had been the CO in another battalion. There was a body of an NVA soldier lying outside one of the bunkers.

"Hey," the CO hollered to his RTO, "Help me string this little bastard up against that tree. I haven't had the opportunity to fire my .45 lately; I need to brush up on my skills."

After the body was tied to the tree CPT Waller fired 15 to 20 rounds before putting away his firearm. The RTO pointed out a skull beside another bunker and the CO told him to put it on a stick and then, as he popped a purple smoke grenade under it, said, "we'll just leave these guys here. Maybe the message will get through not to mess with us."

Rollo, went to the skull and said, "Hey, Bad M, "maybe you should carry this on top of your pack, you know in memory of the LOH pilot, or Medic Larry, you know, to warn people that death follows you. I mean, with this on your back, you could change your name from Bad Medic to Badass Medic." Rollo laughed at his own joke.

"What are you, Rollo? Some kind of damn fool? You know as well as anyone that the men who died couldn't be helped anyway." SGT Menetta never could grasp Rollo's attitude. "Furthermore, you never know, you just might need him yourself one of these days!"

"I'll settle for a second opinion myself. Second platoon has Doc Spenser."

SGT Menetta threw his hands up. "I'd like to arrange for you to go to second, but you know what? Their LT doesn't want you! Now just shut the fuck up!"

Brad set the skull-resembling carving on the concrete slab and picked up a sledge hammer. "Damn you!" he hollered, swinging the sledge downward. "I said, damn you!"

CHAPTER 69
Romancing Across the Table

Todd called Julie the next morning around ten and asked if she had a full hour for lunch.

"I can do that. Where do you want to meet?"

"I'd say at Fat Boys Donut Shop, but it sounds a little too stereotypical. Besides, I'd rather have something a little more solid, and healthier. What do you think about the soup and salad bar at the Bear Tales All-You-Can-Eat? And, if I do get a call during lunch, I can just leave."

"Sounds good to me. What time should I be there?"

"12:15? We can touch base if there needs to be a change of plans."

At ten minutes after twelve, Julie was sitting in the parking lot at the Daniel Boone Bear Tales All-You-Can-Eat-Come-Back-Soon Steakhouse. It had an aged barn wood exterior with a porch running along the front and halfway down both sides. The wood-shingled porch roof was held up by poles that looked like they were direct order from the front of a Dodge City saloon. There was a hand-carved wooden black bear standing guard on one side of the entryway and a wooden Indian on the other. About twenty rustic wood rocking chairs were spaced out along the porch. Julie waved at Todd as he pulled into the lot and parked in an empty spot next to her.

Julie got out of her car and went around to the driver's side of the Oldsmobile as Todd opened the door and got out. After they kissed, she asked him, "So, do we dare leave Franken County unsupervised for a few minutes while we grab lunch?" They walked toward the Steakhouse as Todd answered that he had done it before, and things hadn't come crashing down.

"That's hard to believe, but possible because Phillip's out there to keep the world in order."

"There you go," Todd said, "picking on Cordella again."

"He asks for it."

"You have a point, but I still feel for him sometimes. Yesterday he seemed really down."

Julie defended herself. "Well, you have to admit, when Phillip first started duty at the 58th, he was quite full of himself."

"Remember, key word, was."

Inside, Todd and Julie were led to a booth, where they waited for a waitress. Todd commented on Julie's last statement about Phillip. "I agree, Phillip set himself up for your nickname, but hopefully, he's starting to learn what we all should ... eventually ... maybe."

Julie laughed. "And just what is that, Mr. Decisive?"

"Well, I know that if I were to get shot by some crazy this afternoon --"

"Don't even joke about that," Julie interrupted.

"I'm not, I'm making a serious point," said Todd. "Now, as I was saying, I know that if some crazy shot and killed me this afternoon Post Commander Ratliff would say two things: first, 'that's terrible', and second, 'who will take his patrol tomorrow'? That's about how long I'd last."

"Maybe with Ratliff, but not with me," said Julie. "What do you think about that?"

Todd thought a moment. "A wise king, Solomon, said in Ecclesiastes 'there is no remembrance of most people or things from the past, and even of those who are yet to come, most people and things will not be remembered by those who follow.' You would remember me, for a time, but after your time was up, then what?"

Julie scrunched her face and twisted her lips as she replied, "I thought we were meeting for lunch. Are you trying to depress me? How the hell did we get to talking about yours and my deaths?"

"I guess I'm saying hopefully Phillip's learning what everyone needs to; the world doesn't revolve around them. Did you see him today? Hardly would say anything; looked like his world had stopped revolving, period."

The waitress appeared to take their orders for drinks, and Julie said she wanted root beer and the soup and salad bar. Todd added he also wanted the soup and salad bar, but would have coffee and a glass of water. The waitress told them to help themselves at the bar and she would be back with their drinks in a moment.

When they sat back down, Julie resumed the conversation. "Todd, what you're saying about the world not revolving around us, I think maybe you've learned that one a little better than me."

Todd swallowed the bite in his mouth before answering. "If you're correct, it's probably due to two reasons; first, different circumstances shaped us; the second I've been hoping to avoid talking about."

"Which is …?"

"Uhm, the fact I have at least a couple years' experience on you."

"Haven't noticed, hoping you hadn't either."

Todd laughed as he said, "Your nose is going to grow on that lie, Ms. Pinocchio. Who was it that said the other night, 'will you promise not to stop seeing me just because I'm twenty years younger than you' huh?"

"Got me," Julie laughed, "but you're lying about trying to avoid the topic. Seems I remember something about your trophy-girl? I don't think you want to avoid that, do you?"

"Not if it means losing you."

About that time the waitress brought their drinks and set them carefully off the tray asking if she could get them anything else. Todd replied he was good for the moment and asked Julie if she was okay. Julie said she was fine as she popped the paper off the straw and stuck it down into the drink. The waitress said she would check back in a few minutes to see if they needed anything, and then walked off to wait on other customers.

Todd looked at Julie. "Back to what I was saying," he started, "Avoiding? No way. I don't want to lose you."

Julie smiled. Todd couldn't have said anything more comforting to her. "Not a chance," she said, and then continued. "Todd, I have a serious question. I really am almost blown away about how much I feel I have learned from you over the past couple days. I really am seeing you as my teacher, or mentor, or something like that. But I also love your arms around me, and when we kiss. Can these two roles you are in merge for me?"

Todd became serious as he responded. "I think they already have. I sure hope so. And don't think that I'm not learning from you."

"About what," Julie replied. "Quick judgments and smart-ass comments?"

Todd chuckled. "You now, or at least, you up to a week ago, were me in the military. Then, particularly after the wreck eight years ago, I turned into the man who went inside his shell, thinking that reflection and losing oneself in work was the only answer. I believe I'm learning from you the balance is somewhere in between us. I think we both have a hold of it, coming from different directions."

Julie liked what she heard. She took a sip of drink and then replied, "Good, because, if you're going to be my teacher, since you have years of experience on me, I want that to enter into the romance department, too."

"One nice thing about being human," Todd laughed, "is we can think hypothetically. And even though I want to immediately respond to your wishes, I think they'd throw us out of here if I romanced you on the table."

"But you are teaching. Teaching me to wait. And, don't be male-dense, Todd. You are romancing me across the table, believe me."

The lady in the booth behind them half turned around and said, "Put a lid on it you guys. Some people want to just eat without listening to fairy tales, okay." Todd laughed and looked down.

Julie also turned part way around. "Sorry," she said as she snorted, trying to hold in her laughter. She turned back to face Todd, paused a couple seconds, then turned again toward the booth behind her. "What I meant was I'm feeling sorry for you, Lady."

The lady indignantly slid out of her seat and started to walk out. As she passed their table she stopped, looked at Todd and Julie, and said, "So this is what law enforcement has come to. Fine representatives for the State Police you two are." She turned on her heels and stomped off.

Julie shrugged as she gave a small laugh and said quietly, "Screw her if she can't take a joke."

Todd laughed as he shook his head. "Julie," he said, "me in the Army, except I was a bit more descriptive. And, by the way, I agree with you."

Todd checked his watch. For the first time in over eight years, he wanted to just sit and visit with someone rather than go to work. "I have enough time for dessert," he said. "Want to get to the unhealthy part of our meal and share a hot fudge cake?"

Julie laughed as she replied, "I hear my Torso Tiger equipment telling me, 'Do it, do it. Then maybe you'll feel the need to visit me more often.' I really can't let my lonely apparatus down, now, can I? Let's do it."

Todd grinned. "Hearing that rationalization lets me know, there will be times I will just have to let your mind take its own little journey, and I will probably be left behind wondering what in hell was just said. Incidentally, I see that as a challenge."

Julie had both elbows on the table, her right arm crossed up to her left shoulder, with her chin resting across the back of her wrist. She slightly cocked her head, and looked at Todd. "I know we don't have a lot of time right now, so I want to hear more about this later, but, if you don't care, tell me about JR and Mindy."

The waitress took their order for one hot fudge cake and two plates, and left as Todd looked down and smiled poignantly. "Miranda, Mindy, was the oldest. I was in the delivery room when she was born, and Julie, there is no other experience to compare with the miracle of seeing a little baby emerge from her mother, and realizing she is part of you. I'm sure it's down a notch on the scale from what the mother is feeling, but words just can't explain those emotions. And she became a 'Daddy's Girl'. I had a child-carrier backpack, and there was a hill behind the house, and I used to take her sometimes when I went hiking, even in the winter. Her mother would bundle her up, and she would throw her little arms on my shoulder, sometimes cupping my chin, and off we would go."

"I remember one night about ten, it was a full moon, about thirty degrees outside, and the wind started to pick up. There was another hill that I usually went up, but I thought I should probably turn back. So I said, 'Mindy, the wind is blowing harder. I think we should turn around and go back down to the house. What do you think?' And she replied, 'I'm okay, Daddy. I think we should keep going'."

Todd continued, "One of my favorite stories about her was the time when she was five, and I was sitting out on the porch steps feeling kind of down, thinking about Rodney Short who had been killed on that date years earlier. Mindy stopped playing in the yard and came up to where I was sitting, looked at me and said, 'You're looking a little sad, Daddy, so I'm going to give you a big hug and sugar kiss to fix it. All you have to do is smile'."

Julie wiped a tear away as the waitress set the cake and plates in front of them, and refilled their drinks while asking if there was anything else that she could get for them. Todd said he thought they were okay and thanked the waitress who said she would be back with their ticket in a few minutes and left to wait on other customers. Julie cut the cake and put a piece on her plate as Todd continued. "Mindy was three when Todd, Jr. was born. She was so excited about getting a younger brother. We were really hoping the ultra-sound was correct. She probably would have adjusted to a younger sister, but once brother was in her head, phew, that was all she would talk about. A couple times I tried to set her up for the possibility that it could be a sister, and she would say, 'No, Daddy, if the doctor said it's going to be a boy, then it's got to be a boy. The doctor wouldn't fib to you'."

"The faith of a child," Julie said. "Sounds like me with my Uncle David."

"Oh yes, the faith, but catch this. One night about a month before JR was born, she said, 'Daddy, I've kind of changed my mind and it is all right if I don't get a little brother. I've been thinking, and a kitten would be nice, too.'"

Julie was sipping pop through her straw and almost choked as she laughed and some drink went up her nose. Todd asked if she was okay, and she said she would be, but in the future she might need a little warning if she needed to avoid drinking during a story. Then she asked, "So, what is your favorite story about JR? I know we have to be going soon, but we have time for one more, don't we?"

Todd glanced at his watch. "Oh, yeah, and by the way Julie, thanks for asking me about them. It's good," he said as he smiled wistfully. "Bitter-sweet, but good, to talk about them."

Julie could hardly believe the words she was hearing herself saying. "And I want to know about them, Todd. I really want to know all about the man I'm starting to love so much."

"And it will be a two-way street, Julie. I want to know you, too. And you already piqued my curiosity when you mentioned the faith of a child being like you and your Uncle David. You will have to elaborate sometime. Maybe Saturday on the way to Carter County and Laurel Cave? But back to your question about a JR story. One time I constructed a small plastic greenhouse in the backyard and instructed the kids to stay away from it unless I was with them. Well, JR was about five or so, and came in to tell me Mindy had been around the greenhouse. I explained to him I didn't want him to be a tattle-tale trying to get his sister in trouble, but also that I didn't want him to lie if I ever was asking him if Mindy, or he, had done something. Sure enough, a little later JR came up to me and asked, 'Hey Daddy, Do you want to ask me anything about Mindy and the greenhouse?'"

A few minutes later as they headed out to the parking lot, Julie asked, "Saturday morning, Carter County? I can be ready to leave at eight?"

"Eight it is then," Todd replied.

Julie tilted her head a bit sideways. "And, oh yeah, a question. If I split the gas, shall we go in your car? You not only know the way, but I like the full front seat that allows me to slide over next to you, you know, like they used to could be able to do in the good old days."

"Used to could be able to do, huh?"

"Hey, give me a break. I trained for police work, not English professor. So what do you say to my offer?"

CHAPTER 70
We Just Had Some Differences

Phillip decided to try and see if Deanna might be ready to talk to him again, so he called and asked if she wanted to get something at a drive-thru and ride over to the See Forever Overlook.

"I'm sorry, Phillip. I'm still trying to process things in my mind. Why don't I call you whenever I'm ready to discuss things between us? In the meantime …"

"Yes? In the meantime?"

"I don't know Phillip. The more I think on this and your lack of openness, and now my lack of trust, well, I just don't know … if we are really meant for each other."

Phillip was silent a moment, and then replied. "You know what?"

"What?"

"Sounds to me a bit like the prelude to, why don't we start seeing other people for a while."

"That might be," Deanna said. "But I do at least want you to know that I'm not going to be talking to anyone about to why we're not together. If the subject comes up I'll just say we had some differences."

"Yeah, thanks," Phillip said as he hung up.

CHAPTER 71
Why Are You Called Bad Medic?

DeYount was a new platoon leader assigned to third. He was on his first patrol with 3rd platoon when they came upon a large NVA bunker complex.

"Exactly what the CO said he thought we'd find. Third squad, set up security while first and second conduct a search. All of you keep me updated; I'll establish a headquarter location here with the RTO and medic."

As the squad leaders complied with their orders, LT DeYount asked Brad, "I've heard a couple guys refer to you as Bad Medic. Why is that?"

"Well, Sir, it started over playing around with my name, Brad, to Bad; you know how nicknames get thrown around out here, or at least you'll find out, but I've had a couple situations where I might could have made different decisions, and lost a couple guys that might have made it; I don't know."

"How many lives have you saved?"

"Quite a few, but they don't make up for bad judgment calls."

"Have you ever intentionally made a bad call?"

Brad looked intently at the LT. "No, of course not. But a couple times I reacted without taking time to evaluate more thoroughly."

"Did you have time to evaluate?"

"Hell, I don't know. I just know I fucked up."

"I'm not condemning you, Brad," LT DeYount said, "I'm just curious how it affects you now."

"I try not to think about it, Sir. I want to get through the next month without any more problems so I can get the hell out of here for a while and go to Australia on R&R, come back for the remaining four months, and then go home. I've been Bad Medic long enough."

Brad set the large bench knife aside and looked his latest creation over. He had expended a lot of time on energy on this piece of wood and thought it might be his best face yet. He felt like the old man's eyes were seeing right into him, *and then the lips moved slightly. "Where is SGT Quarles?" Brad's chest tightened in fear.*

Suddenly a bevy of mourning doves settled around the table cooing in unison, "Fat Billy, Chuck, Lonnie, Lonnie Quarles, Chuck, Billy, Billy, Fat Billy."

Brad thrashed his arms as he hollered, "Medic! I need a medic over here!"

"How 'bout a Bad Medic?" the old man snarled. "What do you guys think?"

Brad realized the mourning doves had given way to a pack of coyotes interspersed with raccoons. "I survived a Loach crash," one of the raccoons hissed.

"But," all the coyotes howled in unison, "You didn't survive Bad Medic, did you?"

The doves returned and were mournfully cooing in medley, "But you didn't survive; survive Bad Medic; Bad Medic, did you?"

The coyotes all howled in laughter as the raccoon hissed again, "I survived a Loach crash."

And the doves replied, "But you didn't survive Bad Medic, did you?"

"Stop!" Brad jerked around at the sound of Peter Rabbit's voice.

"Where did you come from?" Brad asked his old friend. "Remember I buried you a while after Vietnam? You're, you're not supposed to be here."

"He's not a bad medic; believe me, I know!" Peter shouted at the gathered menagerie, ignoring Brad's question. The mourning doves took flight as Peter shouted again, and the raccoons scurried away. The coyotes surrounded Peter and Brad. "Guess it's down to us against you," the leader of the pack snarled.

"He's not a bad medic," Peter quietly repeated.

"Did you see him abandon Doc Larry, help blow up Fat Billy, and what about the Loach pilot?" As Rollo asked the question, a coyote lunged at Peter and bit him behind the throat in the jugular area.

"Medic! I need a medic over here!" Peter weakly called out before he died of shock.

"No!" Brad yelled as he jolted himself free of a daytime nightmare. "Mother of God, what's going on?"

CHAPTER 72
Enter Herpes

Tira almost broke the porcelain dove because she was gripping it so tightly. She looked into Jesus's gentle wooden eyes, and wondered, *How could this have happened? I thought you would take better care of me than this!* She debated calling Pastor Brock, but decided against it. She was just going to have to face Albert alone on this one.

She was sitting at the kitchen table crying when Albert came into the house. She looked up at him and asked, "Where have you been, and who have you been with?"

Albert used to occasionally call Tira and let her know when he was going to be late, but recently he had just started arriving home whenever he got there and saying something like "a Division meeting" in response to her queries. He wondered sometimes if she suspected he was having an affair. Ever since he and Delayah had started their relationship, Albert didn't even try anymore to reconcile differences between himself and Tira. But by the accusing tone in Tira's voice, Albert felt a storm coming on. "What do you mean?" he asked. "What's wrong, Honey?"

"Don't Honey me," Tira screamed. "I just came from Dr. Gravitt's office, and I've got herpes! Now I haven't been screwing around, and herpes doesn't just float through the window and decide to crawl into you! Would you care to tell me how I got it?"

Albert felt like he had just run up a fire escape with ninety-nine steps, except he wasn't breathless. But the rest of the symptoms were there as Tira angrily asked again how she had gotten herpes. Albert quickly noted that her volume level had decreased a few decibels between questions, so he replied, "We need to talk, I agree, but we need to be rational."

"Rational?" Tira lashed back. "I am about as rational as I'm going to be! Now if I were a gambler I'd bet anything the herpes came from that little twerp in your office who was talking with you about her Fuck You project."

Albert reddened.

"Yeah, I thought so," said Tira. "And I'll have you know it makes me sick just thinking about it." Albert decided to leave and ride around awhile to try and get some thoughts in order.

Soon after he went out the door, Tira was on the phone, crying, to her mother. When her mother asked her what was wrong, Tira broke down sobbing. Karen Esterbean told Tira that she had a doctor's appointment in a few minutes, but she would stop over on the way to it. By the time her mother arrived Tira had composed herself somewhat and was again facing her crucifix clutching her porcelain dove. She told her mother what had occurred but when she said she was going to leave Albert, she was surprised at her mother's reaction.

"Tira," Karen said "have you thought this through?"

"Mother," Tira had spent hours talking with her mother about how frustrated she was over Albert's late hours and the growing distance in their relationship. So she was not ready for the question; she thought her leaving Albert would be understood. "Mother, of course I've thought it through. Haven't you been listening these past few months?"

"Yes, dear, I have," Karen responded, "and what you've been saying sounds like something many marriages go through. Provided," she continued, "both partners stick around. Now I believe you know about that kind of home, so we won't even go there today."

"Mother," Tira began again. "Hello? I just said Albert cheated on me. Albert's consort is the woman I mentioned earlier that was working on a special project and now I have confirmed what the project is." She asked her mother if she would have stayed with a man who had cheated on her.

Karen Esterbean thought a moment. She loved Tira, but was not blind to the fact that all relationships were a two-way street, and she knew Tira's near obsession with Pastor Brock and the church were also factors in the marriage. She chose her words carefully. "Tira," she began, "I guess my response is that it would depend on who the man was. Now you know I've told you on many occasions Albert is a good man, but even good men stray sometimes. Women, too. And sometimes a mental or emotional straying is as bad as, or worse, than a physical one. Now you know I have said before that when you married Albert, you were taking on the Furcologna name, which means something in this part of the state. I still feel that way, and I think you need to take that into your considerations."

"So you're saying I need to put up with his little whore who gave me herpes just because my husband is a Furcologna?" Tira couldn't believe that in her moment of deepest distress her mother was letting her down.

"I'm saying," said Karen, realizing she had failed along the way to get the two-way-street concept across to Tira, "that Albert may see the way you hold Pastor Brock up on a pedestal as a form of mental cheating on him."

"Mother!" Tira exploded, "Are you trying to tell me you are taking sides with Albert and condoning his evil behavior? Besides, you know Pastor Brock is married, and I would never even think of trying to hurt his marriage." Karen Esterbean reassured Tira she understood what Tira was saying, but also understood human nature, and that every deed of misbehavior was not evil. Tira fought back. "That may be true of some misbehavior, Mother, but there are some areas that are evil. Just last week Pastor Brock preached on the evil of adultery."

"Well, Tira," Karen said, "Remember, I love you. And all I'm asking of you is that you think a little bit more before you make any decisions with major consequences all way 'round, and try to think of all the little unintended consequences which sometimes tag along. But in reference to Pastor Brock and his sermon on adultery and what I said a minute ago about pedestals, I rest my case."

After Karen left for her doctor's appointment Tira angrily went back to the mantle and got down her dove. As she held it in both hands, Tira meditated on why her mother had failed to support her at the moment most needed. Tira signed the cross, returned the dove to its spot on the mantle, and then went to sit on the couch, where she immediately fell asleep from exhaustion.

CHAPTER 73
It Most Likely Involved Sex

The next day, Albert sat in his office with the door open, and, as usual, Delayah knocked with her three - one – two pattern before she walked in. "Still just me," she said as she came in and closed the door.

Albert smiled and asked if she was doing okay.

"I am; how are you?"

"I've been better," Albert responded. He drew in a deep breath and slowly blew it out and repeated, "I've been better."

Delayah asked if it was the ringing and Albert sighed and said he wished that was all it was, the ringing, but it was much more.

"So, what's the problem?"

"Tira," Albert responded.

Delayah felt tightness in her chest as she asked, "So, just what is the problem with Tira?"

"Well," Albert began, not sure exactly how to say what he had rehearsed a couple dozen times, "I have been cheating on her as we both know, but I am ninety-nine point nine percent sure she has been sexually faithful to me. I know she has a religious infatuation with her pastor, has him a pedestal, but I'm sure that, well, that she's not been doing anything like, like us, I mean, like, well, you know." He paused, as he realized his rehearsed script had deserted him and was some-where long gone out the window.

"So, what are you trying to say?" Delayah asked. On the one hand she didn't really want to hear what she was pretty sure was coming next; on the other hand, Albert's verbal floundering was almost funny.

"Well," Albert tried again. "Tira has genital herpes, and swears it couldn't been from anyone else but me, and she's probably right, and, I have not been with anyone but her until … well, until … we … " Again, Albert was flailing about.

"So," Delayah helped him out. "What you're trying to say is you think you got it from me?"

"Delayah, I'm so sorry." Albert was near tears. "I don't know what I'm saying. Things are a mess, and I don't know how it happened."

In the midst of a serious moment, Delayah managed a little smile as she said, "Well, somewhere along the way, it most likely involved sex. That is how genital herpes happens, you know."

Albert misread her tone and replied, "You're upset with me, I know."

Delayah rested her chin against the palm of her hand. "No, I don't think so. If it has come from me, I want to know so I can be treated. And when Gerald and I broke up, well, he said it was because he thought we needed to see others. And then the next day I saw him with another girl. So, maybe … " She broke off.

Albert slowly shook his head and said, "So, you're thinking there is a chance he was with her before he broke off with you, and he may have gotten it from her?"

"Honestly," said Delayah, "I was a virgin when I started going with Gerald, so I had to have gotten it from him. Maybe it wasn't from that girl, who knows. He might have been seeing others before her. You know how it goes."

"Yeah, I guess I do," said Albert a bit touchily. "Is that a put-down?"

"I don't mean it as one; I spoke before I thought; I'm sorry."

"So where are we in our relationship? Do you think we can survive this?" Albert asked.

Delayah sighed. "Hundreds of people before us have survived; hundreds haven't. It's up to us which category we're going to fall into."

Albert pursed his lips and then said, "To be honest, I was initially angry because I thought you were keeping something from me, but what you just said sounds like the plausible explanation."

Delayah shook her head. "I read once people have herpes with no symptoms for some time; I just didn't think at the time I was reading about myself."

"Well," Albert said, "Tira guessed about us, so she knows. But, I don't want to break off with you. And," he paused, reflected a moment, then thoughtfully continued, "It may well soon be over between her and I."

Delayah gave herself a silent, fist-clenching *Yes*, and then responded "I don't want to sound callused, but that won't break my heart. Sorry."

Albert said they were in a rather confused situation at the moment but he had made a doctor's appointment for later, and then asked Delayah if she was going to make one.

"Oh most definitely," Delayah responded. "And I suppose the responsible thing would be to call Gerald and say something to him, but he would most likely deny it could have come from him, so I think silence will serve me best there. So, I guess if you have a doctor's appointment, our time together is postponed. I guess it should be until we both have our visits, anyway."

"Yeah," said Albert, "besides, I'm not sure if I'd be much good for anything today anyway."

Delayah wryly smiled. "I guess our conversation hasn't exactly been good foreplay, has it?"

"Not exactly," said Albert, reaching toward her. "But I want you to know I do love you."

"I love you, too, Albert." Delayah let his arms close around her and snuggled tightly against him as she whispered, "We'll make it though, Sugar, I know we will."

CHAPTER 74
This Complicates Everything

Several weeks later, Delayah and Albert were sharing a couple of recent "tinnantical" writings they had felt compelled to put on paper.

Delayah smiled. "The other morning I was sitting on my little porch, and a little bird started chirping. It sounded good, but it didn't interrupt silence, you know how it is. And this came out. I called it 'Sitting in the Silence'.

> *Sitting in the silence, even though it isn't so,*
> *Occasionally some birds speak, they don't even know*
> *That their cheerful sounds interrupt a peace that isn't there,*
> *As I start another day of non-quiet in the chair."*

"I like it," Albert said, "and the birds make a nice metaphor for anyone who doesn't know. I like your phrase, too, 'interrupt a peace that isn't there'. Sure captures what I'm feeling a lot of the time."

"So, does it make the cut for our book?"

"Easily. Listen, I have some more I wrote, last night actually. Tira and I were at odds again over church, and my attitude about going, and she was going on again about how 'Pastor Brock says this', and 'Pastor Brock says that', and I was tempted to ask her why she doesn't just ask Pastor Brock if she could marry him."

"He's already married, isn't he?"

"Oh, sure, but I don't know if that matters. I swear sometimes, if he said to come to church with a squirrel in the one hand, and a penguin on a leash, you'd have to call animal control the next Sunday."

Delayah was feeling a bit annoyed lately over the fact Albert was becoming quite regular in his voicing his frustrations with Tira, but not in voicing what he could do on his own to eliminate those frustrations, so she decided to hint more strongly to Albert about divorcing Tira. "There's an answer to what's bothering you, you know," she said. "And it's your choice, not hers. But you know that." Delayah decided she would settle for the drip method to try and get her point across and not come on too strong, so she continued, "But enough of that; I want to hear what you wrote."

Albert responded that he heard what she was saying; he definitely was giving it serious thought and the option seemed more viable every day. Then he told Delayah regarding her listening request, he had a couple poems; the first one was called, "Running out of Options". He paused, then read,

> *Running out of options, choices narrow down.*
> *Rooms are getting darker,*
> *Smaller gets the town.*
> *Mind is getting foggier, ears are mocking me.*
> *World is closing in trying to press my sanity.*

"Well, that's almost on target," Delayah responded. "But I thought with me in your life it was opening up options, not narrowing them down. But we can talk about it later this afternoon. Right now I want to hear what else you wrote."

Albert felt compelled to clarify the previous poem. "It's nothing personal when I say 'running out of options'. That's just how I feel in relation to listening to the noise."

"Yeah, I'm sorry. I should have realized. You're right," Delayah said.

"Sometimes it's like my next one, like a wall of flames consuming me. That's what I call this one.

> *"Walls of flames around my mind trying to wear me down.*
> *Sanities are wearing thin with pressures all around.*
> *Noises circle constantly, driving through my head.*
> *I know relief's in sight though, for someday I'll be dead."*

"Well," Delayah commented, "I understand, but I don't like to think of the dark side too much."

Albert shrugged as he said, "I guess I was totally on the dark side last night. I have another one, in the acrostic mode I called 'Death'."

Does it seem so horrible
Even though it finalizes
A life here on this earth
That daily wonders
How to go on."

"Holy shit, Albert," Delayah said. "Where did your head go last night?" She was quite concerned. This was the darkest Albert had sounded since they had started seeing each other romantically. She continued, "Death? We need to talk about the options available. You need to think more about me. I mean, me good; death bad. Listen, I have a question about this afternoon. We were planning on going to my apartment? Still on?"

Albert felt the familiar stirring in his groin as he said they most certainly were. As they went toward the door the phone rang. Albert turned back, and even though he saw from the caller ID it was Tira, he felt he should answer it. After greeting her, he asked how she was. Tira told Albert she wasn't doing well and was wondering if he was coming home soon. He told her it would be awhile as he had a meeting.

"With whom?" Tira asked, strongly suspecting the truth.

"What do you mean with whom?" Albert sounded like he was offended Tira didn't believe him. "It's a department meeting. I have to go."

"Right," Tira responded as she wondered what department Student Affairs fell under. "You're still not seeing that girl, are you? Delilah or whatever her name is?"

Albert stiffened. "No, Tira, I'm not seeing her." Delayah smiled and blew Albert a kiss as he continued, "I told you I broke it off. Now, back off, hear me?"

"Albert, I'm sorry," Tira cried. "Like I told you, I'm not doing well. The reason I want you home is Mother just found out she has an aggressive form of pancreatic cancer. She's dying, Albert. The doctor told her she has less than six months."

Along with the prevailing ringing whistling through his head, claiming its dominance once again, Albert felt his emotions scattered to the wind by a tornado as he told Tira, "I'm sorry. I'll be right home."

Albert placed the phone back on the hook, and looked at Delayah. "I'm sorry."

"Sorry?" Delayah was really aggravated over the side of the conversation she had just heard. "Didn't you just use that expression on the phone with your wife a minute ago? Cancel your meeting, right? Albert, we need to talk. You need to decide … whether you are going to … either shit … or get off the pot."

"Delayah," Albert spoke sharply without meaning to. "Tira's mother just found out she is dying of pancreatic cancer, has less than six months left to live. My wife is devastated. That's why I told her I'd come home. Can you understand that?"

Delayah understood, or at least thought she did. She understood she was in the middle of a strange loop that would spiral on forever if allowed to. She decided to take action, so she queried, "Albert, this might not be the best time to ask this, but are you ever planning on leaving your wife?"

Albert was in the middle of a quagmire and he knew it. He loved his time with Delayah, but he felt like he would be committing a serious offense against Tira if he abandoned her in what was a grave time of need. He slowly spoke, "Delayah, I … I love you. But this complicates everything. I can't leave her right now … not under these circumstances."

Delayah decided she was not going to turn back from prodding. "I understand, Albert; a part of you I admire is shining through. You're a good man. Now, I don't want to sound cold, or hard, but let's say the doctors are right, and Tira's mother dies in six months or less. Then will you leave Tira?"

Albert sat back down in his chair, rested his elbows on the desk, and put his head into his hands. A few seconds later he looked up and said, "You know I couldn't immediately. It'll be rough on her. She'll need me."

Delayah knew she was in for heartache no matter which choice she made and so she decided to hurt sooner rather than later. "Albert," she said softly, "I understand what you are saying, I really do. And like I said, you're a good person, and good people often put others ahead of themselves. If you put yourself first, you would include me. Obviously, you don't. I love you, have loved you, but I can't, no, make that, I won't, go on playing second fiddle. Go home to your wife, Albert."

Albert felt a knife cutting across his emotions as he asked, "Delayah, Honey, can you give me a little time?"

Delayah choked up as she answered, "Albert, sometimes, it's the time to make a choice. So, is your meeting this afternoon canceled, or not?"

A few minutes later, Albert turned his car right out of the faculty parking lot and headed up the street toward his house. His mind was swirling and juggling incessant ringing, mixed feelings about Tira, concern for his mother-in-law, and images of Delayah's laughter, and legs, wrapped around him.

CHAPTER 75
Mom, I Don't Want to Lose You

Tira couldn't shake the images from her mind. The hardest thing she was doing so far in her entire life was watching Karen Louise Esterbean die. Despite their occasional differences in how they viewed the world, this was her best friend, her confidant, and her lifelong companion. But cancer didn't care about things like that. More frequently than ever now, Tira found herself getting her porcelain dove down from the mantle. Tira and Albert had arranged for hospice care, and moved her mother into the front room.

"Mom, I don't know what I'm going to do when you are gone."

"You'll have to be strong, Tira. You've got a good husband. He can help you, and you need to be his companion and friend."

"Mom, he will never take your place."

"I don't want him to take my place," Karen retorted. "I'm just saying the two of you can form a friendship. Talk to him more, like you talk to me."

"But, Mom," Tira's voice unconsciously raised a few decibels. "Half the time when I'm talking to you, it's about him."

"True, dear," Karen laughed softly as she wondered how Tira would respond to her next words. "And now you're going to have to figure out a way to tell him some of those things. But," she continued, "as far as we go, you'll always have our memories. I'll always be with you, Sweetheart."

Tira smiled as she asked her mother, "Remember when you climbed the tree to get me?"

Karen chuckled. "Sweetheart, there are some things which can never be forgotten. I swear you were better than all the neighbor boys when it came to climbing trees. But Lord, I'll never forget that day. You were five, and I heard you squalling and carrying on. I tore out of the house, and there you were, about twenty feet high in the old maple tree, hanging by the seat of your jeans, arms flapping in the breeze. It's a wonder you didn't slip off the little stub of a branch you were caught on and break your fool neck."

Tira tried to recall details, but conceded she didn't remember too much about it, except that she was scared.

Karen had a dreamy look on her face as she started, as if she were recalling one of the highlights of her life. "I remember it all, very well. I was in a dress, hemline a couple inches above the knee. I was so scared you'd slip; I just started climbing to reach you. About that time the mailman was making his rounds and asked if everything was okay. Well, I needed some help getting you down, so I was glad he came along. But I figured he was glad, too, because I'm sure he got quite the eyeful. I said 'thank you,' but I have always thought his pay probably came from the view I had no choice but to give him." Karen laughed, "But, I must admit, it took some doing to look him in the eyes after that."

Tira had some difficulty imagining her mother flashing a mailman as she said, "Mom, I'm sorry I put you in such an embarrassing position."

Karen laughed loudly, and then said, "Sweetheart, every time I think of that day it gets funnier and funnier. Giving the mailman a couple cheap thrills was a small price to pay for the memory I have of you hanging from that tree. I may have been frightened at the time, but it has sure brought many a smile to me throughout the years. And yes, I guess I'm glad I was wearing underwear."

Tira smiled weakly through tears as she squeezed her mother's hand and said, "I love you, Mom. Lord knows I don't want to lose you."

***

A couple weeks later, Tira fluffed the pillow behind her mother and smiled sadly. Karen Esterbean laughed. "Tira, you've got to do better than that, Sweetheart. Good, Lord, you look like I'm dying or something."

Tira knew from the many sermons she had heard that death was a somber business. And it bothered her that her mother sometimes seemed almost irreverent about spiritual things. "I'm sorry, Mom," she said as she shook her head, "but how can you joke about this? You are dying, and you're leaving me! I don't find that funny!"

Karen had learned over the years that in order to survive, she had had to adopt the philosophy of an Oscar Wilde quote that was on a little Hallmark Cards, Inc. wall plaque she had of a Panda bear playing around, standing on its head. The words that went along with the picture were, "Life is too important to be taken seriously". Karen also knew there were some areas of Tira's personality and attitudes that were going to make it especially difficult after her mother was gone.

She said with a smile, "Tira, Sweetheart, I love you, but I've always said you got more of your father's disposition than mine when it came to humor. Now me, when I get to those Pearly Gates, I'm only stopping long enough to tell Saint Peter a joke or two, then it's off to pull a prank on, oh, maybe, Jonathan Edwards. I want to see if two hundred and fifty years of Paradise has loosened him up at all, or if he's still hanging by a thread."

Tira dearly loved her mother, but had never related real well to her sense of humor. She had heard references to Jonathan Edwards in some of Pastor Brock's sermons over the years, and she knew his "Sinners in the Hands of an Angry God" sermon was not just some anecdote to be frivolous about, and so she answered with an edge to her voice, "Mother, that's not funny, and I still don't find your leaving me funny."

Karen knew Tira was hers because she had seen and held her right after Tira cleared the birth canal, but she still marveled over their different ways of looking at things. She also realized it was easier to talk about people changing than it was to see them actually make changes as she said, "Don't look at it as me leaving you, Honey. I'm just going on ahead to prepare Saint Peter for your arrival. Make sure he lets you in."

Tira smiled feebly to cover the slight stirring of anger she was feeling as she thought, *How can Mother even joke about not being allowed into heaven?* After Karen Esterbean dozed off, Tira headed toward the mantle. As she retreated into what seemed to be the only place of security and routine left for her, she asked for the ability to deal with her mother's death. Then she asked for forgiveness for her mother, for her lighthearted approach regarding serious matters.

CHAPTER 76
The Only Tangibles Left

Albert and Tira sat across from each other in a booth at the Electric Blue Steakhouse. Karen Louise Esterbean had been lowered to her final resting place earlier in the day. Tira wanted to go right home, but Albert finally convinced her it would be good for them to go out.

Tears came again to Tira's eyes as she lifted her glass of water and said she just couldn't believe her mother was gone. Albert said he knew it had been rough on her, and was going to continue to be so, but he wanted her to know he was there for her.

Tira stared absently. "Did I ever tell you about my first memory of reading?"

Albert was familiar with the story, as Tira had told it to him a couple of times in the early years of their marriage, but he knew she needed to share memories of her mother, and so he replied, "Tell me again."

"I think I was four or five," Tira began. "We lived in a two-story farmhouse over on Rooster Creek up near Medina County. I was upstairs in my bedroom, window open, leaning against the screen, looking at an animal book. The screen broke loose, and I fell out just as Mom came into the bedroom in time to see my feet going out the window. She said I landed on a bush below the window. I guess I did, but I really don't remember the fall. One minute I was upstairs, looking at pictures, the next I was walking around the corner of the house, book still in hand. Mom was rushing out to get me, terrified. She came tearing around the corner, bowled right into me, and we both crashed to the ground. I wasn't hurt from the window fall, but from our collision, between us, we needed nine stitches, she on her arm; me on my leg."

Albert smiled, then reached across to lay his hand on his wife's, as more tears flowed down her cheek.

***

It had been almost a month since the funeral of Tira's mother, and Albert felt like he couldn't offer Tira the comfort she needed. He had hoped Tira would be able to accomplish more today than yesterday. It wasn't imperative that the cleaning got done, but he figured keeping occupied would help her deal with her mother's death. Every day Tira seemed to be getting more and more dejected. Albert knew depression was typical, but this seemed beyond the norm. He even tried to get her to make an appointment with Pastor Brock, but Tira kept saying no one could help; it was something she had to work out by herself.

When Albert entered the house, he found Tira as she had been the day before when he came home, sitting in her recliner holding the porcelain dove her mother had given her, staring at the wooden crucifix on the wall, tears flowing down her cheeks. Albert went to her and leaned over the chair as he asked, "Tira, Honey. Are you all right?"

Tira looked up at him with eyes red from crying. "Mother said she got this dove from her mother when she was six years old. It was originally her grandmother's. Then, when I was nine, she gave it to me to keep. Why didn't she just keep it, maybe she'd still be here?"

"Tira, that isn't logical. Your mother probably wanted to share the passing of that dove while you were little so she could watch you enjoy it through the years, while she was still here. There is no coherent connection between her giving that to you, and her illness and death."

"Things don't mean anything when it's a choice between them and a person," said Tira, "but when the person is gone all you have left is their things and then they mean everything." Albert reminded Tira her mother's personal things weren't all she had left; that she and her mother had enjoyed many good times together, he had heard the two of them laughing together over numerous things and she still had all of those memories.

Tira looked up as she said, "Albert, I'd trade them all for another day with Mother. But the fact is that this dove, the locket, her china doll collection, the silver tea set, and a few other keepsakes, those are the only tangibles left."

Albert told she needed to be thankful she had those things associated with good memories, and in that regard she was very fortunate, because a lot of people didn't have pleasant memories to recall about a loved one who had passed.

Tira smiled through her tears at Albert as she said, "Mother always said you were a good man. Why haven't I been able to see it like she did?" Albert laughed and said when you were number two you had to try harder. "I'm sorry, Albert," Tira responded. "I never meant to make you number two. But I guess I did, because Mother and I were so close. And then when you cheated on me with that little whore…" Tira's voice trailed off.

Albert took a deep breath in and bit his tongue. When he made the decision to stay with Tira during her rough times rather than leave and go with Delayah, it had been the most difficult decision of his life. Sometimes still, at night, as he was lying in bed, he would recall some specific erotic adventure with Delayah, and it was almost always followed by a blood flow to, and a stiffening of, the *corpora cavernosa* tissues. But, rather than respond to Tira's reminder, instead he said, "Hey, let's not worry over things we can't change, okay? Now how about we go to the Daniel Boone Bear Tales All-You-Can-Eat-Come-Back-Soon Steakhouse and get us something for dinner?"

Tira was starting to feel a little better and beginning to think maybe she and Albert could start the long journey back to what they used to have in the early days of their marriage, and so with a glimmer of hope she replied, "All right, Albert, and I am glad I have so many things to remember Mother by. Thank you for helping me to see I have the memories, too."

CHAPTER 77
Vandalism

After they left the restaurant, when Albert and Tira pulled back into the driveway, they knew something wasn't right. "I know we turned off the lights," said Albert, "and the front door is open." Tira said she was certain she had locked it on the way out, and Albert said, "I know, Honey, I was waiting on you. Let's go see what happened."

Tira got to the door first and let out a cry as she walked into the house. She was in pure shock. "Albert! Albert! Someone has broken in, and, and, oh, my God, Mother's dove, my God, Albert, someone smashed Mother's dove!"

Albert stopped in stunned amazement when he saw the mess in the family room. In the middle of the floor, the porcelain dove was shattered. He thought quickly and knew they needed to let the police look things over, untouched, so he told Tira not to handle anything, they needed to call the police who would need to see the house and the damaged items as they were, untouched, so that maybe they could lift some fingerprints.

Tira walked zombie-like into the living room. Her hutch door was open, things were in disarray, and she could see several things were missing. "Albert!" she cried out loudly, "The china doll collection is missing! Mother's china dolls are gone!" Albert rushed in, and held Tira since she looked like she was ready to faint. He helped her to the recliner and told her to just sit there while he got the police on the phone. Tira broke down into shrieking wails as Albert phoned the Frankenberry Police station. Within ten minutes, a City Police Officer, Jasper Williams, arrived. Albert met him at the door and said they might have to take care of looking the house over at a later time as he was quite worried about his wife, and he thought he should take her to the emergency room.

"No," Tira stopped her crying, and suddenly became cold and hard. "We need to do a complete inventory, so we can catch the wicked people who have done this. Officer, the dove you see there was given to me by my mother, a fourth generation heirloom. Someone who is evil is the only kind of person who would do this. Mother's china doll collection was stolen; I don't know what else has been ruined or taken."

Officer Williams said over the years he had seen a lot of things that didn't make any sense, which more often than not, were done by people who were either high, or looking to get high. He asked Albert and Tira if they knew anyone who might have any reason to vandalize their home, and Tira said, "There's a chance this was done by a girl named Delilah." Albert felt anger rising as he told Tira not to make ludicrous accusations; there was no way Delayah would have done anything like what had occurred there.

"But, look at those crucifixes," Tira screamed. "Only a person with a heart headed for hell would, or could, do such a thing. My mother gave the one on the left to me, so I hung it with the one that I already had. And someone has desecrated them. Just look!" Officer Williams looked at the large, wooden crucifixes on the wall. The vandals had used tape to attach a fork in the left hand of one, and a knife in the right hand of the other, and where the two utensils formed a slight "X", a swastika on a chain was dangling between the two wooden figures. And dangling from a piece of picture hanging wire, around the neck of each was a banana pepper. Officer Williams and Albert looked at each other and shook their heads.

Tira ran into the bedroom and Albert and Jasper Williams heard a loud, anguishing cry. They rushed in, and found Tira kneeling by the bed, lamenting loudly over a picture of her mother. The frame and glass were broken, the picture had a large mustache scribbled on it, and the eyes had been poked out by the point of a pen. "I really think I need to get her to the hospital," Albert told Officer Williams. "I'm afraid she's going to have a breakdown. Can we finish this later?"

"We'll have to," said Jasper, "I think you're right about your wife."

CHAPTER 78
Australian R&R

Brad thought about his five day R&R to Australia. He had been so ready to leave Bad Medic behind for a while and just unwind. Flying over coral reefs had been a beautiful sight and quite relaxing.

After arrival in Sydney he registered at a hotel in the Kings Crossing section then went out and walked around the area for a while. He saw a club called the Red Garter and thought, That's an intriguing name. Think I'll give it a look.

On Brad's third day in Australia he crawled out of bed around noon with one hell of a headache from self-medication the night before. He went downstairs to the dining room and ordered something to eat, and afterwards went to the hotel bar and ordered a beer. When it was almost gone a man sat down next to him and asked, "Hey, Mate, will a vet let me do him the favor of buying him another round?"

"Sure. Thanks. I'm Brad. You?"

"Paul."

They made small talk for a while and Paul seemed somewhat knowledgeable of units and places in the Nam, and Brad also had questions for him about Australia. He admitted that he'd spent his whole life in Sydney and basically knew about the rest of the country by what he read in the newspapers.

After a couple more beers Paul asked Brad if he was interested in something to eat, and then maybe they could get a couple girls for the night. "I've got a nice little flat with two bedrooms just down the street," he said, "and I know some girls; I think you'd like one, or maybe even both, of them." Brad had had enough to drink that what Paul was saying sounded good, really good. "Tell you what," Paul continued. "I'll call Christine and Sharon to see if they can come over, and I can fix something to eat at the flat."

That sounded good to a just turned twenty-year-old who was regularly saying he wouldn't live to be twenty-one anyway, so Brad blindly agreed, never thinking of the lessons of the past six months from Vietnam; that ambushes could happen anywhere.

Paul's flat was on the third floor, and when they got inside he pulled a bottle of milk out of the small refrigerator. "Something to drink while we wait on the girls?"

"I don't know how well milk will sit with what I've been drinking," Brad replied. "As a matter of fact I've got to drain off a little; can I use your bathroom, or loo; whatever you call it?"

"Sure. Right there," Paul replied. "I'll get you another beer."

When Brad came back out, Paul handed him an opened beer. "Drink up. The girls are on the way."

"Thanks."

Paul lifted his bottle of milk. "Cheers."

A couple slugs later and Brad turned, set the beer down, and leaned against the counter.

"You okay?"

"Yeah. Guess maybe I've been drinking a little fast. Feel a bit light-headed."

Paul moved in behind him and reached for Brad's wallet. He bent the index finger on his left hand and pressed the knuckle hard against Brad's kidney area. "I've got a gun, so just hand it over and there won't be a problem."

Brad flipped out as his head went clear. "What the fuck?" He grabbed the milk bottle and could see the shock on Paul's face as he raised it. "Mother fuck, what do you think you doing?" he yelled as his heart beat faster and he gripped the bottle more tightly.

"Look, I'm sorry! I didn't mean anything! I was just kidding about the gun." Paul cried out as Brad brought the bottle down across his face. Blood started to flow as he dropped to his knees, again crying, "I'm sorry! I'm sorry! Look, you can leave, all right?"

Brad hit across Paul's face a couple more times before dropping the bottle to the floor alongside where Paul was, who by then was sobbing and curled in a fetal position. Brad kicked him just above the belt line and *headed to the door. Once outside he ran his shaking hand up the bridge of his nose to his forehead, took some deep breaths to settle down, and started walking back in the direction of his hotel, the ringing in his ears providing background noise to the words running relentlessly through his mind, Bad Medic, Bad Medic, Bad, Bad Medic!*

CHAPTER 79
Not Safe until He's Dead

Roscoe and Heather were working on a shopping list for Food Village. He told Heather he wasn't used to shopping that way, that he usually just went through with a cart and got what looked good. Heather said since they would be on a limited budget for a while they needed to plan carefully, and besides, she found when she was in the grocery it all looked good, especially if she shopped when she was hungry. She added it really was more cost effective grocery shopping with a list.

"Whatever," said Roscoe.

"Okay," Heather started, "we need two dozen eggs and … oh damn, Roscoe! Damn, damn, damn!"

"What's wrong?" Roscoe felt a Shoney's kind of panic shoot through him as he looked around. "You didn't see Jackson looking through a window, or anything, did you?" He was really starting to freak out over near misses.

"My chickens!" Heather panicked. "Roscoe, I can't believe I forgot my chickens!"

Chickens? Roscoe thought. *I don't remember anything about chickens except that she kept some and a damn skunk raided the coop.* So he asked Heather, "What do you mean forgot them? We weren't supposed to get them, were we?"

Heather was shaking her head in total disbelief and disgust with herself. She remembered something from a psychology class in high school to the effect that under stress sometimes even the most stable routines were thrown out of kilter, but she couldn't believe she had not once thought about the well-being of her chickens, not even while telling Roscoe about Jackson hitting her for the last time. "Roscoe, I told you about Jackson and the skunk, but then, I was so mad about him hitting me again, I never even thought about the fact there's no one to take care of my chickens. I can't believe I totally forgot them until right now!"

Roscoe tried to speak quietly, hoping that would settle Heather. He said staying calm and figuring out their way through the next few weeks was a lot more critical then a few chickens. Heather said she knew that, but still her chickens were not going to be taken care of.

Roscoe interrupted. "Maybe Jackson will take care of them."

Heather seemed almost as disturbed thinking about her damned chickens as she had been when Jackson pulled into the Shoney's parking lot. She desperately replied, "Jackson won't feed them. Roscoe, I would have thought you would have figured that one out by now."

"I don't know," said Roscoe. He was a bit miffed that he seemed under the gun again, "I suppose it depends on whether he likes chickens or not."

"About the only thing he likes is to eat them or their eggs." Heather started to settle down. "I'd call Marquita and see if she would take care of them, but that'd be a sure give away to Jackson I was in touch with people here." Roscoe agreed.

Heather became more settled and thinking more clearly as she said, "I hate the thought of staying cooped up here like my chickens for awhile, but it's a necessity. I do believe if Jackson got a hold of me now, he'd try to kill me, for real. He's a dangerous man, Roscoe. I mean, really dangerous."

Roscoe said he would take her word for it and Heather replied, her emotions rising again, "He is. Once, he was gone for a night, and the next evening when he got home, I insisted on knowing where he had been. He got mad and hit me so hard he knocked me out. When I came to, I was still lying on the living room floor, and that son-of-a-bitch was sitting on the couch, drinking a beer, engrossed in Monday Night Football."

"That's cold."

"No, Roscoe, that's Jackson. Now you see why I really have to get rid of him. I'm not safe until he's dead."

"Sounds like it," Roscoe said, thinking, *dealing drugs is one thing, and talking murder is another.* He slowly continued, "I just wish there was another way ... one that wouldn't hurt us if we got caught."

Heather didn't like the look crossing Roscoe's face and said if they planned it right, they wouldn't get caught. Heather was starting to realize the impact the abuse had had on her psyche. Her recurring dreams of Jackson being in the sights of her rifle bringing a fatal conclusion to the intersection of their lives had been more than just dreams, they had been premonitions, and Heather was starting to believe they foreshadowed a preordained mission that must be fulfilled.

Damn it, she thought, *I'm in this way too far to turn back now,* and then she realized the simple facts were, that her chickens were a minuscule matter when stacked up against what she had to follow through with concerning Jackson. *People do get away with murder,* she thought. *Only the dumb ones get caught.* But she also realized it was imperative to have Roscoe helping her, so she again put on her innocent-sounding voice as she said, "Roscoe, look Baby, look at you and the Infiniti. You not only didn't get caught during the chase, you were smart enough to wipe down the steering wheel and door handle so you wouldn't leave any prints. I need you. And you might have been caught if I hadn't come along. We need each other. And we can do it, Baby, we can do this."

"I'm with you," Roscoe said. "And it does look like luck has been with us, too. We just need to make sure we're careful, that's all."

"That's my Baby. Now Roscoe, let's finish this list up so you can go to Food Village. Tell you what, when you get back, I'll help you put the food in the 'fridge, and then before I fix us something to eat, I think I ought to serve you an appetizer. Does that sound good?"

Roscoe caved in to Heather like some people did to meth and said, "Okay, let's get this list done so I can be on my way. Where were we, two dozen eggs, right?"

***

The next day, Heather curled her legs under her on the couch, and picked up the afternoon edition of The Franken Daily Times. Roscoe had gone out to run some errands, and she decided to read the paper before starting on supper. She missed being able to go outside, but she knew this was a necessary evil she would have to endure for awhile. She wondered about her chickens, and desperately fought off the urge to call Marquita.

There was a front page article about the man on trial for holding up the local National Waffle Barn restaurant. Heather remembered the initial reporting on the incident about four months ago. The man had entered the restaurant around two a.m., pulled a gun and demanded money from the cash register. Then he had all of the customers line up and empty out their pockets. An off-duty police officer reached into his jacket pocket, and without pulling it out, fired a pistol at the would-be robber. He missed him due to not having a specific aim, but the bullet whistled within two inches of the would-be robber's head. It had startled him so that he dropped his gun, and the officer was able to overpower and arrest him.

As Heather read the article, her mind drifted to the only time she had ever been threatened by Jackson with a gun.

He was cleaning his .45 caliber pistol. Heather was watching television and asked him why he had been out so late the night before. He responded he had just stopped to have a couple drinks at Rourke's, and Heather asked why he couldn't just bring in a six pack and drink his beer at home.

Jackson didn't like Heather trying to tell him what to do and so he snarled, "Because maybe I like the company there. The conversation might be a little better, you know, football, trucks, what's going on in the world."

Heather didn't want to be slapped again like so many times in the past, but she thought maybe she could argue common sense with Jackson and so she countered his remark. "Well, I thought maybe, since we are married, that we might be part of what's going on in the world. You know, Jackson, I'd like to be one of the ones that can say, 'I'm married to my best friend.' It really doesn't feel like that, though."

"You want your best friend," Jackson said, "go find Marquita. But if you're going to do anything with her, do it here, and let me know. I'd like in on a little of that."

Heather angrily replied, "Jackson, you are disgusting. Marquita is not my friend that way, and I didn't even mention her. I'm talking about us, and our marriage. I barely feel like we have one anymore."

"Maybe I like it down at Rourke's because the girls down there don't nag all the time. They know how to treat a man right."

That set Heather off, and she screamed, "Jackson, don't you dare complain about how I treat you. You've got far more here with me than all your little whores down there put together." As she said it, Heather realized she might be making a mistake.

Jackson kept cleaning on the gun, but pointed the barrel in Heather's direction. "Bitch, one thing the girls down there know how to do is shut their fucking mouths, so if you don't want me to permanently shut you the hell up, then you'd better start doing it now, all by yourself!"

Heather was scared to death. Jackson had hit her before, but had never threatened her like this. She hung her head and meekly replied, "Yes, sir."

"What'd you say?" Jackson asked.

"I said, yes, sir."

"Meaning, just what, exactly?" Jackson wanted to make sure he put Heather in her place and that she had no further doubts about where that place was.

"Meaning, yes, sir, I'll be quiet, and I'm sorry I said anything about you spending time with your friends."

"Do you mean that?" Jackson asked.

"Yes, I do, Jackson," Heather answered.

Jackson laughed, "Well, hell, girl, I was just funnin' with you. I would never shoot you; you know that, don't you?"

"I hope you wouldn't. I want to be a good wife, Jackson, I really do."

"Now you're talking, girl," Jackson said, "Now you're talking."

Heather jarred herself back to reality. She looked at the clock, and decided to read a little more before cooking. She skimmed the Police Blotter and did a double-take. There in the latest arrests was Jackson. He had been picked up for solicitation down in the Hedgehog Brook Street area.

Heather laughed out loud and thought, *I'm missing, and he's out looking for a piece of ass. Life for him just carries on as usual. Well, the bastard's going to die, because I don't dare let him live. He'd kill me for sure this time. I've got to figure out how to do it, but that bastard is going to die.*

CHAPTER 80
Roscoe, We Need a Gun

Heather was standing at the stove and Roscoe was sitting at the table. He wasn't real happy as he had just confirmed through a friend that Charlie Cameron had been stopped by the police and booked for possession. He was thinking if there were any more interceptions he might have to give serious consideration to getting into a new line of work. The thought bothered him as he hadn't gone to college and he wasn't anxious to look for work in whatever industry with openings at his skill level.

Heather brought a plate to the kitchen table and placed it down in front of Roscoe, then stood behind him with her hands on his shoulders and told him to dig in. Roscoe's mouth watered as he looked down at two smoked pork chops, creamy mashed potatoes and gravy, sweet peas, and buttered rolls. *It has been way too long,* he thought, *since I have had my lips smacking around a simple, home-cooked meal.* He used both hands to lift one of the pork chops and started eating. "Mmm," he said between bites, "these are delicious."

"Thanks." Heather felt good inside in a way that she hadn't experienced in a long time. She knew she was a good cook and she planned on using the skill to add icing to the sex cake. She continued, "They say the way to a man's heart is through his stomach."

"I don't know," said Roscoe. "You started to get to my heart when you paid tribute to something about a foot below the stomach line." He belched loudly, then added, "But, don't get me wrong, I like the attention my belly's getting, too."

"Good." Heather was quiet a moment. It was time to move plans to the next level. "Roscoe, I really do appreciate everything you've done for me, too."

Roscoe scooped in a large bite of potatoes, wiped his lips with the back of his hand and spoke with his mouth half-full. "Hey, you scratch my back, I scratch yours."

"I'm starting to get some ideas about how to take care of Jackson," said Heather. "We need to have a gun that can't be traced. What are the odds of you stealing us a good one?"

Roscoe thought a moment then took another bite of smoked chop. "I'd rather not steal one."

Okay, Heather thought, *this must be a first for him, not wanting to steal.* "Well, do you think you could buy us one fairly cheap?"

"Oh, I think it can be managed," he said. "Are we going to shoot him?"

"I don't think so. I'm thinking more in terms of the gun being used to keep him in line while we render him immobile."

"And how will that be?" Roscoe asked.

"The more I think about it, I want to see him suffer. Revenge, I guess. Handcuffs and leg cuffs. Then, I like your idea of duct tape. Around the mouth. Rag stuffed in so he can't be heard. Duct tape over the cuffs so he can't move. Tied to a tree. Cut away his pants so I can squeeze his family jewels until he blacks out. Then we duct tape his head till he smothers. I'm still working on how we'll get him, and then how we'll dispose of him. I just need a little more time to plan this out."

Roscoe gave in to an urge and put his hand over his crotch and rubbed a little to ease the uncomfortable tingling sensation he felt when Heather had been talking about squeezing sensitive areas. "Heather?" he asked, "Are you sure we can get away with this? Isn't there something else we can do to just teach him a lesson he'll never forget?"

Uh, oh, Heather thought. *Cracks in the sidewalk are starting to appear. It might take more than pork chops and sex to keep Roscoe between the lines.* Heather knew by now Roscoe wasn't dumb; overall he seemed a logical thinker. She decided it was time to move the game to that section of the field. "Roscoe," she said, "I think you need to really understand what Jackson is like. This is not a game. If he catches me now, he would either kill me, or beat me so severely I would probably wind up as a vegetable."

Without thinking through all the implications, Roscoe asked, "Can't you get a restraining order?"

"Roscoe," Heather sat in the chair next to him and scooted closer so that she could lay her hand on his thigh to reinforce her verbal efforts at persuasion, "Roscoe, remember, the police are looking for me as an accomplice to your getaway after you stole the Infiniti. Ring any bells?" Roscoe answered he hadn't really thought that one through. "Plus," Heather went on, "there was a story a couple years back, I don't know if you saw it or not, but a woman was going through a divorce with her husband, and he kidnapped her. Well, she managed to escape, and in court the judge sentenced him to five years. He told the judge it didn't matter, as soon as he got out; he was going after her again. I remember thinking to myself, Yep, that's Jackson, all the way. That's why he has to die, Roscoe."

Roscoe sat in silence a moment before he said, "You've really had it rough with him, haven't you?"

"That's what I've been trying to tell you, Roscoe," Heather said, thinking, *I believe that he really may be starting to see the light.* Roscoe told her as soon as he was finished eating he would call a friend of his, Burlap Blankenship, and see what he could work out.

About a half hour later Roscoe walked back into the living room where Heather was watching Survivor re-runs and told her he thought he could get a gun without too much trouble. Heather's heart skipped in a combination of fear and excitement as she asked when that would be and he told her it would probably be in a week or so. He said, "My friend says it will take a few days to make sure we get a good handgun with no trace. Now you're sure we won't be using it to kill Jackson?" Heather assured him that it would be only used to keep Jackson quiet and in line. Roscoe still had little shivers in his groin every time he thought of how Heather had described wanting to squeeze Jackson's testicles until there was a black out. "You really want to do what you said earlier?" he asked.

Heather thought quickly. "Part of it was your idea, the duct tape part, Roscoe, and I think it's a good one. And yes, I want to do what I said earlier. Tape around the mouth with a rag stuffed in so he can't be heard. I know it may sound bad, but I will squeeze until he blacks out. That bastard has been cheating on me since almost Day One and I want him to die having last memories of pain with the same little objects that he used to cause so much grief for me. Then, like I said, your idea, but a good one, we duct tape his head till he smothers." Roscoe grinned as he asked if she really thought his idea was a good one.

"Sure," said Heather, thinking, *And if we get caught, it was all your idea.*

For some reason, Roscoe thought the rest of his idea was good, too, so he asked if she was still opposed to getting rid of him in a porta-potty. Heather shook her head as she said the only reason she didn't want to do that was because, like she had said earlier, she thought the body would be found too soon. She reinforced they really wanted to put it somewhere where it might never be found and Roscoe agreed with her. "You see," Heather went on, "With Jackson, it may be similar to the Goodbye Earl song, or whatever it was; it may be a while before anyone notices he's missing, other than at work, and they might just think he quit." Roscoe asked Heather if there was anything in the paper about her missing, and the minute the words came out of his mouth, he was cognizant that it sounded like he was implying no one missed her either and realized it hadn't been a good question to ask. Heather did not want anything to deter what she was now seeing as the mission at hand, so she chose to not say anything about Roscoe's *faux pas*.

"No," she answered, "But I doubt if Jackson's notified anyone yet either; too proud. But let's get back to talking about getting rid of him. How about somewhere in the Swisher Glenn Forest section of the county? Lot's of places there, I think. It may even be where we want to take him to kill him. And as far as getting him, I'm starting to get some ideas there, too. But you got to help me, Roscoe. Help me think."

Heather reached over to Roscoe and put her hand over his crotch, and again, ironically, said, "You got to help me think, Roscoe," knowing that that would no longer be able to happen for awhile.

Soon Heather was laying back and saying, "This feels good, Roscoe." She thought to herself, *It really does, too.* Suddenly she was struck with an inspiration. "I've got it," she said, sitting bolt upright. "I know how we can do it!" Roscoe said she ought to lie back down because he had thought they were doing it. Heather was too enthused with her sudden inspiration to think about sex at the moment, so she said, "No, Roscoe, I'm not talking about this. I'm talking about how to get Jackson." Roscoe sighed and sat up. He figured that he might as well talk with Heather about how to get Jackson, or he was never going to get her, and so he asked her what her idea was.

"Okay," Heather started, "we get him to a motel. See, I call Jackson and tell him I just had to get away for a few days to think things over. I tell him I just can't take him hitting me anymore, that we need to talk before I can even consider coming back to him. I'll give him the location of the motel room where I'll be at and tell him to come over. You'll be there, too, of course, behind the door with a gun, and when he comes in, you stick it to him, and I'll cuff him and tape his mouth. We'll wait until after dark to get him into the car. We have to plan it all down to the nth detail, but it'll work, Roscoe, it'll work."

"Are you sure that Jackson will show up?"

Heather laughed. "Are you kidding? I know Jackson. All the way to the motel he'll be thinking that as soon as he sees me he'll slap the daylight out of me. He'll be there, Roscoe, believe me."

"Well, if you're sure the scenario will work out the way you think then maybe it's a good idea."

Heather looked over at him with an evil eye. "Good? Roscoe, it's better than that. We are going to get the bastard back for everything he's done to me. And we're using some of your ideas, too. Keep thinking, Baby. I need your help. We need to still figure out how and where to dispose of him. I need to get disguised again so we can go out to Swisher Glenn Forest, and look it over."

"Now?" Roscoe asked ruefully, looking down at something that had done the complete opposite of bolting upright.

"No, Baby, later. Right now we have business to get back to. And I'm going to compensate you in advance for everything you are going to help me do." Roscoe lay back down and pulled Heather to him. In a minute he closed his eyes in pleasure, thinking that Heather having ideas wasn't so bad after all and he especially liked the rewards program she had him enrolled in.

CHAPTER 81
McDonald's, No Fries, and a Kel-Tec

Roscoe decided not to tell Heather about the meeting arrangements where he was going to buy a small pistol popular for concealed carry, a Kel-Tec P-11. She would think the plan was insane, and the fact was, he would have to agree with her. However, Burlap Blankenship said he had a standard, fail-safe format he used in gun transactions and filled Roscoe in on what to do. So Roscoe parked in the McDonald's lot and went in to order something to eat. He noticed Burlap sitting at a booth, and lifted his index finger in acknowledgment, a sign that he would join him as soon as he got his food.

There was one person in the shortest line and so Roscoe got into it. *Oh hell,* he thought as he caught sight of a Kentucky State Trooper walking through the door. Todd Truitt also checked out the lines and sauntered over and stood behind Roscoe, who glanced at him and nodded.

Todd nodded back and asked, "How you doing?"

"Okay. You?" Roscoe answered as he thought, *Not worth a damn now that you're here.*

"Just fine, thank you."

I guess, Roscoe thought quickly, *we just stick with the plan. I've gotta trust Burlap knows what he's doing.*

"Sir?" the waitress repeated, "May I help you?"

"Oh, sorry," said Roscoe. "Yes. Let me get a Fish sandwich and a medium Coke."

"Fries with that?"

"No thanks. I think that'll be it."

"Okay," the waitress said. "Your total is five thirty two."

Roscoe gave her a ten and waited on his change. Then he glanced back at Todd. "You know the old saying. 'I got lost in thought, and it was unfamiliar territory'."

"Been there, done that," Todd replied.

Brad came into the McDonald's and got in line behind Todd. Todd saw in his peripheral vision someone was there and so he turned part way around. Then he greeted Brad, "Hey, haven't seen you in a while. You doing all right?"

After his order came, Roscoe went to the table where the accoutrements were located, got a straw, stuffed a couple of napkins into his left pants pocket, and then went to the booth where Burlap was sitting with his Big Mac meal, large drink, and a gift bag on the seat beside him. After he sat down, he lightly banged the end of the straw to break the wrap, put the straw into his Coke, and then took a couple of neatly folder napkins out of his right pocket and set them on the right side of his tray. A few seconds later he reached into his left pocket and placed those napkins on top of the ones he had just set out.

Trooper Todd Truitt went past their booth, nodded again to Roscoe, and then sat a booth beyond them.

"I hate we're going to miss your wife's birthday party," Burlap said at normal volume level. "But Gail's Aunt Rosie's been getting worse, so Gail's mother asked her if we could make it to Cincinnati this weekend. Gail wanted me make sure I got this gift to you," he said as he handed it over.

"Thanks," said Roscoe as he took the bag and involuntarily glanced over at the State Trooper. Fortunately Todd was squirting ketchup over his fries.

In a minute, Burlap said, "Forgot to get napkins. Care if I take one?"

"No problem," Roscoe replied, a bit nervously. He was getting uneasy over the sight of a State Trooper sitting less than ten feet away from an illegal gun buy. Roscoe watched as Burlap took the napkins, and then returned one. "Sorry, didn't mean to take them all," he said.

Burlap used his left hand to wipe his mouth with one of the napkins Roscoe had taken out of his left pocket, and at the same time, with his right hand, slipped the napkins glued to a small envelope into his left shirt pocket. The party invitation-sized envelope contained partial payment for the gun; Burlap had established that the second payment come later as meth. Burlap had wanted it part of the current exchange, but Roscoe insisted he would not take a chance on jeopardizing his business with public transactions, and finally Burlap had agreed. He had known Roscoe for some time, and trusted him as much as he did himself, which he knew meant he was taking a slight chance on getting screwed.

Roscoe was beginning to sweat a little, but he was grateful for two things: first, the cop was a booth away from them, and second, that at least the other night at The Roasted Bread and Gravy while overhearing about his Infiniti escapade, he had not had panic like he was presently feeling. The thought comforted him and he started to settle down. He began to eat his fish sandwich, hoping his stomach wouldn't insist on instant rejection as he tried to listen to Burlap ramble on about the upcoming weekend.

"Told Gail if she didn't care, I was going to see if I could get a couple tickets to a Reds game," he said. "Maybe her brother will want to go watch some Hunter Greene with me. I mean, I'll go visit with her Aunt Rosie awhile, but I don't particularly want to spend the whole weekend there. I know Gail will though; she was pretty close to her aunt growing up, and it bothers her now that Aunt Rosie's not doing so well."

Roscoe thought, *This would all explode if that SOB in his Kentucky State uniform over there knew Burlap isn't married or particularly fond of baseball.*

A couple minutes later Roscoe crumbled his sandwich wrapper into a ball, and told Burlap, "Well, I need to be running along, but thanks for the gift; I'll get it to Samantha this evening." He nodded at Todd, stood, and started toward the door, and then remembered. "Oh, wait a minute. Let me get my tray," Roscoe said, thinking, *Idiot, Roscoe, idiot. You're melting down into an idiot.*

Todd was thinking to himself that Roscoe seemed a bit unsettled, but knew he had no grounds to check anything out as he watched him head toward the door.

God, that was close, Roscoe thought. *Burlap and his so-called fail-safe format damn near blew up in my face. And what good would the gun be to me; wrapped in gift paper and set down in a Birthday bag. If I* had needed to use it I couldn't have gotten to it. Then he reflected, *What the hell am I thinking? The last damn thing I need to do is add cop killer to my resume, especially a State Trooper.*

Todd leaned forward with both elbows on the table, his mouth resting against the rough triangle shape formed by his index fingers and thumbs, and continued to watch with pursed lips as Roscoe went out to the Toyota Camry, unlocked the door, set the gift on the passengers seat, got into the car, and then left.

Todd looked at Burlap but couldn't detect anything out of the ordinary.

Sometimes I wonder if I have been at this job too long, he thought. *Maybe it is time to look more into what I was talking to Julie about the other night.*
***

A few minutes later Roscoe said "Good news, Baby," as he came through the door. Heather slowed down her fantasizing about wrapping duct tape around Jackson's head long enough to ask what it was. "Things with a gun went quicker than I thought," Roscoe replied, reaching into the gift bag he was carrying and pulling out a small package. He unwrapped the Kel-Tec.

"Oh, Roscoe, I love you, I just love you," Heather said, hugging him.

"I'm glad, but you almost lost me," Roscoe said, shaking his head. He told Heather about the gun buy with Burlap and said he didn't know if his system could stand any more close calls like the ones he'd been having over the past few days.

"There have been some nerve-wracking moments," Heather said, "but God must be smiling on us; everything is working out the way it should."

"Nerve-wracking? That's about the mildest expression you could use!" Roscoe released some of his pent-up emotions. "Why don't you try exchanging money for guns with a State Trooper sitting right next to you watching the whole damned performance?"

Heather realized she needed to get Roscoe calmed down, and soon. "But, Baby, if you think about it, Burlap was a genius, proven by what you just said. You did conduct a gun deal next to a cop and he didn't even know. Now, I know," Heather continued, "you have been taking some risks on my behalf, but I've been sitting here thinking about how my little body can best pay you back, okay?"

Roscoe thought about the fact that he had enjoyed more sex the past couple days than any prior year periods as he answered, "Not going to argue with you."

"And I've also been thinking about our trip to Swisher Glen Forest yesterday, and I think you're right. The perfect spot to dispose of Jackson will be in that small ravine. We can drive the car up the fire lane road."

Roscoe was starting to settle, and beginning to agree that Heather was right about Burlap's ingenuity, and so he replied that he thought if they buried Jackson well enough with the rocks that were there like she wanted to, the body might never be found.

"Then," said Heather, "we go to my house to get my things together, then back here to finish getting ready to leave for better territory. I'll empty my savings and checking accounts which should hold us for awhile until we get settled somewhere else. Unfortunately, for legal purposes, Jackson will be just missing, so there won't be any insurance money. Oh, and naturally, when we go to my house to get my things together, I'll drive Jackson's truck so it won't just be sitting at the Jackpot Motel, which would raise questions. I mean, people will also wonder where he went from the house without his truck, but I don't think it will be noticed as quickly, and by then we will be well on our way out of the state."

Roscoe asked when they should kick off the operation and Heather replied, "Tomorrow morning. At first I was thinking maybe we should wait for nightfall before taking Jackson from the motel room to the car, but, now I'm thinking that if you go by Backstage Outfitters in a while, you can buy a very realistic-looking Halloween mask that we can put over his head so we can make the transition to the vehicle without standing out. With a handkerchief stuffed in his mouth and duct tape over it, and the threat of a gun that he will know we have, I think we'll find Jackson to be very compliant. Oh, and you need to go by the Army Surplus Store and get a set of hand and leg cuffs. We still have several things to get ready, but first, I'm going to give you more reward. Oh, we're about to finally be rid of Jackson, Roscoe. I'm so loaded with energy, I feel like I'm going to explode with excitement, and I want my body melted tight against yours when it happens."

Roscoe grinned. "Then let's go explode, Baby. Together. Afterwards, we'll shower and get ready for the big one. Got to tell you, Baby, I'm still nervous over McDonald's and the cop. But maybe you can help me get over it. Then afterwards we can make reservations for a room for tomorrow."

CHAPTER 82
The Silver Star

Brad was pulled back to another night when he had saved, and lost, lives.

Delta was settled into a perimeter for the night, foxholes dug, Listening Posts set out, something off the C-ration menu consumed, and Brad was with some guys in the platoon sitting around playing cards. Suddenly, with no warning they came under fierce attack, and men from around the perimeter immediately returned fire. The LT received a frantic call from a man on the LP that had recently gone out that they were pinned down in crossfire and Highball was shot in the leg.

"I'm going out," Brad called as he grabbed his medical bag, dove into the underbrush and started low crawling in the direction of the LP, moving as quickly as he could while trying to stay as low as possible as he heard bullets whistling right over his head. After fifty meters or so he could hear someone trying to stifle cries of pain. "Hey, guys, it's me, Brad," he called as loud as he dared.

"Over here!"

When he got to where the men were, he saw Rick had cut off a sleeve and was using it to try and stop the bleeding from Highball's leg. "Good job," Brad said. "Let me get it bandaged so we can get back in. Here's some Tylenol for right now; I'll give you a shot when we're back in the perimeter." After bandaging the leg Brad said he was going to carry Highball back.

"How the hell you going to do that alone? Let me help." Rick said.

"Okay," Brad said. He spoke to the other two men. "You two take mine and Rick's stuff and low crawl your asses back in! Tell the LT we're coming, and for God's sake, don't let them shoot at us!"

The two men took off toward the perimeter and Brad thought quickly about how to get the wounded man back in. "Highball," he said. "Put your hands over your chest and interlock your fingers tightly. Rick and I are going to be on hands and knees on both sides of you and will each slip an arm through your arms. We're going to have to drag you probably a foot or two each pull, but we'll get you there while keeping us all low as possible and hoping we don't take a bullet."

Highball gave a painful laugh. "For you a bullet; for me another one."

"Keep that humor going," Rick said. "It'll help you heal."

A short time later they were back with the rest of the company. Brad treated Highball's wound and then left to go treat the platoon sergeant who had taken a large chunk of shrapnel in the chest. Rollo was working on him and growled, "Where the hell have you been, Bad Fuckin' M?"

Brad just shook his head and started to open SGT Crosby's fatigue shirt more to better see what he was dealing with. He desperately prayed the wound wasn't as serious as it looked. There were other men needing treatment for less severe wounds, so after he did all he could for the SGT he left to attend to them. After treating all who needed care, he went back to spend the night with SGT Cosby. The LT said it would be morning before they could call in medevac.

During a lull in the attack, Brad was sitting on the edge of a foxhole next to where SGT Cosby was resting. A recently arrived FNG came up to where Brad was sitting and asked for help.

"Sure, what is it?"

"Well, earlier I thought I made out the outline of someone sitting in a tree, but a few minutes later it was gone, so I'm sitting there wondering if maybe my eyes are playing tricks with me. Then what I saw is back again. Wondering if you could tell me if I'm nuts or not," he said, pointing to an area some 50 meters or so in front of the perimeter.

Brad told the squad leader on the foxhole to hand him the starlight scope. "Holy shit!" he said to the squad leader. "Call the LT and tell him we need more artillery!"

"What's going on?"

"I'm looking at an NVA sitting in a tree looking right back at me with what looks like his own scope." Brad's hands were shaking as he handed the piece back to the squad leader.

Hmmm, Brad thought. I wonder why after a few artillery rounds we noticed the guy disappeared. In the bigger picture, I also wonder why he wasn't able to do something to me before we took him out.

Brad's fingers were interlocked together as he leaned forward with his hands between his knees. He had been recommended for and received a Silver Star for his actions going out under fire and bringing the LPs and Highball safely in. But SGT Cosby had died the next morning on the Huey en route to the hospital.

Later they had found out that papers taken off dead NVA bodies indicated that an NVA Battalion had orders to overrun and completely annihilate the company, even indicating that such an event would have strong impact on the U.S. media reports and make the war even more unfavorable to an already vacillating public opinion. Brad shook his head and sighed.

CHAPTER 83
Carter Caves State Resort Park: The Caves

Saturday morning at eight a.m. sharp Todd pulled into Julie's drive. She came out of the house immediately carrying a small day-pack and two trekking poles.

"Picked up these yesterday at Freddie Turner's General Store. He has a barrel of them in there. Carves them out himself. I decided to call them Hope and Hanging in there. That all right with you?"

Todd laughed as he said, "Got mine in the trunk. I was going to let you use one, but guess I don't have to now."

"Nope."

The first question Todd asked Julie after they pulled out was about her Uncle David. Julie shared about some of their times together, and cried at a couple points.

"I don't mean to be all weepy on you," she said, "but this is the first time I've felt able to talk with anyone about him since he died. That happened soon after my brother started abusing me, and it has been a 'don't talk seriously to anyone, downhill slide' ever since then. Well, actually, let me change that, until just a few days ago, thank you Trooper T."

In a few minutes, the Kentucky Bourbon Parkway intersected with I-64 near the 152 mile marker. Todd exited the parkway and followed the interstate east to Exit 161 and then turned toward Carter Caves State Resort Park. From there it was just a few minutes until he turned into the Welcome Center parking lot. Todd told Julie that even though the caves they would be going into were not pay caves they needed to get a permit.

"I guess that makes me feel a little bit better," said Julie. "At least if I'm buried alive, someone will know where to start digging."

"Actually, I guess that's the general idea," Todd replied.

He had told Julie earlier sometime they could take the pay cave tours, but today he really just wanted to take her to the Laurel and

Horn Hollow Caves. He had asked her if it would be okay to do the caves first and then the short hikes afterwards and Julie had said the plan sounded good to her.

"Believe me, I have real mixed emotions about the caves," she said, "but I want to conquer the fear, so let's go ahead and get the hardest part over with."

Todd was still wondering if he wasn't pushing Julie into something she wasn't ready for, but she seemed quite sincere in saying she wanted to attempt it. "Okay," he said, "then Laurel first. It's a little longer, but not as wet or as low."

After he got the permits, Todd turned his Oldsmobile left from the Carter Caves Welcome Center and headed back down the road about one half mile to where there were a couple pull-off parking areas on the left hand side of the road.

"The only things we'll need for this are the flashlight in my little waist pack and our trekking poles."

Julie gave a nervous laugh. "and Zoloft?""

"You'll be fine. Trust me."

"Yeah, right."

"No. Seriously. I believe I already know you well enough to honestly say that."

Todd unzipped the largest pocket of the waist pack to double check the LED flashlight was in it. Then they got out of the car and reached into the backseat for their trekking poles.

"Come on Hanging in there," Julie said. "You too, Hope. Let's get this thing underway."

At the opening to Laurel Cave they had to climb over some rocks to where there was a small pool of water that looked as though it could be circumvented on the right side.

"It's not but a few inches deep," said Todd, "and I've discovered there's no way to avoid getting wet feet, so we might as well just traipse on through and get it over with. By the way," he asked, "you still okay?"

Julie followed Todd and carefully used her trekking poles to help maintain her balance. She was rather surprised her nervousness had settled; that she found herself curious as to what came next.

They soon came to a spot where the cave narrowed and it looked as though they were going to have to walk one foot in front of the other as the floor had a small five to six inch wide, maybe eight inch deep, gully carved into the floor. Todd stopped.

"Look at the wall, how different."

Julie observed most of the walls were pitted in a way that looked almost like a huge alligator skin, but then Todd shone the light on a section right next to it which stood in drastic contrast due to lines running vertically, somehow etched quite differently by Nature.

"Look at how beautiful this is. But it's showing this particular perspective only because we are seeing it exposed minimally to a very specific light. We wouldn't even see it this way if it was in full, or even partial, sun."

Julie sighed. "A little irony, perhaps. I've been afraid of caves and dark places, and in fact, I'm beginning to see that's where I've been living all along. Todd, I almost want to kick myself for failing to see some things earlier. So much misspent time."

Todd laughed.

"What?"

Todd told her misspent time was not a phrase one heard very often. He said it took him back to when he had heard it used several years earlier. "Samantha had a niece who sang in a college choir and once they performed at the Second Presbyterian Church in Frankfort when it coincided with a trip we were making to the Kentucky Capital, so we attended the church services to hear the choir."

"There was a short sermon after the performance, and the preacher, I can't recall his name, told the story of a man he had once known who had lived what many called a rough life. When the man was in his mid eighties he took ill and was dying. He called for the preacher and made his peace before he passed on. The pastor said someone commented to him it was a shame that the old man had wasted his whole life and engaged in so much misspent time. The preacher said he asked how it could be called a wasted life and misspent time as it all led to the old man making peace before he died."

Julie looked into what little that she could see of Todd's eyes in the semi-darkness and said, "Kind of like us sitting at my table eating subs together, right?"

"Kind of like that," Todd answered as he bent down and lightly kissed Julie.

"Mmm, I like that," said Julie. "However, shall we continue on to our next adventure, or lesson, or both? Maybe look for a light at the end of this tunnel?"

A couple moments later Todd stopped, turned off the light, and told Julie to look straight ahead.

"So, that's what they mean when they say there's light at the end of the tunnel."

"That's what they mean," said Todd, adding, "Whoever they is."

After they exited Laurel Cave they climbed a small but relatively steep banking on the left side of the creek bed.

Julie almost slipped, but caught herself with her poles. "Now I'm really starting to see the value of my two assistants, Hope and Hanging in there."

"Make a difference, don't they?"

Part way up the banking they came across a footpath and Todd said they needed to follow it to the right to the shorter, wetter, and lower Horn Hollow Cave.

CHAPTER 84
Carter Caves State Resort Park: The Hike

When they came out of Horn Hollow Cave they followed a small trail back up the left bank to where a trail junction had signs for the Welcome Center, one mile each way. Todd said they'd take the trail to the left as it would soon circle close to where they'd left the car.

After a short ride, they parked again and then picked up the beginning part of The 3 Bridges Trail that would take them almost immediately to Fern Bridge. After they descended the thirty plus steps leading to the bridge, they walked around to where they could look up through the double arches that framed a split where they could look through and see sky. The area also had a lot of fern and many tiny clover-like plants. They saw no one else in the vicinity and Julie felt free to talk to Todd.

"This is nice, coming back," Julie said. "I remember my last time here. My brother had been abusing me for almost two years at that point, and I vividly recall looking up through there," she pointed with one of her trekking poles to the place between the two arches, "and imagining the answers to my questions were up in the sky. And this is so ironic. Now that I sense I just might be finding some of those answers, here I am, back where I used to think they were. Todd," she continued, "sometimes I can hardly believe it's me I hear talking; I feel like I've changed so much over the past few days."

"Well, be careful not to change too much; I still want to recognize you."

Julie lightly swung one of her trekking poles against his butt. "And there's more where that came from," she said, "if you don't behave yourself and stop picking on me."

There was a small wooden bridge under the arches, and when they reached the middle of it, Julie gazed down to her left at the small ravine bursting with undergrowth. "This is heaven," she said.

Todd was behind Julie, and being careful not to jab her because of holding a pole in each hand, he reached around her and gently pulled her back into him. She leaned her head back against his shoulder.

"If I died right now, I'd die a happy woman." Then she tightened in the pit of her stomach as she thought, *Julie! What kind of village idiot are you? You are being held by a man who is dating for the first time since his wife was killed, and you're talking about if I died right now; you stupid, stupid bitch.*

"Well," Todd answer interrupted her thoughts, "I'm going to have to ask you to reconsider that idea. Number one, I like the happy woman part, but, more importantly, number two, those are a lot of steps I'd have to carry your dead weight back up, and I'm getting too old for that."

Julie laughed and decided not to say anything or even apologize for what she had just seen as a foolish remark on her part as it hadn't seemed to bother Todd, and also, she realized that she needed to allow herself to be part of the normal human race, imperfections and all.

At one point, about twenty feet ahead of them, a possum scurried across the trail. Todd commented. "I'm surprised seeing one; they're pretty much nocturnal."

Julie shook her head as she said, "Possums. Part of God's Divine sense of humor, the strange side, that is. I mean, I don't know. When I was in college, I think I got the basics of English, Math, Science, Literature, and even a little on the whys and wherefores of human behavior. I generally understand the concepts of light years, dwarf stars, and Economics. But what I have never been able to understand is why a possum, when confronted with car headlights, always thinks he can make it across the road without being hit. Always."

Todd laughed. "Now who's raising the philosophical question? The answer is a relatively simple one. Possums were around long before cars and headlights. I remember reading their reaction to a threat is instinctive and sometimes they get hit because they lie on the road and play possum. They can't help it; it's just an involuntary response."

"Back to my comment about a strange Divine sense of humor; I mean, didn't this Overseer of the planet know when he, or she, first came up with the idea of possums and protection, and humans who would eventually think about cars, that there might be a problem? And I guess I'm sounding again like the night we first made subs at my place, but what I'm saying about possums and cars is not at all unlike this same Overseer knowing about a seven year old girl being fucked by her fifteen year old brother. Just not right, and that should have been foreseen."

"Like I've said before, the more I know, the more questions I have. And although I don't always like it, I can live with that."

"I don't think I can say I'm at that point right yet," Julie responded, "but I honestly think I can say I want to be. Will you keep helping me get there?"

They continued on their way and soon went down a small hill bringing them back to the trail intersection that completed the loop. They turned left and retraced their steps back to the car.

"Todd," Julie said, "I'd really like to walk some more. Do you care if we go back and hike the rest of The Three Bridges Trail? It's still early afternoon, not sweltering hot, and I'm just not ready to quit yet."

"Okay with me," Todd answered. Approximately two and a half hours later they completed the trail and again headed back down the road toward I-64 and the Kentucky Bourbon Parkway.

"This has been a long time coming," said Julie. "It's been a good day."

CHAPTER 85
Gazing at the Southern Cross, Wondering

Brad reflected on the remainder of his time on R&R in Australia. After the incident with Paul he went back to the Red Garter and got drunk; and that remained his pattern for the remaining time in Sydney. Then the return flight north to Vietnam with another glimpse of coral reefs. They were still beautiful, but didn't trigger the same sense of relaxation as they had a few days earlier.

Upon arrival back at Long Binh Brad learned that he could not catch a Huey to the field until the next day. He asked if he could get a pass to town and it was approved with instructions to make sure he was back well before dark. Soon after he got there, a little girl who appeared to be seven or eight years old came up to him, and asked, "Hey, GI. You wanna fuck, GI?"

Brad was taken back as he said, "No."

The little girl replied, "No, no, not me, GI. My big sister."

Brad's thoughts were so screwed up by this time that he just followed her into the house and made payment to the sister who looked somewhat closer to his age of twenty. What the hell, he thought, Australia didn't pan out, I'm on a brief reprieve in the middle of a fucking war, and not really sure what is going on as far as my life. It took him a little while to get near an orgasm as he decided he would try and redeem himself of being a bad medic, and take her into consideration.

But then he heard, "Come on, GI. Not take so long. Hurry up."

Brad shook his head. Good Lord; that had really helped.

While waiting on the Huey to the unit after R&R Brad realized he had forgotten about dropping off eight rolls of film at a PX for development, so he threw them into his pack. Some guys carried an ammo can in their pack to protect letters and film rolls, etc. not Brad. Extra unnecessary weight in his opinion, one which turned out to be rather faulty.

The company was digging in for the night when Brad opened his pack to get out some C's. "Well, shit!"

"What's the matter?" Steve asked.

"I don't think I screwed the top on my bug juice tight enough. It came off and the juice squeezed out."

"Don't look at me. Tried to tell you the weight of an ammo can was worth it."

"I know, damn it. I should've listened to you."

"Is anything ruined?"

"Leaked all over my rolls of film. Doesn't look as if they're any good. Totally soaked. I'm just gonna toss them."

"Sorry about that," Steve said.

"Fuck it. Don't mean nuthin'."

Brad stared at the stars like he had so many other nights wondering where he belonged in the whole thing called a universe. It always took him back to many nights trying to fall asleep in southeast Asia, looking up at a starry sky, oft times gazing at the Southern Cross, wondering, trying to fit things into some sort of sensible pattern.

CHAPTER 86
Have to Let God Know She Loves Him

Albert brought a cup of hot chocolate to the kitchen table where Tira was sitting and set it carefully down in front of her. She smiled weakly up at him as he asked her if she was feeling all right. "One thing has been bothering me a lot," she started.

"What's that?"

"Well, a few days ago when I was in Wendy's, I really think I should have convinced that girl at the cash register to avoid the coming judgment. As a matter of fact, I know I could have if you hadn't interfered."

Albert shook his head and sighed. "We don't need to talk about this again, Tira. You know the break-in and loss of your mother's things have been rough on you."

"Things? They were more than things, Albert. You know that!"

Albert immediately realized his careless choice of words. "I'm sorry, Tira. I know they were irreplaceable memorabilia. And I know it's been hard on you."

"But you still think I only went there because of what happened. It's more, Albert. I have been chosen to receive revelations. And that girl at the register; I just can't get her off my mind, Albert. I just can't. She needs to be given another chance, she really does."

"Tira." Albert spoke rather harshly. "Just drop it. You don't need to be wandering into Wendy's again, or anyplace else, for that matter, spilling nonsense about earthquakes and floods and what have you."

Tira stared coldly at Albert and asked him if he would just go do something else and leave her alone for awhile because she needed to pray and meditate in peace. After Albert left the room, Tira faced her crucifixes as usual. Naturally, she had removed the silverware from the wooden outstretched arms, but now, in addition to the shattered pieces of the porcelain dove, she had those damnable swirling images tumbling through her mind of the lost locket, the destroyed music box, the missing ruby ring, the slashed evening gown and other dresses, the missing Revolutionary War era silver tea set, and always, the image of her mother's picture with the large mustache scribbled on it; eyes poked out with a pen. In the course of her prayer ritual she still held the porcelain dove with both hands, but much more carefully so she wouldn't cut herself on its jagged edges. At the conclusion of her prayer for guided concentration during the task she had to accomplish, Tira carefully transferred the broken dove as usual to her left hand, and then made the sign of the cross. More than ever now she had to let God know she loved him with all her heart, soul, mind and strength.

CHAPTER 87
Prissy Up a Tree

Monday around 7 a.m., Phillip got his first call as he was arriving at headquarters. "Phillip. Julie. You're familiar with the area going North on 473 toward Armstrong County, right? I just got a call from some guy on a cell phone, lives at County Road Bricken, Box 124, but he's next door on his neighbor's property. Tried to get his cat out of a tree and said his neighbor is carrying on over him trespassing; trying to set the tree on fire. I'll notify the Sheriff's Department, but we probably need to check it out, too."

Phillip shook his head and laughed as he headed out. About a mile down Bricken, he had no trouble figuring out where the situation was as the Scarbo Volunteer Fire Department was already on the scene. He pulled into the yard and got out of his cruiser. He recognized one of the volunteers and went to him. "What's going on?" Phillip asked Mike Banner. "I got a call; woman trying to set a tree on fire with her neighbor in it?"

"Your call was accurate," said Mike. "Bitsy Wagoneer and Ralph Henderson. I've lived in these parts all my life. Seems to just get worse between these two. Married eighteen years ago and Ralph moved into the house there with Bitsy. Got a divorce after fourteen weeks. Bitsy stayed in her place and took back her maiden name; Ralph bought the property next door and moved a double-wide onto it. Most people think it was just so he could aggravate her. They ain't never got along as far back as I can remember, though the past couple years folks round here thought maybe they was settling down a bit."

Phillip asked what was currently going on and Mike replied, "Ralph's still up in the tree. We got the fire out, and now some guys are getting him down. Bitsy's right over there on the steps. We told her to stay there, that she was awaiting arrest. Now Bitsy's the kind of gal who will give you a lot of verbal trouble, but if you tell her to wait for the police, she'll wait."

"If I remember right, I have heard those names before," Phillip said. He looked over to the tree in question. Boards had been piled around it, teepee fashion, and, evidently, from the smell, doused with kerosene. The tree was singed to a height of about fifteen feet. Phillip shook his head and walked over to where a rough looking woman was sitting. She may have been younger than forty, but if so, the years hadn't worn well. Bitsy Wagoneer glared back and forth between Phillip and her ex-husband who was being helped down a ladder. Phillip furrowed his brow as he asked, "What's going on?"

Bitsy jerked up straight and bellowed, "I'll tell you what's going on! Trespassin', that's what's really happening. Here you are, arresting a woman on her own property, and the evidence for the real crime is still up there in the tree! 'Course you guys are helping him down now, so the evidence ain't gonna be in the tree no more. But why don't you let me go, and arrest him?"

Phillip told Bitsy there might be charges against Ralph too, he didn't know yet, but since Bitsy had set a tree on fire with Ralph up in it, she should know the charges were at least felonious assault, wanton endangerment, and who knew what else. Bitsy asked what about Ralph trespassin' on her property, was Phillip going to get him for that?

"Wasn't he after his cat?" asked Phillip.

Bitsy snorted. "May have been. That's what he says. But it's his responsibility to keep his cat on his own damn property. Not my fault if it gets stranded up in a tree. I don't really give a flipping screw about his cat. Of course," she continued, "any cat worth nine lives ought to know how to get its own whiskered-assed self out of a tree." Phillip asked Bitsy what she would suggest Ralph should have done and Bitsy responded, "Let it starve to death, for all I care. But he shouldn't have come onto my property. Up that high, mighta been tryin' to look in my windows, I don't know. I just know he was trespassin'!"

Phillip remembered working one summer in his teen years for a house painter, and one old woman who had told them to make sure that they didn't try to look into her bedroom window while they were painting her house. The memory forced a smile.

"Are you laughin' at me?" Bitsy asked.

"No, Ma'am," said Phillip.

"Better not be," said Bitsy. "I may be wearin' old clothes, but I'm damn still all woman underneath."

"Yes, Ma'am," Phillip replied, biting his tongue to keep his facial muscles under control.

The volunteer firemen had Ralph out of the tree, so Phillip told Bitsy to stay where she was and he walked over to the group. Ralph had a small Siamese kitten in his arms, soothing it and Phillip told him he wanted to hear his version of what had happened. Ralph said about four months earlier his Calico had died.

"I take it Calico was a cat?" Phillip asked.

"Of course," Ralph said, rolling his eyes. "Anyway, about a week ago I went to the Frankenberry Animal Hospital and Shelter and got me this little Siamese kitten. Named it Prissy 'cause it seemed to fit her. Earlier today I noticed she wasn't around, and then I heard her squalling and carrying on from way up in that tree. Well I scrambled over the fence, 'cause it was the quickest way, and climbed up to get her. I could tell she was scared. Next thing I know, Bitsy's hollering at me about trespassing, and waving a pistol and telling me to stay put. Saying she's gonna set the tree on fire. Good thing I had my cell phone on me. That crazy bitch was trying to kill me!"

Phillip went back over to Bitsy, read her rights to her, placed her under arrest, and took her to the cruiser. He told her to stay in the car until he returned, then walked over to Ralph and cautioned him to stay off of his ex-wife's property. Ralph asked what he should do if his cat ran away again and Phillip told him he could probably try to recapture it anywhere with the exception of anyplace owned by Bitsy Wagoneer.

As Phillip was walking back to the cruiser a Deputy Sheriff arrived on the scene and hollered over to Phillip. "I see Ralph called you, too."

"Yeah," Phillip laughed. "Things are under control, but you can take over with Bitsy here. Probably more under your jurisdiction, anyway, but hey, if I had been Ralph up in that tree with those flames working their way up, I'd have been calling every department in the county out too."

CHAPTER 88
Enter Scooter and Little Bit

Brad stopped by Frankenberry Animal Hospital and Shelter. After his dream with Peter Rabbit in it the other night he was overwhelmed with the desire for another small animal. He decided to look for a cat. He was met by an attractive middle age woman who introduced herself as Mia. She said there were nine awaiting adoption. One pair caught his eye. The larger black one was stretched out and the small orange tabby was curled up against him. They both stood up and eyed him as he approached.

"These don't look they come from the same litter," he chuckled. "Their stories?"

"They started out in cages next to each other," Mia said, "and they kept sleeping as close to each other as they could, so we decided to put them together. They're inseparable."

Brad felt something and looked down. The cats were standing on their hind legs, both with a paw through the wire touching him, one on each hip. "I think I've been adopted," Brad said. "They'll take me." He looked at the name tags on the cage and said, "Okay Scooter and Little Bit, you're moving to a cabin in the woods."

Mia said, "A cabin in the woods. Sounds interesting. Might want to keep them inside until they become adjusted to you being their human, although it looks like they have already claimed you as Dad. When they realize you're the food source then they'll be more likely to stay near. Once, or perhaps I should say if, you do let them outside, you might want to have some of their food in a bowl right near the door."

"I'll do that. By the way, how much does Scooter weigh? He looks twice as big as Little Bit."

Mia laughed. "You have a good comparative eye. Scooter weighs just a couple ounces over twenty pounds, and Little Bit is a couple ounces under ten."

"He looks big, but not fat."

"Muscle; stroke his neck and back you feel how solid he is. By the way, we have a full-time veterinarian here, so they are fixed and up to date on all their shots."

"Then I guess I'm ready to sign any paperwork, pay the fees, and take these babies to their new home."

CHAPTER 89
I'll Overlook Your Sinful Ways, Albert

Tira held her broken dove in her hands and stared questioningly at the wooden figures on the wall. "Was Pastor Brock right?" she asked. "You didn't protect me from evil. Was mother wrong?"

Tira reflected on the peace surrounding her mother even in the midst of difficult times, and knew it had to have come from her meditation times. So she clasped the shattered porcelain and quieted her spirit. After about five minutes, Tira knew what she had to do next. She still couldn't erase the image of the girl who had been behind the counter at Wendy's several days earlier and, furthermore, she didn't care what Albert said, or thought. The girl had a sweet face and seemed to be exactly the kind of person who needed to be taking advantage of the escape plan God was revealing to Tira. Tira knew it was not necessary for everyone to be swept away in the soon to be earthquake and resulting floods. Albert was in the back room, so after asking her crucifixes blessings, she quietly wandered out the door, turned east, and soon arrived at Wendy's. She went in and approached the counter, where, to her great delight, Kari Turner was again at the register.

"May I help you?" Kari asked at the same split moment she recognized Tira from a few days earlier and inwardly groaned.

Tira knew the timing was perfect. "Honey," she began, "I have been so worried about you since I was in here the other day. You really need to make sure you're ready to meet Jesus. His day of judgment is almost here. God is still revealing to me what is about to happen to this town and to the people in it who don't repent."

"That's still nice," said Kari, "and I'm so glad you are having the opportunity to be a chosen one. But this is still Wendy's, and I'm still here to take orders for food and drinks. Would you like something to eat?"

Phillip Cordella was very much a man of patterns. As so often before, he decided he would get small Fries and the Jr. Bacon Cheeseburger off the Value Menu, and then wash them down with a cold beer at the house. As he came out of the restroom, he couldn't believe he was behind Tira again in line. If he had a bad Karma in conjunction with Tira, it was associated with Infiniti chase and Prissy cat times.

Tira decided she would have to show Kari the same patience as Job as she answered, "It is still not a time to be eating." Phillip shook his head, and then asked Tira if there was a problem. "Big problems," said Tira, as she turned to face Phillip, recognized him, and then added, "Oh, it's you again."

Phillip told her, "Yes, I believe we've met before."

"Tira?" Albert Furcologna came up behind them. "I'm glad I found you. I came out into the kitchen and you weren't there. After last night's conversation I thought you might have come back here." He looked at the girl behind the register. "I do so hope that she wasn't bothering you. I'm sorry."

"I'm okay," Kari said, hoping Albert would take Tira home and put her down in the basement on a chain or something. Albert apologized to Kari again, nodded sheepishly at Phillip, and then steered Tira toward the door.

Phillip watched Albert and Tira Furcologna go out to their car and then placed his order. As soon as they were out of Wendy's and in the car, ready to start home, Albert exploded, "Tira, what the hell are you doing?"

Tira reacted back just as strongly. "I don't have to answer to you, and don't you dare curse when you talk to me! You have been good to me, Albert, but it's just been out of guilt because you had been so evil earlier!"

Oh, Lord, here we go again, Albert thought as he told Tira he had not been evil, he was human, and he had made some mistakes.

"Mistakes!" Tira screamed. "You cheated on me, Albert. I think the only reason you stayed was because you didn't want to leave me while mother was dying. That was nice of you, but how do you think I felt, knowing you were still thinking of that little twerp you had been screwing? The one I might add, who gave us the gift of herpes!"

Albert knew what Tira was saying had some elements of truth in it, but that she was also unaware of just how difficult it had been for him to choose to stay with her. He decided he would answer her for awhile, even though he was quite sure that it was a losing proposition. He replied, "You have no idea what I was thinking, or why I decided to stay with you. For God's sake, Tira, it really could have been because I loved you and wanted to be with you!"

Tira picked up on Albert's semantic choices and quickly pointed them out. "Could have been, not was. Don't lie to me, Albert. God's going to sweep you away in his judgment just like he will with the rest of the evil people in this town!"

Albert sighed and told Tira to stop it, she was suffering from a small breakdown because of the robbery and the loss of some of her mother's things, but the town wasn't evil, and there weren't going to be any earthquakes or floods.

"You don't know that," Tira retorted. "And there's no way you could know because your eyes are blinded with lust and passion for your Delilah girl! Furthermore, your ears are filled with noises you deserved because you betrayed me!"

Albert felt at his rope's end. He was tired of listening to the ringing, Delayah had moved on with her life, and Tira had gone off the deep end. He lashed back. "Oh, I deserve the ringing? And because I betrayed you? Tira, I believe I had the ringing long before I even met you. Explain that."

"I don't need to explain anything, and I don't want to fight anymore. But I do want you to know I will be here be you in the unlikely event you decide to repent and want my help."

"Oh yeah, it sounds like you really want to help," Albert's sarcasm spilled over.

Tira sighed as she thought of how difficult it was to live with someone who kept resisting any efforts to help him exist in this world in a good and decent way. She decided to try one more time, and said, "Pastor Brock says you might repent, if I hold steady in my believing."

Albert flashed back to something he'd said before, and had an image of Pastor Brock's congregation passing through the vestibule into the church holding squirrels in one hand with penguins on a leash with the other. He laughed as he said, "Pastor Brock, Pastor Brock. Is there anyone in this world with anything of value to say besides him? Tira, I have said it before, and I'll say it again, if your precious Pastor Brock said to come to church with squirrels and penguins in tow, I'd find you climbing a tree, then heading out for Antarctica."

Tira's face darkened. "I'll overlook your sinful ways, Albert. At least Pastor Brock speaks wisdom which is more than you do. You just talk about some stupid ringing no one can hear but you, and cheat on me with one of your students!"

Albert decided it was all over but the ringing as he lashed back, "Well, Tira, let me tell you something. The thing that attracted me first to Delayah, before we even got involved, in, what I might add, was fantastic sex, was the fact she understood about the ringing. Really understood. You see, she has it, too."

Tira smirked. Albert had finally admitted out loud he'd been having an affair; she'd been right all along. And it seemed so appropriate the Delilah girl should have the curse of this noiseless ringing, also. Tira felt righteousness bubbling over as she realized what Pastor Brock had said was true; God's ways were mysterious and so far beyond mortal comprehension. She told Albert of course Delilah should have the ringing because she had been having an affair with a married man, and naturally, she deserved it. Then Tira decided to make Albert choose. "So," she asked him, "Why, if this Delilah was so good, especially in the bed, why don't you just go back to her?"

"Well, you see, Tira," Albert countered, "first off, you are just so limited in your imagination. Bed? Do you think we only made love in a bed? Try in the woods at the Quick Break Rest Area on the Bourbon Parkway. And in many other ways besides the good old missionary."

Tira did not want to hear any details. "You are evil saying all this to me. Why don't you just leave and go back to your Delilah?"

"I can't," said Albert, "because she left me. Left me because I wouldn't leave you."

"Well isn't that a shame, but don't worry, because, along with you, Delilah is also going to taste the judgment coming on this town."

Albert thought, *There's no way that I can talk to her, she's so irrational, and I've already said too much to ever repair this marriage. And Delayah, gone too, twisting in the pieces of my shattered mind as I try to reason out a reason. Sometimes I wonder if minds and reasons and shitheads all crawled out of the same divine concoction of murky madness and piss water.* He pulled the car into their driveway and told Tira, "Just go on into the house; I just need to drive around a little."

"Right," said Tira. "You just enjoy yourself, Albert. And don't forget to say hello to your Delilah for me."

CHAPTER 90
Tell Delayah I Love Her

As he drove away from the house, ears screaming, mind tossing around, unable to settle anywhere, Albert told himself he was too much of a coward to outright kill himself; he would have to make it look like an accident. He decided to go around a hundred miles an hour down the straight stretch near Hacker's Mill Pond and go into the curve without braking. It would be difficult to prove it had been a suicide, and Tira would then collect a nice chunk of change. He thought at least he could do that for her in his passing.

Albert turned onto Highway 28 and headed west. Near the Hacker's Mill Pond stretch, he pushed the accelerator to the floor until he hit one hundred. On a side road halfway down the stretch, the driver of the Chevy Impala was texting, and not paying attention to the fact there was a stop sign to comply with before crossing Highway 28. Albert had no chance to brake, and broadsided her at full speed.

Eloise Brock, Pastor Brock's wife, died instantly.

***

Sometime later, Albert regained consciousness, and looked up at Tira who was standing next to his hospital bed. He crumpled his brow and tried to figure out where he was, and why. He asked Tira what had happened. "You were speeding; Albert, and you ran into Eloise Brock. You killed her." Sobbing, she bitterly asked, "What were you thinking of, to be going so fast? And how could you do this to Pastor Brock?"

Albert groggily remembered why he wanted to die. "I'm sorry," he said. "I didn't mean to hurt anybody besides myself." He scrunched his face again, paused, and then asked, "Tira?"

Tira stared down coldly at him as she asked him, "What?"

"Tira," The words came weakly, but Albert wanted to make sure he got them all out. "Tira, do me a favor, and tell Delayah I'm sorry, and that I died loving her."

With that, Albert slipped back into his coma, and, one hour and eleven minutes later, at exactly 11:11 p.m., he died.

CHAPTER 91
The Pain in Your Eyes

Tuesday morning. Todd called Aaron and asked him if they could get together for lunch. They agreed to meet at Shoney's at 12:15. Aaron arrived a little early and nervously waited in the lobby. When Todd came in, they shook hands and then Todd asked, "How have things been going?"

"Quite well," Aaron replied, "And I have to thank you for that." They followed a hostess to a booth, and when a waitress came for their drink orders, they both ordered the food bar.

After serving themselves and sitting back down Todd asked Aaron if he had talked with Toolbox, his former boss.

"I have, and again I need to thank you for helping me get my job back at Brakes and Buggies." Aaron bit into a chicken drumstick, chewed, and then asked, "If you don't mind my asking, do you help everyone you arrest for DUI like this?"

"No. It'd be nice if I could." Todd was quiet a moment before continuing. "The reason I can't is probably two-fold. First, I deal with a lot of people on a daily basis and there's just not enough time to follow up with everyone; second, not everyone is ready to be helped." He looked directly into Aaron's eyes and said, "The circumstances were such that I believed, I believe, you are ready. That doesn't mean it will be an easy road, I just felt like you were ready to start the journey. You are, aren't you?"

Aaron affirmatively shook his head and asked, "How can you tell when someone is ready?"

"I can't always, but with you there was something that made me feel like I had to try."

Aaron replied that what he still couldn't get out of his mind was the look Todd had had in his eyes as he had told Aaron his wife and children had been killed by a drunk driver. "I guess," Aaron continued, "what really got through to me, even though I was drunk, was the realization that the pain I saw in your eyes could have been caused by me under different circumstances."

Todd thought about all of the ironies in the whole situation; Aaron seeing the pain in his eyes, Julie sensing that something was going on with him, he and Julie going out and now falling in love with each other, and as a result, the pain in his eyes being reduced. He thought, *I'd try to understand, but like so many other things in life, it's beyond me.*

Todd and Aaron continued to eat and talked about things for Aaron to do to counteract the urges to have a drink he would most likely be having in the days ahead. Aaron told Todd he had already been experiencing some; the hardest one when he had been tempted by who he had thought was his new roommate at Angel Windows.

"I realized that would most likely be a difficult test for you," Todd said. "I'm just glad you passed it. When they finished eating they arranged a time when Aaron could come by the 58th Headquarters in a couple days and learn more about the State Trooper side of the DUI experience. They went to the cash register and paid for their meals, and then went out to their vehicles to go their separate ways. As he turned right out of the parking lot, Aaron was nearly numb, overwhelmed with thoughts he didn't fully understand, including feeling better than he could ever remember feeling before. He decided to go by and visit his Nana for a few minutes and follow up what had been a good meal with something even better, homemade cookies and milk.

CHAPTER 92
Demon Chasers

Brad smiled as he watched Scooter and Little Bit playing around the cabin. He had a covered rain barrel and they loved to chase each other around it, occasionally jumping to the lid and wrestling until one fell off and one remained Feline of the Mountain. Usually Scooter won, but this time Little Bit managed to hold her own and made him the one to slide off.

After he brought them home he had set up an area for their litter boxes; three, as he had read somewhere that you should always have one more box than the number of cats. He placed out their water bowl and food dishes, and they wolfed down the dried food he fed them.

Later, when he was ready to retire for the night he had been pleasantly surprised by two fur babies jumping on the bed. He lay on his left side and Little Bit came up to the top of the blanket and burrowed down next to him, and Brad put his right arm over her. She snuggled her head back against his chin and cuddled tightly against him. Scooter seemed content to curl up against his back. Brad sighed and thought, *Maybe they'll keep the demons away*. He also had an image flash through his mind; Mia's fingers had no rings on them.

The next morning Brad awakened from the most restful sleep he had had in some time.

CHAPTER 93
Jackpot Motel; Room 123

Wednesday, at 6:30 a.m. Heather picked up her cell phone and told Roscoe to wish her luck. On the fourth ring Jackson picked up and said, "According to Caller ID this is your cell, Heather. Where the hell are you?"

Heather knew that in order to be successful she had to keep from showing her hand, she had to let Jackson be Jackson, and so she just responded, "Jackson, I need to talk to you and maybe even see you later today. I've got to go now but I'll call you back at ten a.m. Bye."

She quickly hung up as Jackson recovered from her message and hollered into a non-responding handset, "Bitch! I asked where the hell are you and ... Bitch! I can't believe that you just hung up on me!"

"Are you sure that was enough?" Roscoe asked.

"I know Jackson," said Heather. "He'll be waiting by that phone at ten, trust me."

***

At precisely ten, Heather called back. "Heather, damn it, don't you dare hang up on me again! Now, where are you, and where the hell have you been?"

Heather felt old patterns of fear and submissiveness but she took a deep breath and responded, "Jackson, let me talk a minute and I might tell you what you want to know. Now I'm sorry I left, but I was upset after you hit me and I needed to just get away and think for awhile."

"Think?" Jackson interrupted. "Heather, what are you talking about? I've hit you harder than that before and you didn't leave. Besides, you were laughing at me. And it all happened because of your damned chickens. Now, when are you coming home?"

Heather felt the conversation was going pretty much the way she had thought it would and she was starting to feel good about her plan. She knew the need to control her rendered Jackson as helpless as Roscoe eating a plate of home-cooked pork chops while she had her hand over his groin promising dessert. So she replied, "Jackson, I'm not sure if I want to come home. I mean, I ... I'm thinking I'd like to talk with you first ... in person ... if you promise not to hit me."

As he thought, *I'm going to slap the shit out of you as soon as I see you,* Jackson replied, "Okay, no hits. Now, where the hell are you?"

"Promise me?" Heather asked.

"Yes, damn it. Now, where are you?"

Heather smiled at Roscoe as she said, "Jackpot Motel; Room 123."

***

A few minutes later Roscoe shifted position behind the door as he heard what he assumed was Jackson's RAM truck park outside. If things went as Heather calculated, and Roscoe was feeling like they would, Jackson would be theirs in about a minute. He shifted again, winked and nodded at Heather, and tightened his grip on the gun. There was the sound of a vehicle door closing and in a few seconds, a knock on the door. Heather opened the door a crack and then quickly stepped back into the room as Jackson pushed through the door and hollered, "Where in the hell have you been, Bitch?"

The look on his face shifted from anger to surprise as Roscoe grabbed Jackson's hair and jerked his head back hard against the gun barrel. Heather quickly closed the door as Roscoe said, "Freeze, dumb ass, and don't try anything stupid. I've got a gun, it's loaded, and I won't hesitate to use it."

"What do you want from me?" Jackson growled, still half dazed from his head being slammed against the barrel of the Kel-Tec P-11.

Roscoe told him he'd find out soon enough as Heather smiled and asked, "Did you miss me, Jackson?" As he looked at her, Jackson flashed back to something that had been a turning point in his behaviors toward others. He'd always been a little larger than most other boys his age, and gained a bit of a reputation as a bully.

In the seventh grade, he found it easy to pick on Bruce Prentice. Bruce looked effeminate, but damned if the girls didn't hang around with him.

One day Jackson pushed him hard in front of about five or six girls. As Bruce fell backwards, Jackson said, "Hey, Wimpo, maybe you'd better get some of your girlfriends to protect you."

The next day on his way home from school, Jackson was laughing to himself because Bruce had been absent. *Probably afraid of what was going to happen next*, he thought. He stopped short when Bruce stepped out from an alley, and stood in front of him, wielding about a three foot length of pipe. Jackson felt panic quickly rising.

"I couldn't make it to school today, because I had to look for just the right weapon," Bruce said. "Did you miss me, Jackson?"

He was able to fight off some of the blows, but still Jackson took a pretty good beating. He had decided right then and there he would not pick on anybody unless he was sure he had all his bases covered.

Now he was thinking that, as with Bruce, he must have overlooked something.

"Where the hell have you been, Bitch?" Jackson again hollered at Heather, and then immediately cried out in pain as Roscoe smacked his head with the gun barrel, lowered it, and then jabbed him hard in the kidneys.

"Shut up!" Roscoe said. "And you'd better start talking nicer to the lady if you know what's good for you. Heather? Ready?"

"Ready for what?" Jackson asked, apprehensively, "and who are you?"

"Don't worry about who I am," Roscoe said, "although you might remember me from Shoney's a few days ago. I saw you in the lobby. Doesn't mean anything though." Roscoe told Jackson to shut up, lean against the wall, spread his legs, and put his hands behind his back as he jabbed him hard with the gun again.

Jackson did as he was told, and Heather stepped behind him. As he felt her starting to put on handcuffs, he rolled to his left and tried to grab her. Roscoe jammed the gun hard against Jackson's neck, right below his chin. Jackson groaned in pain and fear.

"Son of a bitch," Roscoe snarled, "I said don't try anything! Now the lady's gonna cuff you, or I blow your brains out! Your choice!"

As he felt the cuffs click into place, for the first time he could re-member since Bruce, Jackson felt panic. "What are you going to do?"

Heather smiled at the obvious fear in his voice. There was going to be sweetness in this, just like she'd been playing through her mind ever since she'd decided to kill her husband. It was a little surprising to her he hadn't put up more of a fight, and then she realized he was the kind of guy who was macho only in situations where his com-petition was weaker. She had suspected this but had never had the opportunity to really observe it until now.

"We'll tell you in a minute. In the meantime, hold tight. Oh, and forgive my lack of social graces. Jackson, this is Roscoe, my new friend. And by the way, he's right, we did see you at Shoney's a few nights ago, but decided it just wasn't the proper time or place to talk."

*That's an understatemen*t, Roscoe thought.

Heather told Roscoe that since Jackson was cuffed, she was ready to tape his mouth so they could move him to the car. Before they started, Roscoe showed Jackson that the gun was loaded and told him to behave accordingly. Heather got two of Roscoe's hand-kerchiefs she had taken from the dirty linen basket and stuffed them into Jackson's mouth. He struggled slightly, but kept his eyes glued to the gun in Roscoe's hand. Then, Heather duct-taped a few times around Jackson's head, covering his mouth, but leaving his nostrils clear for breathing.

"There," she said, smiling as she reached into a bag and got out the Halloween mask Roscoe had bought the day before and put it over Jackson's head. She undid the top three buttons of his shirt, smoothed the bottom of the mask, and then re-buttoned the shirt. *All in all,* she thought, *Roscoe did a real good job of picking out the mask; it's a very realistic looking older man.* Then she un-cuffed Jackson's hands from behind him and re-cuffed them to the front. "If I'd have been thinking, I'd have done it this way to start with," she said. "But, Jackson, I was just so excited at seeing you again, under control of course, I guess I just couldn't help myself." She laughed.

Then Roscoe jabbed Jackson a couple more times with the P-11 and told him he had best realize that if he made any false moves while they were moving him to the back seat of the Camry he would not live to tell about it. Roscoe asked Jackson if he understood, and Jackson nodded "Yes".

After they got everything into a carry bag, Roscoe told Jackson, "Heather is going to put the bag into the trunk, open the back passenger's side door, and then you and I are going to walk out to the car without incident. Again, do you understand me?"

Jackson thought he'd better play along for the time being as he really did not want to chance that the maniac holding the gun might actually fire it. And even if this Roscoe didn't shoot; Jackson was not feeling up to any more blows to the kidneys. He figured Heather was just out to give him a good scare in hopes he would let her walk away with, apparently, her new boyfriend. And at this stage of the game, Jackson was thinking that might be a good option.

Before going to the car Heather draped a shirt over the cuffs to hide them and told Jackson to hold it so it would look like he was carrying it.

CHAPTER 94
Chloroforming Jackson

After leaving the motel and getting onto the highway, Roscoe spoke. "Jackson," he said, "Get on the floor and just lie there quietly. Now we are going to pull off a side road in just a few minutes, and then we will let you get a little more comfortable and tell you what we want to see happen in the future. You see," he continued, "Heather is much too nice a lady here to be hit around."

Jackson made a low growl through the mask, duct tape, and dirty handkerchiefs. He thought that if Roscoe was telling the truth then there would be either the opportunity to fight back, or maybe even listen to what they had to say and decide if he really even wanted to hassle with Heather anymore. So he fell sideways over onto the seat and tried to get comfortable.

"Oh, no, no, no," Roscoe exclaimed. "I said onto the floor. Now I don't know what part of that you didn't understand, but if you want me to stop and explain it with the barrel of the gun again, I can." Jackson still felt stinging in the kidney area, and so he quickly rolled off the seat onto the floor. He groaned as he landed uncomfortably on the middle hump.

Heather leaned back over the seat and said, "Hey, Jackson, did you hear what he just said about me being too nice to be hit around? You see, here's a man who cares about how I feel. Sorry you had to be so slow in your learning process." Jackson struggled to no avail and tried to say something. Heather just laughed and continued. "Sorry, I'd try and figure out what you're attempting to say, but I need to help Roscoe keep his concentration on the task at hand. And, actually, I think I need to slide my hand over his crotch to help him do that."

Roscoe grinned as Heather talked to him, making sure that Jackson overheard everything. "You know, Roscoe," she said, "I believe once I am a free woman I can let myself go with you like I never have before." Roscoe thought that sounded like an experience he definitely wanted to partake in, but he also worked hard at focusing on the task at hand, mainly, keeping on his side of the road in order to avoid any head-on collisions.

Jackson lay on the floor and silently cursed both what Heather was saying and the center floor hump uncomfortably distorting his body. He thought of all the times in the past he had hit Heather. He had felt a little bad about it occasionally but had certainly never imagined she was up to reaching for this level of revenge. *Perhaps*, he thought, *maybe I should have brought her some flowers sporadically to make up for hitting her.*

Jackson was feeling anxious, but, also beginning to settle his thoughts, and he figured Heather had probably been seeing this Roscoe guy for some time, and they were just going to put a scare into him. It was working to a degree, and Jackson knew he might have to consider letting Heather go. He knew he could find someone else, and he sure didn't want to have Heather surprising him again.

About ten minutes later Roscoe pulled onto a gravel road to the right that went up into a wooded area where they were out of sight of the main road. He was very familiar with the area as he had conducted business deals there more than a few times. More often than not, it had been one of the occasions where he had been letting a female score drugs for the half-price special. There was a place where the road widened with grassy areas to either side and Roscoe swung the car around to face the direction they had just come in. He opened his door and got out, opened the trunk and lifted out a carry bag. Then he went around to Jackson's door and told him he would help him out of the car. Wondering what was coming next, Jackson decided to comply, and a few moments later, with Roscoe and Heather's help, he was standing upright.

Heather reached into the bag for a roll of duct tape, stood behind Jackson, reached both her arms to the front, and started to wrap the tape around him. "Oh, while I'm doing this, Jackson, Sweetie, you could remember things like the time I was lying unconscious on the living room floor while you drank a beer and watched your Monday Night Football, okay?"

Jackson jerked in anger as he realized he was not being made more comfortable, but a hit to the side of the head with the gun barrel stunned him back into submission. Heather completed seven thicknesses of duct tape around Jackson's body which held his front-cuffed hands and arms tightly in place. She then told Jackson to sit sideways in the front seat of the car, while keeping his legs out on the ground. He hesitated, so Roscoe jabbed him again, and then he followed directions.

Heather went to where Jackson was sitting and pulled the Halloween mask off his head. Then she taped his ankles together. "Hope I'm not bothering you too much, Jackson," she said. "And by the way, you don't need to answer if you don't feel like it." She reached up and tapped the duct tap covering his mouth.

"He really is a quiet kind of guy, isn't he?" asked Roscoe.

"With a little help from Mr. Duct Tape, yeah," said Heather. "Though, quite frankly, I believe this is the first time that I've known him to be this way. I kind of like it."

Roscoe realized he was actually starting to enjoy the situation. "Really," he said. "First time you have ever known him to be this quiet? Too bad for him he didn't practice it earlier. By the way, Jackson, I think you are a stupid son-of-a-bitch, mistreating the lady and all. I've been treating her right, and you know what? She's been real nice to me. I mean reeaal nice, if you catch my drift."

Roscoe took Heather's hand and said, "Show him where, Baby." As Heather put her hand over Roscoe's crotch, Jackson struggled and tried to say something, but stopped as the gun once more was wedged tightly against his chin.

"Yeah," said Roscoe, "too bad you didn't know how to treat her. I mean, Jackson, the way she responds to me, well, sometimes, she just blows me away she's so nice; just blows me away. Know what I mean?"

Heather decided to add a couple more thicknesses of tape to Jackson's ankles and then Roscoe directed him to get out of the car and hop to the back door. Jackson followed directions, and lay back down on the floor. Roscoe gave thumbs up to Heather and then she turned to talk through the seats to Jackson. "You know, Darling," she began. "I'm thinking … " And she had been, too. Heather had thought quite a bit about what she was getting ready to say. "I'm thinking you're probably quite upset because I have been committing adultery with Roscoe, but look at it this way. You see, Jackson, I'm thinking I could go to a Super Bowl, screw all the players and half of their coaches, and still be 4th and twenty-five down to you." She continued, her voice rising with anger. "And, come on, Jackson. I was reading the paper the other day and ran across the police blotter report about your little visit to the Hedgehog Brook area. For all you knew at the time, I could have been dead somewhere and all you had on your mind was fucking. You're sick, Jackson, and you're going to die. I want you think about that."

Roscoe shook his head as he added, "You see, Jackson, this is just further evidence of what a nice lady we have here. She's giving you the opportunity to repent before you go. A lot of people wouldn't be that good to you."

There were sounds of Jackson trying to say something from the floor of the backseat. Heather said, "You know, Roscoe, you should have been a preacher. I think we have a man trying to ask forgiveness back here. It's too bad he waited so long." Then she added, "Oh, and by the way, Jackson, when I got two of Roscoe's handkerchiefs out of the dirty clothes hamper, I tried to avoid ones that were too messy. Now wasn't that nice of me?" She laughed as Jackson dry-retched against the duct tape.

Roscoe wasn't aware Heather had done that, and his throat constricted a little as he swallowed hard.

Before they took off, Roscoe took a bottle of chloroform from the bag, poured some into a handkerchief, and then held it over Jackson's nose until he blacked out. They had decided it would be best to have him out of it while they traveled, and regarding any odor, they would put windows partway down. Roscoe climbed back into the driver's seat, turned the ignition, and started driving back down toward the main road.

CHAPTER 95
DUI Apprehension

About 10:30 a.m. Todd was parked in a graveled turn-off, thinking about the previous night's conversation with Julie. About that time a car weaved past him. He sighed as he turned on his lights and siren, and pulled out behind it.

The driver of the erratically moving vehicle pulled off to the side. Todd called in to Headquarters, and then got out of his cruiser. He saw the driver of the vehicle reaching for something and so he instinctively put his hand on his holster and walked toward the stopped vehicle.

"Whoa, Officer," said the driver. "You can take your hand away from your gun. I ain't dangerous, and I ain't gonna try to give you a hard time. I was gonna try an' hide this bottle, but then figured, 'What the hell, why bother?' You caught me dead to rights after a coupla beers."

"So you're admitting you've been drinking?"

The driver pursed his lips sideways and, with a slight slur in his voice, said, "Ain't no sense denying it. You got me."

"Well," Todd started "I appreciate your honesty, but I'll warn you right now, when you're drinking and driving, you are dangerous. Furthermore, I don't want to hear your shit about 'you just had a couple beers'. Now, how many have you had to drink?"

"Well, Sir," the driver hesitated, and then answered. "I'm thinking about what you just said, and it's like this; I may have had one, and I may have had three or more, but I damn sure know I didn't have two."

Todd bit his tongue to conceal a smile as he told the driver to get out of the car. There was another trooper in the area that arrived as Todd was having the man try and walk a straight line. He said he was headed back to Frankenberry, so he asked if Todd wanted him to transport the driver back to jail. Todd thanked his coworker and completed the on-site paperwork associated with the arrest. After his colleague left with the man apprehended for DUI, Todd decided it was time to move on to his next point he'd selected to monitor traffic from for awhile, so he headed toward the northeast sector of the county, in the direction of County Road Bricken. He chuckled as he thought of Phillip's incident with the cat the day before.

***

As he walked into the 58th headquarters Julie said, "Hey, Phillip, Tell me about the cat in the hat. I mean, I've heard some versions of the story from others, but I'd like to hear about that pussy straight from the Tomcat's mouth, so to speak."

Phillip laughed, but also couldn't help reddening a little. "Well," he started. "I don't think it beats Todd's incident with the John Deere lawnmower, but it may come in a close second. These two once-married neighbors apparently have not gotten along as far back as folks in that area can remember. So the guy noticed his recently acquired kitten wasn't around and then he heard her squalling and carrying on from a tree in his ex's yard. He went over the fence, and climbed up to get her. Next thing he knew, his ex was waving a pistol, hollering at him about trespassing, and then she set the tree on fire. She piled boards around it, teepee fashion, and doused with kerosene. It was singed to about fifteen feet. If the guy in the tree hadn't had his cell in his pocket, he actually could have been killed."

"Isn't it crazy," Julie said, "every time we think we've seen it all, someone comes along with a new one?"

CHAPTER 96

Lost in the Sixties Tonight

Brad thought sometimes that one incident from his time in Vietnam summed up how the world was managed by whatever powers might be in the great vast yonder.

Delta made a combat assault into an area which turned out to be hot.

"Get your men into the tree lines and get into position!" the LT yelled.

Third platoon was part of the first sortie, and by the time the whole company was on the ground, the enemy had either left the area, or was quietly observing from a distance. Fortunately, despite the hostile gunfire, there were no casualties. After a brief consultation with the LTs the CO ordered the company to move out. Delta humped about 500 meters when a halt was called, and the CO called for the LTs to come to his location. Third platoon leader gave the gist of the conversation later.

"Have any of you noticed anything funny so far about the terrain we are in and where we are supposed to be on the map?"

"Well, since second is point platoon and I'm the one who radioed back, you know I have."

"And what's different?"

"Jungle's supposed to be a lot denser, and the terrain have more change in elevation."

"Exactly," the CO responded. "I just called back to Battalion and it seems there was a slight fuck-up; we made a combat assault into the wrong landing zone. I say we did, but the fact is the chopper pilots dropped us off where they were told, and it turns out that some fuck-nut at Brigade made a mistake. The problem is, he's not sure what the error was, so we don't even know where the fuck we are, or what the fuck we're doing!"

"So what's next?" the LT said he asked.

"Brigade said we have a change of mission. We're to hump a couple thousand meters more north, and then look for a place to dig in."

"So what's our mission?"

"Said they'd let us know in the morning."

Seems like the morning that establishes my mission is still over the horizon, Brad thought. I mean I've done a lot of woodcarvings, but I think my mission in the medic area fell rather short of the mark. Of course now I have Scooter and Little Bit to care for, and I'm thinking that along with the regular food I been feeding them, they'd also like it if the next time I was in town I picked them up some treats. I'll try those Temptations, see how they like them.

CHAPTER 97
Need an Ambulance Right Away!

Wednesday, sometime around 11:30 a.m. Todd turned on his lights and siren and called in that he had just pulled out after a Toyota Camry he had just clocked at sixty-eight in the fifty-five zone. Roscoe sped up, and Todd did likewise. He closed in on the vehicle, when suddenly Roscoe braked hard and started to pull off to the side of the road. Heather screamed, "What the hell are you doing, Roscoe?"

Roscoe hollered back, "We're in a rural area and I'm planning a getaway, okay! Things have changed since this asshole behind us entered into the picture!" He pointed at the gun on the console.

Heather panicked. She had her mind set on killing Jackson, but they weren't supposed to get caught. Killing a cop, State Trooper, no less, was a whole different ballgame. "Roscoe! No!" she screamed. Roscoe told her to shut up, that they had no other choice. Heather crossed her left arm across her stomach resting her right elbow in the hand, and her head leaned forward into the palm of her right hand as she sat there softly muttering, "Oh, damn. Damn, damn, damn!"

When Roscoe suddenly braked and swerved to the side of the road, Todd reacted quickly enough that he avoided hitting the Camry as he pulled right behind it, but he was angry. Then for no reason whatsoever, he rolled down his window, and without calling for back-up, angrily got out of his cruiser and walked quickly toward the driver's side of the stopped vehicle. As Todd approached the car, he thought to himself that it looked familiar.

Roscoe slowly went into action. He kept his right elbow locked tight at his waistline so that he could slowly reach over and grasp a hold of the pistol. Then, without moving the upper half of his right arm, he clicked the safety off as he moved the gun over his lap and in front of his stomach, and then with his left index finger, pushed the window button forward to further lower it. As he came alongside of the Camry, Todd remembered it was the Camry he had watched pull out of the McDonald's lot the day before as he simultaneously glanced through the rear side window and saw Jackson lying bound on the floor. Roscoe looked out his window and saw Todd's hand starting down to his holster. Roscoe quickly raised his barrel and pulled the trigger. Todd felt a burning sensation in his left side and noise pounding his ears as he fell backwards. Roscoe floored the Camry and spun black marks as he took off and Todd surrealistically watched the car disappear out of sight before blacking out.

Brad had to swerve to miss the Toyota Camry speeding down the middle of the road in the direction he had just come from. *Dumbass son-of-a-bitch,* he thought. *What's his problem? And where the hell is a cop when you need him?*

As he rounded a curve he saw the flashing lights on Todd's cruiser, and then a crumpled body a few yards from the car. As he drew up to the scene of a State Trooper lying in the road he quickly assessed the situation, pulled off to the side, and kicked into medic mode, thinking, *God, if you're up there, and even give a damn, it would be nice if I didn't lose one this time.*

From where the blood was oozing through Todd's shirt, it looked like maybe the bullet had missed the heart. He had grabbed a hunting knife and first aid kit from his truck, so he quickly cut the shirt to expose the wound. Looks like this might be a keeper he told himself; I've got to stop this flow. Since there was no way of knowing if there was a spinal injury or internal bleeding, he didn't try to move Todd and proceeded to press a piece of gauze against the wound with the palm of his hand.

Brad heard the sound of the radio and immediately decided to stop treating the wound so there could be help on the way. He ran to the cruiser and heard a woman's voice calling, "Todd! Todd! If you can hear me, please answer! Over."

He reached through the open window, got ahold of the radio and said, "This is Bradley Miller. I just came upon an officer lying in the road who had been shot! I'm a former Army medic so I'm treating him, but I need an ambulance right away! I'm about a mile north of the Highway 473 Triple Creek intersection near County Road Bricken. Out toward the Swisher Glen Forest Preserve. Over."

Julie felt her chest tighten as she replied, "We'll get help out there right away! Where is he hit? What happened? Over."

"I don't know what happened, Ma'am. I just came upon the scene a moment ago, although I passed a car speeding away just before I got here. Now get help out here stat! I need to go back and stop the blood flow! He's hit in the chest, but I think the bullet missed the heart. Over."

"Okay. Tell him to hold on; that Julie is on her way too! Over."

Brad ran back to where Todd was and started to press against the wound again. *Former Army medic*, he thought. *If they knew my record they would have that ambulance out here five minutes ago.*

A thought flashed through Julie's mind that there really was a God and he was working overtime to insure her life didn't have much happiness in it. She turned to Phillip in panic as she cried out, "Todd's been shot. He's about a mile north of the Triple Creek intersection on 473. Let's go!" Phillip and Julie raced for his car, Phillip turned on the lights and siren, and they sped off. He told her they were going to the same area where he'd had the cat in the tree incident.

***

Brad heard yelling, looked up, and wondered if he was hallucinating as he watched a red-bearded man running toward him chasing what appeared to be a Siamese kitten.

"Prissy!" Ralph Henderson called out, "Come back here!" The Siamese kitten stopped alongside of the cruiser and Ralph picked it up. "Prissy," he scolded, "you shouldn't have run away again, but maybe you did a good thing this time." He stopped at Brad and said, "I was further down the road chasing my Prissy through a field and I saw what happened, Sir. When the car went past I got the license plate number. I hope it helps you. And, by the way, have you called an ambulance, yet?"

Brad told Ralph help was on the way, and then asked him if he would stay there to watch for any traffic as he didn't want to risk moving the Trooper from where he was lying. "Plus, you can give them the tag number of the Camry when they get here."

CHAPTER 98
We've Got to Change the Schedule

As Roscoe flew down the road Heather hollered, "Dammit, Roscoe! This wasn't part of the plan!"

"I know that!" Roscoe yelled back, "But it happened and now we've got to change the schedule. Take different routes." He thought quickly and then said "Look, I know this area. We'll take a right on County Road Bricken to Kneeland Road east, and then cut through Medina County to Armstrong. We'll go to my mother's place, get your Mustang and leave the Camry in the barn. We'll spend the night and tomorrow circle back around to Swisher Glen, same spot, same plan."

Heather was aware she was in the middle of much, much more than she had bargained for a few days earlier when she had decided to embark on an adventure and parked her Mustang behind the Infiniti Roscoe had appropriated. She also knew the shooting of a State Trooper meant high priority allocation of law enforcement resources. She was near tears as she asked Roscoe, "Roscoe, how do we get out of this?"

"What I just said," Roscoe replied. "We have to follow through with killing Jackson now, for sure. If he were to be set free and figured any of this out, he would be twice as dangerous to us." Heather agreed, and decided that Roscoe seemed to be exhibiting two things important to the immediate circumstances; quick thinking, and also concern for her situation, so she just patted Roscoe's leg, leaned back, and decided to leave the driving to him.

In about a quarter mile Roscoe turned right onto the smaller County Road Bricken lined with a variety of deciduous and coniferous trees. Then a few miles later he turned left on Kneeland Road and told Heather they very well might be able to make it to his mother's before there was a widespread search underway by using the side road they had just turned onto. "With a little luck," he said, as he started to feel a bit more relaxed, "someone stole an Infiniti and has a couple officers in hot pursuit. Hell, I wouldn't even care right now if I had another shipment being intercepted. Anything to keep these guys occupied in other activities." Heather said she hoped he was right and then questioned about the next steps after killing Jackson. Roscoe said there was a chance their plate or car description was already being sent out on an APB. Heather asked how that could be since the only car they had seen was going the other direction.

"You never know," Roscoe replied. "No guarantee I killed the cop. He might have seen the plate as we drove off."

"He was shot at point blank range," Heather said. "I really don't think he could have survived."

"Well I pray you're right; we'll just have to hope for the best." They talked some more and decided that after Jackson was eliminated then Heather would go to the bank to make a large withdrawal as earlier planned. Roscoe said they could work on the details of what to do after that, later, when they were at his mother's place.

They rounded a curve in the road and could see partway down the stretch a truck stopped behind a few cars for a red-light where bridge work had closed the road to a single lane.

"Damn it," said Roscoe. "They picked a fine time to do this! Well it probably won't be more than a couple minutes hold-up and it doesn't look like any of the vehicles waiting in the line have anything to do with law enforcement."

"But what if they've put it out over the radio?" Heather asked.

"Just take it easy. We've got to keep cool so as to think quickly if necessary."

He pulled up behind the large flatbed Utility International truck and stopped. The mud flaps hanging down had a blue world on it, with a white line encircling it and a few white lines indicating latitude and longitude. The word UTILITY was curved across the Earth in red letters.

"Pretty mud flaps," Roscoe said.

"How can you be thinking about mud flaps at a time like this?" Heather was agitated and couldn't believe Roscoe seemed almost unconcerned. But Roscoe was concerned; concerned Heather would panic and draw attention to them and so he told her they really needed to appear as relaxed as any two people out for a drive in the country.

"I would tell you to just look like we are a married couple out for a drive," he said, "but we don't want to draw attention to ourselves over some on-going argument."

Heather smiled weakly. She knew Roscoe was right, and glad he was keeping his cool and trying to help her keep hers. "I'm really trying to look normal."

"That's fine with me because your normal look is hot."

About that time the light turned green and traffic started to move. The cars soon were out of sight and in about four miles there was an intersection where the truck turned left and another mile later they passed the sign for Medina County.

"We'll only be in Medina for about ten miles," said Roscoe, "and then we'll be into Armstrong. Looks like we're going to be okay."

Heather started to feel calmer and leaned back against the seat, took a deep breathe and closed her eyes. About fifteen minutes later she heard Jackson stir and try to move around as the chloroform began to wear off. Heather sat up. "Roscoe, do you think we should administer another dose?"

"No. If we let the chloroform wear off he can move around a little, which will make it easier when we switched him to the Mustang."

CHAPTER 99
Will You Forgive Me?

"Phillip, I'm so scared," Julie said, tears flowing down her cheeks. "Todd and I just recently started going together, and already I know I'm head over heels in love with him. I can't lose him, Phillip, I just can't!" She put her head in her hands and broke down crying. She wondered if she was experiencing some of what Todd seemed to have gained from his combat days; the awareness there were situations you found yourself in where you could just cut to the chase and see priorities clearly.

"He'll be all right," said Phillip. "He's got to be." Then he added, "You know, we never know when we stop someone what it may involve; life on the line every day. God, I hope Todd's okay. Did the guy you talked to say what happened?"

"All I know is he said he was Bradley Miller and that he came upon an officer lying in the road who'd been shot in the chest. He said he was a former Army medic so that's good. Then he told where he was and said he had to go back and stop the blood flow. And, oh yeah, he said there was a car speeding away just before he got there. "

"Brad Miller; older guy, Vietnam veteran I believe, that lives out in the boonies near the Swisher Glen Forest Preserve. Actually Deanna and I saw him in the Roasted Bread and Gravy the other night. He's kind of a loner from what I understand. But at least he's a former medic; that should mean he's in good hands, especially a combat medic. Listen, try to call the cruiser again and see if anyone answers; see if you can find out anything more."

Julie, barely controlling her fears, took the handset asking, "Is anyone there?"

She gave a sigh of relief after a moment when someone answered and said he was Ralph Henderson. "Ralph Henderson," Phillip said. "Are you the man with the Siamese kitten?"

"I am, Sir."

"Well," Phillip said, "How's Prissy? And do you know anything about what happened?"

"Well, the kitten had got away from me again and was running through a field toward the road and I was chasing her when I had heard a siren. I was watching from the tree line. I heard a gunshot and saw the officer fall backwards onto the road and then the driver took off flying. I always have my binoculars with me, so I tried to see the plate; I think it was Kentucky, BAZ 111. Prissy stopped running when the gun was fired, so I managed to get her and calm her down, and then I saw this pickup stop and someone immediately started working on treating the police officer, so I came over."

"Thanks for the info," Phillip said, "We'll talk more when I get there."

"Hurry, there's a lot of blood!"

"On our way!"

Julie paled when Ralph said there was a lot of blood, but she called the plate information in. Ralph had gotten it right. The car is registered to Roscoe Knowles of Frankenberry. "Roscoe," Phillip said, "I heard that name the other day when I arrested Charlie Cameron. He was angry at his wife and said they were going to miss their drop for Roscoe. Then we discovered well over half a million dollars worth of crack under several Teddy Bears, no less. I wonder if we're talking about the same man."

"Bet we are," Julie said. "That name popped up in conversation recently. I believe he's under observation for suspicion of drug-trafficking."

For the next minute or so, they rode in silence. Julie didn't really want to talk with Phillip about apologies right then, not because she wanted to avoid the topic, but because she really was shaken by Todd being shot, which seemed to be a much higher priority at the moment. But she also wanted to clear the air with Phillip, and so she started, "Phillip, Todd and I have done a lot of talking the past few days, and one thing to come out of it, is I am very aware I owe you an apology. I have been so insensitive at times, particularly to you, and much of it came from my own insecurities and fears. The wall I built to protect myself was held together by a smart-ass exterior, a cover-up, so I wouldn't have to deal with people anywhere but at a superficial level."

"Hey, it's all good, Julie," Phillip replied, wondering if he was really with her, or if perhaps a softer, cloned version had somehow slipped into the cruiser. "We all have our areas."

"True," said Julie, "but I still was in the wrong with you. Phillip?" A couple of tears again found their way down her cheeks. "Will you forgive me?"

"Gladly," said Phillip, feeling a bit choked up himself as he repeated, "Gladly."

Julie reached over and touched his hand and replied, "Thanks."

CHAPTER 100
Looks like You Kept This One Alive

Delta Company was almost dug in for the night when there was the sound of something crashing through the underbrush toward the perimeter. All were immediately tensed up on high alert.

"Doesn't sound human. Don't shoot! We've got OP's to the front! The squad leader hollered.

"Fucking deer or something!" One of the OP's radioed in.

About that time a deer-looking creature came running out of the undergrowth and jumped over a foxhole. Walter, who was in the foxhole let out a yell, "Son of a bitch! Son of a bitch! Medic!"

"What happened?" Brad called as he rushed to him.

"That's what I'd like to know!" Walter cried out in pain as blood flowed from a gash on his upper arm where a hoof had caught him. "What the hell was that?"

"Looked like a deer," Brad said as he cleaned the wound and wrapped a bandage around Walter's arm. "Although when God made that critter he must have been thinking like Picasso."

"What do you mean by that?" Walter asked. "I didn't really see what hit me although I could tell it was a good-size critter."

"Its head had white splotches looked like they'd been randomly daubed on with a paint brush. Here, you're fixed up. I'll get you some aspirin, and we'll keep an eye on it. I'll tell the CO you need to go to the rear for a tetanus shot next log bird."

About that time Rollo came over. "I guess congratulations are in order, Bad Medic. Looks like you kept this one alive."

"Hey Rollo," Walter said. "Why don't you go crawl back into your fucking hole?"

Brad smiled at life's ironies. A couple weeks later during a firefight, Rollo had taken a bullet in the fleshy part of his arm, just nicking the muscle.

Rollo whimpered while Brad patched him up, never saying any-thing.

Brad smiled again. He later heard that after being treated in the rear, Rollo volunteered for shit-burning detail at Quan Loi.

CHAPTER 101
Never Been Better

Phillip and Julie arrived at the scene soon after the ambulance. EMT's were already getting Todd onto a stretcher. One introduced himself as Cory and said Todd had just regained consciousness. Julie went to him and an EMT asked her to stand back a little so they could get him loaded. Todd opened his eyes wider and said, "Please, let her come to me. I need to tell her what happened so they can start looking for this guy."

Julie kissed Todd on the forehead as she asked, "What do you remember?"

"I was pursuing a guy for speeding; he braked and then pulled off to the side of the road. I barely missed slamming into him; pulled in behind the car. Just before I was shot I caught a glimpse of a man lying on the backseat floor, looked like he was bound with duct tape. So at least we know the shooting was for a good reason," Todd attempted a laugh.

"Don't joke that way," Julie said.

Todd continued, "Well, it was. Obviously there is a kidnapping or something going on, and he had to chance getting away after he screwed up by speeding. He knew otherwise he'd be facing a long jail term."

Julie shook her head. "That still doesn't justify him shooting you."

Todd laughed. "I just said 'good reason'. I didn't say it was justified. It sure doesn't feel justified. And it wasn't because it was me. He'd have shot Phillip here if it'd been him who stopped him."

"Well, thank you for the mention," Phillip said, smiling, and shaking his head. "That'll help me get to sleep tonight."

Julie asked how they were able to smile and joke in the middle of what had happened, and Todd closed his eyes and weakly replied, "Because we can." Julie realized all the implications of what Todd had just said, and shot up a prayer of thanks to whomever the strange

Overseer of all the ongoing events was; a prayer of thanks that Todd still could.

"You have the basics," the EMT interrupted. "We need to get him out of here. Thank goodness that medic was right on the scene. He saved his life."

A couple other troopers were on the scene as Todd was being put into the back of the ambulance. He opened his eyes again. "Two more things," he said.

"Make it quick," Cory said. "We've got to get you to the hospital."

"Phillip," Todd asked, "Do me a favor?"

"Gladly, name it."

"Contact Aaron and set up a time to walk and talk together. I figure when he hears about me being shot, it might be a difficult time period for him; I feel like we already have a good bonding underway."

"Sure," Phillip said, "but first I want to drive around the area awhile and see if I can find any clues leading to whoever shot you."

"I'd rather you contact Aaron right away; there'll be others looking for the shooter."

Phillip picked up on the urgency in Todd's voice and responded, "Of course, I'll get right on it."

"And, if you would, ask Brad if he would stop by the hospital. I want to talk with him more when I'm more comfortable."

"Will do."

"By the way," Todd told the Cory, "I want this beautiful lady here riding in the back with me."

"Done," Mike replied. "Just don't try anything too strenuous."

Todd painfully gave a little laugh. "Not this trip."

Another Trooper talked with Brad and Ralph. Ralph gave him the car description and then said that after the guy shot Todd he took off still traveling north.

Phillip told Todd he'd swing by the hospital in a bit, after he got up with Aaron. The ambulance driver got behind the wheel, and Cory climbed into the back with Todd and Julie and arranged the IV equipment for the ride.

As the ambulance pulled out with its siren on, Julie held Todd's hand and started crying. Todd squeezed her hand and said, "It's all right, Honey. I'm okay."

Julie began sobbing heavily. "No, Todd, it's not all right. During the past half hour or so, I have realized just how much I love you and need you in my life. I know we've not been seeing each other long, but I felt like my life had ended when I heard you were shot."

Todd flashed back to the sound of the gun at the same moment he saw it pointed at him. He grinned as he said, "You thought yours was ended? That makes two of us, Honey." Julie said she just couldn't stand the thought of losing him. She broke down sobbing again. Todd teared up as he said, "Julie, Honey? I agree, non-work-related, we've not been seeing each other long, but I feel such a connection." Todd couldn't quite believe the words he heard next coming from his mouth, "Julie, will you marry me?"

Julie leaned her head against his hand and wept into it. "You know I will."

Todd was no longer feeling any pain. He was only aware that he was reaching the end of one phase of his life and moving on into the next, as he asked, "How soon?" Julie was feeling likewise and asked if there might be a chaplain at the hospital. Todd laughed. "I don't know how long I'll be in there, but if it's more than a couple days, I say, get the paperwork done, and we'll call the chaplain, yes." Julie leaned over Todd and kissed him. As she sat back beside him, she started crying again.

The ambulance driver called to Cory and asked if everything was all right in the back and Todd said, "Never been better!"

Cory relayed the message in a booming voice, "Never been better!"

CHAPTER 102
Time to Reflect

Brad finished talking with the police and decided to go back home instead of to town. He had told Phillip he would stop by and see Todd in a day or so, so he figured he could take care of his errands and shopping then. And he had to reflect on what had just happened. Maybe things were changing. He knew that the only thing in life that didn't change was the fact that things always changed.

Later as he sat at his outside table he pensively looked over to the little cemetery for his mother and grandfather, plus a few critters from over the years, including his first, Peter Rabbit. Other names and events started to bubble up and tumble through his mind; his mother watching him board a plane for Vietnam, An Khe, New Year's Day 1969, Chuck, Doc Larry, Song Be, Fat Billy, SGT Quarles, Tay Ninh, SGT Cosby, LOH pilot and morphine, burning hooches, rage in Australia, Phouc Vinh, bunker complexes, a severed NVA head with a purple smoke grenade popped under it, "Not me; my sister", and a myriad other occasions. He sighed and buried his face into his hands. *How do you reflect and put in perspective*, he thought, *when you can't break free from the devils in your head.*

He jerked his head up at the feel of Little Bit's rough tongue against his ear. She backed off a bit, then came close again and started to lick his right cheek. Scooter jumped on the table, came over and started making biscuits on his chest. "I may never get rid of the demons," he said to his babies. "But I've got you two here to help me with them." Little Bit started nuzzling her head against his chin.

Brad relaxed and curled his hands over the back of each cat. "And who knows," he told them. "Someone needed a medic and it turned out well, at least it looks like it might."

CHAPTER 103
Them and Those F*%king Skunks

Both Roscoe and Heather gave sighs of relief when about an hour later they were on the gravel road leading up to Zelda's. At the house, they parked and got out of the Camry.

As they went onto the porch, Zelda came out of the house and yelled at Roscoe, "Don't you dare think for a minute you are going to involve me in the dumbass mess you have gotten yourself into!"

Roscoe's throat constricted as he asked, "What are you talking about?" His mother replied she had just seen on a local news flash that the state police were looking for a Toyota Camry registered to a Roscoe Knowles who was the main suspect in the shooting and wounding of a State Trooper.

As Roscoe's mind again switched into overdrive, Heather thought, *Damn. Somehow he survived and got the tag number.*

"Okay, Mom," Roscoe said, thinking quickly. "Tell you what. Do me one big favor and I promise I won't ask you for anything else ever again."

"Do you think I'm as stupid as I look?" Zelda angrily asked.

"No," Roscoe started, "Nothing could be that …" He caught himself. "Sorry, Momma. Now, just listen. Heather and I are going to get her car out of the barn and then she'll follow me out of here. I'll leave my car down the road somewhere. All you have to do, if the police come by, is to say that I came here alone and asked if a friend and I could stay for a few days because they were after us and you said 'No'."

"Tell them after you said that I told you my friend was waiting down the road for the answer; that I said that I was going back down to meet him and I'd probably leave my car there. When you asked who 'they' was, tell them I told you the cops, and I probably wouldn't see you for awhile as I was on the run. Tell them I left and that's all that you know. You don't know who my friend was and you don't even know what kind of car he had because he didn't come up here. If they ask you how you know my friend was a he, just say that you don't know, all you know is I said I was going back down to meet *him*."

"Roscoe," his mother said. "I want to hear this again to make sure I got it straight, and the gist of this is if I tell that story your stupid ass won't bother me again for a long time?"

"You got it right, Ma," Roscoe said.

"Then," Zelda said, "hurry up and tell it to me again so you can get the hell out of here!"

After repeating the story his mother was to use if necessary, Roscoe and Heather went over to the barn, went in, and unlocked the car door. Roscoe got into the Mustang, put the key into the ignition and the engine immediately jumped to life. He put it in gear and pulled it outside. He told Heather to drive, and then went and got in the passenger's side. "Drop me off at the Camry, and then follow me down the gravel road a ways," he told her.

Heather had started to relax some until Zelda told about the news flash. She was relieved the Trooper hadn't been killed due to all the complications that would have involved, but quite uptight over the fact that apparently with his survival he'd been able to pass on information to others leading them to conclude Roscoe was involved in the shooting.

There are too many dots out there just waiting to be connected, she thought. *Roscoe and I have to move quickly and the advantage now is Roscoe has to follow through with me; there is no way he can back out now.* So she followed Roscoe's instructions, stopped at the Camry, and then let him lead the way back down the gravel road.

At a place where they were well out of sight of his mother's place, but still not in sight of the paved highway, Roscoe pulled off to the side. Heather pulled behind him, and then he told her to open the Mustang trunk so he could transfer the tools they were going to use. Then Roscoe opened the back door of the Camry, poked Jackson and told him he was going to pull on him until he could scoot out of the car. After Jackson was upright, Roscoe poked him with the gun toward the Mustang. Roscoe had him back against the open trunk lid, and then pushed on his stomach until he fell backwards into the opening.

Jackson was trying to figure out what was going on and hoped whatever game Heather was playing would be over soon. He had blacked out from the chloroform and when he came to, ached all over. Heather and the guy she was with, Jackson couldn't remember his name, were apparently riding in silence. Then after a while the car turned on what had seemed to be a gravel road. After the car stopped, he heard the doors open and close and then some hollering, but he couldn't make out what was being said. Then the car was moving again. Now he was falling backwards into what he guessed correctly was the trunk of another car. He moaned as his head and feet were shoved in and tried to call out through the dirty handkerchiefs as the trunk was slammed shut.

Roscoe left the keys in the Camry and then he and Heather gathered what few personal items they had in it and moved them to the Mustang. Roscoe told Heather she needed to drive because there she'd be less likely to be stopped since police were looking for a male driving a Camry. He told her in the event any traffic approached he would slump his head against the window as though he were sleeping. "Or maybe even slouch down out of sight," he added.

"So where are we headed?" Heather asked. She was anxious to get the deed done with Jackson and to clear out of the State. She was in agreement with Roscoe; given all the circumstances, Jackson definitely had to be disposed of. Roscoe said at first he was thinking of directing her over very back roads to come into Swisher Glen from the south, but that the more that he thought about it, since they were in the Mustang and traveling south they would probably be just as safe taking 473 almost to Frankenberry, then side loop to the west on County Road Pellwood into Turnquist County and approach Swisher Glen traveling east. Heather asked, "Won't that be too risky?"

"I really don't think so," Roscoe answered. "I think the cops will figure their shooter will head away from, not toward, Frankenberry. And if they check out my mother's place, logic will point to heading north. Furthermore," he added, "we can come back to the fire-road we were on the other day coming in by way of a heavily wooded section of Turnquist County."

"I just want us to get rid of Jackson as soon as possible."

"I agree, but with this unplanned delay we don't want to run the risk of taking care of business with dark falling." Again Heather had to agree with him.

About that time she noticed an animal in the road and swerved slightly, but not enough to miss it. There was a slight thump followed by a putrid odor as the smell of the skunk she had just hit wafted into the car. Heather cringed, and then started laughing.

"What's so funny?"

"Well," Heather replied, "although it wasn't planned, the smell will be a pleasant reminder for Jackson of days gone by."

Jackson was trying to get reasonably comfortable in the trunk when the car swerved and he felt a slight bump as if a small animal had been run over. Then he smelled skunk and dry-retched. He had no idea what was going on and his nightmare included realizing he was sharing the cramped space with what felt like a pick and shovel. Furthermore, he was hurting from a plastic quart container of oil pressing against his back he couldn't seem to shift away from. He was nauseous from the somewhat winding road that his stomach was desperately trying to keep up with; then the swerve. And now skunk. It brought back images of Heather swinging a 2x4 and a scent bag being forced to expel its contents all over him. Jackson's mind tried to wrap itself around the events of the past few days; Heather missing, mini-skirts, phone calls, motels, guns, duct tape, dirty handkerchiefs stuffed into his mouth, and now he was being further confused by skunk smells and chicken reminders. He had always enjoyed Heather's fried chicken, but now he wished more than anything else, that when collecting animals for the ark, Noah had just overlooked the damned clucking fowls. Them and the fucking skunks.

Soon Heather told Roscoe she was getting hungry and he said they could stop at a fast food restaurant along 473 to get something. He added they should probably chloroform Jackson again before turning onto 473 to avoid the risk of him making noise and drawing attention to them. "I just wish," said Heather, "we had put him into the trunk of the Camry."

"Maybe, maybe not," Roscoe responded. "What if the trooper had been suspicious and called for back-up before searching the car?

What happened worked because we had the element of surprise." *It wouldn't have happened at all*, Heather thought, *if you hadn't been speeding.* She didn't voice her thoughts as she knew she couldn't afford to get Roscoe angry.

CHAPTER 104
Big Lovable Golumpki

Brad got out his woodcarving tools and wondered if evaluation of life accomplishments were to be in segments, or in whole. The tormenting voice of Bad Medic had stayed with him over the years, despite evidence to the contrary. But this most recent incident made him wonder if, instead of a wounded NVA soldier, there was a breakthrough lurking around the bend in the trail.

Scooter and Little Bit were at it again, engaged in a friendly wrestling match. Brad had taken to calling Little Bit his Little Demon-chaser as almost every night she invariably wound up cuddling in his arms, leaving out for nocturnal wanderings about the cabin sometime after he fell asleep. And Scooter was his Big Lovable Golumpki. His black fur looked nothing like the Polish stuffed cabbage, but Brad always felt good after making and eating the dish, and it seemed an appropriate name as he always felt good when Scooter jumped onto his lap and started rubbing his head against Brad's chin and making biscuits on his chest.

CHAPTER 105
I Wonder What's Eating Her?

Eloise Brock's funeral was at two p.m., Wednesday afternoon. As Tira approached the casket, her tears flowed incessantly. Pastor Ulysses Brock stood staring down at his deceased wife. Tira touched his arm and he turned to her. Tira was still in shock over the fact that the man who had been such a spiritual inspiration and guide to her throughout the years was in such pain caused by actions of her late husband. "I'm sorry. I'm so very, very sorry," she said.

Ulysses Brock brought his open left hand to his face, covering the lower half of it, and stood staring at Tira for a moment. "The police said that Eloise ran a stop sign. Hannah Bestwick said Eloise was text messaging her when the accident occurred. Hannah's devastated."

Tira said it wasn't Hannah's fault. Albert was the one going a hundred miles an hour. Tira added that Albert deserved to die, not Eloise, and Pastor Brock told her no one deserved to die. Tira gave a quick snort and tossed her chin as she asked, "Pastor Brock, do you know what his last words to me were?"

"I'm sorry." Ulysses Brock was obviously shaken. "Did you say last words? I thought they took Albert to the hospital, then, well, I didn't, I've been …"

"He died the same evening," Tira interrupted. She went on. "His funeral's tomorrow. I didn't want to bother you with anything because of …" Tira indicated Eloise Brock lying in the casket. "But do you know what his last words to me were?"

"Hopefully an affirmation of love for you, and God."

"Right," said Tira cynically. "Try an affirmation of love for that Delilah, his girlfriend."

Janice Taylor, a widow, and President of the Women's Auxiliary Group at the church was standing next to them. "Well," she said, "at least he made an affirmation of love for someone."

Tira glared at Janice, turned, and walked out, thinking she might be able to forgive Albert if it had been Janice Taylor he'd slammed into.

Janice turned to Ulysses Brock and said, "Poor Tira. I wonder what's eating her."

CHAPTER 106
The Coyote Trail

Phillip got up with Aaron Patterson at the Brakes and Buggies Service Center and filled him in on the details of what had happened to Todd. "And, Todd's concerned his getting shot might create extra stress for you that might make it more difficult as far as resisting urges to drink. I'm wondering if you want to go for a hike." Aaron said he would like to. Phillip looked up at the late afternoon sun. "It's about a half hour to the Coyote Trail in the Swisher Glen Forest Preserve, and walking at a reasonable pace, we can complete the Coyote lower loop in a couple hours, and be back with time to spare before dark." After Aaron got into the cruiser, Phillip stopped back at headquarters and quickly changed into a pair of jeans and a T-shirt. Pulling onto the highway, he headed in the direction of the Swisher Glen Forest Preserve and the Coyote Trail.

Sometime later they finished the Coyote loop and were back at the car. They'd had a good talk together, and Phillip felt Todd was right on target sensing Aaron was at an optimum moment for assistance. But Phillip's thoughts were also on his own inner struggles. *This was a good hike*, he thought. *Something I need to do more often. I guess perseverance is the key. And I guess,* Phillip grinned inwardly, and then it spilled out onto his face, *I guess I have just become too proud and dumb to quit. I've got to keep searching through the darkness for the keys. So, back off darkness, look out odds, I'm going to find my place to fit in this universe.*

Aaron looked at him and said, "It looks like you're feeling really good."

"I am," Phillip replied. "I think Todd's going to be okay, so I really am." They got back into Phillip's car and headed in the direction of Frankenberry.

CHAPTER 107
One Hell of a Medic

Little Bit crawled into his lap, and looked up at him. "Baby Girl," Brad said, "you keep squinting that right eye. I may have to take you to the vet and find out what the problem is." He looked slightly up and to his right. *I wonder if Mia works today*, he thought. He was planning on going to the hospital as Todd had asked him to stop by. He wasn't overly anxious to, but since it had been requested by the officer, he thought he should comply. He knew Trooper Truitt probably wanted to thank him, but years of being a loner as he wrestled with his demons kept him on edge about relaxing too much.

He decided to call Mia and see if he could drop by with Little Bit to get the eye checked out. She told him to bring his baby girl in.

Mia was waiting on Brad as he walked into the Frankenberry Animal Hospital and Shelter with Little Bit in a carrier.

"Hi, Brad. Nice to see you again, although I wish it didn't involve a problem with Little Bit. How we doing Baby Girl?"

Mia took a look at Little Bit's eye and said, "Okay. We see this quite a bit actually. I'll let Dr. Rictenburg, our Vet know she needs some drops, they're called Tobramycin Ophthalmic Solution. Should clear her right up."

"That's a relief," Brad said. "Listen. I need to go visit someone in the hospital for a few minutes. I'm wondering if there is a chance I could leave Little Bit here and pick her up afterwards. I'll pay."

"No need to pay; we'd be glad to keep her. By the way, I read this morning's paper. Looks like you've been busy practicing a past profession."

"Aw, they didn't need to write that up."

"So you were a combat medic? Guess that experience served you well."

Brad shrugged. "Just glad it worked out okay."

"Must feel good to know you've saved a life."

A contemplative look crossed Brad's face. "Yeah," he said. "When you can."

Mia picked up on the tinge of sadness in his voice. "Listen," she said. "I get off work in a little over an hour. Want to grab a bite to eat somewhere?"

The question caught Brad off guard, and he replied, "Well, there's still the question of Little Bit. I doubt if any restaurant will let her sit with us, and I don't like the thought of just leaving her in the truck."

Mia pursed her lips sideways with a twinkle in her eyes. "Same answer as while you make your visit; we'll leave her here and you can pick her up afterwards."

Brad nodded his head. "Okay. We can do that."

A few minutes later found him entering the Frankenberry Medical Hospital. *I just hope*, he thought, as he walked toward the elevators, *Trooper Truitt is still alive. My luck, I did something wrong.* The door to 406 was open, so he hesitantly tapped on it. "Come on in," Todd called out.

"You asked for me to stop by?"

Todd and Julie greeted him warmly. "You'd better believe it," Todd said. "The doctors said you saved my life. As I was being loaded into the ambulance I thought I'd like to thank you when we could chat a bit. More so the case now; the doctors told me I most likely wouldn't have made it if you hadn't been there right away and known what to do. I owe my life to you."

"Just glad," Brad replied, "that after all these years I still remembered a couple things to do right."

"Me too. And man, if I had known a couple days ago what was going to happen, you would have been eating for free at McDonald's. Hell," Todd laughed, "I ought to look into a lifetime meal card for you."

"Just did what I could."

"You must have been one hell of a medic in Vietnam."

Brad looked down at the floor, glanced back at Todd and quietly responded, "Quite different there. More situations to have things go bad."

Todd could see Brad was uncomfortable so he said, "Well, I just want you to know we are most grateful for what you did, and if there is anything I can ever do to help, please don't hesitate to call. Julie, would you give him one of my cards?"

They visited a bit more and then Brad left to run his errands.

CHAPTER 108
Getting to Know You

When Brad got back to the shelter Mia greeted him. "Good timing. I'm just checking out. Little Bit is wandering around in our play room so she'll be fine until we get back."

"Care if I pet her a minute." He looked at Mia and grinned. "Yeah, I'm one of those guys who talks to his animals."

"Well, of course; they do understand, you know." Mia laughed. "Besides I'd question what kind of a guy you were if you didn't."

"Baby Girl," Brad said. "We're going to leave you here just a while longer, but you'll be okay. I'm not deserting you. I'll be back." Little Bit rubbed her head against his hand and then ran over to a cat tree and climbed up and rested on a platform.

"See. I told you they understand." As they were going out the door Mia said, "So, next question. Where do you want to eat?"

"I'm good anywhere. Do you have a preference?"

"Well, since you asked, there is a little diner over in Goodman Village called the Roasted Bread and Gravy. Ever been there? It's not that far."

Brad nodded. "I've been there. Nice place and good food."

"Well then, it's settled," Mia said. "If you'll allow me to be a passenger in your pickup, I'll buy dinner. I am the one who asked you out, remember."

Brad looked at her with a little smile. "Let's go then. Since I'm chauffeuring, allow me to get that door for you."

***

While waiting on the waitress to bring their meal, Mia asked Brad what had led him to becoming a combat medic. He told her about his rabbit, Peter, and then briefly mentioned the journey that wound up in Vietnam. Then he changed the topic.

"So what about you? What powers that be led you to working at the menagerie?"

Mia laughed. "Sometimes it does seem like a zoo." Then, with her mouth closed she placed her tongue between her upper incisors and her lip, leaned her elbow on the table, and rested her chin briefly on her closed fist, and then gave a pensive smile. "I guess you would have to say it started with volunteering several years ago, but after my ex-husband decided after twenty five years of marriage that a twenty five year old secretary was more to his liking, well ... I brooded for almost a year, and then told myself that I was free to do whatever I wanted. I attended Consultation Peak Community College and got my Associates Degree and then eight years ago convinced Dr. Rictenburg, that she really needed someone else there full-time."

The waitress arrive with their order and left.

Mia bobbed her head a little. "So, back to you," she said. "In between bites, of course; after Vietnam?"

Brad gave her another brief answer, highlighting the cabin and reason he could stay there and work on woodcarvings, hike, hunt, and read.

Mia placed her hand over his. "Brad, forgive me if I'm being too intrusive, especially since we scarcely know each other, but when I mentioned earlier that it must feel good to save a life, and you said 'when you can', I sensed a sadness come through your reply. Anything you can talk about?"

Brad stared at their touching hands and decided to try sharing a little bit for the first time in his life. He started with the nickname assigned, Bad Medic, before he even went out to the field. Then he gave an overview of New Year's Day, 1969.

There was a tear trickling down Mia's cheek as she squeezed his hand. "And this was in your first firefight, first week."

"Yuh."

"A lot there. I don't want to press you for any more information at this time, I know it's hard stuff, but I would like us to go out together again. Maybe for the rest of this meal we can talk about Peter Rabbit, Scooter, Little Bit, plus all my fur babies."

"Sure. Sounds good," Brad answered. "And I do appreciate your listening. To be honest, I've just shared some things I have never mentioned to anyone else, ever. Not even my ex-wife, which I should mention was a rather short-lived affair, with a lot of arguments centering on my place of residence. Some people aren't too keen on living in the woods. Even with electricity."

CHAPTER 109
Hiking Was Invented for Thinking

Later Phillip called Deanna about the time he knew she usually got off work and asked if they could possibly get together to eat, and talk a little.

"I heard about Todd," she replied. "So okay; you can fill me in on how he's doing."

"Looks like he's going to be all right. Listen, do you want to eat someplace besides the Electric Blue, or just stay there, and let someone wait on you."

Deanna laughed and said, "They'll probably make me serve us, but we can try."

A few minutes later Phillip parked and went into the restaurant where Deanna was waiting for him. After exchanging greetings they waited to be seated at a booth.

Deanna spoke first after they were seated. "So tell me more about how Todd is."

"He's actually doing quite well, and really fortunate he wasn't killed."

"How's Julie?"

Phillip grinned. "Quite well, I believe. I called her a few minutes ago and she said they're getting married soon as possible."

Deanna was a planner and an organizer, so the idea of a spontaneous decision to get married was foreign to her. "You're kidding!"

"Not at all." Phillip shook his head. "I guess this made them both realize just how much they loved each other, and they're getting married right away. Todd said if he has to be in there for more than three or four days, they're getting married in the hospital chapel."

"Wow." Deanna shook her head. "I guess they are serious. Quite frankly, Phillip, that kind of planning, or maybe I should say, lack of it, is a concept I'm not familiar with."

Phillip laughed. "Julie told Todd if anyone was going to kill him it would be her, from loving him to death. And by the way, she apologized to me for all the hard times she's given me in the past."

"That sounds like a miracles never cease to happen moment," Deanna said.

"I know," Phillip replied. "And I've been doing some real heavy thinking since this situation with Todd, and I do want to break this pattern I have been in. It's not from fear of death or anything like that, although I suppose I really don't want to die slumped over a downloaded video from some site like the one you found. But it's more … I'm worried about not living life to the fullest, which I can't do glued to some image on a screen. I know I still do love … and … need you, Deanna." Phillip continued quietly. "And I am so frustrated with myself over what I am seeing more and more as wasted time." He paused, and decided to be honest. "And yet, part of me also has to admit there is a factor of, I like it too, that enters in sometimes."

Deanna looked at Phillip with moist eyes as she quietly said, "I loved you, Phillip. I really did. Actually still do in some aspects. But I have to be honest, something died the other day, it really did, and I'm not sure I can bring it back to life. And you just made the comment, the site I found. Makes me wonder what's still out there that I haven't found out yet."

The waiter approached and asked if he could get them something to drink as he set menus on the table. Deanna said water was fine for her and Phillip said he'd have the same. The waiter left for their drinks and Deanna said she already knew what she wanted, The 'Electric Blue' Chef's Salad. She added, "I'm in the mood to eat something, but nothing heavy."

"So," Phillip replied sadly, "are you saying that you don't see us getting back together?"

"Phillip?" Deanna said. "Back to what you were saying about wasted time. I guess there are two ways of looking at that. If the end results of all that time has brought you to the point of determining to set a different course, then the question is, was it wasted?"

Phillip thought a moment and furrowed his eyebrows before he spoke. "I guess not but it seems like it. Especially since it seems to have cost us our relationship."

The waiter returned with their water and asked if they were ready to order.

"I'm not ready," Phillip said. "Can't decide what I want."

"I'll have the Electric Blue Chef's Salad. Sure you don't want that too, Phillip"?

He shrugged as he replied, "Sure, why not?"

The waiter left to get their order and they both sat in an awkward silence for a couple minutes. Then Phillip spoke. "As soon as we finish I'll let you get on home. I think I'll go hike a while."

"Kind of late in the evening for that isn't it?"

"Hiking was invented was for thinking. I think I need to get some more in."

CHAPTER 110
Going to the Chapel

Dr. Pedigone came into Todd's room and said, "I hope I'm not disturbing anything because it sure looks like good medicine is taking place." Todd and Julie broke away from their kiss and looked around at the doctor somewhat sheepishly. "Oh, no," the doctor said, "Go back to your business unless, of course, you want to hear my news." Julie said they would listen only if it was good. "It depends," said Dr. Pedigone. "The reason I don't mind interrupting you is it looks like you're going to have a complete mend; no major problems. However, you won't be home until sometime next week, probably toward the middle of it."

"Then we want to continue with our plans, and get married Saturday in the chapel," Todd said.

"Based on what you said earlier I thought you might; that's why I came as soon as possible to inform you of the mending schedule."

"And," Todd went on, "we want you to join us for our wedding, if your schedule allows it."

"I'll work my schedule so it does allow it, barring emergencies, of course. Once you set a time with Chaplain Harrison, let me know."

"Doctor," Julie asked, "since you're planning to come would you do me the favor of giving me away?"

"Of course," Dr. Pedigone laughed. "I mean look at you. You've been hanging around the hospital ever since Todd came in, and I can't even send you a bill. If I can't make any money on you, I might as well give you away."

"Thank you, Doctor," Julie said, as she kissed his cheek, laughing.

"Seriously," he said, "I'm honored you asked me." He shook Todd's hand and hugged Julie. "Congratulations."

After Dr. Pedigone left, Todd and Julie kissed again. "Todd?" Julie looked at him with a question in her eyes. "Promise me something?" she asked.

"Depends what it is?"

"Ah," she laughed, "so this is what I'm up against. Okay, have it your way. But seriously, Todd, promise me you'll always call back-up in potentially dangerous situations."

"Trust me; I've been thinking about how foolishly I acted. You're proposing a promise I need to make, and keep. My problem was I got angry and let my emotions take over, and I forgot what one should never forget. Honey, I am truly sorry for being so careless."

Julie grew thoughtful as she said, "I don't know. Now I'm going to sound like you, but, on the other hand, look what's come out of it. We're getting married Saturday. But now you have me, I want to keep you. So," she said rather forcefully, "you had better keep that promise, mister."

CHAPTER 111
Mia Squeezed His Hand

Even with Scooter and Little Bit snuggled in the bed against him, Brad had a restless night. Flashes of a week the company had been on LZ Grant kept tumbling around in his dreams, interspersed with flashes of Mia ... *incoming, no casualties ... the next day two nearby LZs were hit with ground attacks ... several killed on each ... incoming ... "Want to grab a bite to eat somewhere?" ... two artillery pieces knocked out, 8 killed ... 13 wounded ... night ... several trip wires set off ... flares popped with no sightings ... "I was free to do whatever I wanted" ... next day several recon patrols sent out .... Claymore mine accidentally blown ... killed Joe and an FNG lost his right hand ... Mia squeezed his hand ... another FNG had serious leg wounds; Brad doubted the man would ever walk on his own again ...*

The next morning he tried to fit the events of the past couple days together with the Bad Medic days of Vietnam. He did his thinking best while walking through the woods, but he had some chores around the cabin he wanted to get to first.

CHAPTER 112
Prep for the Kill

Roscoe awakened and stretched and threw his arm over onto Heather's. They had slept in the Mustang with the seats reclined, and apparently, the stress from the day before, and the effort of grave digging, added to some robust sexual activity, had taken its toll, and they both dozed off soundly.

After they had pulled onto the fire lane the evening before, they followed it down to the spot they'd come to a few days earlier that they had decided would be a good location to dispose of Jackson. Leaving him in the trunk of the Mustang, Heather and Roscoe had walked to the small clearing they'd earlier scouted and quietly talked through the next day's plans. Then they went down the ravine again to pick and shovel out a shallow grave for after they killed Jackson. They determined that with the multitude of football-plus size rocks in the area, a grave about three foot deep would suffice as they would then pile plenty of weight over the top to keep wild animals from digging, and discovering. However, they soon discovered digging three feet down in a wooded area was a lot easier said than done.

"Roscoe," Heather said, "perhaps my idea wasn't so good."

"I don't know. I think our difficulty digging is actually making it a better idea."

"How's that?"

"Probably no one will even think of someone doing what we're doing."

"You might be right," Heather said, "but it doesn't make the work any easier."

When they were done, Roscoe said, "Let's just leave the pick and shovel here; no one will be down here tonight."

When they arrived back at the car, Heather opened the trunk lid and told Jackson she hoped he was paying attention, laughed, and said, "Jackson, you were a hard man to live with, in the most difficult way, but you can rest easy as tomorrow we'll get everything worked out." Jackson moaned and Heather said she thought they should give him another small dose of chloroform to keep him quiet throughout the night. When she administered it to him, his forehead seemed a bit feverish. "Jackson," she said, "don't you dare go and get sick on us, you understand? Tomorrow's a big day." Jackson just moaned and gave a small twitch before succumbing to the odors again.

After it got dark, Heather told Roscoe she was too wired to sleep and asked if he was up to doing something.

"You mean make love?"

"What do you think I'm talking about? Chasing blue-footed boo-by birds in the Galapagos Islands? Damn, Roscoe!"

When they were finished they got as comfortable as possible in the Mustang's reclining bucket seats and gave way to total exhaustion.

Apparently the seats had been comfortable enough, as they slept for almost eight hours.

CHAPTER 113
The Big Squeeze

Heather moaned as she slowly awakened and asked what time it was. Roscoe rubbed the palms of his hands over his eyes, looked at the clock and told her it was almost nine. "God, I can't believe we slept this late," Heather replied. "Do you suppose some of that chloroform drifted our way? We really ought to get started with our plans, don't you think?"

Roscoe said "I don't know about the chloroform, but I'm going to have PBJ crackers and drink a Root Beer before I do anything."

Heather stretched. "I can go along with that idea."

When they finished with eating they turned their attention to Jackson. He did not look well and Roscoe and Heather struggled hard to lift him out of the trunk. Heather told Jackson she would really appreciate it if he would cooperate a little more but it actually did look as if what little he was doing was truly his best effort. After they had him standing beside the car, Heather undid the duct tape around his ankles, and put leg cuffs on him. Then she took about a fifteen foot length rope and tied it to the chain between his leg cuffs, then up and through his handcuffs and then wrapped the end of the rope around Roscoe's left hand. Roscoe jabbed Jackson with the gun and told him to start moving down the hill to their left.

Jackson wondered how long Heather was going to play the bizarre game before letting him go, and then his stomach involuntarily constricted again and his fears re-arose as he watched Heather take two large rolls of duct tape, some more rope, and a pair of scissors out of the car. She smiled and said, "Jackson, I know you've enjoyed your life to this point, and I hope you enjoy your last few minutes, because I am certainly going to."

Jackson was choking from the handkerchiefs in his mouth and weak from no food the day before. Now fear was overtaking him and he started to have difficulty breathing. He collapsed and Roscoe jerked on the rope leash. "Get up, Jackson; hear me?"

Jackson rolled into a fetal position and then with Roscoe pulling, he was able to sit up. Roscoe and Heather grabbed onto the rope close to Jackson and helped him around to where he could kneel, and then slowly rise to his feet again. He wobbled, and collapsed once more, and Roscoe started the process of getting him onto his feet all over again. Though he felt as weak as piss water Jackson managed to slowly plod in the direction he had been told to go.

About fifty yards down the hill, he collapsed again. When Heather poked him, he moaned, and tears started down his cheeks as he looked at her. She started to feel sorry for him momentarily, and then reminded herself there was no room for weakness; she had to steel her mind for the task ahead. Heather realized she was beyond a point of no return. She remembered studying some Greek tragedy in high school in one of her English classes and the teacher saying something about 'irretrievable actions', and now she knew exactly what her instructor had been talking about. She told Jackson they would let him rest a few minutes, but then he was going to have to walk again. Jackson retched against the duct tape, rolled his eyes upward, and passed out.

Heather rolled her eyes upward and said, "Damn! Damn, damn, damn!"

"This is just fantastic," Roscoe said. "What now?"

Heather rubbed her forehead with her pointer, middle, and ring finger to try and ease the tension she felt. She sighed and shook her head. "I don't know."

Roscoe knew from his business dealings that panic was the key to unlocking big trouble. "Okay," he said, "We've got to stay calm. Go back to the car and get the bottle of water I left there. I think we can get him awake and moving again."

Heather headed back up the hill. She surmised the chloroform was a factor in Jackson's weakness along with two handkerchiefs stuffed in his mouth that had made the last twenty-four hours waterless and foodless for him. *Still*, she thought, *this is not how I thought it would go. But maybe Roscoe's right. If we can get him awake, and let him rest some more, we should be able to get him down to the clearing and* the tree. *I damn sure don't want him to die before I have the chance to kill him.* She got the bottle of water from the car and headed back to where the two most influential men in her life were waiting.

"I know if he dies here we can drag him to the ravine to bury him," Heather told Roscoe, "but I hope we can get him awake. I want him to suffer before he dies."

Roscoe only knew that he really didn't know what all went on in Heather's mind. Although he had used women, especially as far as sex in exchange for drugs went, he never felt like he was taking advantage of them because they were getting something back out of it. And although his father had been an abusive person toward both Roscoe and his mother, still his mother had never voiced any indication that she wanted to see him suffer. *Of course,* Roscoe thought, *on the day of his funeral I was thinking that he ought to suffer in an afterlife somewhere, at least for a little bit. But hoping someone suffers after death and making them suffer here are two different things. At least I think so.*

He looked down at Jackson and told Heather, "You should take some consolation in the fact Jackson is already suffering."

"I know, but it isn't the right kind of suffering. The last thing I want Jackson to feel as he fades away to death is pain, sharp agonizing pain in his jewels."

Roscoe felt a nervous twitch in his own groin area and made a vow to never, ever get Heather really angry with him. He splashed a little water on Jackson's face, and Jackson's eyelids flickered as he slowly started to regain consciousness. Roscoe took Heather off to the side and told her, "Listen, I think that for a while at least, we should stop talk about killing and let Jackson think we're just scaring some sense into him; that his ordeal is almost over."

They let Jackson rest almost an hour before he was again prodded to his feet. Roscoe ran the gun barrel under Jackson's chin, then up into the pinna portion of his ear and then whispered to Jackson, "You'd best cooperate if you want to stay alive. This is all about making sure you can be believed when you promise to never bother Heather again."

Jackson felt a glimmer of hope and decided to fight with what little strength he had for an opportunity to keep air flowing through his lungs. Jackson fell five more times, and after each fall, Roscoe gave him a little time to rest while talking to him about how he really needed to let Heather get a divorce, and to promise he would never hassle her again. Jackson kept shaking his head in the affirmative, and from the bottom of his heart, he meant it.

While they were resting after Jackson's fifth fall, Heather bunched her face up in frustration.

"What?" Roscoe asked.

"I've kind of lost track of time these past few days as far as my cycles go, and I think that my period is getting ready to start."

"Damn!" said Roscoe. "Did you bring any pads, or whatever the hell you use?"

"Roscoe, that's what I mean when I said that I kind of lost track of time. I don't have anything."

"Well, this is just fine. What do you suggest that we do?"

Heather thought a moment and then smiled. "I've got it. We can let Jackson help us out here, maybe earn him some Brownie points."

Jackson was aware enough to wonder what more could happen to him and how he could possibly help with Heather's dilemma. He was thinking that it would have been nice at one earlier point in their marriage if he had picked up some Kotex for her like she had asked. Instead, he was distinctly recalling telling her, "Well, Bitch, it sounds like you have yourself a bit of a problem that you might just need to go to the store and take care of your own damn self." She had never bothered him with it again, but now he was wishing she had. Jackson told himself that if he could go back and change things he would have asked Heather precisely what it was she needed so he could make sure he brought home the exact item. But he hadn't.

"Well, the way I see it," Heather said, "He won't mind letting me cut a section of his shirt from the back that I can fold up and use as a sort of field expedient Kotex pad. Will you, Jackson?"

"Sure sounds like a plan to me," Roscoe replied. "Jackson, you won't mind will you?"

Jackson responded by nodding his head vigorously.

Heather cut a piece of the shirt large enough to accommodate her needs and then went off to the side to install her improvised blood-catcher into her panties as comfortably as possible. She went back to where the men were waiting, thanked Jackson for being so considerate of her, and then asked him if he was ready to travel again.

Jackson again nodded "yes" and awhile later he led the way on his leash into a small clearing with a large oak tree bordering it which stood out from all the rest. Heather told Jackson to stop and put his back to the tree. He complied and then his eyes widened as she and Roscoe took his rope leash and used it to tie him around his chest to the tree and then used the other rope they had brought and, likewise, bound his feet to the oak. Heather knelt in front of Jackson with the scissors in her hand, smiled at him, and instructed him to listen carefully so he would understand just how he was going to die. Jackson's hopes for freedom were fading fast, but he still felt he knew Heather well enough to know she was not a killer.

"Jackson," Heather said, "Those little balls of yours have visited many women in this county, and I would like to pay proper tribute to them. So what I am going to do is cut away the front of your trousers and shorts and then I am going to massage them." Her voice grew hard and angry as she continued. "Oh, excuse me, did I say massage? What I meant to say, you lying, cheating, shit-assed wife-beater, what I meant to say is that I am going to squeeze and twist them until you pass out, which will actually be good news for you, because then I am going to duct tape your head until you smother." Heather looked up at her husband as she talked and received great pleasure from the look of distress embedded on his face.

"Now don't worry," she went on, "we already have the spot for your body picked out. Actually, Roscoe and I came down here and dug the grave last night, down that little ravine there. And you will be so well covered with rocks, that, quite frankly, my Dear, I just don't think you'll ever be found. Oh, and by the way, as far as earning Brownie points for letting me use your shirt, I lied."

As Heather grabbed the front of his trousers and started to cut, Jackson groaned and tried to jerk his hips around, but quickly stopped when he was stuck with scissor tips. Heather finished cutting a large hole in his trousers and under shorts, and as she reached toward him, Jackson became very aware of the fact that for the first time ever in his life, he did not want his testicles to be recipients of feminine touch.

CHAPTER 114
Hidden Observer

Tira sat in the front row of the church pews alone with her thoughts as she stared at Albert lying in the casket. Had he died eight to ten years ago in the early years of their marriage she would have sent him off with the best Watonga Funeral Home had to offer, even if she'd had to ask her mother for help. But he was soiled now, had soiled himself with the Delilah girl, and had even lobbed some of the dirt her way. Tira wryly smiled. When Karen Esterbean passed, she left Tira a goodly amount of money. Tira could easily afford to give Albert the best now, but there was no way she was going to. She couldn't quite bring herself to have him cremated, which would have been a lot cheaper, but at least, she thought, she could take some comfort in the fact she hadn't wasted too much money on him.

Ulysses Brock approached Tira and asked if she minded if he sat with her a moment. Tira smiled sadly and said, "Not at all. And I need to apologize to you again for what Albert did to Eloise." Pastor Brock started to say something and Tira said, "No, it was his fault. He left the house after saying horrible things to me about what he and that Delilah girl had done, and the police said they estimated he was going around a hundred miles an hour. His fault; no other way to look at it."

"I do understand how you feel. It's still hard to lose someone, even if they have not been fully supportive of you." Tira wondered what he might be implying, but before she could say anything else, Ulysses Brock continued. "What I want you to know is I appreciate all the work you have done for the church. My prayers are with you during this most difficult time."

Tira nodded, and then felt she needed to clarify something. "Pastor," she began, "there are a couple more things I feel I need to apologize for. First, I would have had you involved in Albert's service, but I knew it would not only be difficult for you because of your own loss, and also I didn't want you to have to try and think up good things to say about the man who had caused you so much pain." Her pastor reached over and touched her hand and told her he appreciated her consideration. "And another thing I really need to apologize for," continued Tira, "is the fact that, over the past few months especially, I have not been as helpful around the church as I should have been. What with problems getting much worse with me and Albert, and then the loss of my mother, I just lost focus, and I'm sorry."

Ulysses Brock poignantly smiled and told Tira, again he understood, perhaps more than she knew; that everyone had trials and times of losing focus. Tira wondered what he meant, and then she was struck with another thought.

"I know money doesn't solve things," she said, "But from Albert's insurance money, I think he had about a million dollar term life policy through TIAA, and, anyway, I will make sure I pay my tithes to the church."

Pastor Brock squeezed Tira's hand and commended her for thinking of the church when she was going through such a difficult time. He told her he would talk with her more about her tithes at a later point, but there were some renovation projects he'd been thinking of recently; that maybe they could even name a new youth wing Furcologna Hall.

"I don't think so," Tira said. I wouldn't particularly want that. It would remind me too much of Albert. But we can think of something."

"Sorry I can't stay for the service," Ulysses Brock said. "I'll talk with you later. I really do need to leave right now, but I just want you to know you have me, and your church family, for support." He stood, and then spoke again. "There is another project we have to give some attention to at the church fairly soon," he said. "I know it sounds trivial, but in the steeple bell tower area we have a bit of a predicament which actually could spread and become a fire hazard. It seems we're having a problem with squirrel infestation."

Tira did not take any comfort in the fact that if Albert was listening from somewhere in a world beyond; he was probably enjoying a good belly-laugh. Pastor Brock told her again he would soon be back in touch with her, excused himself, and left the room.

Tira thought it was nice to think she had a church family supporting her, but she wondered how many of them were blaming her in some way for what her husband had done to the preacher's wife. She wondered if the truth be known, that behind all his kind words to her, Pastor Brock was still seeing her as somewhat accountable. Her thoughts brightened as she began to see what a wonderful irony it would be when she donated some of Albert's insurance money to Pastor Brock and the church.

A short eulogy was delivered by the pastor of a nearby sister church, and when he was done speaking, Tira realized she hadn't heard a word. After the services she shook the preacher's hand and said, "Thank you for your kind words; they were so appropriate."

Only a handful of people came to the graveside service at the Frankenberry Sweet Peace Memorial Park. As Tira listened to another brief oratory, she thought the only thing could bring her peace would be if Albert's Delilah girl was also on the receiving end of the words being spoken. Then she breathed a prayer requesting strength to make it through the coming days and for the continued guidance along the pathway of showing others the love of God, not the path of wickedness taken by Albert and Delilah.

When the services were over, and the few people had dispersed, Tira rode back to the church with the funeral director and signed a few more necessary papers. She thanked him for his services, went out and got into the car her mother had left her, and then broke down sobbing. After a few moments, she decided to ride around awhile and try to sort out the images making razor cuts across her mind and emotions. She turned left onto the highway with no particular conscious destination in mind. Some minutes later she realized she was headed toward the Swisher Glen Forest Preserve where she and Albert had walked a lot during the early years of their marriage. Tira figured her subconscious was pulling her toward a time when they had been happy.

Less than twenty minutes later she approached a large field that sloped to a beautiful wooded area, and she thought, *This is the place Albert said years ago we needed to do some hiking where we wouldn't have a trail but instead would have to rely on a compass.* Tira remembered specifically saying, "Okay, as long as we don't get lost," But, she thought, *We never did come out here and do it.* She decided at this particular moment she was feeling lost, and she got the urge to hike into the woods to see if maybe somehow she could find a little of herself. She looked for a moment at the crucifix her mother had dangled from the mirror, then relaxed and wryly smiled at the fact she was dressed for church.

Karen Esterbean had been a bird-watcher and always kept field binoculars in the car. Tira decided to take them with her, so, forgetting to lock the car door, and attired in a dark gray skirt and blazer and shoes that made for very difficult walking, she headed for a wooded hill across the clearing. Once in the tree line, she climbed a gradual incline for what seemed a half mile or so, and then it ascended quite sharply. Tira stopped a moment, looked down at her shoes, stared at the hill, and then decided to climb it. *I'll pretend Pastor Brock is waiting at the top for me*, she thought; *waiting to say that although we are both having hard times right now, if we persevere everything will be okay.*

Tira drew in a deep breath, sucked in her stomach, squared her chin resolutely forward, and started up toward the wooded crest. It became increasingly clear to her the shoes one wore to funerals were not necessarily the shoes one should wear to go hiking. After strenuous exertion which left her gasping for air, she reached the pinnacle. Tira stopped to catch her breath and then started down the other side of the hill. Suddenly she stopped dead in her tracks as she heard what sounded like a woman talking, followed by a muffled, yet bloodcurdling, scream. Tira put the binoculars to her eyes and scanned with limited visibility in the direction she thought she had heard the noises from.

Through the undergrowth, she saw what appeared to be a small clearing not too far away, and in it Tira caught a partial view of two men and a woman. She gasped as she brought her binoculars into clearer focus. One man was tied to a tree with duct tape wrapped around the lower half of his head. The stifled scream she had heard had obviously come from him. The front of his trousers and undershorts was cut away, and the woman was kneeling in front of him, squeezing his testicles. Over and over, Tira heard the muffled sounds of agony. She couldn't believe she had stumbled upon such acts of evil personified.

*****

Brad finished his work and got ready to go wander around for a while. He got his pistol and holster from the cabin and strapped them around his waist. He decided to take the pick-up and park along a tree line of a forest near the Coyote Loop Trail area where he occasionally hiked.

CHAPTER 115
They Were Doing Evil Things to Him

Trembling, Tira turned and quietly but quickly headed back in the direction she had come from. As she started to descend the steeper incline which had taken her breath away just minutes earlier, Tira picked up her pace. In her haste, she slipped and fell forward with a small cry, and then panicked over the fact she had cried out. Her pantyhose were torn and one knee was skinned and hurting quite badly, but she managed to get back onto her feet. She looked fearfully toward the top of the hill behind her and expected to see someone appear at any moment. She decided she would make better time if she took off her shoes to carry out her escape from the evil while barefooted, so painfully she continued in the direction she thought she had come from, glancing behind every so often.

A few times she fell down and panicked as she prayed desperately for deliverance from evil. She saw a clearing ahead, and grimacing through tears running down her cheeks, lurched toward it. When she reached the field, horror overtook her when she did not see the car anywhere. Tira quickly decided she must have come too far to the left during her stumblings and so she decided to follow the tree line to the right. After a couple of minutes she discovered to great relief she had been correct in her calculated guess as she saw her vehicle about a quarter of a mile away. Even though her leg and the bottoms of her feet were hurting her terribly, Tira gripped her shoes more tightly and broke out into a run toward the car.

When she got there she put her shoes back on and reached into her blazer pocket for her keys. Her chest tightened again with fear as she realized they weren't there. Tira broke down crying at the thought of having to look for them, which meant heading back toward the evil she had just seen. She pulled on the door handle and to her relief, realized she had left the car unlocked. She quickly slid behind the steering wheel and decided to meditate with the crucifix again before embarking out on her hellish quest for the missing keys.

She settled her mind and tried to retrace exactly what she had done since first pulling into the clearing.

Okay, she thought. *First, I parked. Then, I reached down and --* Tira almost passed out from relief as she closed her hands over the keys still in the ignition. She breathed a prayer of thankfulness over her discovery, and that she had not locked the car door.

Tira looked in the direction she had just come from to make sure there was no one following her and then she started the car. Before she could back out onto the road her chest tightened in fear as she saw a pickup pulling in behind her. She started to panic and then realized it wasn't the evil man she had just seen out in the woods. She got out of her car and ran back to the truck. "Please! I was just walking in the woods and saw a man and a woman torturing another man! They were doing evil things to him!"

"What kind of evil things?" Brad asked.

"Just evil," Tira replied. "I've got to notify the police. May I use your cell, please?"

"Didn't bring it with me; left it at home. Sorry. Now, where is this happening?"

"On the other side of that hill there is a small clearing and they had this man tied to a tree and were torturing him!"

Brad wasn't sure what kind of weirdness he was encountering, but he told Tira, "Okay, you go for help; I'll go check out what's going on. I'm familiar with the area. I believe I know where you're talking about."

"Be careful!" Tira said. "These are evil people!"

Brad pulled back his shirt a little to reveal the holster. "I think I'll be okay." He pulled his pickup around Tira's car so he could park right at the tree line.

Tira pulled onto the road, but after a minute or two, she realized she didn't really know if she was going the right way or not, and so she pulled off into the small parking area for the Coyote Loop Trailhead so she could call for help on her cell. She fumbled in her purse for her phone, and when she couldn't find it, dumped the purse contents into the passenger's seat. Panic returned as she realized she had not brought the cell when she left for Albert's funeral; she must have left it on the charger.

About that time a man, who looked to be in his mid-thirties, driving an older model Buick Skylark, pulled into the parking area. Tira froze and watched in fear as he got out of the car. When she realized he also was not the man she had recently seen in the woods, she pulled over to him, rolled down her window, and asked if he had a cell phone she could use to call 911. Aaron Patterson said he had a Tracfone, pulled it out of his pocket, and asked if there was anything he could do to help.

Tira was overwhelmed by everything that had just happened and became near hysterical. "Please! I was just walking in the woods and saw a man and a woman torturing another man! They were doing evil things to him!"

"What kind of evil things?" Aaron asked.

"Just evil," Tira replied. "Now there's another man on his way to check it out, but I've got to notify the police. May I use your cell, please?" Aaron handed her the Trac phone and she dialed. She was relieved at an immediate response.

"911, May I help you?"

Tira told what she had just seen in the woods, and when the dispatcher asked her where she was, she told him she was at the parking area for the Coyote Loop Trail.

"Okay," replied the Dispatcher, "you're in the Swisher Glen Forest Preserve. Wait where you are for a police officer. Are you alone?" Tira responded she was with a man who had just pulled into the parking area and she was using his phone. The dispatcher told her to ask the man if he would stay with her until an officer arrived. Tira replied she was scared and wanted to know what to do if the people she had seen in the woods came by. She reiterated that they were evil and might try to kill her.

"Ma'am," the dispatcher said, "we need you to show an officer where this torture is taking place." Tira said she would wait and asked the dispatcher to please tell the police to hurry. "Stay on the line," the dispatcher told her, "until I get in touch with someone and then I can let you know approximately how long it will be before help arrives."

"Okay," Tira said, and then turned to Aaron. "Sir, 911 wants me to wait on the phone until they can tell me how soon an officer will be here. Is that okay?"

"Sure," Aaron said as he wondered what in the world was happening in his life now. The woman seemed serious enough, and was definitely scared, but he also felt like he was experiencing something from La-La-Land. As Tira had talked to the 911 dispatcher Aaron recalled some guys he was with one time discussing LSD, and he wondered if maybe this lady holding his phone had taken something hallucinogenic before hiking in the woods. Nonetheless, he could see she was truly scared to death, and thought he should try to help her if he could.

"My name is Aaron Patterson, and I'll stay with you until the police arrive."

"I'm Tira Furcologna, and thank you."

The dispatcher came back on the line and told Tira a State Trooper, Phillip Cordella, was less than ten minutes away, and she should stay at her present location. Tira thanked the dispatcher and gave the phone back to Aaron.

"A State Trooper named Phillip Curdle, or something like is on his way," Tira told Aaron.

"Phillip Cordella?" Aaron asked.

"Yes, that's the name."

Aaron shook his head in wonderment. "Phillip Cordella and I were out here hiking this trail yesterday afternoon. I hope he won't use his siren and tip off the people in the woods, but then, I guess he's been doing this stuff long enough that he knows what not to do."

All of a sudden Tira sucked in air through her teeth and put her hand to her forehead. Aaron asked if she was okay and she said, "Yes, I'm fine. I just can't believe I didn't think of this earlier; it would have been a lot easier."

Aaron asked what would have been a lot easier, and Tira replied, "Hiking."

She went to the rear of her car, opened the trunk and moved a couple items, and smiled as she held up a pair of tennis shoes. "This was my mother's car," she explained, "and she was a birdwatcher so she always kept these in the trunk. If I'd remembered them earlier, I wouldn't have been falling down in my high heels." Tira realized she must be quite a sight to Aaron in her church clothes, knees covered with scratches, torn pantyhose, hair disheveled.

Mother's probably laughing at me now, she thought as she kicked off her heels, tossed them into the trunk of the car, and put on the tennis shoes.

CHAPTER 116
Let's Just Get Him Buried

Roscoe was worried Jackson might be making too much noise with his muffled screams and told Heather to hurry up and make him black out.

Heather responded, "He's not being loud enough to be overheard, Roscoe; we're in a perfect location. Now I know we can't take all day, but this man has caused me so much grief with these little babies that I am going to enjoy seeing him suffer just a little bit longer."

Roscoe breathed in deeply, and then, with his cheeks puffed like the clouds on an old-time map, blew out. He decided that, since they were out in the middle of nowhere, and since so far, Heather had overall made good calls, he would continue to trust her. He also thought once again that he was quite certain he never wanted to be on the receiving end of Heather's wrath.

Heather stopped squeezing Jackson's testicles and then started to rub gently over his groin area. She turned and winked at Roscoe and then said to Jackson in her little girl voice, "I'll bet you've been scared, haven't you? Do you really think that your Heather girl would kill you, Baby? I just want you to know that I am not someone to be pushed around anymore."

She leaned forward and blew lightly over his groin as she massaged him. Jackson was barely conscious by this time, but he breathed a sigh of relief as he began to comprehend that maybe his torture was coming to a point of closure. Heather's continued attention to his groin area was having, for him, an unintended, but, for Heather, not an unexpected, consequence. "Mmm," Heather moaned. "Roscoe, look at what is happening to my Jackson-Baby."

Jackson had never been into masochism, but at the moment, under the circumstances, it seemed to be working for him, and he started to eagerly wait for more. He somehow relaxed a little, while continuing to rise to the occasion, and decided to get all that he could from the new pleasure that was driving away his aches and pains and bad memories of the past several hours. Heather looked up at Jackson with a loving look in her eyes, smiled tenderly at him, and then said to Roscoe, "Can you believe that I have had the kindness of heart to give this … this … male whore bastard one last little bit of gratification before he dies?"

With that she grabbed Jackson's testicle sack and started to twist and squeeze until with a final scream coming from somewhere deep around Roscoe's dirty handkerchiefs, Jackson slumped forward, unconscious.

Heather told Roscoe to hand her the duct tape so she could wrap the rest of Jackson's head.

"Hell," Roscoe said. "Let's just get him down to the hole so we can bury him."

CHAPTER 117
Faster and Faster into Loony-Town

When Phillip Cordella pulled his Cruiser into the Coyote Loop Trailhead parking area, Tira ignored her still-smarting knee, and ran to his car. Phillip felt concern as he observed a woman running toward him with frazzled hair plastered around her perspiring head, a scraped knee and ripped hose, wearing a Sunday-dress outfit and old tennis shoes. "Officer, I'm so glad you're here!" she cried. "I've been scared to death!" At that moment Phillip recognized her from the two prior Wendy experiences and thought he must be having another bad Karma day, minus the Jr. Bacon Cheeseburger.

***

Brad quietly approached the clearing he believed was the one Tira had referred to, but he didn't see anyone. There was a piece of denim that looked like it had been left there recently. He left it alone as he thought it might turn out to be evidence. He listened carefully and heard some talking below the clearing down a bit of a gully. Carefully he crept toward the voices.

"Your idea about this little gully was a good one," he heard Roscoe say. "With all the rocks in the area we can cover him good, and I doubt he'll ever be found. And I'm also glad we dug the grave last night. Between getting Jackson from the car to the tree, and then dragging him down here, I'm about worn out."

"I can hardly believe we've done it, Roscoe", said Heather. "I'm … I'm finally free. All we have to do is get him into the hole and get the rocks over him."

Brad quickly assessed the situation and decided that even with his pistol and the element of surprise he still might not be able to control things as it was a two to one situation, plus, he saw Roscoe was wearing a gun. He decided it might be better to withdraw to a good hiding spot closer to the clearing and hope the lady he had encountered was getting in touch with the police.

***

"You the lady reported the torture?" Phillip asked, trying not to smile. Then he looked at Aaron and said, "Small world. I thought we were just out here yesterday. What brings you back?"

"I decided to come back out and do some more hiking. When I pulled into the parking area this lady asked if she could use my cell phone. I agreed to stay with her until help arrived, and when I heard it was you coming it just reinforced my decision. She's seems scared enough that it looks like something really bad has happened."

Phillip looked at Tira and asked her if she remembered him from Wendy's a couple days earlier. Tira rolled her eyes and said "Yes, and I hope you'll help me this time."

Phillip sighed and said, "I have to check out what you said so I can give a report back to headquarters. Aaron, why don't you come along and I can drop you back here afterwards, okay?" Aaron said that was fine with him and then Phillip told them to get into his car. "Ma'am," he said to Tira, "you can ride up front with me and tell me what happened on the way." Aaron opened the door for Tira; she got in, and then he went to the rear door. As he climbed in he heard Phillip saying, "I'm Trooper Phillip Cordella, and, if you would, tell me your name again."

"Yes, sir; I'm Tira Furcologna, and, believe me, I'm so glad you're here."

"Furcologna, that's right," Phillip thought, *That name sounds familiar from something else.* Then he asked, "Wait; are you and your husband related to the guy who wrecked the other night out near Hacker's Mill Pond?"

"That was my husband," Tira replied. "He was buried earlier today." Phillip told her he was sorry for her loss and remembered that, just before the first Wendy's incident, Tira had also been under traumatic conditions. Tira continued. "After the funeral I decided to come out here to ride around the area where Albert and I used to walk after we were married, in our happier days. I saw a real pretty place where we talked about hiking several years back, and I decided to walk there to see if I could find any peace."

"So what did you see?" Phillip asked. Tira described what she had observed a few minutes earlier and Phillip said, "That sounds like pretty bizarre stuff. Are you sure that what you just described was what you saw?"

"Please don't doubt me," said Tira. "I know you're probably thinking because of what happened at Wendy's, and because my husband just died, that I'm unstable, but I know what I saw. We're talking evil people, Officer."

Phillip thought, *Naaaw, why would she even think I'd think like that? Evil people. Let's see, where have I heard this before?* But he just responded to Tira, "Sorry. Didn't mean to sound like I didn't believe you."

"Also, there was a man pulled his pickup in behind me just before I left, and he said he would go check it out."

This story just drives faster and faster into Loony-Town, Phillip thought.

In a minute he pulled his car into where Tira said she had parked and they could see Brad's Chevy near the trees. "See," Tira said, "that truck belongs to the man who said he would go see what was happening."

"I believe that's Bradley Miller's truck," Phillip said.

When they got out Tira said they needed to be really quiet, as she started to lead the way across the field. Phillip looked at Aaron, smiled, and put his finger to his lips. Tira led them up the small hill and into the woods, toward the spot where she had seen the torture taking place. As they started climbing the steeper incline, Tira winced from the pain in her knee and thought, *I'm sure glad I remembered Mother's shoes.*

After cresting the hill, Tira recognized the location, but wondered if her mind really was playing tricks with her as she whispered, "They're gone. They were right down at that tree, Officer, I swear to it."

Phillip was thinking he couldn't believe he had to follow through on what was obviously a wild goose chase as he said to Tira and Aaron, "Well, let's go down and look by the tree to see if these people left anything we can use as evidence to trace them. And, yeah, we need to be as quiet as possible." As they started he added, "These people sound dangerous," thinking, *Dangerous, right, as dangerous as Prissy, Ralph Henderson's kitten.* Then he thought, *Okay, just fifty more yards of playtime, and then I can ask Aaron if he wants to go to Wendy's with me for a Double Jr. Cheeseburger Deluxe … Hey, what's my problem? I like to hike. Maybe I can ask Tira if she was sure it was this tree; perhaps we should look around a little more.*

As they approached the tree, Aaron thought he heard something. "Shh," he whispered. "Down that ravine, I hear talking." Then he looked at the tree where Tira said the people had been, went over and picked something up, and came back to Phillip and Tira. He showed them denim cloth that had been cut away from, most likely, a pair of jeans.

Holy shit, Phillip thought, *Tira may be right, and, if so, it looks like we could be dealing with a couple of psychopaths.* He drew his gun and, this time seriously, put his finger to his lips.

About that time Brad came toward them and softly said, "Don't shoot. I'm Brad Miller, the man she sent ahead of you. The two people you're looking for are right down in that gully getting ready to bury a man they just killed."

CHAPTER 118
Freeze! You're Under Arrest!

When they had first started out across the field, Phillip had muted his radio as a precaution he figured he really didn't need to take, but now he was thinking he was extremely glad he had done so. He didn't dare get on it now to call for back-up, so he whispered to Aaron and Brad, "We're going down, and I'm going to need your help. I am deputizing you. Brad since you have a gun you can help cover them while Aaron handcuffs them. Aaron, let me show you quickly what I'll want you to do."

He quickly demonstrated the procedure to follow while cuffing, then he told Tira he wanted her to stay at the tree and to be absolutely quiet while he, Brad, and Aaron followed the gully where it was obvious something, actually confirmed by Brad as someone, had been dragged down. Phillip told Brad and Aaron he would be referring to them as Deputies.

As they slowly crept closer to where the voices were coming from, Aaron felt like he was caught back up in another mind tornado. A few days ago he had been sitting in jail for DUI after his arrest by Trooper Truitt, and then he was admitted and released from Angel Windows. After one time of meeting with Trooper Truitt according to his shock-probation terms, Todd had been shot and hospitalized. Now, the day after he and Phillip had walked the Coyote Loop Trail and had their talk, here he was, with the handle of Deputy Patterson, following State Trooper Phillip Cordella and some other guy down a ravine toward two people who were apparently killers.

He knew it was happening, but he also wondered if somehow, he wasn't just having a case of some real bad DT's. They all slowly picked their way forward and then Phillip stopped and held up his hand as he caught sight of Roscoe and Heather carrying rocks toward a small burrowed out spot with what looked like a body lying in it.

They edged a little closer, and then Phillip called out, "Freeze! State Police! You're under arrest!"

Roscoe dropped the rock he was carrying, and reached for the gun in his pocket. Phillip fired a warning shot, and Roscoe's hands immediately extended heavenward. "Don't shoot!" Roscoe cried out. "Oh, God, please don't shoot!"

As Phillip approached them, he sternly warned, "You two, don't move, or the next bullets have your names! Now, Deputy Patterson, cuff them together. Deputy Miller, check out that man being buried." Aaron's own hands were shaking slightly as he fumbled with the handcuffs, but he managed to get them on Roscoe and Heather while Phillip recited their Miranda Rights.

Phillip double-checked the cuffs, then called on his radio for assistance and an ambulance and gave the location. He kept his gun trained on Roscoe and Heather as he looked down at the body of Jackson Lamech. Phillip had seen a few things in his time as a State Trooper, but never anything like this. Brad had started to work on the man lying on his back with bands of tape still around his ankles and arms. Brad was pulling off the several wrappings of brownish-maroon duct tape the lower half of his head was enclosed in. Apparently he had expired by suffocation. The most bizarre sight was his exposed testicles, bruised and swollen and near the size of grapefruit.

Brad checked the body for any signs of life and noticed a slight movement of the chest.

"He's still alive!" he called out to Phillip. "Barely!"

When Brad finished tearing away the duct tape over the lower part of Jackson's face, he pulled out the handkerchiefs and Jackson gasped for air and twitched. Phillip told Roscoe and Heather the charges were attempted murder, upgraded to murder if the man died.

Heather smiled at Phillip and said, "But, Officer, you don't understand. This man here, he had the gun. He was forcing me to help him cover up a crime he committed."

"What?" Roscoe screamed. He felt like he'd just been caught selling meth at the Policeman's Ball, and he realized he was riding a big rubber duck in a swimming pool that was draining out fast. His life had been totaled up again, and it looked like the final score was going to be worse than when he was being chased in the Infiniti, probably somewhere in the vicinity of minus fifteen. He hollered at Heather. "You double-crossing bitch! Officer, this was all her idea!"

"Oh, no," said Heather in her innocent-sounding voice that had worked so well with Roscoe and Jackson. "You see, Officer, Roscoe, here, a car thief and drug dealer, by the way, came up with the ideas. He threatened to kill me if I didn't help."

"Well," said Phillip. "You will both have the opportunity to tell your stories to a judge, and, of course, we'll have to include the testimony of our eyewitness."

"You're bluffing about any eyewitnesses," Heather said.

Brad raised his right hand slightly with the index finger raised. "I'm one," he said, and then Phillip hollered for Tira to come down to where they were. When she got there, he asked her if Roscoe and Heather were the people she had seen earlier at the tree.

Heather looked at Tira and said, "Damn, damn, damn, damn, damn."

Then Heather drew in a deep breath as Tira looked at her and said, "Evil. You two are just evil."

Heather again tried to get out of the mess she had created and told Phillip that she would be glad to provide both him and his deputies with a little pleasure. Phillip contemptuously looked at her and said, "Some pleasures … aren't."

Phillip asked Tira if she thought she was okay to go with Aaron to where the cruiser was parked, wait for the ambulance and police reinforcements, and then if she could wait at her car while Aaron showed them the way back.

"I'm not only okay," Tira replied, glaring at Heather and Roscoe, "I will be glad to."

Phillip told her to make sure she waited for him to get back out so he could get her statement, to be careful, and he watched as she started back up the way they had come in. He felt remorse for brushing her off twice at Wendy's, and decided he would make sure she had the opportunity to avail herself of counseling if she so desired.

Brad asked Roscoe where the keys to the cuffs on Jackson were.

Roscoe shrugged and nodded toward Heather. "Ask her."

Heather snorted. "As soon as I thought that whore-loving bastard was dead, I tossed them as far as I could. If you look for them hard enough you might find them."

"Want me to go look around?" Brad asked Phillip.

"No. If the ambulance doesn't have bolt cutters, I do in the Cruiser. How's he doing?" Phillip asked, pointing to Jackson.

"I'm doing all I can, but I'm glad other medical personnel are on the way."

In a few minutes Brad felt relief as he heard the sound of sirens approaching. When Aaron returned with three other state Troopers and two EMT's, Phillip quickly briefed them on what had occurred. He said he was also pretty sure they had in custody the man who was responsible for shooting Todd Truitt.

The EMT's said although it looked like Jackson was in extremely critical condition, he just might make it because of Brad. Then they and the reinforcement troopers loaded Jackson onto a stretcher and started to carry him out. Phillip and Aaron went on ahead with Roscoe and Heather, while Brad stayed with the medical team.

Several minutes later, at the cruiser, Phillip and Aaron cuffed Roscoe and Heather individually, and then they put them into the back seat. Phillip told Tira and Aaron he would take them back to where their cars were at the Trailhead, and they could follow him back to Frankenberry to the 58th State Police Headquarters. He asked Tira if she was all right to drive.

"I think so," Tira said, "As long as I'm following you."

Phillip told Tira and Aaron to squeeze into the front seat, dropped them off at the parking area, and told Tira he would see her in a few minutes to get her statements. As Phillip drove off with Roscoe and Heather in the backseat he thought to himself, *These two in the car with me, evil people; these two are evil.*

CHAPTER 119
Under a Paradox System

Phillip told Todd and Julie about the events of the day. He laughed as he related how he had felt when following Tira through the woods. "I would have bet you a month's salary I was on a wild-goose chase. I think the depravity we encountered shocked me even more because I was so sure Aaron and I were just out for an afternoon stroll with a wild-eyed woman from Frankenberry."

Julie shrugged. "After your Wendy's experiences, who can blame you?"

Phillip soberly replied, "The circumstances surrounding Tira are really quite sad. I hope she'll get the help she needs; when I talked with her briefly after she gave her statement, she seemed open to counseling." After a few more minutes he bid Todd and Julie farewell, telling them that he would see them for sure on Saturday at the wedding. Phillip had gladly agreed to be Todd's best man and Julie decided to ask Tira if she would be her bridesmaid.

"Maybe doing that will give her a certain sense of normalization or something after all she has been through."

After Phillip left, Julie reached up and stroked Todd's chin. "You know, since this shooting incident I've given thought, quite a bit actually, to what you said the other day about wanting to run a halfway house for recovering alcoholics just released from prison."

Todd gave a thoughtful smile as he nodded and said, "Yeah, me too."

"I'm sure there will be inherent problems, maybe even some danger involved, but somehow I think I would rest easier if you were in that line of work."

"Do you want to know what discourages me from it the most, besides lack of money and organized plans?"

"What's that?"

"I'm thinking it would be a real time-consuming enterprise, and I want to figure out ways to have more time with you, not less."

Julie felt good inside. Good like she had never felt before, as she said, "Todd, I love you, you and your unselfishness."

Todd grinned. "I think I'm being very selfish when I say I want more time with you."

Julie knew from experience there were struggles in every relationship, but she didn't want to even think of those times at the moment. She liked what she was hearing from Todd, and the only thing she wanted to continue to hear, was more of the same. She responded to his comment that he wanted more time with her. "That's what I'm paying you to say, and, Honey, you're doing a good job. But seriously, Todd, you are an unselfish guy. Were you born that way, or what?"

"Probably what," Todd laughed, "I really don't know."

"I swear," said Julie, "the more I learn about life, the more convinced I am that the world does operate on a paradox system."

Todd grinned. "Think of our walk through Laurel Cave the other day. There was a beauty we could only see with limited light. You and me and whatever all this is leading up to is similar to that." He smiled again looking down at his bandages. "Although I think I would have chosen a less painful method of learning if it had been left up to me."

"Like I said," Julie repeated, "I'm becoming convinced we're functioning under a paradox system. It seems like you don't learn anything good unless you wade through the textbook of bad. The Yin and the Yang, if you will."

Todd smiled broadly as he said, "All right. Now you're really starting to sound like the woman I want to call myself married to."

***

The next day Phillip stopped by to see Todd and Julie for a few minutes and found Brad was in visiting him again. Philip told them although Jackson Lamech was still on life-support, he had been upgraded from extremely critical condition to serious but stable. He looked at Brad. "And they say if you hadn't been there to treat him, there would have been a funeral instead. Congratulations."

Brad nodded as Todd said, "Glad to hear it. I don't know what all he did to get his wife that mad at him, but no matter what, it didn't justify what she did. Actually, I believe that's why divorce courts were created."

"Agreed," Phillip replied, and then he proceeded to tell Todd about the charges against Roscoe Knowles and Heather Lamech. "So along with attempted murder, Roscoe is being charged with aggravated assault for shooting you, plus stealing the Infiniti, and Heather is charged as his co-conspirator. They will be in front of Judge Leahy, so you know what that means."

"Let me guess," Todd said, "No bail."

"You got it," replied Phillip, "and, if convicted, about which I have no doubts, I also expect, no leniency."

Julie looked a bit worried as she asked if there were any chance Roscoe and Heather could beat the raps. Phillip replied, "I did everything by the book, and they were caught dead in their tracks."

"But," Julie questioned, "Is there any chance a couple of good defense lawyers could get a jury confused about who actually was responsible for the idea?"

"I seriously doubt it," Phillip replied. "First, Brad overheard them both talking about the grave, and Heather saying she was finally free. Plus she mentioned she threw away the keys to the cuffs when she believed Jackson was dead. And we have Tira Furcologna as an eyewitness, and what she says she observed lines up exactly with the injuries. And they both had to drag Jackson down that gully. Then Aaron, Brad, Tira, and I all heard them both make further incriminating statements. No, Julie," Phillip grinned, and reddened a little as he went on, "Now I don't want to sound like a First Beat Officer you used to be acquainted with, but I really think this case is about as airtight as you can get."

"I do so hope you're right, Phillip," Julie said. "I really do."

"What about using Brad and Aaron?" Todd asked. "Can Defense claim they had no right being a part of the arrests?"

"Already been over it with the Prosecutor. She says they were duly deputized, and necessary."

Before Brad left, Todd and Julie said they wanted him to come to the wedding, and to bring a friend if he wanted.

CHAPTER 120
The Wedding

Phillip wheeled Todd to the hospital chapel where some friends of Todd and Julie, along with Brad and Mia, eight nurses, and a few other hospital personnel were waiting. Tira had agreed to be Julie's bridesmaid, and they were down the hall in another room. Dr. Pedigone was pacing outside the chapel. "Why am I nervous?" he asked Todd. "I've never done this before, but as I see it, that's no reason to be nervous. You maybe, but not me."

"I don't know," said Todd, laughing. "Perhaps you should go see a doctor. I believe there's a mirror in the restroom down the hall." Dr. Pedigone replied he didn't have an appointment and Todd said, "You won't need one. I know this guy. He takes walk-ins."

Dr. Pedigone laughed. "Well, you can't turn anyone away, can you? Car payments and all. You know how it is." Todd laughed and said of course one couldn't, especially a Porsche. Dr. Pedigone put his hands on his hips and smiled as he replied, "Trooper Truitt, give me a hard time, I'll charge you for it on your bill."

Todd bantered, "Well I'm thankful State Police have good insurance benefits, and I think hard time charges have just a small co-pay."

Phillip asked jokingly if they were going to go to a wedding or not and Todd grinned as he responded that he wouldn't miss it for the world.

"Now, let me out of this wheelchair," he said. "I am walking down the aisle." Phillip asked if he was sure, and Todd replied, "I was shot in the chest, not in a leg." Phillip laughed and said as best man, he was just double-checking. Soon Phillip and Tira joined to start their walk into the hospital chapel. Then they went down the aisle together and took their respective places.

As Julie came through the door on Dr. Pedigone's arm, tears came to Todd's eyes as he thought, *I am marrying the most beautiful woman in the world, and, JR, Mindy, Samantha, I love you, always will, but I am also moving on. And I know you all three are probably saying, "It's about time."*

As Tira looked at Todd standing there with bandages, she was overwhelmed with the dangers he and other law enforcement officers faced on a daily basis and shot up a quick prayer. *Dear God, thank You for taking care of Todd, and please protect State Troopers and all Law Enforcement Officers everywhere. They need your protection as they fight against evil people; they really do.*

The group was small, but united in spirit as Chaplain Harrison began, "Friends of Todd and Julie, welcome, and thank you for sharing in this celebration of the joining together of Julie Wright and Todd Truitt. And before we start the ceremony I want to give a couple of special thanks, first to Brad Miller for being with us today; thanks for saving the life of Trooper Truitt. Without your actions, we would very likely be holding a different ceremony today; a somber one. And secondly, Ms. Tira Furcologna, thank you for being instrumental in the capture of the man who shot Todd. We owe you both, Brad and Tira, a debt of gratitude."

***

Later, back in the hospital room, Todd was in bed propped up with pillows, and Julie was lying next to him. A nurse knocked, then came in, and Julie quickly sat up. "I'm sorry," Julie said. "I hope you don't mind my lying here."

"Honey," said the nurse, laughing, "It's your wedding day. Are you sure you don't want to be doing anything more than just lying next to him?" Todd and Julie laughed as Todd said there were some things that probably should wait. The nurse shook her head and said, "Well, now, kids, unless it's an emergency, I don't plan on disturbing you two again tonight."

Julie laughed as she said, "Well, I hope you'll pardon us if we disappoint you, but there are some things I believe we'll just keep private, between him and me."

"Don't blame you. I'm not saying you have to, you know, just clearing the way in case you're thinking of it."

"Oh, don't get us wrong," Todd interjected, "we're thinking of it, trust me."

The nurse laughed. "Now Officer Truitt, I'm just delivering your medicine. But call me if you need anything else." Then she kissed Todd on the cheek, hugged Julie, and went out.

CHAPTER 121
The Arraignment

Roscoe and Julie were arraigned the next day. They both pled "Not guilty" and their looks toward each other were missing the lustful affection which had characterized so many moments of the prior few days. They also proclaimed their relative innocence in the assault of Jackson, each claiming the other one was behind what had happened, and that they were being forced to go along with the situation for fear of their life. Judge Leahy told them to save their stories for a jury.

CHAPTER 122
Brad and Mia

Brad and Mia drove around for a while after the wedding, and he talked quite a bit about his combat medic days.

"I don't know why I feel so comfortable sharing all this information with you," he said. "I feel like some kind of wall is coming down."

"Well, I'm sure glad you came by and adopted Scooter and Little Bit. And I'm really glad to be here listening to your information breaking through that wall."

"It may have started with the babies," Brad said. "They started cuddling up their first night with me, and overall I've been sleeping better. Listen; do you see what I see up ahead? Want to grab a bite at Shoney's?"

"Sure."

CHAPTER 123
As Good as Fettuccine, or, Q-Tipping Ears

Mr. and Mrs. Todd Truitt went to her place after he was released from the hospital. They had decided to get take-out en route. Todd asked Julie what she wanted and she said she had a yen for chicken or something.

"Do you want me to take care of your yen?"

"Which one?" Julie laughingly asked.

"Something?"

"That sounds good, right after we eat."

Since they both liked it, they got chicken fettuccine from the Electric Blue.

As they were sitting at the small kitchen table, Julie drew in a deep breath of contentment, moaned, and said, "Mmm. This is delicious. The perfect delayed honeymoon meal to give me energy to take you to our bedroom and, carefully of course, assault you."

Todd laughed as he said, "I don't believe you can assault a willing soul."

Later, after they had made love, they lay there, and Julie rested her head carefully against the non-wounded side of Todd's chest. She sighed with what she was sure was the deepest feeling of contentment she had ever felt in her life, and said, "Oh, God, that was well worth the wait. Todd Truitt, I love you. I love you so much."

"And I love you, too," Todd said, "But, and I think we need to be honest with each other, Julie, I know you were fantasizing. You sounded exactly like you were enjoying another plate of chicken fettuccine."

Julie burst out laughing and said, "Okay, so I got caught. And, this is it, isn't it? I guess we're just going to have a kinky relationship, right?"

"That's all right; I had my own fantasy going on. It felt so good I could swear I was Q-tipping my ears."

Julie Truitt laughed, stretched up, and kissed her husband on the cheek.

EPILOGUE – THREE YEARS LATER

Todd Truitt retired early as a Kentucky State Trooper to start and manage Sunrise Shelter, a halfway house for recovering alcoholics recently released from prison. He and Julie have twins, age two, Rodney and Rochelle. Todd recently published a book, *Lifelong Lessons from Combat Zones and Other Traumatic Events*.

Julie Truitt resigned her position as a dispatcher for the 58th State Police Headquarters to be a full-time Mom to the twins. She and Todd have became good friends with Brad and Mia, and every couple of months they get together for an evening of homemade sub sandwiches and playing Canasta. Even though the twins limit her spare time, Julie does some volunteer counseling at the Frankenberry Total Care Center, working with abused children.

Brad Miller and Mia dated for a few months and decided to marry. They live in his cabin near Swisher Glen Forest. Todd convinced him that he should market his woodcarvings, and he sold all but a few favorites. Word started to spread about his work and he soon found himself with an ever-widening market area.

Mia Miller still works full-time at the Frankenberry Animal Hospital and Shelter. She enjoys hiking with Brad and loves the cabin and its surroundings. Before they got married they added on an extra playroom for the cats, which of course included hers, Loki and Luna. Fortunately all the cats have acclimated to the larger family unit quite well.

Phillip Cordella was recently promoted to Lieutenant. Within the 58th State Police Headquarters he has become widely respected by his superiors and colleagues. He finds that every so often he still has a strong impulse to visit nastywatchers.com, and most of the time he manages to beat it. He also still enjoys taking hikes, and eating at Wendy's.

Deanna Wilson started dating someone new and eventually married. She was recently hired as a Communication Instructor at Consultation Peak Community College and stays quite busy with her class load. Since she loves to cook, she always has a delicious meal awaiting her husband, Howard, when he arrives home from work. However, she refuses to ever set the table, stating her aversion as a former waitress.

Pastor Ulysses Brock waited until after what he deemed was an appropriate period of mourning, and then took Tira Furcologna to be his wife. He told himself that her shapely body had nothing to do with his interest; it was more the fact she was twenty-seven years younger than he, which would help keep him relevant for the church youth group. Besides, she adores him, and, for whatever reasons, is a virtual tiger in the bedroom.

Tira Brock assists her husband with the church work on week-ends and jealously protects him from admiring women in the church. The most valuable of her mother's heirlooms were recovered at a lo-cal pawn shop. Because of that, during the week, she owns and man-ages "Tira's Treasures", a pawn shop which cooperates fully with the Frankenberry Police department. Although Tira outwardly expressed regret, inwardly she rejoiced, when, shortly after she and Ulysses Brock were married, the widow Janice Taylor announced her decision to transfer membership to another church.

Aaron Patterson completed paying his restitution to Mrs. Walk-er for her damaged fence within three months after his release from Angel Windows, and then started a savings account. He earned an Associate of Arts degree from Consultation Peak Community College, and now works for Todd Truitt at the Sunrise Shelter. His services are divided between maintenance of the shelter and as a counselor.

Heather Lamech was sentenced to twenty-five years in prison and knew that with good behavior, she could eventually expect pa-role. She filed for, and was granted a divorce from Jackson, but having had her fill of men, she decided to make the best of a bad situation and became the bitch of the head prison trustee, Barbara Baybee. Oc-casionally when just the two of them are together the ecstatic sound of Heather screaming, "Damn, Oh, damn, damn, damn," can be heard throughout that part of the prison.

Roscoe Knowles was two years into his thirty-three year sen-tence when he got a new cell mate, Isaac Wells. About a week after Isaac's arrival, Roscoe couldn't resist stealing a pack of cigarettes from him and the next morning was found hanging from a sheet tied to a bar in his jail cell window. Isaac said Roscoe had seemed depressed and apparently committed suicide during the night.

Jackson Lamech was in an intensive care unit for a month and then moved to a regular room where he remained for two weeks. However, he was moved back to intensive care for another week after a nurse hit him in the head with a bedpan for pinching her ass. After his eventual release from the hospital he went on disability and later moved in with a home health care nurse who liked to sleep in provocative, hot pink, form-fitting T-shirts which showed off her long legs to perfection.

Delayah White finished her degree in Psychology, and graduated *summa cum laude*. She works at the Frankenberry Total Care Center, and has organized a local Tinnitus Sufferers Support Group. She finished the book of poetry she and Albert had started to work on, and dedicated it to his memory. To date it has sold over 10,000 copies, although she has yet to receive any of the royalties as they remain frozen until litigation by Tira Brock is settled. One of the regular attendees of the Tinnitus Sufferers Support Group is a divorced Iraq War veteran, Reggie Baker. Reggie asked Delayah for a date the evening she showed up to the support group wearing an olive colored jersey dress with a mid-thigh hemline and side slits. She and Reggie have been going together ever since.

Charles Cameron was sentenced to prison for five years but was released after two years for good behavior and time served awaiting trial. He was back selling drugs less than a week after getting out.

Rita (Cameron) Tolheny managed to get an all female jury to believe that she really didn't know anything about the drugs in the car; that she really had thought they were delivering toys to the Safe Shelter for Women in Portsmouth, Ohio. She divorced Charles Cameron as soon as he went to prison and then married a high school sweetheart who was a pharmacist and activist for recreational marijuana legalization.

Chantillee continues to be an aggravation for her policeman brother, Josh, as she regularly returns to her street corner. Due to a series of strange dreams she had, she has recently begun her solicitations in a pink mini-skirt.

Bitsy Wagoneer was charged with wanton endangerment and received a year's parole. She sold her long time County Road Bricken home and moved to another part of the county up a hollow called Mongrel Dog Branch, figuring that by being located in such a named place she wouldn't have to worry about being bothered by any of her neighbor's cats.

Ralph Henderson lives with his now full-grown cat Prissy. He has her fully acclimated as a house cat to such extent she has a cat seat for one of the bathrooms where she has learned to use the potty and then flush after herself. Ralph exercises daily by climbing trees.

\
Myriad Pro and Chiller on 50# LSI Archival white
Type and Design by Karen Paul Stone

www.ingramcontent.com/pod-product-compliance
Lightning Source LLC
Chambersburg PA
CBHW050310030726
47505CB00003B/643